"Beautifully blends lyrical prose, a prop
characters into a tale that will be sure to er
as she is brave and empathetic, and her story is utterly unputdownable.
What a brilliant addition to the young adult fantasy canon."—Ayana
Gray, *New York Times* bestselling author of *Beasts of Prey*

"Romantic and full of high-seas action and adventure. Brimming with
fantasy and lore, *Compass and Blade* is a story that poured out from
the heart."—Gabriela Romero Lacruz, author of the #1 *Sunday Times*
bestselling novel *The Sun and the Void*

"An addictive blend of lyrical prose, shimmering magic, and whip-
sharp pacing—fans of *Fable* and *Daughter of the Pirate King* will devour
this."—Laura Steven, author of *The Society for Soulless Girls*

"A gripping, atmospheric fantasy of saltwater kisses, sharp-edged
secrets, and the siren call of the deep sea—I couldn't turn the pages fast
enough."—Kika Hatzopoulou, author of *Threads That Bind*

"A pulse-pounding, seafaring adventure steeped in magic, romance,
secrets, and betrayal. So immersive and exciting and richly atmospheric—I
couldn't put this story down."—Aisling Fowler, author of *Fireborn*

"A heart-pounding sea adventure, with descriptions so visceral, you can
taste the salt on the wind. *Compass and Blade* will drag you under the
waves and you won't want to come up for air."—Cyla Panin, author
of *Stalking Shadows*

"I devoured *Compass and Blade*. I flew through each page of lyrical prose
and swashbuckling adventure. Readers will be truly captivated by Mira
and her journey to find her father and herself along the way. I know I
was. A magical, seafaring tale with a lot of heart."—Alexandra Christo,
author of *To Kill a Kingdom*

"This bloody, romantic adventure will sweep you away faster than the
tide. *Compass and Blade* will be the new obsession of readers who love
Adrienne Young and Alexandra Christo."—Megan Scott, author of *The
Temptation of Magic*

SHADOW and TIDE

ALSO BY RACHEL GREENLAW

Compass and Blade

One Christmas Morning
The Woodsmoke Women's Book of Spells

RACHEL GREENLAW

SHADOW and TIDE

HARPER
An Imprint of HarperCollinsPublishers

For Rosie and Izzy, always

THE CONTINENT
The Spines
Innish Tar
The Straits
Mines of Valstra
Hafenged
Stanvard
Skylan
FIVE PRINCIPALITIES OF THE MIDDENWILDS
Nestra
Bergstat
Kir
Hindelmach
Lorra
Gelve
Mavena
The Southern Ocean

SHADOW and TIDE

CHAPTER ONE

EVERY NIGHT, I TWIST THE SHEETS BETWEEN MY fists. I watch the light as it shivers across the ceiling, the moon and stars chased by clouds across the sky. I fight to stay awake, staring until my eyes burn. But it still comes for me anyway.

The nightmare.

At first I believe we will escape. That the mist draped over us will cloak him and keep him safe. *Phantom* dances on the waves, and beyond, the isle of Rosevear. A shimmering outline in the distance. I break into a run across the old quay on Penscalo, sure I will beat them this time, that the men at my back won't steal him from me. I reach out, my fingertips just brushing his green wool jacket, his pale blue eyes locked with mine.

Then it happens.

I watch, my boots glued to the ground, a gasp lost in the roar of the drowning sea for the moment my father falls.

The moment I fail to catch him.

The roar intensifies, pulsing, keening in my head, and I sink to my knees on that old granite quay, the pain a knife in my chest. I claw for him, the distance between us growing, but I can't move. I'm trapped.

And when I look around, I see Seth. The son of Captain Renshaw. My betrayer, my enemy. His mouth widens into a taunting grin, brown curls swept back from his forehead, a crow of laughter on his tongue as my father dies. Fury erupts in my chest, wild and untamable, ferocious.

I leap for him, nails like claws, a monster in human form just as they all feared, and I cannot control the siren inside me, the feral creature wanting vengeance, wanting his beating, bloody heart, wanting them all to suffer as I do.

And then I scream.

My eyes fly open, scanning the near-dark, my chest rising and falling. I bolt up, scrambling from the bed, fists raised, ready for them, my entire being throbbing with pain and rage, ready to fight, ready for blood.

That's when I realize.

The truth slamming into me, again and again.

My father's not coming back. He's not dying at my feet. There are no men with rifles and blades, no Seth or Renshaw. There is no blood. And that terrible roar, the deafening howl of the sea dressed in pain, isn't coming from the ocean at all.

That deafening roar . . . is me.

I wipe my hands down my face, pulse crashing in my ears as I remind myself where I am. *Who* I am. Not a monster, just a girl on my island, in my bedroom, in the cottage where I grew up on Rosevear. I take a deep, soothing breath, frowning as something bitter sweeps down my throat . . .

smoke. And not just a gentle whirl in the air from the lingering embers in the hearth and extinguished candles . . . It's cloying and insistent.

Stumbling to the window, I rake back the curtains and fumble with the latch, panicking as I cough and cough, needing fresh air. But there's something barring it. I narrow my eyes, not believing what I'm seeing at first. A plank of wood, attached to the window from the outside. Then I hear it.

The screaming.

I shake my head, clearing the fog of sleep, and move from the window as a cloud shifts. The moon's light, brimming and full, drenches the room in silver. Foreboding shivers down my spine.

All I see is smoke.

"No." I throw an arm over my mouth. All at once I'm wide awake, scanning the darkness, finding that the light is not just coming from the full moon. It's also coming from the other cottages.

I scramble around the edges of the bed, coughing again as the smoke fills my lungs, my hands flying to the drawers next to my bed, where my mother's notebook, the map, and her letter are tucked inside. I hurriedly slip them into my nightshirt pocket as I stride for the bedroom door and thrust it open. I gasp, stumbling back in shock. The front room is ablaze. A wall of heat forces me to take another step back, sweat prickling over my skin, heart thumping too fast and too hard against my ribs.

Kai had warned us in the last meet, only a couple of days ago, when Bryn and Pearl arrived for a visit to collect his things. He had posted lookouts along our shores; he'd sent

Terry and Lish to Port Trenn for information.

He knew what was coming for us.

The watch.

Only a month after I had intervened, saving Bryn and my father from the gallows, when their other prisoners had escaped the noose too, the watch is here to punish us. To make us suffer as Captain Spencer promised. More terrified cries cut through the sound of crackling flames, and I whimper, knowing others are trapped as I am. Trapped in their cottages with no way to escape.

I rush back into the bedroom, grabbing a scarf to tie around my face, pulling my jacket over my nightshirt in case I need to shove anything burning out of my way. Finally I lace my boots, whispering feverish thanks to any old god who is listening that I left them in my bedroom when I changed for bed.

Then I turn back to the doorway, back to the front room and kitchen beyond, alive with ravenous flames, and step over the threshold.

"Mira!" a shrill voice howls. "Mira! I can't get through, I can't get *through*—"

"I'm here!" I shout, hacking instantly. My eyes sting, water filling them, turning them to slits. I barrel for the door, through the licking flames, the heat, and the thick smoke, finding it smoldering and scorched. There are two chairs piled in front of it, already crumbling to ash and fire. Like someone placed them there.

Like someone wanted me to die in this cottage.

I wedge my jacket sleeves around my palms, pulling the chairs away, the scent of burning fabric mingling with the smell of wood. I hear muffled sobbing, then a heavy thud as the door bursts open, drenching me in cold air.

Agnes is on the other side in her nightshirt and jacket as I am, her red hair a tangled thicket around her pale, tear-stained face. "Mira, *thank goodness* . . ." she hiccups, pulling me toward her. We stumble away, arms around each other as I hack up all the smoke from my aching lungs.

"What—what happened? Is the watch here?" I say, voice grating with gravel.

"They were."

It takes me a moment to wipe the sting from my eyes, to push my hair out of my face and really look around. And when I do, I almost fall to my knees, the horror of what I'm seeing hollowing me out. Fires rage in the cottages surrounding us, smoke billowing in gray, smothering sheets. People, stumbling and wailing, call for fathers, mothers, sons, daughters. . . . The watch has come in the night, prowled through our village, and torched our homes while we slept. I claw at Agnes's arm, a strangled cry rising inside me.

Rosevear is burning.

CHAPTER TWO

"NO, NO, NO!" I GASP, FORCING MY LEGS TO MOVE. I get away from my cottage, toward the others stumbling and huddling in clumps, the crying, the *screaming*.

"Water!" I shout, running for the nearest group, scanning their eyes in the dark, reaching for their shoulders, shaking them out of their shock. "We need water!"

Agnes appears at my side, pulling the only person who isn't holding a child away from another group. "To the well, to the well!" She sends out a call, whistling like Bryn used to. For a heartbeat, my breath catches, and I stutter. But then I snap back, locking all that pain away. And I run to find the six others who swim out on the rope alongside me, my team on nights filled with the sounds of the dying.

I find Kai first, directing three of the others.

"Mira, you're here." He rests his hand on my shoulder, relief softening his tone as he turns to face the group of cottages before us. One of them, the one on the right . . . is the healer's. "Lish is working through the houses, making sure everyone is out. Eight cottages aflame from what we can see. Have you seen Agnes?"

"She's safe," I manage, covering my mouth as I wheeze, the smoke sinking its claws into my lungs. "She's gone to the well."

"Good." He eyes me, then points to a group clutching children to their sides. They're all in nightshirts like me, their eyes wide moons in pale, terrified faces. "Get them to the meeting house. Gather up anyone you can find. There are still people trapped."

I can't wrap my head around this. That some of my community, the people I've grown up with, known every day of my life . . . are still in these cottages. But I nod, falling into my role when we search a wreck. And I realize that Kai has slipped into Bryn's role. Our anchor. The one who directs us, who makes sure we all get out alive.

"Follow me!" I call to the fathers and mothers, the scared children clutched to their chests and sides. "To the meeting house!"

I settle them in, a few already crying quietly, hugging their shivering babies. Pearl hurries between them, bandages tucked in the crook of her arm as Bryn talks in low, soothing tones, trying to instill calm. My heart wrenches, cracking inside me at the sight, and I quickly leave to find more survivors. The meeting house is set apart from the cottages, and the wind has swung to the opposite direction. The people will be in no danger from drifting sparks. And as I find Old Jonie, arms clutched around her niece, both of them hacking, bent almost double, I'm glad I can lead them straight to sanctuary.

"Go inside, stay warm, no going back to the cottages. I'll . . . I'll be back."

An explosion rips away my words. I whip around, scanning the land and darkness, and my heart thunders in my chest. The nearest cottage, just down the lane, is a furnace. I choke out my shock, taking a step back from the blaze. The meeting house is away from it, but the heat and light are intense.

Too intense.

"Kept the seal blubber in there. All that oil and fat," Old Jonie says, her voice thready with the smoke churning up her lungs. "Won't be any survivors from that one."

I gulp, my feet already moving. I scan back and forth, the flashes of burning casting chaotic snaps of bright light in the soft, predawn haze, as I desperately search for people in need, anyone who is still alive—

When he steps from the darkest shadow.

"Elijah," I choke out, his name a sob on my tongue. I run to him, unsure if I'm seeing things, if the haze of flame and smoke has made me see what isn't real in the swirl of shadow and dark. But as I stop a few feet away, I know it's really him. I know it from the quickening of my heart, the way his midnight scent wraps around me. I know it from the way his eyes find mine, dark and ringed with those soot-black lashes, his arms and chest strong and lethal, rippling with muscle. His white shirt is unbuttoned at the top, as though hastily thrown on with dark breeches and boots, his hair sleep tousled, blending with the near-dark. It takes all of me not to close the distance between us and lean into him, to feel those arms come around me like they did aboard Renshaw's ship.

He looks around, assessing, chiseled jaw clenched, before settling his gaze back on me. He takes a step closer, his hand finding my cheek, worried eyes darting over my face, my body. That feel of home somehow wraps around me like a spell as my thundering heart begins to calm. "Are you all right? Are you hurt?"

"I'm fine. You're here. You came."

His hand tenses against my skin, then drops back to his side. "Not nearly soon enough, it seems." He swallows, gaze drifting to the carnage surrounding us. "It's the full moon, Mira. I came to take you to Ennor, as we agreed in our bargain. . . . What happened?"

Of course. The full moon. The bargain. My fingertips reach for the bargain mark etched into my skin, brushing over my wrist, and I glance down, finding it blazing in the near-dark. The compass, shot through with a blade. "They must have come while we slept, the watch, torching cottages. Eight are ablaze, maybe more now, and there are . . . people trapped."

Fear sharpens Elijah's gaze as he looks around again, taking in the chaos. Then his eyes snap back to mine, steady and sure. "I can only traverse with two at a time. Point out the cottages where there are people still inside."

"I . . .Yes. Yes, of course." I blink, clearing away the relief at his sudden presence, locking away that desperate, afraid part of myself, and set off at a run toward the heart of the village. He moves alongside me, focused, running along the lane, cutting through the bracken and heather to reach the village quickly. "Kai's leading; he'll know!"

We find Kai shouting orders, trying to tame the cottage next to Agnes's with a steady supply of buckets of water from the well. But it's just spraying steam and smoke, the true fire untouched and raging. My breath stutters as I regard the cottage, the hunkering granite walls and small windows, the one I know contains a family. They exchange a few words and Elijah turns toward the cottage. Then, in the space of half a heartbeat, he vanishes into a fold of shadow.

"The father's still in there," Kai says over the crackling roar of the flame, eyes sliding to mine as he rubs sweat and ash from his forehead. "Went back in for the youngest. Rowena's out with the older two. Shit, Mira. What if they . . ."

"Kai . . ." I say, placing my hand on his arm, the pain wrenching me apart. There are no words I can say to dress this up in anything but what it is. Devastating. I glance back at the mother, Rowena, holding her two children to her. She's crying, silent tears tracking down her cheeks, eyes fixed on the doorway just like ours are. Everyone around us stills, watching as seconds creep toward moments. I bunch my hands into fists, wondering if I should try the smoking wooden door. If I can somehow get through, if Elijah can find them—

He appears at my side.

And with him, one hand clutched around each of theirs, are the father and a toddler, no older than two. Little Eliza, with the blond curls. She sags at his side and her mother gasps in anguish. I dart for her, wrapping my arms around her tiny body, pulling her away from the heat. Her father sinks to the ground, retching and coughing, and Elijah looks to me, to the bundle in my arms. Her mother follows a few steps away, and I lower her carefully to the ground.

"My girl, my little one . . ." Rowena keens, and my heart-beat thuds in my ears as I kneel beside her, clearing away the curls plastered to her cheeks—and all at once her eyes fly open. She coughs, her little body creasing in the middle, and her mother has her arms around her, crying her name over and over.

I get up off the ground, tremors running through my entire body. And when I look up, I find Elijah's gaze on me. Dark and serious, a night devoid of starlight. I murmur a thank-you, too quiet for him to hear. But his mouth parts in the smallest smile, before he turns back to Kai, back to the next cottage, to the others who need him.

Elijah slips between pockets of shadow again and again as I shepherd survivors to safety. Kai rallies the able-bodied, Agnes at his side as they drench as much as they can with bucket after bucket of water from the well. We're all coughing as the world wakes around us, the sun rising past the plume of smoke to reveal the stark reality of Rosevear. I stumble my way back from the meeting house and see what no one will admit—the water, carried in buckets, is not dimming the blaze. We need more. We need an ocean, a *storm*. . . .

I grip my hands into fists, desperation pouring through me as I watch Kai and the others fight all those fires, ten cottages now burning, as the flame has caught and spread. It's not enough. We can't hold back this tide of ravenous flame. A sob racks my throat, and I turn my eyes to the sky, to the clouds, and will them to swell and split apart. Will them to fall upon us, to drown us and save us. I will it with everything in me, picturing the terror in every face in the night, the children clinging to their mothers and fathers. I close my eyes, taking a shuddering breath, and something inside me stills.

Then a raindrop, a single tear from the sky, falls on my chapped lips.

When I open my eyes, tilting my chin up, I find the clouds are plump and heavy. More raindrops fall, marking my face, my clothes, lightning flashing in a fork to the earth, before thunder rumbles.

And a torrent of rain crashes down.

Too tired to feel anything but the ache in my bones, I raise my arms skyward, closing my eyes with a sigh as the sky cleaves open. Rain. Lifesaving, endless rain. I've never been more grateful, more relieved, as I watch the flames in the cottages begin to dwindle into ribbons of gray and ash. Somehow I willed it and the storm rose to my call. Perhaps some forgotten old god listened on the wind to the cry in my desperate heart.

"Mira . . ."

I blink, turning to find him standing beside me. Elijah Tresillian. And it hits me in this moment what he is. *Who* he is. Wanted by the watch. Lord of an isle. Boy with a strange and powerful magic. The one I am bound to. His white shirt is a painting of rips and streaks of soot, telling the tale of our harrowing night. His eyes meet mine, heavy with exhaustion, with pain and sadness. My heart beats once, twice, and I can no longer contain the tears inside me. They mingle with the rain and storm, and without a word, I pull him to me, burying my face against his chest. His arms come around me, sure and steady as the anchor I need, and I let him hold me as I shake and shake.

CHAPTER
THREE

"TWO DOZEN WOUNDED. SIX DEAD," KAI INTONES
a few hours later as we gather outside the meeting house.
Inside is a hive of activity around the wounded; the healer is
propped in a corner, where volunteers ask her gentle questions for guidance. The dead are at our feet, covered in white
shrouds. Two of these bodies are the healer's brothers. The
storm has abated, leaving only the bitter scent of charred
wood and acrid smoke, the cottages down the hill still smoldering.

"Is everyone accounted for?" I ask quietly, eyeing the bodies. They remind me of my father before we laid him in his
coffin. I look away, closing that door on the part of myself
that is weeping. I have to hold it together today, despite the
tired drag of my limbs and the heaviness in my heart.

Kai looks uneasily to Bryn, who is leaning against a walking stick Kai fashioned from an old oar. Bryn's features are
unreadable. He's giving Kai the space to lead, to manage this

situation himself. A lump sticks in my throat as Kai squares his shoulders, facing all of us. "Gilly Matthews is missing. She was on lookout duty when the first fire went up—in your cottage, Mira, and the healer's. We found planks of wood fixed to the windows to bar escape . . . and furniture piled up inside, as though someone climbed through a window in the night, set the fires, and blocked any means of getting out."

I hiss with fury as a wave of curses rolls around us.

"That shrew," Agnes spits, face contorting. "That miserable, murderous little *shrew*."

"We don't know for certain," Bryn rumbles, exchanging a look with Kai. "But we do know it was no accident. We'll continue searching for her. Kai, I think you'd better pass it around."

Kai's eyes bore into mine as he unfolds a sheet of parchment. He hesitates, then sighs deeply, passing it to me first. I unfold it slowly, my hands still dancing with tremors from the long night and all the horrors I've witnessed. It's a note. A demand of sorts. From the watch.

I clear my throat. "Kai did not want to read this out loud, because he is protecting me," I say, smiling sadly at him. "But *I* will. I owe too much to this island to hide it from you all."

I feel Agnes slip to my side, like a faithful shadow, and her presence bolsters me, as it always does.

"It says the people of Rosevear are harboring a person of extreme interest to the watch. A person who goes by Mira. If I am not delivered to the watch's prison on Penscalo for questioning by the next moon turn . . ." I lick my lips. "They will start a door-to-door search, and round up anyone who may know me, to be held in the prison and be questioned in my stead."

"Mira . . ." Agnes starts, placing a hand on my arm.

The sheet of parchment flutters in my fingers. We all know what questioning really means. Torture. And when the watch rounds up these people, *my* people, they won't let them out of their prison. Not alive, anyway. "It says . . . that this is our warning."

Silence whistles through the crowd around me. Wind gusts up from the village, reeking of smoke, of death and damp and violence. I breathe it in, the bite of my guilt shaping me, molding me. When I look into the faces of the people surrounding me, all I see is emptiness. Like they've stepped out of the rooms they inhabit, through a doorway deep within themselves. I brought this upon them.

Six deaths.

Two dozen injured.

My fault.

"Mira . . ." Agnes says again, trying to turn me to her. "*None* of this is your doing. You didn't—"

"Don't say it." I pass the parchment to her and run a hand over my eyes. "We all know who is to blame for this."

I look up and find Elijah watching me, arms crossed, Pearl at his side. She murmurs something to him and he nods, expression unreadable. When the parchment reaches him, passed from hand to hand, he refuses to look at it and strides away from the gathering. They're all avoiding looking at me, gazes fixed on the ground or the middle distance. The pressure builds in my head, with the bodies at my feet, my community around me. A child quietly begins to cry, a thin, ghostly wail, and I just . . . I can't take it.

★ ★ ★

I hunker down next to his grave. It's simply marked, a chis-eled wooden headstone sprouting from the earth with his name and the date of his passing carved into it. Kai crafted the marker with a border of waves around his name. I touch my fingers to it, needing that connection to him. The sea thrift, his favorite, is all around me, pale pink and delicate. There seems to be more here along this stretch of cliff than there was in years past. I like to think that's him, encourag-ing spring along. Giving us a wild place where we can still find each other.

"If I stay on Rosevear any longer, more of them will die," I say quietly, staring out to the ocean. The sea is rougher today, showing her white-tipped edges in the wake of the storm that emerged at just the right moment to save us. The breeze lifts and tumbles her, the sun lighting stark pockets of deep navy. I bite my lip, watching the waves form and re-form. "But if I leave, if I make sure the watch knows I'm no longer here, will they come and take them for question-ing, just because they can? Will they die anyway?"

I draw my knees close, the tempest swirling beneath my ribs making me feel so very small. "Tell me what to do, Father," I whisper. "I can't find myself anymore. It's like all of me vanished when you . . . now that you're gone. I can't find my way."

I feel a presence at my back, a shift in the way the air moves around me. Looking over my shoulder, I find Kai walking toward me, face set in patterns of deep gloom.

"Mind if I join you?"

"Not at all," I say as he presses his fingertips to my father's marker, a sign of respect. Then he hunkers down on the other side of the grave, as if it's the three of us in a row. For a few moments, neither of us says anything. We let the peace and the sea wash over us, and I realize Kai needed this place too. That maybe the weight of the island isn't just squarely on my shoulders.

"Pearl is going to stay on for a time, to help the healer."

"Pearl healed me aboard *Phantom*; my foot was cut and she bound it with herbs. . . . She'll be a great help," I say. I don't mention the healer, her two brothers resting in their shrouds. Not with the snapping jaws of my guilt just waiting to swallow me whole.

Kai draws in a breath, then releases it slowly. "Agnes is right, Mira."

"Don't."

"I won't," he says, flicking a glance to me. "But you'll know it, given time."

I don't say anything. There's a hollow opening up inside me, pieces of myself falling in. I'm scared that if I look too closely, if I admit to it being there at all, I'll fall in and never find my way out. It will grow to consume me and coat me in eternal cloying night. It's devastation and grief and guilt, and it's only getting deeper, wider, this hollow. It's where the people I love used to be.

"We can't salvage anything of your cottage. Your father's things . . . your mother's and yours . . . I'm so sorry."

"It's all right," I say, my voice a frail rasp. "I have the map and my mother's letter. The other things . . ." I swallow, a knot forming in my throat as I picture my mother's chest full of her clothes and notebooks, my father's pipe and his favorite mug. "The other things were just anchors."

"We all need anchors, Mira."

I shake my head sadly. "If I am to protect you, I have to cut you all away. You know it, Kai. Agnes knows it too. I just . . ." I look at the grave marker. "I needed to come up here. In case I can't make it back for a while."

Then I roll up my left sleeve and hold my arm out to him. The silver lines of the bargain mark are faint in sunlight, but he sees the shape of them on my wrist.

Kai's eyes widen. "That's a bargain mark."

"I stood here a month ago and made a bargain with Elijah Tresillian to avenge my father and protect Rosevear. We sealed it with this mark. I was to go with him on the next full moon . . . which was last night. That's why he was here. To collect on the bargain we made."

"I thought . . . We've always heard that only witches—"

I shrug, replacing my sleeve. "Elijah is no witch. I don't know what his magic is, where it comes from."

Kai is quiet for a moment. "So you're going with him."

"I made a bargain."

"He's already upholding his side of it, isn't he? He came to collect you, but he stayed instead of taking you. He aided us last night. But if you ask him, maybe he will release you from this bargain. We can find another way."

My fingers stray again to the bargain mark. "I don't want to be released from it. I want to fight the watch. I need you all to be safe. And I want to be free."

He breathes in through his nose and I glance at him, seeing the storm I feel under my own skin echoed in the lines of him. The way he holds himself, the way his eyes are clouded and grim.

"Without Rosevear, I am no one," I say quietly. "You're my kin, my home. I would give anything."

"That's what I'm worried about," he says, finally turning to fix his gaze fully on me. "You would give *everything* for Rosevear. You already have."

"I'm going with Elijah," I say, releasing my knees to stand on shaking legs. I take one last look at the frothing navy-blue sea, the delicate pink sea thrift, my father's grave. I brush my fingertips across the marker, silently saying goodbye. "I'm fulfilling my side of the bargain. Just . . . take care of her for me. Tuck her heart inside your own."

Kai stands, placing his hand on the grave marker, and for a moment, I see the anguish he buries. The weight of fear, the deep love like a pool in his soul. He knows who I mean without me uttering her name. My sister in all but blood. Agnes. "I promise I will."

I am about to turn and walk back to the village when I see a flash of light in the distance. I squint, raking my eyes back and forth across the sea. "Did you see that?"

"What?" Kai is instantly alert.

"A flash. A sail, perhaps."

"No one would chance a crossing today, not after that squall, surely. . . ."

I gasp as there is another. And another.

Kai swears under his breath, running for the village. "They don't know where the rocks are; we never shared the markers on this side of the island!"

I tear my eyes from the sea, sprinting after him. They are boats. A dozen of them. Fishing vessels, gigs, punts. They are just like ours, but their sails tell us where they hail from. Our fellow islanders, the people of the neighboring Penrith.

They are about to wreck themselves on our shores.

CHAPTER
FOUR

KAI SENDS THE WHISTLE SKITTERING THROUGH the village.

The whistle that rouses us. Rallies us to go into the tide.

"With me!" he shouts as the six of us gather at his heels. Seven, including him. We now have a new seventh, a new member to replace Bryn. Grier is small and nimble with dark hair and skin and a full, serious mouth. She is fifteen, older than Agnes and I were when we first went out on the rope, swimming to shipwrecks in order to help survivors, but also to find the goods our island takes to survive. Yet my heart still twists as she blinks back at me. From the moment she agreed to be one of the seven, to swim out in storms and brave the sea in all her forms, her childhood ended. I wonder if she has realized that yet.

"We're going to reach them before they meet the outer teeth," I say as Agnes peels off from the group to drag the boat shed doors wide. "We will work as one, as always. But we will try to steer them clear."

The others nod as Kai issues a burst of instructions. The tallest and broadest in the middle of the gig to power us through the choppy waves. The slightest at the edges, Agnes at the front to set the rhythm on stroke side, and me behind her to set it on bow side. Kai will cox us, guiding the rudder, facing us in the gig. I shiver, wishing I could dive into the sea. But for once, we will not be swimming out on the rope. We need the people of Penrith to see us, and they're too spread out.

I take my place behind Agnes, putting my weight under the side as the others take up places around the gig. We drop it onto two pulleys on wheels that Kai has configured with his brother, Arthek, who even now darts around us, handing out gloves so we do not get blisters from gripping the rough oars. When we get to the water's edge, it froths over my calves and at once my blood ignites.

The sea cries out to me, and I want to listen. I want to swim as an arrow to the people of Penrith. But I know I would not reach them all in time. We need to work together. Old Jonie passes the end of the rope to Kai, who loops it around his forearm. He nods to her as more islanders scatter over the cove. I climb into the gig, taking my seat in position five as Agnes clambers into position six ahead of me, the others hopping over the planks that act as our seats at my back. I pull on my gloves, slotting the oar between the pins and weighing it in my hands, pushing my feet against the stretcher, a piece of wood below Agnes's seat in front of me, to test if I can push against it and pull a good stroke as the others take up their places. We pull out, Agnes turning the gig about on stroke side as we hold water on bow side, our oars cupping the water. Her feet dig against her stretcher as she leans back, pulling the paddle through the water so the end of the oar rests against her chest.

"Arms out." We all lean forward, arms out straight, the tips of our paddles resting just above the water. "On my count. Three, two . . ." Kai grips the rudder, his features set on the course. As one, we lower our oars and row.

The sea is fickle today, hurling her might at us. But I grit my teeth, keeping with the rhythm of the others, the pace Agnes sets, my gaze trained on the line of my paddle, on the way it hits the water. I keep Agnes in my peripheral vision, checking, as I lean back and drop my shoulder at the same time, that we work as one in the water. We gather pace, setting a careful rhythm that has us gliding through the worst of the chop. I fall into a trance, focused only on my breath, on the pull of the water under my hands, the churn of my stomach at what will happen if we fail.

"Keep it steady. . . . They've spotted us," Kai says.

I chance a look at him, then behind me, and swear as my paddle falters, missing a stroke as it judders on the surface. Kai's jaw is set, his eyes pinned to the horizon, and I push back my growing fatigue. We have to work as one, on the rope, in a gig, in every part of our lives.

It's how we survive.

"Reached the inner teeth!" Kai says, and we whoop, Agnes never letting up the pace. My whole body is screaming, exhaustion clawing at me. But I know the others will be feeling it too—we're all on borrowed time after last night. "There's a drifter. . . . I'm bringing us round; they're too close to the rocks. . . ."

I crackle with fear at Kai's words, but keep to the rhythm,

not daring to look over my shoulder. We all fall silent, the whoosh of our breath the only sound. We have to make it. I can't stand to lose even *one* of these people. Not today. Not after the horrors of last night.

Kai calls a stop, standing abruptly. The small sloop is dangerously close to a hidden rock of the outer teeth. I can make out six people, too many for a single-masted vessel that size. They're huddled together, waving to us as if in greeting.

"I'm going," I say to Kai, wrenching my gaze to look back at him. He nods once and I pull my paddle in. Then I dive into the deep.

At once my breathing settles, my arms cutting close to my body as I use my legs to power through the water. I take deep slashes with my hands, pushing myself through, finding the quiet and the closeness to dim my exhaustion, the sea igniting the flame in my blood, my siren side. I let everything slip away and follow a thread of current over to the shadow of the sloop above.

I dart through the outer teeth, pulling myself up on one of the rocks and lifting myself out of the water. Balancing on the rock, I call to them, and they turn to me as one. "It's all right!" I shout, cupping my hands around my mouth. "Pull in your mainsheet, you're drifting to the rocks!"

A woman, a full shoulder taller than the others, nods first, reaching for the main mast. "The others don't know!" she calls back as a man helps her, pushing his gray hair from his eyes. I realize the others are children, young and gawkish, staring at me with terror and interest.

I turn, searching the cresting waves, and spot my gig. Then I see where Kai is heading, and my heart flies to my throat. "Keep east of this outcrop, navigate slowly, keep to the marker of the big rock to the left of the boat shed. Line up with that and never stray from it. There's another set of rocks before you reach the cove!" I call over. The woman nods and I turn, already diving again.

This time, I begin to feel the fatigue, even here in the sea. As I cut through the water, following the shadows of the boats overhead, I feel my arms weakening, my legs failing to kick as hard as they might. I need rest. I need sleep. And tracking the progress of my gig, they're losing their rhythm. They're waning too.

I surface near a trio of punts. "Slow!" I say, waving my arms in a steady motion.

"Mira? Bloody hella . . . you'll catch your death!" a familiar voice calls from the nearest punt, all broad with a soft burr. The accent of Penrith.

I grin at Feock as he pauses his rowing. I've met with him every year on feast days, when our communities had more to share. He would journey over with his uncles and cousins, celebrating with us until the dawn. He was my first kiss, the first boy I thought of as anything other than a brother or cousin. But we always met them when they sailed over, and guided them in past the outer and inner teeth if they approached our island on this side. They never arrived like this.

"You know very well I won't, Feock Gent!" I say, a laugh of relief bubbling up my throat. I swim for his punt, gripping the edge of it to hold my fist out to his. His light brown hair has come loose from its twine, fanning out around his features in a cloud. "Catch my death indeed. What are you about?"

His face darkens momentarily, before he blinks it away.

"We'll explain when we're on land. Will you guide us in? I've got a little one; she needs your healer."

I peer past him, seeing the tiny body of a baby cradled in the lap of a young woman. I nod at her, and she nods back, her eyes rimmed with tiredness. I turn, whistling to Kai, three sharp bursts. He whistles back, already with the leader of the other set of vessels, and I turn back to Feock. "Stick close to where I swim. Make sure the others follow you."

The bone-deep ache sets in before I reach the shoreline. Moving slower through the water, staying on the surface so Feock can see me, leaves a thumping in my head that rattles my teeth. By the time I've guided them in, my whole body is spasming, and it takes everything I have to help drag the punts up the sand past the tideline.

"Get Pearl," I say to the nearest person I can find—Arthek. I help Feock to lever the woman and her little one from the punt, one of us on each side. The child looks to be no older than a year and is barely moving, blue lipped, eyes lidded, and covered in a layer of frost-filled veins. It turns my own blood to ice.

The woman is babbling something in a string of sentences, but it's a language I only have the thinnest grasp of. When she notes my blank expression, she switches to Arnheman. "Please help. Please. Feock said you would, that you could . . ."

"She's Leicenan," Feock says, wrapping his arm around her waist before replying to her in perfect Leicenan, reassuring her, then turning to me. "Rescued them both from a storm five months ago. She wanted to stay on Penrith, she was escaping a bad situation, and we fell in love. . . ." He sighs. "Tricina . . . she's my everything."

I nod, understanding immediately, seeing the fierce bond between them as Pearl sprints down the trick steps to the cove. More of the boats are landing at our backs, but I only have eyes for this tiny infant. Pearl kneels, indicating that the woman should place the child on the sand. Pearl speaks in a string of accented Leicenan, enunciating certain words with a lilt. The woman cries and nods, giving Pearl permission to help her child as Pearl pulls a flask from her jacket, uncorks it, and holds it to the infant's lips.

We hold our breath. Feock hugs Tricina to his side as she sobs quietly. At first nothing happens, and the silence is heavy. I can't bear the sight of more death, especially in one so helpless. Tricina keens quietly as Feock's eyes dart to mine, desperation and horror filling them. I press my lips together, counting down the seconds that the child fails to breathe.

Then, finally, she stirs. Pearl smiles, slowly pouring in a few more drops as her eyes meet mine, relief edged with pure exhaustion as we both take a breath as well. "Witches' brew. No more than a few drops, or it will act as a poison, especially for one so young."

She removes the flask, secreting it in an inner pocket as Tricina scoops the child into her arms, a wail escaping her in a warble. Feock pulls them both to his chest, crying quietly. I lean away on my heels, then fall onto my back. I stare up at the sky, tracing the shape of a scudding cloud. Agnes falls to the ground beside me, taking my hand in hers, and we lie like that for some time, tiredness and shock overtaking us as more people come down to the beach to help the islanders from Penrith up the steps.

Kai comes to join us, sitting with his knees against his chest on Agnes's other side. "It's not over yet," he says wearily, watching the people of Penrith trail up the sand. "Gather yourselves."

CHAPTER FIVE

"THESE WERE EVERYWHERE," FEOCK SAYS, SLAP-ping a sheet of parchment on the table. We're gathered in Kai's cottage, which is still whole and intact. I look around me, all of us soot and salt stained, clutching wounds, our features drawn and haunted. Agnes, Kai, Feock, Bryn, Pearl, Elijah, and the village leader of Penrith, Gwalin. Elijah is directly across from me, and my gaze snags on his. He's been in the village all morning, helping my people salvage what they could from their homes when Kai found him to pull him into this meeting. I note the tremor in his fingers before he thrusts his hands into his pockets. He is like the tide before a storm today. Troubled and restless.

I peer down at the parchment as everyone falls silent. It's much the same as the parchment left on our own island, with one exception. The writer left her mark upon it: two bloody fingerprints with an R slashed through them. The sight of it ignites the embers of fury inside me, and I grit my teeth.

"Renshaw," Kai spits out.

Captain Renshaw. The woman who kidnapped me, prepared to spill every drop of my blood to release the secrets of the map my mother left for me. The woman who sent her son to find me and trick me, to lure me in so they could steal the only pieces I had left of my mother. And then . . . surrounded us on that quay on Penscalo and took my father's life. The loathing I hold for her swirls just below my skin as I stare at her mark on the parchment. Now they've burned our homes, chasing our people from their island. I was not wrong to want vengeance, I realize.

Renshaw *must* be destroyed.

Elijah snarls and turns, making for the farthest corner of the room. He folds his arms across his chest, watching us, his features narrowed and pinched. I wonder if he is trying very hard to check his temper. If merely the mention of his rival's name sparks a rage in him that takes everything he has to reign it in. Just over a month ago, Renshaw captured me and his crew, tormenting us before he could launch a rescue. This isn't just about power or control of the routes. This is personal. For both of us.

"You saw her?" I ask Feock.

He shrugs. "I can't be certain. I saw her crew torching two cottages. Wasn't fast enough to catch any of them, but I did see one clearly. He was standing by their skiff on the beach as they made their escape. Tall with messy brown curls, wide-set features."

Seth Renshaw.

I bite back the growl that rises within me, running a hand down my face. Of course. Renshaw sent her son to ensure that the message was delivered, loud and clear. Even now, she still uses him to do her dirty work, and he complies.

"Does Renshaw have an argument with you?" Agnes asks of Gwalin. His features are steeped in shadow, craggy in the way that Bryn's are now. Yet his intelligence bleeds through, his way of weighing a situation and seeing the multiple outcomes.

He shakes his head, white hair, normally combed and tied back neatly, now stringy round his face. "We've never had cause for trouble with her. She sticks to the routes from the straits, while we watch the merchant ships passing from Leicena up to Port Graine. Never had a need to be at odds."

"Then we can only assume one thing," Kai rumbles.

I place my finger on the parchment, directly over one of the bloody fingerprints. The anger inside me simmers, picturing Seth, that day on the old quay on Penscalo. How they all melted away as the watch appeared, none of them caught in the crossfire. I bunch my hand into a fist. "She's struck a deal with the watch. They're working together."

Agnes draws in a sharp breath. "That callous, *devious*—"

"Clever," I say, stepping back. "Cold, calculating, tactical *banshee* of a woman."

"Now you see why you can't underestimate her," Elijah says softly, walking back to join us at the table. We all turn to him, and he stops a few feet away, eyes on the parchment. "She would send her own son to torch an island. She would make an alliance with the watch, when they've always been on opposite sides of the law. She won't stop. She's driven by something deeper than a lust for power."

We fall silent again, and my fingers stray to the bargain mark. To the compass, shot through with a blade. I can't see it in the dim light of Kai's cottage, but I know it's there. I know that if I stepped out under a full moon, it would blaze luminous as it did last night, reminding me of my tie to Elijah Tresillian. Of my promise.

For vengeance.

Now, keeping Rosevear safe and destroying Renshaw are one and the same, it seems. If she's banded together with the watch, they both directly threaten the isles, my home, my people . . . and we need to remove them all before they can remove *us*.

I raise my head, fixing my gaze on Elijah. His eyes meet mine, and I find he's at that final point, just before the world tips over into a tempest. Calm and sure, the slip of quiet before the storm.

"It's time, isn't it?" I say quietly. "I'm ready."

He nods only once, his gaze never leaving mine. "It's time."

The smoke still rises from my cottage like mist. The roof has caved in, collapsing in on itself. The outside walls stand firm, but inside I know the only charred remains I will find will be pieces of my broken heart.

Agnes comes over to lean her head on my shoulder, winding an arm around my waist. We've both had a few fitful hours of snatched sleep at her cottage, and time to bathe and ready ourselves before tearing into a small meal of her father's baked bread, carrots flavored with island herbs, and eggs from the chickens in their yard. No meat—no pork or chicken or pheasant, not even rabbit. It's springtime now, so the fields will begin to provide a slender bounty. But the stores are low, the animals scarce. We have to be careful with what we slaughter, especially now that there are so many more mouths to feed.

"You can have some of my things. I have clothes that will fit you. You still have my blade," she says quietly.

I heave a sigh, leaning into her. Just standing here, staring at this cottage, feels like a chapter of my life closing. This cottage holds all my memories of my mother, my father, their few possessions. It was the place where we prepared meals, where we told stories, where we mended Father's fishing nets. It was the place I fell into dreams and nightmares. Where my father told tales of wild, vicious things when my mother would leave us to slake her thirst.

It was where I was born, and where the Mira of before, the one who knew nothing of her true self, died.

"If Father was here, he would already be talking of looking for a new place to build, keeping his sights set on the future." I swallow. "Mother would have left him to it, gone down to the sea to wash away her tiredness. Maybe she would have taken me with her, to sink for a time beneath the waves."

Agnes's arm tightens on my waist. "It's all inside you still. They're all there. We carry them with us, don't we? My mother would have been up at the meeting house, nagging Pearl for her tonic recipes."

"She would have had you following her around all day with a great heap of bandages cut from her own shirts, demanding you keep up."

A small laugh falls from her lips, and she unwinds herself from around me. "I suppose the ghost of them is here today."

"You're probably right." I sigh. "And I know what both my parents would say to me."

Agnes squeezes my hand, then releases it. "They would tell you to be strong. To have hope. To fight for what you believe in."

My breath catches, and I thrust my hands into the pockets of my jacket. "I've felt so empty. Like a bowl, all hollowed out. I kept hoping it would turn, that I would somehow find my way back to myself. . . ."

"Maybe there's no going back to what we were before."

I look at her staring at the charred embers of my cottage, the tendrils of smoke. Her red hair is clean now, but still unbound. A wild thicket of fire frames her freckles, her cheekbones. I've barely seen her smile in weeks. Everything that has happened has changed her too. Perhaps she's right—there is no going back. If I can't find a thread, a tether, what will stop me from being consumed by that dark hollow in my chest if that's now my true self? What will stop me from becoming the creature lingering in my blood, seeking only revenge?

"The nightmare never leaves me," I confess. "I don't know if it ever will. I'm either so numb or so filled with fury, I can't see past that moment to anything good from before."

Agnes sniffs, facing me. Then she throws her arms around me, hugging me fiercely. "You will. Give it time. You're doing the right thing by leaving. I know it doesn't feel that way, but we'll see each other again. And when this is all over, we'll still have Rosevear. We'll still have each other. You might not be the person you were before that day, but if you hold on to why you're leaving, that you're finding a way to protect what we have here, then you'll find yourself again. Even when you're angry. Even when you're numb." She whispers in my ear. "Remember that dream you used to have? Remember flying through starlight?"

I picture the dream, the velvet-soft night, the stars and the unknown hand wrapped around mine, guiding me through the dark. "Because it's from before all this?"

"Because it's your dream of being truly free."

I hug her back, burying my face in her hair. I breathe in the scent of baked bread and rosemary, cut with the slightest hints of lavender and smoke. I want to believe her, that we'll get through this. But I'm not sure anymore that we'll still have Rosevear after this is over.

I'm not even sure we'll still have each other.

I release her, not wanting to prolong our parting. If I do, I don't know if I'll be able to leave this time. She gathers clothes for me, a couple of shirts and breeches and some undergarments. Then she swipes an apple-studded bun from her father's bakery, slipping it into a cloth bag. My favorite.

When I walk to Eli, I feel like I'm walking to my end. Like I am dropping off a precipice into deep, unforgiving waves. I stare at the gathered islanders, my people and the people of Penrith. They touch their hands to their hearts in farewell, eyes round and tainted with fear. I pick out a few of them in the crowd: Kai with his broad shoulders, Arthek at his side. Bryn leaning on a walking stick, and Pearl not far away from him, arms brimming with jars of salve. They're staying for a couple of days to help, then heading back to a safe house, far from the eyes of the watch. Then I look to Agnes, sweet Agnes, trying to hide the tears leaking from her eyes, and Feock, his arm around Tricina, her arms around their little one. All these people I can't let down. My home, my kin, my heart.

"Are you ready?" Elijah asks, his hand extended toward mine.

After the briefest hesitation, I take it. I feel his warmth curling around my skin, the scent of midnights enveloping me. I look up into his eyes, finding the storm inside him has receded. That he is still the safe harbor I found a few weeks ago, at a time when I was so desperate and adrift. And I know, in that moment, that I am doing the right thing, putting my trust in this boy. That making the bargain was the right thing to do.

"I'm ready."

He smiles, cracking a small window into the heart of him, and the warmth from our connected hands sends sparks fluttering in my veins. "Then hold your breath. And don't let go."

CHAPTER
SIX

WE STEP BACKWARD INTO SHADOW. I DRAW IN A tight-chested breath as the faces around me bleed into darkness. All at once, I am submerged, ripped from the ground, flung forward as if by some frenzied storm. The only thing I can feel is Eli's hand around mine. I grip his tighter, needing to feel his presence, to know I will not be left in this hurtling, empty maw of night. I can't see, can't breathe, and as panic begins to claw at my chest, I can do nothing but open my mouth to scream.

The world snaps into focus.

I fall to my knees, gulping down shuddering, desperate breaths as my whole body shakes. Elijah releases my hand, and I bring them both to the floor before me, the sharp cold of flagstones piercing my flesh.

"It gets easier each time," Elijah says, and I hear him as if through a tunnel, as though I am still very far away.

Gradually my heartbeat drops to its usual patter, my eyes

adjusting to the dim light in this place. A long room, paneled in dark wood with high windows drawing in thin light from outside. A heavy wooden table lined with chairs takes up much of the space. I count twenty on either side. There are portraits on the walls, painted in muted tones with gold accents, one of a family with a dog as big as a wolf at their feet. This has to be a formal dining room. It must be the castle atop the hill, star shaped and towering over the main town of Ennor below.

"Welcome to my home, the seat of House Tresillian. Ennor Castle."

Elijah leans against a wall a few feet away. His mouth is curved into a grin, arms crossed over his chest, but instead of the swagger I imagine he's trying to pull off, he sags against it and I note the strain in his eyes, the color drained from his skin. I blink again, swearing under my breath, then force my limbs to move as I stand to face him. "I am *never* doing that again. *Ever.*"

Elijah merely shrugs, his grin growing wider. "Suit yourself. You're welcome, by the way."

"For what?"

"For making the journey as smooth and swift as I could. It's not always that pleasant as a passenger."

I gape at him. "*That* was pleasant?"

"Almost enjoyable. Like I said, *you're welcome.*"

Before I can retort or bludgeon him over the head with whatever I can lay my hands on, a door flies open in the corner of the room. Elijah unfolds his arms immediately, his taunting grin turning into something more genuine, something even . . . warm.

"Caden," Elijah says, indicating me with a wave of his

hand. "Meet Mira. She'll be staying with us for a time."

Caden's grin is the mirror to Elijah's own as he looks me over. I find a boy similar in stance to Elijah, broad and tall with a warrior's frame. He has golden-blond hair, a crook in his nose as if it has been broken and reset badly, and eyes as blue as a summer sky. He strides over, offering me his hand. Where Elijah is aloof and secretive, as though hewn from midnight itself, Caden is the complete opposite, like rays of glinting sunlight. I reach out instinctively, a smile springing to my mouth.

"Well met," he says with a nod before releasing me and stepping back. "Hope Eli hasn't been inflicting one of his moods on you. He can be a tad grumpy if he misses a night of sleep, or a meal."

Glancing at Eli, then back at Caden, I swallow. So similar, yet in some ways a little different. Not quite brothers then, but he's definitely a relation, a member of House Tresillian, the family that has owned the isle of Ennor for generations. "Are you a Lord Tresillian too?"

"Unfortunately," he says, rolling his eyes. "I promise I'm far better than this one in every respect though. Only get irritable if I miss breakfast."

"It's true. You may as well know that now."

I blink at them, trying to place Caden. "Are you . . . cousins?"

Caden nods. "Our mothers were sisters."

"Were?"

His gaze slides from mine, and I wonder if I've misstepped. For a beat, all is silent before Caden frowns at Elijah. "We didn't realize you'd be gone so long. And you look . . ."

"There was a . . . complication," Elijah says with a sigh. "I had to traverse several times. More than I had prepared for."

Caden's frown deepens in concern and he opens his mouth, as though about to say more, but Elijah quickly cuts him off. "I'll ask Amma to show you to your room, Mira. You can join us for lunch after you've freshened up."

"My room?"

Elijah raises an eyebrow. "Where did you think you'd be staying while we scheme?"

"Not in a *castle* . . ." I murmur, turning to the door and finding a woman beside me. "Oh!"

"You'll get used to that," Caden says, cracking a grin. "This is Amma."

Amma tuts at Elijah, then Caden, reaching for my sleeves to straighten them. Her assessing gaze sweeps over my clothes, my hair, a slight frown etched in the middle of her forehead. I cannot guess at her age. She seems at once a young girl and an old woman, with silver hair and pale skin. And when I look at her properly, I find my eyes turned away, as if I am not supposed to look fully at her. Only from the corner of my vision do I see the color of her eyes—a deep, leafy green. She flits to Elijah's side, reaching up to touch his cheek. Oddly, they bear a resemblance too, a similarity I can't quite put my finger on. "You need to eat more. And rest. You've used too much of your power."

"Amma . . ." Elijah grumbles, pushing her hand away gently.

"What? We both know it. Fancy bringing the girl to the formal dining hall. It's like you *wanted* to sneak her past me."

"Wouldn't dream of it."

I watch the exchange, finding Amma growing almost filmy, translucent as a dragonfly's wing, as I watch them both. I squint, wondering if it's just my exhaustion, if my eyes are playing tricks. Then Amma is by my side again, taking my elbow in her bony fingers. "First, your room. I'll have a bath drawn. Then, you must eat." She cuts Elijah a look. "*All* of you, nothing but bags of bones . . ."

Amma leads me from the dining hall, and I just catch a shared eye roll between Caden and Elijah before the door creaks closed behind us. Amma releases my elbow, moving in quick, flitting, birdlike movements down a wide flagstone corridor. She is slender, the dress she wears a light blue, and I swear I can see the corridor through her spine as I pin my gaze to her back.

I keep pace with her though, realizing I could soon become lost in this castle. There are doors upon doors, with staircases half-hidden behind heavy curtains, spinning upward, or leading down in sharp turns. Seth said this place was magic, that it contained riches. . . . It doesn't appear this large from the outside. Does this sprawling castle somehow tuck itself into a smaller space? I hurry after Amma as she takes a right at a fork in the corridor, and almost collide with her.

She eyes me with a twist of humor in those piercing green eyes. "Your room." She hands me a key, silver and long, that feels as light as air. "Lock it after yourself. The castle sometimes plays tricks on visitors until it's gotten used to them."

"It . . . plays tricks?"

She shrugs, as if it's entirely obvious. "With generations of witches making up the Tresillian family, what would you expect?"

Witches? Elijah hasn't spoken of this. But with what I've seen of him, the way he can step in and out of shadows, the strange magic he commands . . . would others in his family not also possess some kind of power? I wonder again what he is, where his strange command of magic and shadow comes from. Amma pushes open the door, indicating that I should walk inside. "Thank you. Do I call you Amma?"

"Yes," she says, revealing a full set of far-too-perfect teeth. "That will do very well. The bath is nearly run, best turn the taps off before it floods."

"Oh . . ." I say, turning to the room. And when I look back at the doorway, she's vanished.

I heed her warning, pulling the door closed, and turn the key in the lock. There's a faint click, then the room almost seems to ruffle itself, and my feet skitter on the floorboards. I barely take in the bedroom before remembering Amma's other instruction. Dropping my pack to the floor, I bolt for the door set in the wall to my left, finding a bathroom complete with a claw-footed bathtub, steaming and nearly overflowing with water.

I lunge for the taps, twisting them, and breathe heavily as I stare into the pool of warm water. It's sweet scented, like the flowers in Old Jonie's garden that she cuts and places in brimming jugs around the meeting house. Like violets and sweet pea and roses. I gather another deep breath, allowing the steam to curl inside my lungs, warming me from the inside, all the way through to my bones. Then slowly I undress, slipping into the water. I sink all the way down, past my shoulders, my throat, and finally lower my face under the surface.

After I have bathed, I find a towel waiting for me. I wrap it around myself, padding out to the bedroom to look at my quarters in this strange place. There is a huge four-poster bed, the likes of which I have only seen by peering through the windows in rich merchants' homes in Penscalo, all solid oak with a heavy quilt embroidered with tiny blue forget-me-nots. There is a large wardrobe, a chest with spare linens stored in it at the foot of the bed, and a dressing table set with a comb and a looking glass. I give myself the briefest of glances, knowing I will find only a drawn face and a fog of golden hair, damp around my shoulders.

But what calls to me the most is the window. Set with diamond-shaped panes of glass, it looks out over the sea and the main town of Ennor spread below. A window seat is set into it, with a stack of cushions scattered on top, and I sit down on the edge, gazing out at the tapestry of houses and market squares. It's beautiful in the spring light, with its quay stacked up with lobster pots, the people milling slowly about their day. For a while, I just stare, wondering what it would be like to be one of them. What it would be like to just have everyday cares. To have a family around me that loves and cherishes me. To have a home and a hearth and a hearty meal to enjoy in peace and safety, without the watch and Renshaw ready to snatch it all away.

I close my eyes, then open them onto this empty, lonesome room. I cross to the pack containing the clothes Agnes lent me, pull on one of her worn shirts, and sink into the middle of the bed. The shirt smells like her: lavender and herbs and bread, with the slightest tang of the sea threaded through it. My heart twists. I don't know when I will see her again, or Kai, or any of my island kin.

I've left Rosevear smoldering in my wake, and now that I'm alone, I cannot hide from the needling guilt of it. I clench my hands into fists, reminding myself of why I'm here, the bargain Elijah and I made. How my heart craved vengeance, how I *will* extract it at the end of a blade, and then we will all be free. The suffering and the hardship will not all be for nothing.

I pull the cover up over my head, reliving every moment of the night before, the flames, the frantic search for survivors, the fear as I guided the people of Penrith through the hidden rocks. I close my eyes and sink beneath the surface, deep into the ocean of nothing inside myself, and finally I sleep.

CHAPTER
SEVEN

TWO YEARS HAVE PASSED, AND THE FAR ISLES
are not as she remembers.

Brielle arrives on a Wednesday afternoon, the sea restless
and foaming, reaching toward the deck of *Florian*. It's a merchant vessel, sturdy and built for long journeys, on its way
from Hail Harbor in Arnhem to travel back along the straits.
It is the only ship that agreed to carry her and set her down
on the Far Isles, for a generous pouch of coin. No one wants
to stop here anymore. There are too many stories of ghosts
in the surrounding waters, of glimmering lights that should
not exist. And now a nest of pixies plagues the islanders that
remain.

She disembarks on the main isle of Egan, pack slung across
her broad shoulders, instructions written on the parchment
in her jacket pocket.

But the isle of Egan holds an eerie stillness.

Where once there were huddled groups playing dice on

the quay, pickpockets weaving, maids selling hot buns for a copper, now there is only the watch. She swallows, eyeing them quietly, these men checking the merchant ship, nodding her past with a gray slyness to their features. She walks into town, heart drumming a little too quickly, but not with fear. The watch has changed Egan, stolen the life from its throat.

Her heart drums with fury to see it.

She makes for the Inn Melusine first, a place she knows has kept its head afloat. It gazes back at her sleepily, a lumbering sort of place with squat windows and a bowing roof. It is named after a monster that lingers in the rivers of the owner's homeland. Brielle asked her once, a few drinks in, why she would name her inn after those gruesome creatures. The owner leaned her elbows on the bar and whispered, *The Melusine isn't just gruesome, hunter. She's eternal. Cut off her head and she'll grow another. Pierce her heart and she'll cackle with glee. She cannot be killed off. Rather fitting for my business, don't you think?*

Brielle turns those words over now as she eyes the faded gold lettering on the swinging sign above the door, a depiction of the river creature swirling in blues and greens around the words. She touches her fingers to her heart, feeling the outline of the pendant hidden under her shirt before ducking beneath the lintel and stepping over the threshold into the solid gloom beyond.

"No fare for travelers today," a lisping voice calls from behind the bar. "Nor tomorrow, or the day after that."

"Even for an old friend?"

The woman turns sharply, squinting at Brielle. Helene still wears her hair in the Leicenan style of her youth: black ringlets piled high atop her head, thin tendrils hanging around her jutting cheekbones. She has lost her plumpness, her skin sagging under her eyes. But as Brielle steps into the watery light stretching from the windows, a grin creases the woman's features into something almost youthful. She hasn't lost that steely glint, at least.

"Hunter," Helene breathes, placing the glass she's polishing on the bar with a clink. "You've returned."

Brielle crosses to the bar, matching her grin before clasping Helene's hand. "At last."

"You're looking taller. But too skinny. You like rabbit still? *Kell!*" She shouts from the corner of her mouth, her sharp eyes never leaving Brielle's face. "Got a beautiful brace—Kell set a trap yesterday. Made a lovely pie this morn."

Footsteps, fleet and skittering, sound from the side of the bar. A boy a little younger than Brielle appears, wiping his hands on a cloth and blinking quickly. His brown hair is scruffy, a streak of flour across his forehead, and as he notices Brielle, he begins to laugh. "You took your time! Where's my winnings? You owe me *at least* a silver."

"Cheeky shit," Brielle says. She doesn't like how bony they both are. How sunken their eyes, how pale their skin. She digs a hand in her pocket, flicking a silver coin into the air, which Kell catches deftly. "Have I ever not paid up?"

"There's always a first time, hunter," Kell says before moving back toward the door he entered through. He points at Brielle, raising his eyebrows. "Pie? Tatties and neeps? Don't tell me your coven's cooking is a patch on mine."

Brielle pats her stomach with a grin. "I've only been waiting two years for your cooking, Kell."

Helene places a brimming glass in front of her. "Draw

yourself up. Tell me the news from Arnhem."

Brielle takes a deep gulp, the bitter, thick drink warming every corner of her. She wipes her sleeve across her mouth, sets the glass back down, and begins to weave the tale of the last two years. This is how it works. The real currency on her assignments isn't coin. It's stories. It's talk of the shiftings and stirrings on the continent. The news people like Helene crave, that carries them out of their small worlds and into the farthest reaches of Brielle's.

"And yourself?" Brielle says, pausing to accept the plate of rabbit pie and all the trimmings from Kell. Her stomach rumbles, and she picks up the fork to cram a piece into her mouth. Meaty and rich, salty and flavored with wild garlic. She almost groans as she sucks the meat juices from the tines of her fork. "How fare the Far Isles?"

Kell leans on the bar next to Helene and they exchange a brief look. Brielle busies herself with a gulp of her drink, letting them work out where to start. How much to tell her. How many secrets they are willing to impart to a monster hunter, a witch.

"The only visitors we have are the ones the watch will allow to reach our shores."

"Quiet then?"

Kell hesitates. "There have been . . . disappearances. People leaving, of course, when they can get the permits together, or slip past the watch. But also people just . . . not turning up." He shrugs. "I don't know how else to put it. It's not the place you'll remember, hunter. It's . . . haunted."

"Have you considered leaving? Getting back to Leicena, or moving on?"

Helene shakes her head quickly, chewing on the inside of

her mouth. "Three folk stowed aboard a passing merchant vessel without a travel permit a moon ago. The watch found them all."

Her words hang in the air, a mist Brielle can't blow away with hearty cheer. She's heard of the watch checking travel permits that seem almost impossible to come by. Forgeries have begun circulating, bad and good, all of them costing a small fortune, just so people can travel freely between Arnhem, its isles, and the continent. The ruling council, it seems, does not like its people to leave. Only the merchants and witches travel freely, and then only if they are favored by the ruling council, pay the tax, and are granted permission. "I'm sorry. Truly."

"'Tis not your doing," Helene says with a small sigh. "We all know whose doing it is. But no use harping on. You're here on an assignment, yes? That coven of yours sending you over here?"

"Yes," Brielle says, adjusting her seat before fixing her gaze on Helene. "What can you tell me about the pixie nest?"

The trick with a nest like this is to find the queen. Brielle scours the eastern reaches of the island, carefully blending in to the landscape with her hunkering steps. She finds evidence of the nest three hours in: a scatter of fish heads and bird bones, and a glint of gold. She crouches down low in the drifts of heather and bracken to examine the leavings. A gold bracelet with a broken clasp. A pendant with a fragment of glitter at the center, the shaped glass that Highborn high society goes wild for. And a ring, the kind that would sit on a pinky finger.

With the finger still attached to it.

Brielle huffs a breath, narrowing her gaze on the pale bones. A bird skull, fractures fissuring through it, and the spines of several midsize fish, possibly pollock. She bites her lip, assessing the finger. Definitely human, most likely belonging to a member of the watch. The fingernail is too clipped to belong to an islander, with no dirt embedded around it to indicate hard work. No wonder she'd been given this assignment. She reaches into her bag, fishing out a bottle containing a delicate pink plant.

Frost flowers.

They grow in the northern mountains of Arnhem, known for their beauty, taste, and scent. They are used in drinks at decadent parties in Highborn, a way to display wealth and power. But they are also used by hunters like her as a lure.

"You're close, aren't you?" she says softly, eyeing the surrounding heather. "We'll see if you have a penchant for more than just gold, glitter, and bones."

Brielle unstoppers the cork on the top of the bottle, pulling out one of the pink stems. She crushes it in her fingers, letting the petals scatter in the wind. At first there is only silence. Like the very island has held its breath.

Then she is engulfed.

She crouches lower as a stream of pixies goes for the bottle. Her gloves protect her hands as the pixies bite and tear, sharp needle teeth flashing in blue gums. A shriek, hideous and scraping like claws on granite, rips through her mind, and she turns quickly, eyeing the swarm of tiny bodies.

"There you are." The queen. No larger than a hand, but luminous, glowing like phosphorescence. Brielle reaches for the smallest dagger in the sash across her chest, flicking it at the queen. It strikes her in the middle. Brielle watches as the tiny pixie screams, pale green hair flying around her sharp little features. Her wings slacken, body dropping to the ground. The entire swarm drops down with her.

Brielle sniffs, pushing a strand of hair behind her ear, and brushes herself off as she stands. One of the little buggers has gnawed through her jacket sleeve, leaving tiny holes where its teeth met something too solid beneath. She nudges the tiny bodies aside, stepping across the heather to scoop up the queen. She leaves the dagger in, not wanting to lose any of the queen's precious pale blue blood. Then she begins the careful extraction.

Selecting a dozen vials from her bag and a syringe, Brielle drains each and every pixie. Most of the creature blood will be kept by Coven Septern and her malefant, the coven leader, while the rest will be handed to a courier of sorts, to be distributed to a web of apothecaries in Arnhem and across the continent. It keeps their magic fed for creating the hexes, curses, and spells they sell, will generate learning and study for the more academic witches in the coven and make the coffers full from the trade with the courier. But some will be given as a tax to the ruling council of Arnhem, just as with every creature Brielle hunts.

When her work is done, she removes the dagger from the queen's chest and cleans it carefully before placing it back inside the holder on her sash. She sniffs again, eyeing the frail little bodies, their iridescent wings, their pale blue-and-green features. When she received the assignment, she had been told by her malefant of the horrors they had wrought. Stolen toes in the night. An eyeball. And worst of all, the smallest finger of a baby's tiny fist. She suppresses a shudder, leaving their remains scattered among the heather and bracken for the crows to find.

She has no mercy for creatures like this, magpies and tricksters, or worse, the monsters that kill just for sport. With one final check that all the glass vials are properly stoppered in her pack, she sets off back for the Inn Melusine.

CHAPTER EIGHT

SLIPPING THE SLENDER KEY INTO MY POCKET, I check that my bedroom door is locked. It's afternoon, and somehow I have slept through the middle of the day. I curse, turning to the web of corridors. My bedroom sits at a fork: a corridor before me, and one to my left and right. I hesitate, trying to remember the direction Amma and I arrived from a few hours ago. But the corridors and half-hidden staircases twist in my mind, and I realize I haven't a clue where I am in this place.

I say a quick rhyme under my breath, pointing to each corridor before settling on the corridor that leads to my left. It twists into darkness around a far corner, but so does the right-hand one. I set off, my boots ringing too loud, echoing off the flagstones. I try to remember what I know of Ennor Castle. It's shaped as a five-pointed star with ramparts and towers at each point, and yet seems so much bigger than it appears from the outside. When I was last on Ennor with

Seth, he spoke of a great bounty hidden within its walls.

There's magic there. And riches. More than you'll see in a lifetime of wrecks.

But so far all I have seen is vast, echoing corridors and the kind of decor and furnishings that may have existed here for more than a hundred years. I force the cadence of Seth's voice from my mind, focusing on the corridor. Perhaps he also knew of the line of witches in House Tresillian, and that is why he believed there was magic and wealth here.

The corridor is lined with paintings, mainly portraits of men and women depicted alone or in groups. There is one that catches my eye, just before the turn into the shadow beyond. It's huge, taking up a vast section of the wall, painted in golds and pinks as though aflame. There's a beautiful old-fashioned galleon, the likes of which I've only heard about in tales or seen sketches of. Certainly not the kind of ship the merchants sail past the Fortunate Isles. With three masts and billowing white sails, she's a beauty. But she's listing in the water, the sea rising up to swallow her, and from a murky corner, I spy something that shouldn't be there—a tentacle, massive and poised, lurching toward the ship. I squint, stepping closer, noticing shadows in the sea beneath the galleon. And I realize why she is listing. She's in the clutches of something huge, something *horrific*—

"The kraken."

My heart judders and I spin, finding Elijah lounging against the wall. He's freshened up since this morning, and the telltale signs of fatigue have nearly been swept away. He's wearing a navy-blue shirt, dark breeches and boots, and a teasing smile that tells me he's got some of his swagger back. I track the movement of his fingers as he pushes a few strands of dark hair away from his eyes, the piercing depths of them seeming to glitter as they meet mine. My pulse quickens, a flush creeping up my throat as I catch a hint of his scent, cedar and citrus, laced with sea salt. I breathe it in, finding it all too intoxicating, and irritated with myself, I cross my arms and scowl at him. "Are you always lurking behind people?"

He ignores my question, looking over my shoulder at the painting. "It was my great-grandfather's pride, that galleon. She sailed once along the southern coast of Leicena, and that was the last time anyone ever dared navigate that stretch of sea."

I turn to the painting, eyeing that creeping tentacle. "Because of the kraken?"

"Yes, and others. Teeming with monsters. That's why the straits are so carefully patrolled and protected by Arnhem and Skylan fleets, and why islanders like *you* . . ." He comes to stand next to me. "Are rather a thorn in the ruling council's side."

"I see."

We both stare at the listing galleon, and my gaze dips to the shadow that lies beneath.

"I was on my way to collect you."

I turn to him, eyes sweeping over his profile, pausing on the dip at the base of his throat, the top button of his shirt. "Yes?"

"You missed lunch, but I've called my inner circle together and Amma is putting out food for us. Now you're rested, it's time we got to work." He hesitates, eyes flicking down to mine. "My friends are . . . looking forward to meeting you."

I raise my eyebrows. "That sounds ominous."

He smiles, saying nothing, and I fall into step beside him as we walk through the castle. There are more paintings, more doors and walkways, but everything is old-fashioned and frayed at the edges, like the fading beauty of that galleon. "I'm surprised the watch isn't beating down your door to investigate this place."

"The watch governs the lands the ruling council owns, but this is a private island . . . and one they are dissuaded from landing on, with a hefty bribe in the right pair of hands every now and again."

"The watch is guided by money and power."

"One could argue by a misguided sense of duty also, but yes. I wouldn't say they're above corruption, would you?"

"They must want to root you out too though. Must be looking for a way onto this island. Or have they not connected the dots that the Elijah on their wanted posters is also Lord Tresillian of the House Tresillian?"

"My operations are entirely aboveboard—"

I snort.

"—on paper." Elijah clears his throat. "Piracy is a terrible crime. One Renshaw indulges in, but I hold certain routes and have licenses for transporting particular goods. Just like any decent merchant. The ruling council gets its cut, and the watch is told to look the other way."

I narrow my eyes. "What kind of goods?"

"If you're referring to the hold of *Phantom*—"

I suppress a shudder, remembering the rows and rows of vials of blood. I still can't help equating it to my own blood, and my mother's, even though Pearl assured me they had never carried siren blood. "I am."

Elijah stops and I pause, turning toward him. "Apothecaries

are not against the law. Nor is magic. We pick up the vials from a coven in Highborn that I have an arrangement with, and we spread them between the apothecaries that I—or rather, that House Tresillian—own. As I told you before, that hold was from a particularly vicious nest of wyverns that were bent on killing an entire village of people in the Spines for *sport*. I do not feel sorry for the damn beasts, nor am I sorry their blood is made into remedies and potions that keep human beings, normal people, *alive and well*. Even as we speak, Pearl is using some of those potions on Rosevear to heal your wounded."

I lick my lips. "You don't own the witches then? Or their hunters? You own an inherited isle. . . . Would the witches in your family not have inherited . . . a coven?"

He smiles before continuing on down the corridor. "No one owns the witches. Their covens are . . . ancient. And yes, the Tresillian witches form part of a coven, one I deal with to this day, but they do not own it. They are the only ones who can extract that blood from the monsters of our world. Their hunters do that." He spreads out his hands. "They hunt the creatures, bottle the blood, use it for what-ever spells and hexes they're creating for the highest bidder, or just for themselves and their academic interests, and I take the rest from the coven in Highborn that my house has ties with. The apothecaries distill it into a powder for human consumption. Drafts, tinctures . . . just like my apothecary, Howden, who fixed up Seth in Port Trenn." He raises his eyebrows. "It's an honest trade."

"More honest than claiming salvage from passing ships, is that what you're saying?"

He pointedly ignores my question, and as we round a

corner, he pushes back one of the heavy curtains hiding a staircase. "Before we go on, I need you to know something about the people I work with here. They work for me in name alone; in reality they're my partners. Equals. When you speak to them, think of it as . . . extending our bargain. We need them on our side, but they may have their own opinions."

We descend the spiral staircase, hearing voices bubble up from below. The staircase leads onto a wide landing, the main staircase in the center. And there, waiting for us in a grand entrance hall in front of a set of double front doors, is a group of people.

Elijah Tresillian's inner circle.

Merryam with her arms folded across her chest, hair falling in ringlets around her face. Caden standing with his hands clasped at his back, feet firmly planted in a warrior's stance. And there's a woman I haven't met yet, chestnut hair half up, half down, cascading in wavy rivers past her shoulders. She peers up at us with huge brown eyes that are a touch amber. They seem to . . . glow. She smiles, hovering delicately next to Caden, her white shirt neatly tucked into a dark gray pinafore dress, hands in the pockets of her skirts. I search their faces and realize they're all the same age as me, or perhaps just a little older. Elijah must have chosen an inner circle of people he's grown up with.

"Amma is having kittens," the woman in the pinafore dress says in a melodic voice. I look back at her, noting her delicate features surrounding those arresting amber eyes as she scrunches her nose. She's beautiful in a way that I've seen in artists' renditions of sirens. Haunting and secretly deadly. I wonder what this woman brings to the inner circle. "You're late."

Eli takes the staircase two at a time. "Mira overslept."

I pinch my lips together to keep from retorting, walking unhurriedly down the staircase to join them. Merryam comes straight to me, throwing her arms around me in a fierce hug. I return it, closing my eyes briefly as she murmurs in my ear, "You owe me at least three letters. You didn't answer a single one. Forgotten how to hold a pen?"

"I'm sorry," I say, breathing in her scent, sea and salt and smoky tea. "It's been . . . difficult."

She loosens her grip on me, her eye fixed on mine. "It's good to see you here."

I step back, throat suddenly thick, heart a little heavy, as Caden nods to me, eyes twinkling, and this new young woman . . . she assesses me intently. Her lips part as if she is about to say something, but just then, a huge door similar to the main front double doors opens to our right, and Amma stands in the doorframe. She gestures to the room beyond. "The tea will be tepid."

"Apologies, Amma," Eli says, touching her arm as she steps to the side, allowing him past.

I follow the others, then feel an arm slip through mine. "They're all bluster, but never annoy Amma. You'll find your tea and bathwater tepid for life," the young woman says. "I'm Tanith, the librarian."

"Mira," I say.

"Sit by me," she says, and I realize it's not a request. These people may be loyal to Eli, but I have yet to win their allegiance. I swallow discreetly, tamping down my nerves as I prepare to argue for my people.

CHAPTER
NINE

"HOW MANY?" KELL ASKS, LEANING OVER TO PEER inside the bag at Brielle's feet. "Lose any fingers?"

Brielle slouches back in her chair, holding up her hands. "All present and correct. And there were two dozen in the nest."

Kell whistles, eyes lighting up as he places a bowl of soup in front of her, then half a loaf of thick sliced bread. Brielle's stomach rumbles, the sweet and savory notes of the gingery soup mingling with the scent of warm, fresh-baked bread as she lifts her spoon. The inn is quiet again today, a couple of locals with heavy brows and frayed clothes seated at a table in the corner, murmuring into pints and playing a game of checkers.

"I wish I could go with you. When you have to leave again."

Brielle sighs and places the spoon back on the table with a clink. "I wish that too."

She has no words of comfort for him. That's just not who she is. But if she could, she would scoop Kell up, take him back to the coven, and train him. She would teach him how to be a hunter, how to follow his instincts, how to use magic in order to disable, disarm, and drain. But they both know that can never happen. Kell is human, not a witch like her, and if she tried to smuggle him off the Far Isles, he would meet the same fate as the others who had tried to leave without a travel permit.

"I've been practicing," he whispers, glancing across at the two locals in the corner, then over his shoulder at the windows looking out on the street. "Remember I told you, last time you were here. I swear, I can do magic like you."

"Kell . . ."

"Just look. Just *look* and tell me this isn't true magic." He squints, holding his hand out in a fist in front of himself. Sweat glistens along his hairline, a frown mark deepening between his eyes.

"Kell, we've talked about this—"

"*Look.*" And in the span of a charged breath, he twists his fist, opening his palm to the air.

Pale fire ignites in his hand.

Brielle thrusts her chair back, leaping up to put the table between them. She blinks, breathing heavily, watching those dancing lilac flames lick his fingers. "It's not . . . it's not *possible.* . . ." The boy hadn't uttered a word, not a single word of magic. The flames just . . . ignited from his *thoughts.* Witches could only cast with the right word, after years of careful study and practice, and only with the blood of a creature acting as a catalyst for the magic in their veins. But this . . . this is different.

Kell grins, triumph breaking his concentration as his gaze flits to Brielle and the fire gutters out. He shakes out his hand and Brielle reaches for it, examining his fingers, his skin, finding them cool to the touch. Unmarked. Unharmed.

"It *is* possible, hunter," Kell murmurs. "Maybe it's not only you witches that hold all the magic in this world. Have you ever come across another like me?"

Brielle knows a lie is kinder, that the truth would only give Kell hope, and he would try and leave Egan to find the others hiding their magic on the continent, nurturing secret power that their communities either revere or shun them for. She's seen both sides of it; she knows how a crowd can turn against a boy like Kell. And she knows the ruling council will either exploit him or kill him.

She shakes her head and swallows, closing her hand over his. When she speaks, she has to work hard at keeping her tone measured and steady. But the fear laces it anyway, fear for him, for what they would do if they found him. She knows he's an orphan, dropped off here as a youngling and nurtured by luck and Helene. He isn't a threat. He isn't a monster in human skin; she would know. She would smell it, or sense it. But that wouldn't matter if her next assignment was to take his blood and drain him. Magic like this disrupts the order of things, the careful balance of power, and if her coven or any other hears of a boy that can raise fire with a mere thought . . . the risk is too great to bear.

"You keep this secret, boy. You don't show a soul. Not one *single* person, do you understand?"

"But Helene—"

"Even Helene," she growls, releasing Kell's fist and folding her arms across her chest. "What do you think would happen if the watch found out?"

Kell presses his lips together, that glint of triumph turning dull as an old copper coin. "They'd lock me up and send for a hunter."

"A hunter like me."

"A hunter like you."

She shakes her head slowly. "Don't put me in that position. Not ever. You don't want to be hunted. You know what those vials in my bag contain."

The first slice of doubt and fear cuts across Kell's features. "All right. I'll keep it secret. I won't show anyone. But, Brielle . . ."

"Yes?"

"If there's me, if I can do this, then maybe there's more like me. Wherever I came from before I was left here, there could be others. Maybe . . . maybe it won't be me you're hunting next. But if magic's changing, then it could be someone *like* me. Someone human. And maybe everyone just needs to know we're not a threat. That it's just change, and change isn't always terrible."

Brielle chews over Kell's words all evening. The next morning, they are still harrying her, and when she grasps his hand in farewell, she has to contain her flinch. She's heard murmurs of children like Kell across the continent these past couple of years, children born to human parents who can do more than a human ought. Not changelings, not monsters like she hunts, but true humans, ordinary children with magic sparking in their veins. Magic that doesn't need feeding with monster and creature blood, or to be coaxed out with words and spells. Those murmurs usually reach for her in the quiet corners, the villages in the Spines, the principality of Lorva—or the desolate towns surrounding the mines of Valstra.

She's even met one or two, and helped hide them, trodden on the embers of rumor and speculation so they could slip away, or live in peace. But not here. Not so close to Arnhem and Leicena, where covens like hers have their strongholds, where a whole web of apothecaries sell magic to the masses. Magic means wealth and power, and there are rulers and witches that will not want to give up their control of either. Mostly she's afraid of it getting back to the covens and, through them, the watch and ruling council. That some other hunter will find a child such as Kell and haul them back to their malefant like a prize.

She breathes out through her nose, long and burdened, as she stands on the quay waiting for her merchant ship, *Fair Rosamund*, to be ready for departure. It isn't luck this time, but coin that compelled this ship to stop here. Coin paid by the head of her coven, her malefant, to ensure her swift return to Highborn.

"A coin and a feather for them," Helene says at her shoulder. Brielle glances down, finding the woman staring, as she was, at the merchant ship, the members of the watch lining the quay, the wide, gray sea beyond.

"I was thinking about the last time I was here. How much has changed."

Helene smiles wryly. "Do you ever see him?"

Of course Brielle knows who she means immediately. Even the merest mention of him stirs the bitter bile in her blood. "Not if I can help it."

"Cut a fine figure though, did he not? Captain Spencer Leggan. You know, we do not blame you. We were all fooled to begin with by him and his grand words."

Brielle snorts and pats Helene's shoulder. "Kind of you. But we both know I was the biggest fool of us all."

"For believing he was good?"

For loving him, she wants to say. *Loving him, when all along, I should have hated him and all he stood for.* "For believing he wanted to create a better world, when all he really wanted was to carve it into his own vision."

Helene turns to her. "You are good, hunter. But something troubles you, something greater than your guilt over what happened here. What that captain did to these isles."

"I—" Brielle begins, stopping short. She wants to tell Helene so desperately. To confide in someone. About the assignments coming in now for her coven and how some of the creatures she hunts do not seem so monstrous to her. About the whispers, about the watch and how she mistook ruthless ambition and the desire for control for passion. Mostly she wants to talk to Helene about Kell, about the magic erupting where it shouldn't. She wants to make Helene promise to protect him, to find a way for them to leave this place, to find somewhere safe from witches like her.

But she just shakes her head. She can't say any of those things, not to this shrewd-eyed woman, not to anyone. "I'm to return straightaway, Helene. No extra nights by your hearth, I'm afraid. I have a new assignment awaiting me. My malefant commands I return."

Helene nods, her eyes narrowing. For a moment, she says nothing. Then the breath she expels ends on the slightest smile. "Take care of yourself, Brielle. Don't take this the wrong way, but I hope never to see you again. Not on Egan . . . and not anywhere near my boy."

Brielle looks at her sharply and realizes she knows. Maybe

she's known since she took him in as a small child. Maybe those pale flames in his fist are not the first sign of what he can do, and how different Kell truly is.

"Here, take this. In case you can purchase a travel permit. Travel as far from here as you can, somewhere quiet and safe. Invent new identities, new histories. Tell no one." Brielle slips the few gold coins she has from her own purse into Helene's fingers.

Helene closes her eyes briefly, pocketing the coins. "I am not so proud as to refuse your gift, hunter. Maybe once I would have, but now . . . now I have little choice. Thank you."

Brielle watches Helene leave the quay, walking back to the Inn Melusine, a slight limp plaguing her right leg but her head held high. She looks down at her hands, the hands of a witch. A hunter. The ebony nails, the solitary faint black vein tracking down her thumb, the scars flecked over her flesh, a map of the creatures she's fought and killed. She closes her hand into a fist over it all and strides toward the merchant ship. Her pack, now filled with blood vials, clinks against her back, and as they cast off, she turns from the isle of Egan and faces northwest. To Arnhem. To her next assignment, waiting to be delivered to her at her coven's stronghold in Highborn.

To home.

She believes in her work as a hunter. She believes in what she does, how she has been trained to slay the monsters plaguing their world. She's a weapon wielded by her coven, a sharpened blade, a nocked arrow. She knows the blood she drains will be used for good, just as she's always been told. But lately . . .

Lately she is troubled by those murmurs.

Lately she is questioning more.

CHAPTER
TEN

WE ENTER A LONG ROOM SET WITH WINDOWS down one side, a huge fireplace at the center of the opposite wall. There are worn, rosy-colored rugs strewn over the flagstone floor, side tables stacked with books and oil lamps, and comfortable, lived-in sofas and armchairs arranged in groups. Elijah and Caden sink into two armchairs by the fireplace, which roars to life as if by its own volition. I remember what Amma told me—Ennor Castle likes to play tricks. Does it also like to reward those it is loyal to?

"Don't mind Maggie," Merryam says, launching herself onto a sofa and snagging a slice of saffron cake from the sprawl of simple, filling food on the low table between the armchairs and sofas. "She's a softy."

I look down by the fireplace and see who Maggie is. A giant wolfhound, gray and shaggy, with doleful eyes and a thumping tail. She lumbers to her feet, sniffing around me, and her head comes up to my chest. I reach out, brushing my hand over her head, and she nudges me, as though in greeting. Her eyes meet mine, and I grin. She's just like the giant wolfish dog in the portrait in the formal dining room where I first arrived this morning. "I think we're going to get along just fine."

I take a seat next to Tanith, directly across from Elijah. He picks up the teapot from the coffee table, pouring tea into everyone's cups before nudging a small milk jug toward me. "If you take it with milk."

I let a small amount of milk color the amber tea before stirring in a drop of honey. Then I take a sip, letting the lavender notes wash over me. It tastes like Agnes's blend. It tastes . . . like home. In fact, a lot of the food Amma has laid out for us is the kind of food Agnes and her father sell in their bakery. Saffron loaf studded with currants, apple cake, thick-sliced brown bread and butter. It's homespun, and as I reach for a Chelsea bun, thick and doughy, I wonder if their lives are so very different to mine, even in a castle. I raise my gaze to meet Elijah's, and he nods to the food as Merryam fills her plate, already squashing a second saffron slice between her lips. "Go on, or you'll offend Amma."

I don't wait to be told twice. I pick up scones, butter, apple cake, and have another swig of tea before taking a big bite of the saffron loaf. It's just like Agnes's, and my heart twists. Tanith's hand bumps mine and I smile at her, allowing her to take the last cheese savory scone. She picks it up and drops it on my plate. "Now you owe me a visit."

"Where?"

"The library. Second floor." She nods her head to the wolfhound, who is once more sprawled next to the crackling fireplace. "Maggie knows the way."

When I've eaten my fill, I look to Elijah. He takes a drink of tea and says quietly, "We eat as the rest of our island does here. Nothing is wasted. Nothing is taken for granted."

I nod, contemplating past winters when our island stretched every resource we had, sharing and bartering so every family survived. It seems that in this, Lord Tresillian is no different from Bryn. He doesn't take more than his share, doesn't try to set himself apart, despite this castle where he lives.

"Mira is here for a reason," Elijah says then. "She and I have an agreement. An understanding." He sits back, allowing me the space to speak, and I realize it's on me to convince them. This may be his isle, his castle, but he does not command these people. Another way he is like Bryn, and now Kai.

I clear my throat and place my teacup on the table as I rub at the bargain mark on my wrist, picturing everything that has come before this moment. The journey aboard *Phantom*. Seth's hand in mine in the bowl of sea. The sirens, with their claws and pointed teeth. The letter my mother left for me, and the map that I carry right next to my heart. Then I picture him, my father. That final moment. The one that haunts my nightmares and banishes my dreams.

"I am," I hear myself saying, gathering it all inside me. Every moment. Every heartbreak. Making me stronger, surer. Ready. "I mean to destroy Captain Renshaw for all she has done. I'm going to drive away the watch before they bleed the Fortunate Isles dry. And I need you." I focus my gaze on Elijah Tresillian. Lord of Ennor. Wielder of a rare and dangerous magic. The boy I am trusting now with my life, and that of my people. "I need your help to do it. It seems Renshaw and the watch have formed an alliance, one that aligns their interests in only one way: to take control of the Fortunate Isles."

"Eli told us what happened on Rosevear and Penrith last night," Merryam says quietly. "I'm so sorry that it's come to this, Mira."

I swallow and smile sadly at her. "Pearl helped as many as she could. She's a wonder."

"She really is," Merryam says in agreement. "And you have my support, always. Mine and hers. *Phantom* and my crew are with you."

"So Captain Renshaw and the watch have banded together and sprung a two-pronged attack in the night," Caden says, sitting back. "Interesting alliance, especially with her on every wanted poster between here and Hail Harbor."

"Interesting, and fatal for the Fortunate Isles," I say. "Including Ennor. If Rosevear falls as Penrith has, they may turn their attention here next. There's too much at stake to do anything but fight, and *win*."

"Oh, I don't doubt it," Caden says with a grin. "She's a wily one. But we'll be ready. You have my blade. I'll begin training, Eli. Sharpen up the crews, prepare the people on the island in case the fight comes to us."

"Is that what you do? The training?" I ask.

"Training, fortifications . . . Merryam here oversees the drops and runs. I make sure the crews know what to do if they get into any trouble. Eli throws his weight around as Lord Tresillian, brokers the deals we need for our coffers, and wrangles information."

Eli chuckles. "When I'm away, I know the island and operations are in good hands."

I look to Tanith, who is eyeing me steadily, those soft, wide eyes reflecting the flickering glow of the firelight. "Come see me when you have questions about what *you* can do," she says. "Something tells me Eli didn't just bring you here to beg for help." Her gaze strays to Eli. "Something tells me he has brought us a weapon."

I hesitate, sharing a look with Elijah before pulling it from where I keep it hidden, against my heart. The map, and the letter from my mother. I place them on the coffee table, spreading them so that everyone can see. "From my . . . kin."

Tanith smiles knowingly. "No wonder Renshaw was after you."

"You can see it?"

"Not exactly," she says softly, leaning forward to place her fingertips on the parchment of the map, which appears blank to all but a siren. "I can feel it. The hum of strange magic, it's like a song of the sea. A siren song. It's a map, isn't it?"

My eyes dart to hers as she leans back. "It is. A map of the knowledge a siren would hold in her head, passed down from mother to daughter, inked in their blood."

"And you can read this map?"

"Yes. I can see every inch of the Fortunate Isles, the coastline around Arnhem, stretching across the straits, past the Far Isles."

Merryam whistles and grins.

"I've never come across any records, but . . ." Elijah begins.

"You want to know what our weapon here is capable of. I'll research," Tanith replies, gaze not leaving mine. "But if the library doesn't hold anything, you know where you'll have to turn."

I frown. "Where?"

"The witches. Coven Septern," Elijah says, waving a hand. "But one step at a time. Let's focus on what we know. Renshaw has made an alliance with the watch, and if she's working with them, she may well have made some kind of agreement with the ruling council. I'll begin working my contacts, testing the temperature of our great rulers. In the meantime, we train, we make ready, and we work out how to weaken Renshaw and the watch before they weaken *us*."

Caden rubs his hands together, grinning. "I've wanted to take her out for years. This map of yours, Mira . . . Can you find her strongholds?"

I nod, running a finger over a secret cove I've been eyeing, a secret place I'm sure is hers, unmarked on any other map I've seen, sitting between Port Trenn and Port Graine. As the map moves and alters with the tides and weather, it also reveals the positions of the vessels crossing it. There are times when her vessels have hunkered in this secret cove over the past month; I've studied their movements whenever I've unfolded the map to scrutinize it. "Here," I say, describing the coordinates. "This is where I'd like to start."

Merryam nods. "I'll check it out."

"Take Joby. Have you found a replacement for Pearl?" Elijah asks.

"A *temporary* replacement?" Merryam shoots back.

Elijah inclines his head. "Of course. I assure you, you will not be parted for long."

"Will you also keep a watch over Rosevear, Mer? I don't like to think of what would happen, if . . . if . . ."

Caden and Merryam both nod. "I'll put a couple of crews offshore. Caden can switch them out for training. Don't worry, Mira. We'll know if they attack again."

Relief floods me. "Thank you. I can see if any vessels move too close," I say, glancing down at the map, at the spread of ships across the sea. "But sometimes Renshaw's ships move unnaturally fast."

Elijah and Tanith exchange a look. "There are five main covens in Arnhem," she says. "None of them above taking good coin for a spell. The witches don't involve themselves in politics; they take on work from those who pay well, and they expect discretion."

"I'll look into it," Elijah says grimly. "If there's a coven working with Renshaw or the watch, someone will know something. Someone will talk."

After the teapot is drained and the plates stacked ready to carry back to the kitchens, Tanith and Caden make their excuses, stretching and moving from the room. I nod to each of them in turn, wondering how much I can rely on them. How invested they'll be in what is to come. It's not until Merryam leaves the room, briefly dropping her hand to my shoulder before exiting, that I look to Elijah. The one person who could truly decide the fate of Rosevear, the one I made a bargain with.

"That went well," he says, lounging back on the sofa.

I release a breath, rubbing my hand down my face. "Did it?"

"They listened and agreed with you."

"I was honest."

He nods. "I'm sorry I didn't get there in time to save your cottage. Your mother and father's things. That must feel like a great loss."

I bite my lip, avoiding his eyes. "You showed up at the right moment, and decided to stay and help. That's what counts."

"I'll always help, whenever I can, Mira."

I meet his eyes, finding truth in the smoldering depths. It jolts me, pulling me into this room with him, into the now. I realize I've been in survival mode since I awoke to the scent of burning. Leaping from crisis to crisis, disconnected from the horror in order to keep going, keep fighting. But we made a bargain, sealed it with a mark, and he must be referring to that. "You let them decide for themselves, don't you? Your crew, your inner circle. You don't command or force them. You're a team."

He shrugs. "It's up to them, always. It goes both ways, loyalty. If Caden disagrees with me, we talk it out, or we take it to the practice courtyard. And if Tanith does, I have to seek her out in the library, and wait until *she's* ready to talk. And Merryam . . ." He shrugs, grinning. "She might tell you I'm her boss, or her captain, or however she decides to frame it in a given moment, but the truth is she does whatever she damn well pleases. If she doesn't want to do a drop, she refuses, and I have to plead with her and fix things until she's happy. She's a pain in the ass, and I value that above all else. She questions, she calls me out on things. The business runs like clockwork because of her instincts. The moment she starts agreeing with everything I say or ask of her is the moment I'll know I've seriously messed up and I've lost her trust. I'd take a blade to the chest for any one of them, and they'd all defend Ennor without question if it came to it."

I swallow, seeing how his eyes have shifted, the smolder in them burning now. He's loyal. He loves these people, fiercely. They're his family. It's how I feel about Agnes and Kai. Perhaps we are not so different after all.

I shift in my seat, tiredness weighing down on me. No,

more than tiredness. It's that hollow in my center, growing and deepening, as though hungry for more of me. More pieces of me. It fills my entire being with a weariness I can't seem to shake. "If that's all . . ."

"Wait."

I'm halfway to my feet. "Yes?"

"There are no restrictions here. You can go where you like, do what you want. But, Mira . . ." He pauses for a heartbeat. "I want you to train. If you're going up against Renshaw, I need you to be ready. You're a target for the watch now, and it won't be long before our friend Captain Leggan sends a report to the ruling council about what's happening here, if that hasn't happened already. I would bet anything you'll be named in that report. And once they know your name . . ."

"I'm a liability. To you and your inner circle. To . . . everyone." Elijah doesn't disagree, doesn't so much as shift in his seat. That's what I like about him, his calm and his tenacity. Some might call it ruthless, but I call it pragmatic. In the time I've known him, I haven't once seen his emotions get the better of him. Sometimes I'll catch a glint of something lurking beneath, but he hides it well.

"You're untrained. Right now I need you reading that map so we can monitor any movement and hunt down Renshaw's strongholds. I need you forming a strategy with me. But I think there's more inside you, if you can unlock it. And I won't be the only one thinking that. So . . . I'm asking you to train with Caden. But I'm also asking you to come with me to find information."

"What are you planning?"

He smiles, teeth wolfish and predatory. "Renshaw wants

you. The watch is after you. I think we need to traverse to a mainland port and use you as a lure. See if we can't rattle some secrets from a few people."

I smile back. "Now that sounds . . . dangerous."

"Dangerous and worthwhile?"

"I'm in."

"Good," he says, getting to his feet. "Now I want you to understand Ennor. Take a walk with me. It's time you see my island and what I hold dear. And why I'm prepared to fight as hard as you."

CHAPTER ELEVEN

THE CLOUDS PART AS WE STROLL DOWN THE HILL into the main town on the isle of Ennor, Elijah nodding to people as we walk. The main town winds up from the quay, bordered on each side by beaches. Cottages and shops line the streets, opening out onto a series of market squares. The air is thick with the scent of buttery pastry, the pollen from cut flowers, and the morning's catch.

I drink it in, reveling in the industry, the clink of coin, the plumpness of the faces we pass. Treading the sun-warmed streets now, with Elijah at my side, is so very different from my experience the first time I visited, just over a month ago. No longer am I met with barely contained hostility and suspicion. The people smile at me, make jokes with Elijah, and seem perfectly at ease with their young lord among them.

"I need to check in with the apothecary and a couple of merchants who've recently returned from Port Graine," Elijah says. "But then I'll give you a tour. Show you the side of

Ennor you probably didn't see on your last visit."

"All right," I say, stepping around three children playing a game of dice on a doorstep. "Lead the way."

When I was last here, I lingered outside the apothecary, not daring to go inside. The polished glass windows glint, showcasing a display of tinctures and potions. The jewel-colored bottles and jars glow and wink, and if I had any coin to part with, this would be the shop I would visit. I can just imagine sending some of these wares back to Rosevear, how they would line the healer's stores.

A bell clatters over the door as we enter, and Elijah steps over to the counter, leaning against it to chat with the apothecary. It's a woman, brown hair caught in a bun at the nape of her neck, a little girl sitting next to her with her nose buried in a book. Elijah chuckles at something she says and I turn away, not wanting to look as though I'm listening in.

The shelves are deep, honey-colored wood lining the walls, and each set of jars is labeled with navy-blue ink on pale parchment tied with twine around the lid. There's a section for hair care, one for body and bath, and another for remedies. I surreptitiously sniff some of the jars, closing my eyes as I'm swept away in a haze of gorse flowers, blue-bells, and lavender. A few people wander in, picking up jars and carrying them to the apothecary, who exchanges a few words with each of them. It's all so . . . relaxed. So ordinary and unhurried, the people of Ennor purchasing lotions and oils to make their everyday lives gleam and glimmer.

I wonder how it would be if we had this on Rosevear? If we had time and coin to spend on simple, everyday pleasures such as this?

Elijah takes his leave and I walk out after him, waving at

the little girl, whose eyes crinkle in a smile before ducking her head back to be consumed by the story she's reading.

"Henny manages the shop and her partner, Berrin, blends the remedies and potions they sell. But Berrin isn't well, and he's the only person who can combine the essential ingredient in the apothecary blends."

"The . . . magic?"

Elijah shrugs. "You can call it blood with a judgmental frown if you like. Anything else and I'll grow suspicious."

"Maybe your opinions on the matter are swaying me," I say carefully, bending to scoop up an apple that's rolled off a market stall. I place it back with the other green and red fruits and turn to him. "Maybe I'm listening and turning things over."

Elijah raises his eyebrows and plucks something from my hair, passing it to me. It's the small white feather of a fledgling, all soft down. A flare of heat fizzes gently in my veins as I regard him, this boy of secrets and shadows. Except here, today, he doesn't seem so secretive. In fact, he merely seems content. An island leader quietly checking in on his people. "That's good to hear, Mira. At least you no longer believe me to be a villain."

"Oh, I wouldn't go *quite* that far," I say teasingly. "Perhaps you're a villain with a heart."

He chuckles, and the sound is like sunlight trickling over warm stone. "Come on, we still have two more stops."

The merchants are a man and a woman twice his age, who treat him with deference. As we sit in their office, which is housed in an imposing granite building, built beside a workshop where metalworkers craft the wares they trade in, I marvel at the way Elijah works. He twitches the ledgers toward him, asking questions about their latest acquisitions of metals at the auction house in Hail Harbor on the mainland, and studies the figures before listening to their answers. The merchants talk of the rising price of bars of silver, how the ruling council is sending agents to buy it up and make it into weaponry in the factories in the north.

"Our esteemed leaders are preparing for something," Elijah murmurs, tapping a finger on the desk. "And your experiments with tin?"

The woman nods, turning to pick an item off a shelf behind her. I lean forward, examining the metal can, which appears to be completely sealed. "Going well. We've found this size keeps its shape, and it preserves foods better than jars."

"Doesn't shatter like glass either," says the man gruffly. "Joby will be glad of it for your crews."

"I'll send him down," Elijah says, passing the tin can back. "Good work."

"Lord," the woman says, pride flushing her cheeks, "we've struck an agreement with a mine in the south of Arnhem that's found a good yielding seam of tin. Tremelethen, near Port Graine. Only a small venture, but the prospects look sound. We're acquiring direct, cutting out the agents. With your initial investment, we're thriving."

"Excellent," Elijah says quietly, smiling at them both before rising. They all shake hands and we leave the office, the sounds from the metal workshop ringing in my ears as we cross through an alleyway and leave the main streets of the town behind.

"You invest in the businesses here?" I ask as the street becomes a stony path, hedges bordering fields on either side.

"And then you . . . what? Collect on your investment?"

"Not exactly," he says as we take a left turn, then skirt a field hugging the pale sand beach. "The House Tresillian only begins taking a cut when the ventures are thriving and supporting the workers and their families. Until that point, there's little use in crippling them by demands for repayment."

"And what of the ruling council? Does the watch not collect the dues for Arnhem?"

"Not on my isle," Elijah says. "I pay direct to ensure our freedom and the islanders' individual prosperity. It's worked so far, but in these times . . ."

"Everything is shifting."

"Exactly." He stops and rounds on me. "Mira, I wanted you to see that side of Ennor, because I want you to know there are ways Rosevear can prosper. With the right investment, with a will and some creative thinking—"

"You're forgetting one thing," I say with a humorless smile. "No investment. And Captain Leggan pocketed all the glitter that might have helped set us up for better times."

"I'm offering it," he says softly. "As part of our bargain. I see protecting Rosevear as more than just staving off the watch. How will that help you and yours in the future?"

"That would be . . ." I blow out a breath, imagining coin for tools and materials, for Kai to build seaworthy crafts to order, for Agnes's bakery to expand, for the fisherfolk to invest in better nets and pots. And that would only be the start. I look at Elijah, really look at him, and see a boy who is becoming a man. Those dark eyes, so serious now, the way he's studying me, gaze flickering over every corner of my features. I take a breath, pulse fluttering at my throat, and as a breeze ruffles my hair, his scent drifts around me, ensnaring me.

I swallow, blinking quickly, and carry on walking along the path. He's offering a way out, but not just for me. Freedom for the whole of Rosevear. Everything I want, all we need. I rub my fingers over the bargain mark, not wanting to believe that it's this easy. That a real future, where we do more than exist but *thrive*, could actually be within reach.

"I'll think it over."

Elijah shows me a cove scattered with pearly shells, his favorite as a young boy, and I allow myself the heady joy of dipping my feet in the sea. Heat curls up to my thighs, and when I glance over my shoulder, I find him watching me again, a small smile playing across his lips.

When we make our way back to the main town, dusk is falling. Elijah tugs on my hand, leading me toward the pub near the quay. "Final stop."

The din in the Mermaid hits me like a wall when I enter. No one looks up; everyone is consumed by their own lives, with raucous laughter and chatter rattling around the room. I pull out a stool next to Elijah, perching at the bar, and the boy polishing glasses inclines his head to us.

"Whatever is good today, Marc. Two of them."

He nods, throwing the polishing cloth over one shoulder as he extracts a bottle from under the bar, pouring a small measure of a jade-green liquid into a smoky glass. He pushes one toward me, then one toward Elijah, before moving on to the next customer with a swift "On the house."

I swirl the liquid in a circle and clink the glass against Elijah's. "To bargains and surprises."

He chuckles, inclining his head. "To young women made of storms."

I grin at him and down the drink, feeling the lick of fire and ice. I cough, the burn of it settling, warm and soft, coating my senses. Wiping away the terror as my island burned, the nightmares that haunt me, the lack of control. "Thank you, Elijah."

"For what?"

"For understanding. For knowing."

He smiles, features serious and intent, his thigh grazing mine as he turns back to the barkeep and signals for two more drinks. It's the lack of control over my life, I realize, that creates this sense of deep unease inside me. The watch and Renshaw took my certainty, robbed me of my razor-sharp focus. But somehow, on Ennor, I am returning to myself. Elijah's thigh, just brushing mine, sends flames dancing all through me, sharpening my senses further.

As the sounds of the pub grow more frenzied and raucous around us, we chat about nothing, exchanging stories, and by the end of the evening, when we're walking back up the hill under a glittering spray of starlight, I realize that the hollow in my chest has grown a little smaller, filled with flickers of flame that burn and burn.

CHAPTER
TWELVE

SHE TRACKS MUD AND DUST ACROSS THE POL-
ished floorboards of the entrance hall on her return to the
coven, earning a hard stare from Peony, the witch on duty.

"Good hunting?" Peony asks, flicking her long, inky
sheet of hair behind her shoulder. Her lip curls in distaste
before she smooths out her expression, inspecting her shiny
black nails. "You know, Brielle, I do admire you for all the
assignments you go on. The malefant chose well when she
adopted you. Such a *useful* weapon for the coven."

Brielle manages to contain her snort. She's disheveled and
hungry and has just gotten off the dawn stagecoach from
Hail Harbor. After two stops to change horses, a very quick
meal in an inn forty miles south of Highborn, and a burly
man sitting beside her, talking at great, monotonous length
about the state of the roads for the final stretch of highway,
Brielle's patience is frayed and thin.

"Yes, the assignment was successful, and how lucky for

you, Peony, that you have a place at a coven with hunters like *me* bringing you fresh vials." She raises her eyebrows. "I never forget my place here, but then neither should you."

Peony laughs throatily, eyes glittering. "That's why I like you, Brielle, you don't take any shit. Lowri's downstairs, by the way. Scarce emerged in three days, some spellwork she's fixated on."

"I'll clean up and go to find her," Brielle murmurs, glancing at the door to the basement level, which seems, even to her, to vibrate with vicious magic. "Wouldn't want to offend you *real* witches by tracking more mud through these hallowed halls, now would I?"

What many do not know is that the blood of a creature holds the subtle texture of the magic it possesses. When woven together with other ingredients in careful spellwork, it is possible to create wonders. And horrors. When Brielle descends to the lower level of the coven house, stepping inside the workroom Lowri favors, she finds her friend and adoptive sister hunkered over a scarred wooden workbench, making precise, tiny notes in her grimoire and tapping a series of bubbling glass bottles, all laced together in a complicated web of metal holders. Lowri mutters something under her breath, forcing her hair from her face, and taps a bottle, suspended in a metal holder, the liquid a shade of violet that reminds Brielle of Leicenan sunsets.

Brielle clears her throat, only a few steps away, and Lowri swivels slowly toward her, wearing an unfocused, bloodshot glare. Lowri is an intense, cold sort of witch, a shuffle of awkward, cramped angles, which means she is usually left alone. But she's her true self with Brielle, open like a bloom.

Her features crack apart, losing all that frost, and she gets to her feet, drawing Brielle into a bony hug.

"I thought you'd be back tomorrow. I've lost track. . . . This puca blood is tricksome, cunning and quick. I can't quite pinpoint how to coax it into my working. . . . Anyway." She blinks up at Brielle, assessing her carefully. "You haven't been looking after yourself, have you?"

"It seems that neither have you."

"Fair," Lowri mutters, rubbing her eyes. "Scones? It's nearly eleven."

Brielle's stomach grumbles. "Yes. The mal can wait for the report."

Anyone observing Lowri would believe she was oblivious to all but the delicate nature of her spells, but as she stretches, yawning deeply, and tidies up her workbench, she chatters to Brielle about the last few days she has missed while away. She tells her of the human male Jessemyn lured into her bed last week, and how Cook is keeping a coblyn, trading scraps of silver fabric with it so that it will scrub the pans while she's abed. She flicks her fingers at the workbench, saying a single word—"*Inferna.*" The spare slips of scrunched parchment and the spilled ingredients burst into hot blue flame.

Brielle leans against the workbench, crossing her arms and listening as Lowri tidies away her spellwork, destroying the discarded pieces of her research and workings, leaving behind only a few more dark scars in the wood.

Every so often Brielle hears the cries of the monsters they keep in the basement cells that are fashioned from twisting, spelled iron bars. She observes the monsters occasionally, but finds them disturbing in a way the other witches do not. Her work as a hunter is to find and drain the monsters she hunts.

But sometimes the malefant instructs a hunter to bring one back alive. The cries she hears most frequently when she visits Lowri down here are from a trapped fury, a shape-shifting creature the malefant has kept for study. The fury is a talented mimic, and Brielle is wary of its attempts to lure her from this workroom with the pitiful begging of a human child. She knows what a fury is capable of and hopes that soon the malefant will order it drained so they no longer have to suffer its mimicry.

She glances around, blinking in the low light, taking in the slabs of scarred wooden workbenches, empty save for scatterings of powder and a few discarded books; the pearly glass beakers, bottles, and tubes; the shelves stacked from floor to ceiling with carefully labeled jars, leather-bound books, and odd objects found by hunters. She crosses the flagstone floor as Lowri idly discusses Presentation, the formal examination of a witch's spellwork, and reaches for one such object—a crystal as big as her fist, flame colored and warm to the touch. Brielle found it on one of her assignments, claiming that the locals in a mining town in Valstra believed it held the spirit of a fire sprite.

Brielle closes her fingers over it now, wondering as ever if she imagines the pulse beating inside it. Her thoughts turn from her troubling visit to the Far Isles to Lowri as she chirps away about some answer Peony gave in class that had her in fits of giggles. Brielle smiles.

Lowri is the only witch in her coven she would actually call a friend. The only witch she could count on when they both manifested that night in the northern wilds of Arnhem, when all the covens sent their young to either manifest, die, or be cast out if they did not manifest properly, doomed to become a wandering wraith. Clarus is the night every young witch longs for and fears most, a night that will change everything for them.

Brielle never tells Lowri where she goes on an assignment until she returns, sometimes bearing new scars, sometimes bearing gifts, like this crystal. She sighs, placing it back on the shelf. After they both manifested in their fourteenth year, they went their separate ways in the coven, Brielle to be honed as a hunter, Lowri as a witch to perfect her spellwork.

"You ready?" Lowri asks, interrupting her thoughts.

They leave the workroom through the only door, extinguishing the oil lamps as they go, and Lowri locks the door behind them. She places the iron key on the hook next to the door, and speaks a word over it.

"Lavas."

A vein in Lowri's wrist flares ebony before fading back to its usual pale blue. The iron key is coated in a film of spells, and now it will only unlock the door if held in the hand of a witch of Coven Septern. They make their way up the staircase, Brielle's booted feet tapping on stone. With each step the knots in her back unravel, and when she reaches the ground floor, she finds sunlight streaming in through the stained-glass windows surrounding the main door. This floor and the two above it are all polished wood and neatly arranged furniture with a sense of impersonal purposefulness. Guests of the coven are received in the front rooms, while the guts of the house, the kitchens and laundry and such, are at the back. Lowri's and Brielle's bedrooms, along with the other witches and hunters in training or who are just accepting their own solo assignments, like Brielle, are in the attic, up three flights of stairs that usually leave her a little breathless and lightheaded if she's neglected her stomach.

"I should change," Lowri says, fussing with her black dress, which is smeared with spell ingredients and creased.

"You should *eat*." Brielle frowns, noting her friend's sallow coloring, the way her eyes are a little glazed from a lack of nourishment. "When was the last time you ate? Or slept?"

"Two nights . . . a day?" she says, and swallows. "I have to get that spell right."

Brielle rolls her eyes. "You're worse than me."

A darting black shadow winds its way in a figure eight around Lowri's ankles, and she bends to run her fingers through her familiar's soft fur in greeting. The cat mewls in protest at the length of their time apart, and Lowri bends to pick her up, allowing her to settle like a scarf around the back of her neck. "You know I've been busy, Nova. I'm sure you've had great fun mousing."

Cook shooed me out. Nova's feline purr grumbles. *No mice, no treats.*

Lowri chuckles, reaching up a hand to tap the tip of Nova's nose, which is white and shaped like a newly formed star. "Poor creature."

Indeed. And you smell like puca, all boggy.

"I'll bathe later. The others will have to put up with it."

Not every witch has a familiar, but somehow Nova chose Lowri, and Lowri had shared the story of how Nova came to her with Brielle on the night of Clarus. One rather dreary day in February when Lowri was six years old, Nova had appeared in her bedroom, balanced on the end of her bed. Nova, already full grown, sat licking her paws and waiting patiently for Lowri to wake up and adopt her. Nova spoke, the sound of her purr making perfect sense to Lowri, and they have come as a pair ever since. Usually when a familiar chooses a witch, it's for life, and a good sign the witch will manifest.

Sometimes Brielle catches a glimpse of what lurks beneath Nova's seemingly ordinary feline exterior, something vicious, perhaps monstrous, but Nova has always appeared as a black cat and hidden her nature well. She speaks, but only to the witches she wants to hear her, and so far she has only bestowed this gift on Lowri and, more recently, and only occasionally, Brielle.

The one part of the coven house that Nova is expressly forbidden to follow her witch into is the basement. No familiars, no humans, no visitors from other covens. Only witches who carry out spellwork and study the captured creatures are allowed down there, along with hunters.

Brielle reaches the top of the staircase, Lowri trailing behind her and murmuring to her familiar, just as the grandfather clock in the hallway chimes eleven. She crosses the landing, which smells forever of beeswax and pollen, and enters the door that leads into the sitting room. The room is arranged in clusters of wing-back reading chairs and small tables, the light filtering through large windows on one side. Brielle crosses to peer down at the street below, glancing along the pavement where a few people hurry, then raises her gaze to the buildings opposite, much like the coven's town house but with one notable difference. They do not house any witches.

"What have you been hiding, Lowri?" asks a rather grating voice. Brielle glances to her right, finding they are not quite alone. Peony, the witch who greeted her this morning in the entrance hall, sits in one of the chairs farthest from the fireplace, clutching a delicate china teacup. She scowls over the rim at them. ("It isn't her fault," Lowri always reasons. "It's just her face.") "I hope you don't intend to upstage us all at Presentation."

Brielle hides a smile, crossing to the sideboard nearest the door and helping herself to a plate of apple cake (joy!) and a scone with lashings of sharp bramble jam and clotted cream. Lowri heaps up a plate as well, then pours a saucer of milk for Nova. They both sink into high-back armchairs across from Peony, and Lowri lowers the saucer of milk to the floor. Nova unwinds herself from Lowri's shoulders and leaps gracefully down. Lowri busies herself with the teapot before answering Peony. "Puca blood. Tricky thing to work with, leading me on a merry dance. Any ideas?"

Peony's forehead dimples further, her black nails stark against the cup as she raises it to her lips. "Tried rose thorns?"

"Crimson and black."

"Mint? Spider silk?"

Lowri nods before cramming a slice of apple cake into her mouth. Brielle inhales a scone, then reaches for a second, her stomach finally placated as she swigs at her teacup, moving to refill it.

Peony bites her lip. "A conundrum. What's it for?"

"I want to create a beckoning spell. Something subtle that I can use on Nova and create a want in a person to follow her—much like how this particular puca lured unsuspecting humans into its bog."

"So you *are* planning on winning Presentation this year. Clever."

Lowri blushes, taking another gulp of tea before rising to go and help herself to more apple cake. The witches in training of Coven Septern are mostly academic creatures, prone to long bouts of solitary study with the occasional showcasing of their work, like at the annual Presentation. Seldom have even the more senior witches had to use magic for anything more . . . bloodthirsty. Arnhem hasn't been at war for a hundred years.

But the competition to win Presentation is fierce this year, and the prize highly coveted. A bigger bedroom, a private bathroom, and a personal study. Brielle knows that Lowri longs for such a space, as does every other witch, Peony included. It also indicates something else for the witch who wins in Lowri's year: that you are nearing the end of your training and ready to ascend the ranks of the coven as a fully fledged witch. "I suppose you've already developed your spellwork for Presentation?"

"You suppose correctly."

"But you're not going to divulge any more."

Peony only smiles, her features softening slightly before snapping back into the usual frown. "We'll see who is ready to ascend first, won't we?"

Before Lowri can question her further, the door to the sitting room bursts open, revealing a harried-looking messenger staring wide-eyed. She swallows, scraping a shock of carroty hair off her forehead, and waves an envelope at the three of them. Brielle recognizes her, a young witch who will be sent to the wilds for Clarus on Litha, when the night and day are of equal length. Brielle looks away, not wanting to consider what will happen if the girl does not manifest. "Ruling council wants to meet with you, Brielle. And the mal has a new assignment for you."

Brielle dusts the crumbs from her fingers and takes the

envelope before ripping it open. Her features darken as she takes in the message inside. "Looks like I won't be here long."

"Where this time?" Lowri asks, eyes darting to hers as Peony tries her best to look like she isn't listening in.

"You know I can't say."

"A hint?"

Brielle swears softly, as though her mind is elsewhere, as the messenger mumbles something about the mal wanting an immediate response, before leaving in a cloud of anxiety.

"I knew this was coming. I *knew* things were changing. . . ." Brielle stuffs the letter back in the envelope and gets to her feet, already stalking for the door.

Lowri catches up to her in the hallway outside, tugging on her arm. "Tell me," she says quietly. "What do they ask of you this time?"

"I can't, Lor. You know I can't say."

"Brielle. It's me and you." She crosses her arms.

Brielle sighs, running a hand over her face. That moment in the Far Isles burns in her mind, and she'd do anything to turn back the clock, to force Kell's hands together faster, to hide his magic, to protect him. But there are others like him. More and more who she cannot protect. And now the ruling council isn't only interested in information about them. They want one of them captured.

"A human, all right?" she whispers, eyes fixed on Lowri's. "Not the name of a monster, nor a creature. The next assignment in this message is a *human* name."

CHAPTER THIRTEEN

SMOKE CONSUMES ME.

I cough, fighting against a veil of darkness, screams all around as I try to get free. Stumbling, I trip over my own feet and crash to the floor. I'm back in my cottage on Rosevear. I'm sealed in, the flames eating my mother's chest, my father's things, erasing every part of us, of what little I have left—

Mira.

I cry out, ripping through smoke that feels like cloth or gauze, rending a hole in it and pushing my way through.

Mira.

The shrieks from the dying outside the cottage walls are like nails on slate, and I'm still trapped. I can't reach them, can't save them, I can never save anyone I love, my father, my *father*—

"Mira, wake up!"

A hand closes around my shoulder. I scream, bolting

upright, dragged back from the flames. I press a hand to my chest, breathing heavily.

Just a dream, just a dream, just a dream . . .

I'm drenched from the rain, the howling wind flinging a deluge upon the isle outside. The blankets and pillows are in a sodden, torn heap around me. My bed, the whole room, is in tatters. The door is broken in, hanging off its hinges, the windows in splinters, glass glittering across the floor. And when I look up, I find a boy leaning over me, eyes staring into mine. Eyes containing whole worlds of deep, depthless night.

"What happened?" I whisper, finding my throat is scratchy, as though a scream has lodged in it, fighting its way out.

Elijah looks at me. "You were screaming and lightning scorched the ground, mere feet from the castle. Then thunder shook the whole of Ennor, and the rain came. Mira, it was like . . . it was as though you were calling it."

My breath hitches and I draw my knees to my chest. All I remember is the dream, the sheer terror of being trapped, the scent of acrid smoke, just like on Rosevear, the night of the fires. Just before the storm came that night to douse the flames, a storm I desperately willed into being . . . a storm just like this one.

I scramble for my mother's letter, finding it on the floor beside the bed. I rake my gaze over it, knowing she wrote something I should have paid more attention to. . . .

Be the storm the world needs to right itself.

I swallow, turning to Elijah. "Can creatures of the sea— sirens—do anything more than I already know? They're lethal, quick, hold all the secrets of the sea in their blood like a map . . . but can they also command the weather? Call a storm into being?"

He hesitates for a moment, as though afraid. But for me or for his island and his people, I'm unsure. "Tanith has encountered tales. She researches creatures and their known abilities, but for sirens, her accounts are from witches, second-hand stories. Not conclusive at all."

"So it's possible that I . . . did this," I say with a shiver. "That I somehow called this storm. And that I called the one on Rosevear too." I can see it's already abating, fingers of sunlight breaking through the furious gray of the clouds, reaching for the island as the rain trickles to a drizzle. "Was anyone hurt?"

"No," Elijah says. "The worst damage is in this bedroom. It was focused on the castle, not the town." He steps back, casting around the room. Pale light begins filtering in with a soft breeze, steeped in salt and sun. "Did your mother say anything else in her letter? Anything that Tanith can research?"

"It says . . ." I scan the letter again, then drop it to my lap, pulse thudding in my ears. "'There are those that will hunt you. That will want you to calm the ocean for them, or create a tempest. There are those that will call you a monster. . . .'"

He eyes me carefully. "Mira, you are not a monster."

"How can you be so sure? I don't know how to control this power. When the storm came the other night, I willed it, desperately. I wanted it to douse the flames. But I had no idea that I had caused it. . . . I thought it was luck. But this time I was dreaming, having a horrible nightmare, and this happened. I have no control over this . . . power. What if I do hurt someone?"

I look over at where the window was, at the glass, jagged and cracked around the frame. Horror slowly dawns on me. Ennor Castle is by a town, full of *people*. Innocent people . . . and children. "I have to be able to control this. Whatever it is. I never thought, never imagined I could do any more. I didn't know that part of the letter was *literal*." I rush on in a panic, throat thickening, thinking of what I could have done, what I could have caused . . . death. Chaos. On Rosevear the other night, this storm could have grown, it could have damaged the few cottages left standing, it could have whipped into a tempest and destroyed the homes of the very people I was trying to protect. "I would never have knowingly put anyone in danger—"

"I know, Mira, I know. We'll work it out." Elijah rubs a hand across the back of his neck and I shake my head, tearing my gaze away from him, the violent horror of what I could have done settling into my bones. If I can't control what I am, if I can't keep a lid on everything inside me . . .

I could kill someone.

Elijah clears his throat, breaking me out of my reverie. I notice for the first time his bare torso. He's wearing a pair of dark breeches, slung low on his hips, but nothing else. His hair is mussed, his eyes still crinkled and sleepy as he swallows, throat bobbing. When he heard me crying out, he must have leapt from his own bedchamber and broken down the door to get to me. "Breakfast is in the kitchen. After that, Caden will begin training with you."

"Thank you."

"You don't need to thank me," he says calmly. "Amma will restore your room; the castle will help her. It likes to mend itself. But . . . go and see Tanith. If anyone knows more about what a siren is capable of, about the magic in your veins and why it's manifesting now, it's her."

"We'll begin with a warm-up, then go through some basic drills," Caden says as I enter the courtyard after breakfast. It's in the center of the castle, bigger than the outer walls would suggest, but then I'm coming to expect that of Ennor Castle. Caden is standing with his hands clasped at his back, a small smile tugging at his mouth. "I know you carry a blade. You're an islander, you've grown up knowing how to defend your home if you need to against smugglers and such, so I don't doubt you can use it, but—"

"I've had no formal training," I say, flicking a stray hair from my eyes. I braided my hair in twin braids tight to my scalp, yet the fine strands still spring loose around my forehead. The breeze has kicked up, moaning around the courtyard, and I'm glad of the leathers Caden found for me, tight fitting to move in, but warm and as flexible as a thousand ever-shifting firedrake scales. "And without training, I'm a liability on any mission."

Caden nods. "Precisely. So we'll meet here each morning and go through the same routine. I need you to build muscle memory, to shift and move on instinct. Because when you're in a fight, you don't always have time to *think*."

We begin with stretching and a jog around the courtyard. Caden is a good foot taller than me, the same as Elijah, but he matches his strides to mine. I lose myself in the steady rhythm of my footsteps, the breath warming my lungs.

"So, you tried to cook us all in the night."

I splutter. "Who told you?"

"No one. I woke to that crack of thunder at dawn, then

the rain pummeling the castle walls." He eyes me slyly. "Your bedroom window shattered quite dramatically."

"I was aiming for Elijah's and missed."

Caden roars with surprised laughter. "Two windows over next time, fierce one. And please don't chuck lightning bolts near mine. Let's stop. It's time for drills."

We run through footwork, block and parry. Over and over and over. By the time Caden is done with me, the sun is high in the clouds, and I've almost forgotten about last night, about what I'm capable of, that monstrous side of me lurking in my veins. As Caden calls a halt, I wipe the sweat from my forehead, my limbs already aching.

"Unless you've got something better to do?" he asks, reaching for a carafe of water on a low table by the door I entered the courtyard through. He pours a tumbler of water and hands it to me, then downs one himself. "The Mermaid serves in the day as well, I guess."

I shoot him a look, heat flaring up my throat. "And what does that mean?"

He grins, setting his glass down on the table and crossing his arms. There's no malice, but I can tell he's teasing me. He knows I went to the Mermaid with Elijah last night. I would bet the whole island knows that their young lord was out with a strange girl, chatting and laughing together all night, and she now resides with him in the castle on the hill. I fight back my blush, reminding myself it means nothing. "You were sluggish and slow this morning, and I need you quick and nimble."

Sighing, I place my tumbler on the table next to his. For some reason, Caden's good nature, his sunshine and warmth, is rattling me. I'm like a blade, ready to cut. Spoiling for a fight, and I suppose it's because I'm scared of what I could have done. I am *not* slow; I'm practically vibrating out of my skin with all this pent-up energy, and all at once, I snap. "Show me."

"What?"

"Come on," I say, stalking for the set of wooden practice blades at the side of the courtyard. "Show me how I'm oh so *slow* and *sluggish*." I know I'm rising to take the bait, that he's testing the edges of my patience. But I've never had much patience. The storm of my true feelings is only ever just beneath the surface.

He chuckles and shrugs, all ease as I toss him a practice blade. I wait for him to move, to do anything but stand there, eyeing me, but all he does is crook his finger with a grin. It sends rage, sharp and quick like lightning, through me, and I leap at him.

Blade thrust up, then around, drawing a line to meet his own. My steps are swift as I spin, angling my body around his. But when I try to unhook the blade from his fingers, I find nothing but thin air. I turn, but not fast enough, as his foot swipes around my ankles. With a crash I fall to the ground.

He laughs and I glance up to find him looking down at me. "Want to go again?"

"Are you always this infuriating?" I hiss, refusing his offered hand to stand up.

"I take that as a compliment."

"Of course you do," I mutter, wiping those fine strands of hair from my forehead. But somehow, the tension in my chest is gone, and I need this release. "Again."

He puts me on my back three times before I walk away,

making a vulgar gesture at him. He roars with laughter, and I realize that nothing seems to rattle him. And I swear, as I leave the courtyard, that the nearest shadow holds eyes that crinkle in mirth before vanishing.

My troubled mood does not improve over lunch. If anything, I have more to work out of my system, a knot of molten anxiety that will not cool. I enter the kitchen, which is blessedly near the entrance to the courtyard, and find that my limbs are trembling from exertion as I take a seat at the big wooden table in the center. Amma is fussing with a pot of soup on the hearth, and the fresh-baked bread on the table smells delicious.

"Cut it up into slices, let it cool, and then butter it for yourself and the others," Amma says, not turning to look at me.

"Thank you," I say, doing as she asks. The kitchen is like a larger version of the healer's cottage, copper pans hanging on hooks around the hearth, pots of herbs crowding on the windowsill above the sink, and a cool marble pantry leading off the main kitchen, where I can see wrapped cheeses, preserves, and bottled cider. "Can I do anything else?"

"Get the bowls, girl. And there's a pie from yesterday in the larder. Fetch it along with some cheese. Cutlery is in the drawer over there." She indicates the dresser, full of glasses and mugs and crockery on the other side of the kitchen.

I do as I'm bid, and Amma hums a song, one I haven't heard since I was a little girl. It reminds me of my mother, and I pause for a moment, listening to her. She flits like a dragonfly, half-translucent, dressed in a lilac gown today, and I wonder what she is. If she's a witch, or a creature, or part of the castle given an almost human form.

The others troop in, Caden going to taste the soup on the hearth as Amma nudges him away, Tanith absentmindedly feeding a piece of pie to Maggie at her feet. Then Elijah and Merryam, deep in discussion, slide onto chairs as well. I tear into the meal, listening to them all joke with Amma, and it reminds me again of Rosevear.

"Now we're all here, Merryam has had word about that secret cove you found on your map, Mira," Elijah says.

Merryam leans forward, grabbing an apple, which she begins to peel with her knife in a long green ribbon. "Joby and I took *Phantom* to check it out. Renshaw's men were guarding it. I slipped ashore unnoticed and overheard them discussing a drop, in three nights' time."

"I propose, if everyone is willing, that we intercept this drop," Elijah says. "And we leave Renshaw a very clear message. We know she's sided with the watch against Rosevear and Penrith, and if she turns on any of us on the Fortunate Isles, she turns on *all* of us."

CHAPTER
FOURTEEN

"WE NEED MORE INFORMATION THAN THIS," I say, leaning forward. "A drop in three days' time could be anything. If we really want to hit Renshaw where it hurts, we need it to be the right drop. A precious, *costly* drop."

"Indeed. What would you recommend?"

I bite my lip, thinking this through. If we follow this lead, if we interfere with a drop, Renshaw will have men there, and it's a risk. She'll know that we know about that cove, and she won't use it again. If I was with the seven, if Bryn was guiding us, he'd have gone to Port Trenn. "We need your contacts, Elijah. Who do we know who might be able to tell us what's on the ships sailing the straits that might be in Renshaw's pocket?"

Caden whistles, grinning. "She's good, Eli."

"She's better than good, she's *right*," Merryam says. "We have to run down Renshaw's coffers and burn her options. We need her desperate and cornered, so she makes a mistake the watch can't ignore. She'll flout the law too obviously, and they'll have to break their alliance."

Elijah nods. "Remind me never to get on your bad side, Mer. Ever been to Hail Harbor, Mira?"

Hail Harbor is two nights' travel by boat, and with my face now plastered on wanted posters, along with Eli's and probably half of his crew, albeit under their various aliases, we cannot risk crossing by land. Elijah flexes his fingers as we meet in the entrance hall, both of us wearing long black jackets, breeches, boots, and hidden blades. I have the map tucked next to my heart, not wanting to leave it behind, even well guarded in Ennor Castle.

He offers his hand to me, and my stomach twists at the thought of traversing. But we have to, and I wonder if it isn't just me who wishes there was an alternative. Elijah still seems tired after the night of flame on Rosevear, as though the use of his magic all through that night as he rescued my people took a heavy toll. But he says nothing as his fingers close around mine, his thumb smoothing over my knuckles, as though in silent apology that this is the only way. I nod before stepping with him, and find myself in a world of shadow.

This time, I try to make sense of the chaos as we traverse, the dark abyss whirling like smoke as I tumble and twist. There is no end and no beginning, almost as if we are indeed traveling through shadows. When I feel solid earth beneath my feet, my knees buckle, but I don't fall. I suck in a breath, the feeling of falling swiftly draining away this time. When I look up at Elijah, his eyes meet mine, and he releases my hand slowly, almost reluctantly.

"Hail Harbor is a little different from Port Trenn. Try not to offend anyone. The merchants here have their own private watch to keep the streets clean and clear."

"All that tells me is that there's more to steal," I say, glancing around. We're in a back alley, pressed between two rows of houses, cobblestones beneath our boots. At the end of the alleyway, I can hear people, the clatter of horses' hooves, and the cry of wheeling gulls.

Elijah chuckles. "The merchants here have more than enough to spare, but don't get any ideas."

I raise my eyebrows, saying nothing as we walk toward all that noise and step out onto the street. And it's like another world. There are hardly any women in sight; it's all men and boys, either driving carriages or horse-drawn carts, or walking together in groups, heads bent low in muttered discussion. The houses on either side of the street are all three-story affairs, with pearly windows and polished brass plaques beside glossy front doors, and when I look up, I see the shadowy outlines of desks and bookcases behind the panes.

There are shops with immaculate window displays showcasing leather goods, books, telescopes, and nautical maps. As we journey along the street, I keep my head low, but can't help gazing at a double window display of tailored jackets in forest green and deepest navy, studded with brass buttons and lined in contrasting silken fabric. A man with a carefully trimmed beard and a crisp white shirt steps out, a boy trailing behind him laden with smart-looking boxes of his purchases. Hail Harbor is a town catering to the rich merchant class, I realize. And I do not belong here.

"We'll make one stop before we take tea," Elijah murmurs,

moving to cross the street when there is a gap in the trundle of carriages.

"Tea?"

"Every respectable merchant takes tea, and that's where I will find my contacts and hear the gossip of the town."

"And before that?" I ask, dodging a boy hawking penny newspapers full of sensationalist news of the continent, most of which likely isn't even true.

"A visit to the bank. Godrich and Sons." He smiles at me. "If we are to create a small stir, and loosen some tongues around us so they believe we are just like them, I must make a sizable deposit and then splash some coin. The bank and the teahouse are the places these fine men like to gather."

The entrance to Godrich and Sons is up a flight of wide stone steps, the rooms inside scented with wood polish and tobacco. I stay close to Elijah, trying not to stare, but banks are so far beyond our reach on Rosevear—places none of us has ever had need of. We hide coin in boxes under mattresses and in the crevices in the chimneys of our cottages, not in places like this, full of men in tailored clothes, wearing expensive cologne so they even smell wealthy.

The back wall is a line of tall mahogany desks, clerks seated behind them wearing spectacles and frowns. I only spy one woman in the room, wearing a ridiculously fussy pale green gown, hair cast in glossy raven ringlets framing her dark brown skin. She concludes her business at a desk, accepts a written note, which she places in a bag dangling from her wrist, and sashays out.

"Where are all the other women?" I ask him quietly. "She's the first I've seen."

"At the country estates, preparing for the season in

Highborn and Morgana, or else hidden away in houses and shops, cleaning, cooking, serving. . . ."

I wrinkle my nose. "This really is a place of men."

"Which is exactly why I brought you along. You are *quite* the distraction."

Glancing around, I note the men's brazen gazes, the clerks muttering to each other as they cast their eyes up and down my form. I lift my chin higher, staring down a man who is leering obviously. After a moment he snorts and wanders toward the door onto the street, and I'm not sure if I've won, or if I've just created a whirl of salacious gossip.

Elijah concludes his business, handing over a leather folio that is handed back to him a moment later with a hand-written note. Elijah dips his head to the clerk and motions for us to leave.

"Now the teahouse," he says. "There were several merchants in that bank who I know hold mining interests in Valstra. We should be able to glean something interesting. No doubt they will visit the teahouse as well."

I walk after him, past a candlemaker's, an apothecary, and another shop filled with nautical maps and spyglasses. I slow my steps, looking at the rolled maps, the display of spyglasses, and the compasses set in glinting silver and gold cases. When I look beyond the window display to the patrons of the shop milling about inside, a pair of eyes meets mine, wide-set, under familiar brown curls—

I freeze, blinking quickly as the people inside the shop shift, obscuring my view. Placing my hand on the cold glass, I scan the shop more carefully, searching the faces, the people browsing the shelves, but I must have imagined it. The boy who betrayed me, who sends a jolt of pained fury right to my heart, even now . . .

Seth Renshaw.

"What is it? Mira?" Elijah asks.

"It's . . . it's nothing. Just a reflection."

But as we round a corner, Elijah leading the way toward the teahouse, vengeance burns afresh in my heart.

The teahouse is through a set of double doors leading to a marble entrance hall scented with flowers. We are greeted by doormen who take Elijah's name, and one shows us up a wide staircase to a room wrapped on two sides with windows facing the sea. I realize my hands are still in tight little fists, my teeth gritted, as thoughts of Seth Renshaw flash behind my eyes.

The teahouse is packed, waves of conversation eddying around the crowded space. We are seated at a table to one side of the room and order tea and cakes, which are served on delicate blue-and-white porcelain. The cakes are tiny, delicate little mouthfuls of melting sugar and roses. I've never tasted anything so sweet; the sugar we plunder on Rosevear is used sparingly, if at all.

"The gentleman on your right, Mira, deals in glitter, and the man next to him owns a mine in Valstra. Listen in," Elijah whispers, and I pretend to chuckle, as if Elijah is the most hilarious company, and lean toward the group of men at the table next to us.

". . . Skylan levies are rising all the time."

"Worth it though? Now the Far Isles are under control, there's dwindling numbers of encounters with monsters too."

"We haven't had any issues with sailing the straits in some time. Other than the expense, of course. If there was another safe route, I would use it."

Elijah raises his eyebrows, busying himself with more tea.

"I hear you're entering several lodes for next week's auction, Timins."

Timins guffaws loudly and proceeds to boast about the two ships he's bringing over with full cargos in three days' time, and the partner he's dealing with, someone with a hidden port who's guaranteeing their safe passage in Arnhem waters. I glance at Elijah under my lashes.

Three days' time . . . This has to be the drop. And if Renshaw has moved beyond piracy and is actually partnering with merchants, then she has more at stake than just the goods. It's her fledgling reputation we'll be relieving her of. Satisfaction warms my stomach, and I take another cake, sure we've figured it out.

Elijah shuffles his chair closer, so he's sitting beside me, bending to murmur in my ear, "Are you thinking what I'm thinking?" His knee grazes mine under the table and I breathe in his scent, the lure of the tide and midnights cut with a fresh lemon tang. His fingertips brush mine as he reaches for the bowl of sugar lumps, and my pulse quickens, suddenly all too aware of his closeness.

"I'm thinking we have our answer," I say, noticing the silver fleck of a scar just below his ear, no doubt from a long-ago fight.

"Shall we?" Elijah says, standing slowly, the heat and pressure from his closeness ending abruptly. I nod, my voice caught in my throat, as he leaves a scatter of coins on the table and moves to pull out my chair for me.

I'm too busy congratulating myself, enjoying the feel of a full belly and the anticipation of a win, to notice the men following us through the streets of Hail Harbor. But as we reach the secluded alleyway where we first arrived, I move to take Elijah's hand and see three figures, shoulder to shoulder, blocking the light from the street and the shadow we were to traverse through. My blood runs cold as we pull out our blades. Elijah can't risk anyone seeing what he can do here.

"You've got something our captain wants," the man on the right says gruffly, eyeing the blade in my hand, then Elijah's. "We can do this the easy way, or the hard way."

"There is no easy way with this one," a voice says at our backs. I whip around, finding three more. The one in the middle has wide-set eyes, a constellation of freckles, and brown curls, carefully tousled, half obscuring his features.

"Seth," I hiss, heart thumping in my ears. So I hadn't imagined him in that shop. He was really there, and now he has us cornered.

"To what do we owe the pleasure?" Elijah drawls, taking a step to the side, so his back is against the wall. "Renshaw is not in my favor right now, I'm afraid."

"We're not here for you, Lord Tresillian," Seth says, taking a step closer. His eyes settle on me, a fleeting cloud passing over his gaze before he frowns. "Give us the map, Mira, and we'll spare you both. If not, you won't be leaving this alleyway alive."

"I don't have it with me," I lie, raising my chin. "Take another step though, and I'll finish what I started on Penscalo."

He clenches his jaw, taking another step. "You're lying."

"And you're *bluffing*," I snarl, squaring up to him. "We both know you need me alive."

"Not anymore," he says quietly. "Mother's made a deal with a coven that can reveal the map to her too. It will answer to her blood now, as well as yours."

Elijah's eyes widen in shock as he blinks at me, then at the men. Calculating, weighing up the situation . . . and finding the odds might be against us. "Now who's the liar, Seth?"

He shrugs. "Believe what you want, *Lord* Tresillian."

I take a step back as Seth and the other two advance, bracing my boots on the uneven cobblestones.

And immediately I realize my mistake.

A hand grips my arm, yanking me backward, and I gasp as I'm slammed into the wall. Pain explodes down my back, knocking the breath from my lungs, my vision tunneling before the alleyway drifts back into focus. I look up into the face of one of the men who held me captive on Renshaw's ship. His cruel, cold eyes are coated in malice. "Because of you, my brother is dead."

"No taking liberties, Finch. Get the map, then we leave," Seth intones from a few feet away.

"Lay a hand on her, and you'll join your brother," Elijah says quietly, his voice like the quiet before a tempest. "That's your first and last warning."

Finch's doughy face splits into a hideous grin as he glances behind him, and laughs.

But Elijah's not talking about what he would do. He's warning them of what *I* will do. And with Finch's laugh echoing around the alley, the hold on my temper snaps.

I laugh as well, right in his face, as acid churns in my stomach. Then I angle my blade and thrust it deep into his guts.

CHAPTER
FIFTEEN

I TWIST AS FINCH DOUBLES OVER, AND KICK HIM in the side. He topples into the other two blocking our escape, their shouts and curses ringing out. I turn, seeking Seth, and find his eyes wide with shock, flitting from the hot blood on my blade, to my face.

"I warned you, Seth," I say, pulse thumping in my ears, dragging me back to that day. "I told you what I would do to you if I ever saw your face again."

I get three feet down the alleyway before Elijah grabs me. Thrusting me into a pool of shadow, he turns to Seth. "Go and tell your mistress you let us slip through your fingers."

Then we're gone, consumed by nothing but the dark.

When we slam into the flagstones of the entrance hall of Ennor Castle, Elijah shudders for a moment, swearing viciously. It was a close call, despite our bravado. Too close. Caden appears by the front doors, Tanith at the top of the staircase, as I sway next to Elijah, the world spinning relentlessly.

"What happened?" Caden asks, all traces of sunlight gone. He sees the blade gripped in my fist, a single drop of ruby blood falling to the ground. I look up at him, not bothering to hide what I am. I could have easily taken another few steps and buried this blade in Seth's beating heart. All my hate and grief is just beneath my skin still, simmering and twisting.

"Renshaw," Elijah grits out, wincing, as though the sudden traversing across a wide distance has depleted him. "They cornered us, six of them. Seth claims she made a deal with a witch to be able to read the map herself. Maybe it's true, maybe not . . . but we only just got away."

I take a deep, soothing breath, willing my heart to calm, forcing myself to bottle all that rage and hurt back inside myself. I didn't kill Seth, but I could have. If Elijah hadn't intervened . . . My gaze cuts to his, and I wonder why he stopped me. In the alleyway, I realize now, I did not feel like myself, almost as if another side of me had taken over. I shake away the thought, the tangle of fear growing inside me, and focus on what the others are saying.

"But we know how to hurt her now. Sabotaging the drop in three days will do more damage than we imagined."

"Then we best get to work."

"Again," Caden says as I gather the breath in my lungs. Before this, I had believed myself healthy and swift. But now, in the training session the following morning with Caden, observing his ease and warrior's grace, I realize, grudgingly, that I have much to learn.

I raise my fists and we go again.

An hour later, my whole body is trembling, and as we

stop for water, I notice it. The chalk marks on the wall. A simple vertical line, the letter C on the left, M on the right. And a mark underneath the C. I splutter, pointing at the wall, and round on Caden. "Is that a . . . *scoreboard*?"

Caden raises his eyes slowly to the wall, taking a leisurely swig of his water. "Why, does it bother you?"

"I didn't know we were keeping score!"

"You seem upset."

"I'm not!" I take a breath, seething quietly, willing my blood to simmer down. "I'm not upset. But if I'd known you were keeping score—"

"You would try harder? Interesting." He takes another sip of water, flashes me an easy grin, and places his tumbler back on the low table. "We can finish training. You can go for lunch, or . . ."

But I'm already stalking to the middle of the courtyard.

I hear Caden chuckle before I turn, finding him standing with feet shoulder width apart, hands clasped at his back. This time I'm not fooled. I match his stance. And I wait.

"If you want, we can talk," Caden says, not moving an inch.

"What about? You want to trade tips on hair care?"

Caden flips back his sunny locks. "Sounds like you think my hair looks nice."

I snort. "It sounds like *you* think your hair looks *nice*."

Caden smiles, eyes glittering. And then he pounces. I barely see him move, barely catch the shift of muscle before he's on me, twisting a foot behind mine as I scramble to keep from falling. I bring my fists to my face, but he's already danced back. "If your enemy is talking shit, it's usually to distract you."

"Right, got it," I mutter, not lowering my fists. I skirt around him, reach for a practice blade, and toss him the other one. He plucks it from the air, swinging it in a wide arc, and takes up a fighter's stance. I do the same, and this time I catch the blur of movement before he swings. Wood meets wood in a clap of sound, sending pain shooting from my wrist to elbow. But I don't pause, sweeping around him, keeping my feet light as I slice for his back.

I get in two blows before he trips me. And as I lie on my back, his wooden blade at my throat, I grit my teeth and accept his offered hand.

"Better," he says. "Elijah stopped you in the alleyway because he wants you to learn control. To not give in to your impulses. Don't let them turn you into the monster they believe you are."

I close my eyes for a moment and nod briskly. Caden waits, and I know he's monitoring me for a reaction. But I stay silent, keeping a tight grip on my temper as he ambles over to the scoreboard and flicks a second chalk mark below his own initial on the wall.

"He's trying to get a rise out of you," Merryam says at lunch as I mutter into my meal of fresh-baked bread, soft cheese, and fragrant, herby salad in the kitchen. "It's how Caden operates. First he strips you down, finds where to press to get an emotional reaction. Then he teaches you how to control that impulse to slug him in the jaw. *Then* he hones you. Makes you lethal, a fighter, like him. He wants you to fight with a cool head, not a fiery heart." She winks at me, tearing open some bread, the steam rising from it smelling like Agnes's bakery. I swallow, my heart twisting in my chest.

"And did you?"

"Did I what?"

"Slug him in the jaw."

Merryam grins. "More than once. When I first arrived here, I was so angry, hurt, betrayed. . . . It took me some time to get my bearings on who I am, what I wanted to become. That good-natured, sunny disposition of his? Pissed me right off when I'd landed on my back for the tenth, twentieth time, and *all* I wanted was to slug him in the jaw." She shakes her head, still grinning. "But he's the best, and that's why he trains us. I'd take a knife to the chest for Caden. Any of us would."

"Why?"

"Because both he and Eli took the time to help me heal," she says softly. "Not my body, although Renshaw did a good job of roughing me up before I arrived. My heart. My head."

Her words are an unsettlingly close echo of Eli's own. And it's how I feel about Agnes, about Kai and Bryn and the rest of my island. They've always been the balm to my quick temper, the steady hand when I've been restless. I eat the rest of my meal in silence, feeling every inch of the bruises, but somehow that hollow inside me has closed up even more.

Maggie is waiting for me as I leave the dining hall, tail thumping a steady rhythm on the floor in front of the staircase. I scratch her head and her tail thumps harder, big baleful eyes staring into mine.

"Time to pay Tanith a visit, isn't it?" I say softly. I can almost feel her presence in this castle, watchful and waiting. Elijah said he always goes to her, never the other way around. It seems I must do the same.

The library stretches across two floors. I enter on the first floor behind Maggie, the double doors leading into a space filled with sunlight. Window seats are carved into the windows that rise up, facing out to the sea, and on my left is a winding spiral staircase that leads to a mezzanine level. Every wall, except for the one with the tall windows, is crammed with books. Clothbound volumes, some glinting with gold lettering, some with no titles at all, sitting neatly on dark mahogany shelves. The space in the center of the room is scattered with cracked leather armchairs and low tables, stacks of books on some of them in haphazard piles. It smells of dust and paper and a shiver of something sharper. Like the first frost of the year.

"Maggie showed you the way." I look up to find Tanith leaning on her forearms against the rail around the mezzanine level. She nods at the hound already relaxing in a patch of sunlight. "Eli claims she's more loyal to me than him. Thinks I must give her extra treats."

"Or she loves reading," I say.

Tanith's features awaken with a surprised smile. "I guess you're ready with your questions."

"Sort of." I shrug, moving to the nearest bookshelf. I pull out a book at random, flipping through the pages, and discover it's a history book about the forming of the five principalities of the Middenwilds. Tanith glides down the spiral staircase, coming to stand next to me, and pulls another book from the shelves. "I think this would interest you more."

I take it, the deep green cover slippery and cold to the touch, unlike the clothbound volumes surrounding it. When I open to the title page, I frown. "Spellwork?"

"It's a grimoire. It was Eli's mother's." Our eyes meet, and she takes the history book out of my hands, placing it back on the shelf. I open the grimoire to the middle, finding the pages full of cramped notes in the margins around carefully typewritten words. "The Tresillian witches have a long, distinguished line. Eli's mother, Elena, was the last of the Tresillian witches to have close ties with Ennor."

"But not the last of them entirely?" I ask, leafing to another entry near the beginning. This one contains an illustration, a field of wildflowers, and in the middle of it, the shape of a door made of nothing but darkness. I quickly turn to the next page, a spell of sorts, to rip a name or a secret from another's mind.

"No," Tanith answers. "There is a coven in Highborn that Eli meets with regularly. That coven has . . . strong links to the Tresillian family."

I snap the grimoire shut and pass it back to her. "Did Elijah bring you here too? Like the others?"

Her eyes flare wide in surprise. "Why do you ask that?"

"Because you're not human, are you?" I take a stab at a guess, realizing my instincts were correct. "You're a creature."

She laughs, deep in her throat, and I get a glimpse of the true Tanith. Her amber eyes smolder and her skin glows softly, catching the light through the window like a thousand glinting scales. "If I were to take on my real form, you would run shrieking from this castle."

I swallow. "Has Elijah seen your true form?"

"Only once." She blinks, and her eyes are more human again, with that touch of amber circling them, her skin no longer glowing with hidden scales. She sniffs, replacing the grimoire on the shelf. "Someone he is close with rescued me, gave me a reason to assume this human form, and in turn, I swore an oath to the Tresillian line. To Eli. I've been the librarian ever since. Books are *far* more interesting than most people. And the people, the witches, I have known over the years . . . let's just say that there are not many I would leave my true form for. This is the first time in over a century."

"So you must be . . ." I blink at her, noting how youthful she appears, how gracefully she moves, like water or . . . flame. "You must be hundreds of years old."

"I'm still the equivalent age of Merryam or Caden," she says with a shrug, walking alongside the bookshelf, running a finger over the titles. "As far as we can tell."

"And what would I be? Am I still young?"

She hesitates, looking me up and down, and when she speaks, her voice is soft. "I know you are hoping for answers, maybe even for an account of someone like you, but I have found little information on sirens, Mira. Very little indeed. Some accounts claim your kind live a thousand years. Some a hundred, closer to a human lifespan. The fact that you are part siren, part human . . ." She shrugs. "There is much we do not know about you. Much to discover."

"The storm that formed when I called, not once, but twice—"

"It's a type of siren song," she murmurs. "It's not well-documented. The Tresillian witches speculated in their grimoires, but no human has lived once they have been lured by a siren, or been trapped in a storm a siren called into being."

"But it shouldn't be possible. I do not thirst for human blood. I love the sea, I thrive there, underwater, but that's the only indication of what I have inherited. I have no power."

"You don't? You have magic in your blood, Mira. Look at what Eli can do, and no one understands it. No one knows what he is; even *he* does not know. His mother was a witch, his father . . . we're unsure. There are no other creatures, or monsters, in this world able to flit between shadows, or bend them to their will like smoke. And yet Eli exists."

"So Eli isn't all human either? Like me?"

"I would say not, wouldn't you? Not a witch, but not quite as I am either, a creature in human form." Her smile curves across her lips, as though I'm a particularly interesting book she's just discovered. "Perhaps you are the only two that exist in this world, not quite one thing, not quite the other. But your own thing entirely."

"I'm not quite siren enough though, am I?" I say wryly. "The map isn't a part of me, and I can no longer take it out of the castle. It'll have to be kept under lock and key, and without that knowledge on the move, we no longer have an edge."

Tanith hums thoughtfully. "Siren enough . . . an interesting observation."

"What would you suggest?"

"I . . ." She hesitates. "If the map is the key to success and freedom for the Fortunate Isles, then we need to ensure it's still useful. We need to ensure that you're still the weapon we need you to be."

CHAPTER
SIXTEEN

PHANTOM SAILS ON A DUSKY TIDE. IT TAKES hours to reach the cove, and the route is plotted meticulously to avoid the watch and Renshaw's fleet. Reluctantly, I leave the map behind, Amma promising to guard it within the castle walls. It's too risky to take it with us, despite how much we need the knowledge as we navigate the waves. But as we sail away, I feel its absence like a fresh wound.

I crouch down low with the others on deck as we near the coordinates, making barely a sound. Joby stands at the helm; Merryam, Caden, and I await Eli's signal. Seeing Joby again, with his mop of chestnut hair and quiet ways, I was instantly pulled back to when I first sailed aboard *Phantom*, when I could feel the layers of deceit and secrets like cold mist. Now there is none of that between us, and his warmth and kindness are akin to Caden's. Elijah doesn't just pick people he will find useful for their skills, I realize. He surrounds himself with people who feel like family.

Blood whooshes in my ears, in, out, like a restless tide. I am ready. I feel more alive than I have in a full moon's turn, and as she shows her face, clouds scudding past her eerie glow, the bargain mark flares luminous on the inside of my wrist. I flex my fingers around my blade and glance over at Caden. He's watching me, a troubled look swirling over his features, eyes snagging on the bargain mark. I raise my eyebrows in silent question, and he purses his lips, looking away. I guess Eli didn't tell him everything. Or maybe he disapproves of Eli making a bargain with me at all.

We drift as close as we dare to the secret cove as a cloak of mist thickens over the sea. The sound of voices and whistles rings clear as a bell from Renshaw's crew, and we know that if we are too loud, they will hear us. And we'll be dead.

"Mira, you're first in the water, as we planned," Elijah murmurs. "Mer, follow her, get to the shore and hide in the stack of crates. No risks. Wait for me to carry Caden, and we'll target the crates before moving to the dwelling. Joby, you're with *Phantom*. Keep her hidden."

We all nod, and I check that the laces of my boots are strung tight in a loop around the back of my neck. We're taking a risk with such a small crew, but if we'd brought one of Elijah's larger vessels, it would have been too obvious. This way, we can strike without mercy and escape swiftly. And the first step of my and Elijah's bargain will be fulfilled. The first step toward vengeance and freedom.

On silent feet, I pad to the railings and swing over the side, landing with the tiniest of ripples in the water. Merryam is right behind me. We move slowly through the sea, the warmth soothing my veins, and reach the other side of the cove. I pull myself from the water, then lean down to offer a hand to Mer. We crouch behind a crate, watching the slow patrol of Renshaw's crew, the men and women passing in and out of the dwelling house that looks half storage and half pub. It's lit up within, laughter spilling out into the night, the occasional clink of a glass as though they're toasting their success.

"I never knew of this place," Merryam mutters, narrowing her eye. "Renshaw always was slippery as an eel. Always had the luck of a demon on her side."

"Well, her luck's about to take a turn."

A flash on the other side of the small cove tells us Elijah and Caden are in position. "I'll go for the nearest patrol— you start opening crates?"

"As soon as we see it . . ."

We both watch, eyes raking the dark. Then the dwelling house erupts.

Smoke and heat billow from a side room, shouts echoing toward us. Renshaw's crew streams out, coughing and arguing, blades in their hands. Elijah has placed a witch-crafted device that lit and detonated in an explosion of heat and fumes. It's the signal to move.

Merryam squeezes my shoulder, then leaps for the nearest person, the thump and muffled gasp telling me she's knocked them out cold. I dart for a crate, levering it open with my blade, and sink my hand into straw, searching for the cargo. My fingertips slip over something cold and smooth, and I grasp a bottle and pull it out. Gold and sweet, like honey-eyed sunlight, the finest vintage from the vineyards of the principality of Kir. Their only exported good, from what I remember of Bryn's teachings. It was meant for the tables of the rich of Arnhem.

But now it'll go to the sea.

I pull out the bottles as fast as I can, uncorking them and pouring them over the side of the port. The shouts increase, nearing me, and I duck down, scanning the dark before moving to the next crate, the next part of Renshaw's loot. And with every bottle I empty, the flames licking up the side of the dwelling house and store lighting my path of destruction, the thrill builds inside me. We are dealing a swift blow that Renshaw will feel like a pain in the gut. A warning of what's to come.

A reckoning.

By the fifth crate, Mer joins me and we empty the last of it together. "Such a waste," she tuts gleefully. When we move to the sixth, we find what we came for, what will deal the harshest blow.

Metal bars.

Stacks and stacks of them, all stamped with the insignia of a mine in Valstra. The respectable, affluent merchant and owner Renshaw has formed a partnership with . . . the partnership we are about to set fire to. I haul up the bars, one at a time with Merryam, throwing them into the hungry sea. Even if Renshaw sends her crew down to the deep to find them, she'll never recover them all. And it'll leave her reputation in tatters.

I picture the way she tormented me aboard her ship, how she sent me up the rigging in a ball gown, the fear of heights digging claws deep in my chest. I remember the feel of the lye as it burned my hands bloody and raw from her cruelty. This is all she deserves.

This is my vengeance.

When we're done, I strike a match, checking that Caden

and Elijah have Renshaw's crew well occupied on the other side of the cove, and light the tinder-dry empty crates. The straw catches quickly, smoking enough to make my eyes water as the embers drift up, soon lighting the next crate, then the next.

I want it all to burn.

And like a moth to a flame, the crew spies us through the chugging smoke, shimmering outlines as they burst through, blades raised and furious. I drop back a foot, grit my teeth, and set to work. Twisting and jabbing, I fight my way through the gathering crew, dealing blow after blow as the flames crackle around us. A woman grabs my hair, yanking me back, but I barely feel it. I twist, slicing at her arm, and she moans, sinking to the ground. I am fury, I am rage, and in that moment, it consumes me whole.

I can hear Caden's lessons ringing in my ears, but I don't fight like him tonight. I don't fight with a cool head, following the blocks and jabs he's teaching me. I fight with a fiery heart, brutal and swift, taking my fair share of knocks and kicks as I leave too much of myself vulnerable.

I fight like an islander.

I fight for what's mine.

I fight for survival.

"Mira! Time to go!" Merryam calls, and I see she's slipping into the sea.

The few members of Renshaw's crew left standing are racing for the dwelling house, grabbing buckets of seawater to throw at it. But it's lost now. By morning, there'll be nothing but charred remains. Just like what they did to Rosevear. I'm turning to leave, poised to dive into the water and swim back victorious to *Phantom*.

Then I see him.

Standing at the edge of the port, fists braced at his sides, watching me.

"*Seth,*" I hiss.

There's fire between us, flame and smoke, and no easy way to cross and face him. He smiles, a twist to his mouth like he knows that even here, even now, Renshaw is protecting him. I think about Penrith and Rosevear. I think about my father, and the moment the light in his eyes guttered out. And I think of that alleyway in Hail Harbor, when he was so ready to take my mother's legacy from me, to allow Renshaw's men to leave me bloodied and broken.

I see red.

Then a cool hand comes around mine.

Looking up, I find Elijah's eyes. Dark stars, endless night. Endless, *cooling* night. "Mira, no. Not tonight."

I growl in frustration, glancing at Seth, at the flames dividing us. There's no way through. No way I could reach him without torching myself in the process. But I'm so close. So close to taking out all my anger, all my pain, on this boy, and filling that hollow in my chest—

"Mira," Elijah says again, softly. "When we strike, we strike with our heads. And when the time comes, Seth will know your wrath. He'll know what it is to burn."

I release a shuddering breath, bile coating my throat. Elijah's right. This isn't the moment. However much I want Seth to feel as I do, to know what it is to suffer and be so lost, to lose *everything*, this isn't that time. "Fine," I say. "Take me back to *Phantom.*"

Elijah's grip on my hand tightens, but there's a tremor, as though he's exerted himself too much. But I swear he releases a charged breath before I'm pulled into cool, dark nothing.

Joby's already set sail as we land on the deck. I turn back to the blaze that was once Renshaw's secret cove, gripping the railings until my hands turn numb. I can still see the outline of Seth as he watches us leave, dark against the ravenous flames. And I force myself to turn away, to wrench my gaze from that burning cove, to bask in the waves of victory. Merryam reveals the bottles of Kirish wine she liberated, uncorking one and sloshing it into mugs to toast our win, Caden laughing with Elijah, Joby whooping to the night. I feel more of that hollow in my chest fill with light, and I imagine, for the first time, that there might be a future for us on these isles. That Renshaw and the watch may not rip them from us after all.

"Mira," Elijah says, that wicked grin he used to wear making my heart patter deliciously as he strolls over. He clinks his mug against mine, eyes never leaving my face as he leans in and whispers, "Tomorrow may end in flames, but tonight, *we* are the ones that set them."

I laugh throatily, taking a sip, the honey and fire of the wine warming me as much as Elijah's presence. "To us, then."

"To us," he says.

CHAPTER
SEVENTEEN

A HUMAN NAME, A HUMAN GIRL, AND YET BRI-
elle has been assigned to hunt her. Mira Boscawen, born
to a siren and a fisherman, is less and yet *far* more than she
anticipated. At first she refused, telling the malefant, no, it's
wrong, it's unnatural, we cannot accept this assignment . . .
then she heard a little more. Who wanted this monster captured, what she was, what she had done. And who she was
working with: Elijah Tresillian and his crew. A boy with
strange magic, a boy she and the rest of the coven know
very well, along with his crew. She read the file, the background information; she made sure she knew everything she
needed to. As always with an assignment, her best weapon
is knowledge.

As Brielle crouches on the cliff edge, watching it all unfold
at the secret cove below, she sizes up this creature in a young
woman's skin and the rest of the Tresillian crew. They move
like a pack, striking as one, and she struggles to see how they

even communicate when separated.

"Clever," she whispers, raising the spelled spyglass back to her eye. But not *too* clever, she realizes as a boy with brown curls burnished to copper in the dancing light of the flames appears, a boy she can only assume is the son of the infamous Captain Renshaw, Seth Renshaw. Not clever enough, perhaps. As the flames devour the dwelling house and secret store, Seth steps away from the other members of his crew, distancing himself. He's eyeing Mira as she twists and cuts down his men. And his expression is guarded. Not hateful, as it should be. More curious. And possibly a touch regretful.

Brielle huffs a breath, blinking quickly as Elijah Tresillian appears, disappears, then steps out of a shadow to slit a man's throat. The man drops to his knees, falling forward, but Elijah's already gone. Reappearing beside Caden, who blocks a punch from a woman and sends her flying. Brielle turns her spyglass back to Mira, catching how she moves, how she fights like she's desperate. There's little skill there, little finesse. She's brutal in her simplicity, using whatever's at hand to win a brawl. If anything, so far, she's been lucky. If she's not trained properly, she'll be dead before long.

Brielle smiles. In this, at least, she has an advantage. A hunter trains from the moment she is chosen in a coven, preparing for Clarus, when they will become a full hunter. For Brielle, she was four, and her mother trained her well. A hunter herself, she remembers the scars rippling along her birth mother's arms as she held Brielle, the barked commands as they trained in the practice yard at the back of Coven Septern. That is, until she didn't come back from an assignment in the wild depths of the Spines and the malefant, sensing power in Brielle, chose to adopt her as her own and raise her instead of casting her out of the coven. It took Brielle eleven years to train, to prepare to face the nest of wyverns that had killed her birth mother in the Spines. And at seventeen years old, when she drained them dry, leaving their stinking carcasses scattered over the ice and snow, finally she found some peace.

She watches as Elijah traverses with Caden back to *Phantom*, disappearing in the thick of night to reappear on deck five hundred meters away. Angling her spyglass, she notes how he shakes, how Caden places a hand on his forearm to steady him. The traversing he can do, the way he moves through shadows, it drains him. Just as with any witch or hunter using magic. She considers this. All she knows of Elijah Tresillian is that his mother was a witch. But what his father was, the malefant will not say. Or perhaps cannot say for sure.

She realizes there is one missing, even as Joby navigates away from the secret cove—the monstrous girl. Brielle angles the spyglass for the cove. Surely they wouldn't leave without her. But Mira is still there, blood dripping from her blade. Even as all around her, the crates burn and burn. Seth stands across from her, a furnace raging between them. Mira takes a step, every line of her taut and ready. Brielle holds her breath, wondering if she'll try and cross all that flame. If she'll take the risk.

If she'll go for the kill.

But then Elijah is next to her, taking her hand, speaking quickly, shadows folding around them. Mira breaks away, looking up at Elijah Tresillian. And in that moment, Brielle's heart lodges in her throat. Mira's eyes are . . . so very human. Human and full of an endless, depthless sorrow. Her breath hitches. That expression, that sadness, she knows it all too well. She nurtured that kind of sorrow, until the day she stalked those wyvern through a world of ice and snow and slaughtered them. Only then was she released. Only then could she move on, allowing her tormented soul to heal.

That sorrow, it is her own.

Brielle looks on as Mira and Elijah are swallowed up by shadows, reappearing on the deck of *Phantom* a mere moment later. Brielle clutches the spyglass, needing to see Mira's face. Needing to see, one final time, that humanity carved in the lines of her skin. But *Phantom* moves too fast, shooting away on some ghostly tide, and Brielle lowers her spyglass. She doesn't know what to make of this young woman, this killer, this monster. But Brielle recognizes something in her. She recognizes her grief, her rage.

She recognizes herself.

Brielle journeys through the night and the better part of the next day, arriving back in Highborn by midafternoon. Stiff legged and sore from being on horseback too long, she aches for a bath and a hot meal. But the night before will not leave her. She has to see her adoptive mother, the malefant.

The mal's meticulous assistant's eyes turn wide as she catches sight of Brielle striding up the corridor, and she quickly taps on the malefant's door before ushering Brielle inside. Brielle sinks into one of the armchairs across from the mal's desk, breathing in the scent of parchment. Hillary Tresillian regards her impassively. A petite witch with blond hair, like her son Caden's and nothing like Lowri's, pulled into a severe chignon, stretching her skin at the temples. She wears a prim dark gray cardigan and wool skirt, as she usually does, not a stray thread nor a wrinkle to be seen. To Brielle she is timeless, as though she holds every secret this world has ever possessed in her mind, hoarding every detail like a firedrake, superior, unshakable and wholly unmotherly. Brielle, in contrast, is a creature of earth and blood, smelling of horse and damp grass, her hair slipping out of a hasty plait.

The malefant raises her eyebrows. "Well?"

"She's not what I expected," Brielle admits quietly, hands drumming an uneasy beat on her thighs. She's never been comfortable around the malefant, despite the fact that she raised her. Especially when Brielle's speaking her mind. "I didn't realize she would be so . . . human."

"And yet she has killed other humans in a heartless way that is distinctly *siren*. Wouldn't you agree? Surely you saw evidence of that in your observations."

"I did," Brielle agrees uneasily. She pictures the way Mira sliced and spun, wielding her blade against Renshaw's crew in the attack they had sprung on the secret cove.

The malefant purses her lips. "Need I remind you that this is an assignment, Brielle. You are a hunter, one of our brightest and *best*, and with that comes certain privileges and expectations. We need you on this one. *I* need you on this one. You are given free rein. I turned a blind eye when you went rogue in the Spines just over two years ago, but this is the ruling council. We cannot turn this down, and we *cannot* fail. Our position in this city is precarious enough. We cannot afford to fall out of favor at such a delicate time."

Brielle knows all of this. They have gone over and over it in their meetings, the high witches of the coven hissing over her disorderly appearance, her wayward willfulness, how in the past she has allowed her emotions to govern her actions. And she sat there and took it all. "I know, but—"

"No excuses this time. Remember, the coven stays outside politics. We do not get involved; we simply keep magic alive, uphold tradition, and ensure the survival and prosperity of our witches and hunters. Which means *appeasing* those in power." She sighs, bringing the tips of her fingers to her temples. "The ruling council asks me daily for progress reports, Brielle. *Daily.* They want this monster captured, and from what they have inferred, they want her studied and drained. They have paid handsomely for us to deliver."

A shiver trickles down Brielle's spine and she swallows before continuing. "I also saw Elijah and Caden."

"Did you now?"

"Elijah seemed to be . . . protecting her."

The mal frowns, her bottom lip puckering. "And you think this will be an issue for you?"

"No." Brielle shakes her head. She isn't getting anywhere. Her adoptive mother might as well be a wall made of metal and glass. "Thank you for your time."

Brielle stands to leave, moving for the door.

"One more thing . . ."

She turns, eyeing the mal. "Yes?"

"No mention of any of this to Lowri." The mal's smile barely touches her eyes. "She does not yet understand the choices and sacrifices we must make as a coven to survive. Even when it comes to family."

Brielle nods once and slips back into the corridor. She heaves a heavy breath after closing the door, her thoughts muddied and troubled. It's one thing to hunt down murderous monsters for her coven, and quite another to hunt a creature that appears all too human.

"You're back!" she hears a voice exclaim. Glancing up, she finds Lowri, face flushed, eyes shining. "You've just missed Presentation, but it was all fine. I completed it. In fact . . ." She points to a discreet pin at her shoulder, a thin gold bar shot through with a streak of ebony. "I was commended."

"Congratulations," Brielle says, grinning. "And Peony and the others?"

"All completed, all passed. No one will be leaving the coven this year, *thank goodness*. . . ." Lowri blinks quickly, a shadow shifting across her features. They both know what it means for a young witch to not complete her training. What becomes of them, covenless and alone. "And I won the prize. My own private bathroom and study . . ."

Brielle reaches out and squeezes her arm. "I'm thrilled for you; you deserve it."

"But what about you?" Lowri says, forehead suddenly creasing as she takes in Brielle's disheveled appearance, and she glances behind her, at the corridor beyond. "Has Mother been bothering you?"

"It's fine. I . . . Can I ask you something?"

"Sure."

"The monsters I hunt. That I drain, and the magic we use . . . I don't know. I've been thinking more and more about what makes a monster truly monstrous."

Lowri frowns. "Well, obviously they're monstrous. They are the monsters. That's your role, to hunt monsters, Brielle, and bring back the blood laced with magic so we can study and . . . do good with that magic."

"But what if a monster . . . what if they don't seem so terrible?"

"Lowri!" a girl calls from a gaggle of witches on the staircase. Brielle looks to see a pouting Ellowyn, mouth painted scarlet, eyes glittering chips of ice framed by white-blond hair. "Are you coming?"

"Yes!" Lowri says, already stepping toward the throng of witches. She hesitates for a moment, turning back to Brielle. "Catch up later?"

"Of course. Forget I said anything," Brielle says, forcing as much warmth into her voice as she can stomach. She watches Lowri go with the other witches, all of them with their pristine black nails, their straight, glossy hair, their grimoires and textbooks hugged to their chests. Lowri belongs with them. She belongs with the casters, the ones who create the coven's spells, the academic, beautiful set that preen and glisten with power.

Not with her.

Not with a hunter.

Brielle glances down at herself, her dusty clothes, her careless, bedraggled braid of brown hair, and rubs her eyes. She wishes for a moment that she was one of them. She wishes she hadn't been chosen as a hunter. She wishes, more than anything, not to have this burden of hunting this monster, this Mira Boscawen.

CHAPTER EIGHTEEN

"GUARD YOUR RIGHT SIDE, MIRA," CADEN BARKS as the wooden practice blade slides along my ribs. "Again."

I push my hair from my face, the loose tendrils clinging to my skin and sweat. Muttering darkly, I take up my stance. Every muscle, every fiber of my being, is aching and weighed down with lead. It's hot in the courtyard, the sun beating down with the first real warmth we've had since last autumn. Usually I would bask in it, finding a quiet moment on Rosevear to soak all that sunlight into my skin. But not today. Today is about pain. And apparently, forcing myself not to bludgeon Caden over the head.

"After this, can I have water?" I croak, twirling the wooden blade in my fingers before gripping it tight. "Or do I have to beat you to the ground first?"

Caden grins, white teeth flashing. "The day you put me on my back in this courtyard is the day you can take *off* from training."

"Figures." The door to the courtyard opens, snagging my attention, and I don't see Caden move until I'm on the ground, his blade at my throat.

"Guess you're not planning on *working* for that drink of water."

But I barely hear him as Merryam squares up with Elijah a few feet away. Mer is wearing her usual shirt and breeches, exactly what she wears aboard *Phantom*, at breakfast, even at dinner. And Elijah . . . I swallow. He's wearing the same outfit, but in an entirely different way. His white shirt is unbuttoned to halfway down his chest, revealing the rippling muscles beneath. His breeches, cut tight to circle his thighs, strain as he takes up a fighting stance, grinning at Merryam. She lunges for him, striking up, twisting, sweeping a foot to hook around his ankle . . . and he doesn't miss a single beat.

I realize I've held my breath, eyes glued to his sleek form, when Caden taps his practice blade against my cheekbone. "Focus."

With a small snarl, I leap to standing and drop my foot back, ready. But Caden's looking past me, a small smile on his mouth. I realize the fighting has stopped on the other side of the courtyard. I open my mouth to question Caden, to jab him into concentrating so I can get this over with, when he steps back completely.

"My turn," says Elijah, and I whirl to find him next to me. I force my eyes to stay on his face, even as his own trail down my throat, then up, slowly, to meet my gaze. "Let's see if Caden's taught you anything worth remembering."

I raise my eyebrows, glancing at Caden, then back at Elijah as Caden shrugs and walks over to Merryam. "Good luck, small fierce one."

"Are you going to go easy on me?" I ask, gritting my teeth. Whereas Caden fights like a dancer, I know Elijah is far more deadly. From the first moment I met him, I've known what he is. Lethal. A predator. I swallow again, anticipation flickering in my veins as my heart thrums in my chest.

"Would you really want me to?" he asks, eyes glittering as he raises his practice blade.

"I guess not," I mutter, readying myself.

And we begin.

He barely moves, and yet I am disarmed in seconds. I concede, bending to pick up the wooden blade and drop back a foot. But however fast I move, however smoothly I work through the steps Caden has taught me, Elijah disarms me every time with the most precise and practiced movements. He anticipates every step.

I'm squinting as the midday sun washes over us. If anything, this should make me fear him, or hate every moment as I'm beaten again and again. But I find that I'm enjoying it. As he strikes left, I duck and whirl, slicing the blade along his arm and ending up behind him. He huffs a laugh, turning toward me, and I grin back.

"I think I won that round."

"What, out of seven?" he says, shifting the practice blade from hand to hand. "Let's raise the stakes. First to get the other on the ground."

Heat floods me as I imagine pinning him beneath me, straddling him as I hold him down, but I keep my voice level. "All right."

He doesn't wait for me to be ready. Twisting my blade from my fist with a flick, he disarms me with lightning speed. I duck, rolling away, but he's on me in a heartbeat, gripping my wrists and flipping me to the ground. The sun sears my vision, and I close my eyes. Then darkness shifts behind my eyelids. I open them to find him above me, his body aligned with mine. I can feel every inch of him, his thighs pressing into my sides, his chest just grazing my chest, his heart beating in a rhythm that's a twin to my own. My breath hitches and I freeze, every nerve in my body suddenly achingly aware.

"They won't wait for you to prepare, Mira," Elijah says softly, his mouth close to mine. "Renshaw's crew, the watch. They will disarm you and take you, whether you're ready or not. They will not be kind, and they will not be gentle."

My breath comes in shallow bursts as I inhale his scent, sea and storms and all the allure of a star-scattered night. My entire being softens, molten with heat, and as I blink up into his eyes, I suddenly picture that dream I've had for years. Where I am holding the hand of someone unknown, a stranger, yet a person I seem to trust in my very bones, as we swim through eddying starlight. I haven't had that dream since that day on Penscalo, when my father died, haven't remembered what it is to fly. But now it's all I can think about.

Elijah's eyes shift, growing darker as they flick to my mouth.

Before I say anything, he moves off me, leaving me alone on the ground. I prop myself up on my elbows, watching him as he takes our practice blades. "We're done for today," he says, not turning to look at me but instead looking to Caden. An unspoken agreement seems to be made, and

Caden nods, wincing before moving away again. Eli finally shifts, angling his head at me. "I'll be training with you from now on. We begin tomorrow at dawn."

"What, that's it?" I say, getting to my feet. Confusion wars with reason, wanting his body against mine, and yet wanting to shove him, to yell, to *scream*, as blood beats hot and thick in my veins. It's clear Caden has just passed off my training to Elijah, that I'm not progressing fast enough, that I'm still a liability. The frustration builds inside me, and all I can do is hurl it at the closest person to me. Him. "You tell me I'm not good enough, I'm not ready, that Renshaw and whoever else will not give me an inch . . . and all I can do is *practice*?"

He sighs, crossing his arms. "You're doing enough, Mira. More than enough—without your map, we wouldn't have known about the secret cove. But I can't have a weak link in my crew. I can't—"

"Have me putting the rest of you in danger—yes, I know!" I wipe my sleeve across my face and realize I'm shouting. Merryam and Caden carry on as though they can't hear us, but I know they're hanging on every word. "I know my limitations. I know very well I'm putting everyone, every single person on these isles, in danger with my very *presence*. When they cornered us in Hail Harbor, that was all because of me, and what they want from me. The watch has threatened my home, and they haven't backed down. If I don't turn myself in within three weeks, by the next full moon, their threat still stands against all of us—"

Elijah takes a step toward me. "So fight. Train. Get better and beat them, and we'll work out the rest—"

"But what if it doesn't work?" I say, the heat cooling inside me. I hug my arms around my body. "I was powerless. They torched my island, my home, and I was *powerless*." I turn on my heel, stalking out of the courtyard, as directionless as I was the day I arrived. And yet . . . now there is something filling that hollow in my chest. Anger. Frustration. A sense of impending, unstoppable doom. I've moved beyond that stage of ghostly grief.

Now I want to burn down their world.

"You're back," Tanith says, her voice like a curl of flame as I stalk through the doors of the library. "Let me guess. Training isn't going so well."

"Let's just say I'm highly aware of my very human limitations," I grate out, prowling to the windows that overlook the sea. Looking at the endless cascade of waves, white tipped and restless today, I realize I haven't swum for the sheer joy of it since I arrived on Ennor. "I thought I could find answers here. Not just fulfill the bargain I made with Elijah, but find answers about what I am. What I can do."

"You have to ask the right questions," Tanith replies. "Any fool can wield a blade. But you're more than that. Elijah and Caden are training you and testing you. They're trying to teach you control. Trying to push you to your limits . . . so you can become aware of them. And so you know how to push back, not get rattled, and stay focused."

"They're baiting me."

She smiles. "When Elijah was young, he realized how truly different he was. His mother, Elena's coven would not have him, would not help him to understand the strange magic he possessed. There was no one left here on Ennor except Amma, who is held to this castle with a tendril of

Elena's lingering power. Amma was created to protect the castle and her son. Without Caden, Elijah would have been alone. Amma raised them both, and the islanders helped him become the young lord, the leader he is now."

Alone here, rattling around in this huge castle, two young boys having to cut their own path through the world, to become the leaders of Ennor the islanders needed. "So he wants me to fight back."

"Yes. It's the only way he knows how to reach you, to ignite the fire inside you. By testing you, pushing you. He was angry when he was young. He felt powerless too, until he learned how to control his power, and how to wield it. Fighting with wooden blades serves two purposes. You hone your skills in combat, and you release all your emotion in that courtyard with him and Caden, where any stray magic can be contained. He wants you to react. He can't have you raining lightning on the isle in your sleep. So far, you've only shown that side of your magic twice, and I haven't found any new research left by the Tresillian witches yet. If he can draw it out in the courtyard, then you can start to learn about it." She shrugs. "But of course, he's male and he's Eli, so he keeps his plans and schemes to himself."

I nod slowly, turning from the window. The siren side of me . . . I don't understand it. I haven't done anything like that night when I was desperate on Rosevear and during the nightmare on Ennor, but who's to say I won't do it again if I can't learn my limitations and triggers? If I can't learn control? "He grew up here with Caden. . . . What happened to his mother? His father?"

"That is for him to tell you," Tanith murmurs, reaching out to straighten a book. "Not me. But you should know by now that you can trust him. He *will* help you. In you he sees pieces of himself, his own journey, his own frustrations."

"But it's not possible for me to get all the answers here on Ennor," I say. "However much I can trust him, and however much he might *want* to help me." It dawns on me suddenly, what I must do. Who—and what—I must seek out. I think of my mother's letter, the line I reread a few nights ago. I look at Tanith, meeting her gaze. "The witches might have the magic we need, but not the answers. I need to go back to the sirens. My mother's letter alluded to things, but almost in riddles. I need them to tell me plainly what I am capable of, and how I can learn control."

Tanith smiles, her eyes glowing. "If you're ready to hear what they have to say."

CHAPTER
NINETEEN

OUR POSITION IN THIS CITY IS PRECARIOUS enough. . . .

You are a hunter, one of our brightest and best. . . .

She has killed other humans. . . .

Brielle sinks down, submerging herself in the warm water, wishing she could turn off the torrent in her mind. The bathing rooms on the third floor are blissfully deserted, the rows of tubs divided by curtains, empty but for the cloud of citrus-scented steam. She stays underwater for as long as she can hold her breath, counting down the seconds and reveling in the muffled quiet. When she rises, drinking down great gulps of air, she hears voices at the far end of the bathing room. Two other hunters, older than her, Hira and Shayle. After a moment, she realizes who they are discussing. Her.

"The mal gives her preferential treatment. When was the last time *she* had to hike through the bloody mines? My fingers are permanently singed from those fire sprites."

"You think that's bad? I've got three months in Morgana,

bowing and scraping to those simpering fools with their sharp tongues."

"No . . ." Hira makes a tutting sound. "Hobgoblins?"

"The whole court's infested. Apparently this particular hoard like their rubies. They've claimed the royal court of Leicena as their house, and with every supposed favor, they take a little keepsake in return. It's becoming a problem." Shayle sighs. "Cunning little thieves."

"My uncle had a hobgoblin, up north. Used to make him breakfast."

"Doesn't sound terrible."

"The hobgoblin stole and slaughtered the neighbor's chickens, one by one, to make the breakfast. Cost my uncle an arm and a leg to replace them all, then he had to hire a hunter from a local coven to get the little bugger."

Hira guffaws. "There's always a catch."

"So you're probably off to Valstra again, I'm in Morgana, and meanwhile *Brielle* gets to lord it up with the malefant and ruling council, taking her time over whatever lofty assignment she's been given. . . ." The sound of gushing water cuts off their voices, and Brielle sighs deeply before sinking back under the steaming bubbles.

What Shayle and Hira don't realize, what she can't tell them, is that she would trade places with them in a heartbeat. She would give anything right now to be hunting down fire sprites or cutting herself on the serrated edge of the Leicenan court's tongues as she rounded up mischievous hobgoblins. Anything to avoid this assignment she's been given, to hunt a monster that appears human. It feels less like an honor and more like a test. And if she refuses, or fails . . .

The ruling council could turn against them all.

★ ★ ★

"You must not meet their eyes," the malefant murmurs as they are hurried through wide corridors of gleaming marble. "Only speak when spoken to. Let me do the rest of the talking."

"As you say," Brielle replies uneasily. The court of Arnhem, a stately palace at the very heart of Highborn, used to be occupied by the high royal family. The crown, passed down from father to son, to brother and nephew, still sits on a plump velvet cushion inside the palace somewhere. But the last head that wore it had been decapitated in a bloody coup a hundred years ago. Now the self-appointed ruling council of three resides here. One represents the wild north, one Highborn, and one the mainland and islands of Arnhem. Every coven, be it an ancient establishment like theirs, or a collective of young witches, must give a fifth of the blood their hunters gather as a tributary tax.

Now, instead of holding balls like the Leicenan and Skylan courts each season, these wide marble corridors are filled with leading members of the watch, dignitaries from the continent, and guards everywhere, watching on with stony distaste. Brielle presses her lips together, noting the lack of women as her boots echo against the veined white floor. A lack of women, art, joy, laughter, whispers. Courts she has visited across the continent survive on a staple diet of gossip and intrigue to keep their courtiers sated. But here there is only cool, brooding silence. Brielle cannot wait to leave.

They reach a set of double doors painted gloss black, reaching almost to the high ceiling. Brielle's gaze rests on the guards on either side of the door, eyes hollow, scarlet uniforms pressed and crisp, gold buttons depicting the insignia of the ruling council—the roaring Arnhem lion.

Then the guards fall into position, push open the doors, and a man steps inside to announce them both.

"The malefant, Hillary Tresillian, and hunter Brielle Tresillian, of the Coven Septern."

Then he shuffles back and leaves them to enter the chamber beyond. Brielle's hand instinctively reaches for a blade before she flexes her fingers, remembering she had to surrender her weapons upon entry to the court. Sweat slicks her palms and she blinks steadily, telling herself to breathe. Fear is her enemy. It creates panic, which manifests in stupid decisions. Right now she must remain cool, collected. And yet every inch of her prickles with unease.

The three members of the ruling council have arranged themselves like a painting, one staring out the window, one seated on a sofa, sipping from a teacup. The third stands behind the sofa, one hand braced against the back. They're all impeccably dressed in black suits tailored to accentuate their height, giving them strong shoulders and a fine silhouette. They are all pale faced, with varying shades of blond hair and eyes that shift over you like they can see all of your secrets.

It's only then that Brielle spies the three other people in the chamber. One in an armchair by the sofa, as regal as a queen, red hair spilling in a wave over one shoulder. Another, a boy, tall with the same wide-set features, shuffling from foot to foot behind her, eyeing the rest of them with the same unease Brielle feels. It's the boy she saw in the secret cove as it was ambushed by the Tresillian crew, and his mother, the infamous Captain Renshaw. And the other . . . someone Brielle had hoped she would never lay eyes on again. Leaning against the far wall, arms crossed, features set in a sneer.

Captain Spencer Leggan.

Brielle barely contains the snarl as it builds in her throat.

"Malefant Tresillian. Brielle Tresillian. Please, come, sit," the man on the sofa says, in a deep, plummy voice, indicating the tea set before him, the vacant sofa across from his own. "I hope you like tea. A smoky variety, imported from Hindelmach. Quite lovely."

The malefant clears her throat and sits on the edge of the sofa, back ramrod straight, as Brielle stalks to the other side, hands braced on her legs. Tension crackles in the chamber as they all take each other in, the man on the sofa apparently oblivious as he pours two cups of hot tea. His eyes are a forest green, intense and almost beautiful, while the man behind the sofa has brown eyes. Brielle hasn't caught any features that define the third yet, as he stares out of the window.

"Thank you for accepting our invitation. Malefant Tresillian, we've had the pleasure of greeting you many times before, but for your benefit, Brielle, I am Tiberius. This is Otho standing behind me, and over there at the window, our brother Nero."

Brielle inclines her head to them. "Pleasure."

Tiberius nods, continuing. "And may I introduce our friends, Captain Renshaw and her son, Seth Renshaw? And over there scowling at us all, Captain Spencer—"

"We know who he is," Brielle growls abruptly.

"Brielle," the mal says lightly, holding a subtle reprimand, and Brielle curses herself for showing even an ounce of feeling, staring daggers at the cruel captain who once held her heart in his undeserving fist.

"Excellent," Tiberius says, smiling with teeth so unnaturally white they gleam. "Of course, you assisted with the Far Isles, Brielle, alongside Leggan here. Great stuff. Now we are all *dying* to hear how your assignment is going."

Before Brielle can open her mouth, she feels the mal's hand on her shoulder. She fastens her lips together, knowing what that means. A warning. Already she has gone against orders.

"Your grace," the malefant begins, before taking a careful sip of the tea. "Brielle is monitoring the creature and has already identified her associates and current place of residence. She is tracking her movements and will strike at the perfect moment to ensure success. Everything is in hand."

"Her associates?" Nero asks, turning to face them from the window. Now Brielle can see his features, his ash-colored eyes. So pale, so strange, they almost fade into the whites. She suppresses a shiver, locks her spine, and looks away from him.

The mal hesitates before continuing. "Elijah Tresillian and his crew."

Captain Renshaw snorts.

"And this will not be an issue for you? Your nephew, your blood, harboring this creature?"

"Of course not," the mal says, placing her drained tea-cup decisively in its saucer. "When the time is right, Brielle will act. Of course, the coven itself is a place of sanctuary. If my nephew were to visit, Brielle would only be able to observe. But as witches, we owe no loyalty except to our coven. Familial ties are secondary."

"We know your rules and your ways," Nero says, waving his hand dismissively and turning to stare once more out of the window at Highborn, stretched out below.

"And Brielle knows her assignment. She is our best hunter, a loyal and dedicated member of our coven. She will not fail."

Brielle's eyes rise, meeting Captain Leggan's, and for a moment, his sneer disappears, replaced with something close to regret. She rakes her gaze across all those assembled, landing on the man, Tiberius, seated on the sofa across from them. He seems less dismissive, less impatient, than the one by the window. Otho, the brother behind the sofa, has not said a word. Only stared, leaving the hair on her arms to rise. She clears her throat. "Mira Boscawen has taken human lives. I've seen her fight. I've seen how volatile she can be. At some point, her siren blood will out, and if her mother was as you told the mal—"

"Her mother brought down an entire Arnhem fleet with a single storm some years ago," Otho says, frowning. I see his slender fingers suddenly dig into the back of the sofa. "If her daughter even holds a *fraction* of that power in her blood—"

"Which brings us to why we asked you to visit us here today," Tiberius interrupts, seemingly entirely unruffled and smiling again, as though sharing an intimate conversation with friends at afternoon tea. "The assignment has . . . changed. We no longer wish for you to capture and drain the creature. We wish her brought to us alive and whole. Unharmed, if you can manage it."

"Alive?" Brielle asks, confused. "But if she's dangerous, as lethal as we all believe—"

"Alive," Tiberius cuts in. "I trust this will not be an issue?"

"Not at all," the mal says hurriedly. "We welcome the assignment."

Brielle says nothing, merely breathing the air as it drifts in on an idle breeze, smelling of Highborn, of old stone and secrets. As they discuss trivial matters for a few moments more, Brielle allows the tea to turn cold in the cup in front of her. She has never brought in a monster alive. It's not what a hunter does.

She wonders, as she sits staring at these people, if Mira Boscawen is really the monster they claim her to be. Or if Mira serves some unexplained purpose to them that the ruling council is not sharing with Brielle.

As the mal concludes her conversation with the ruling council, Brielle and the others are told they can leave. She stands, allowing Captain Leggan to move ahead of her as they walk to the doors. She leaves the chamber, directed by the guards to wait for her malefant in an outside courtyard filled with spring blooms and the scent of nectar. She allows the color of the flowers, the floral notes warm and honeyed, to calm her racing thoughts.

Muffled footsteps pull her back to the courtyard as a young man, taller than her, regards her from several feet away. He turns with a small smile, dipping to smell a rose, the petals thick and creamy. "You're a hunter, aren't you?" he says in a deep, melodious voice. "The one they've brought in to capture the human with magic."

Brielle hesitates before jerking her head in a nod. "What gave me away?"

"You seem troubled." He points to a scatter of flowers, tiny and insistent, crowding around the rose. "If the gardener spots them, he'll weed them out. Rip them from the soil and discard them."

She moves toward him, intrigued. He doesn't seem to be

a guard, and yet his accent doesn't indicate that he's from any of the countries that make up the vast, sprawling continent. His hair is short and light brown, almost blond, his nose crooked, as though it's been broken and reset badly, his eyes that forgettable shade that's not quite brown, not quite green. And yet there is a gentleness about him, a quietness that Brielle cannot place. Almost as though he's from everywhere, and nowhere. She stops a few feet away, her gaze flitting to the plant. "They don't look like weeds."

"I suppose it's a matter of opinion," he says, squatting down to brush his fingers over the periwinkle flowers. "What is deserving of life, what has value . . . and what must be pruned to make way for something else."

"Not everything in this world can live. Some things must die; some things are dangerous."

The man straightens, his calm, unwavering gaze resting on her features like dappled sunlight. "And who then is more dangerous? The living being that is hunted and killed, or the hunter performing this noble act?"

"I believe . . ." Brielle hesitates once more, then shakes her head with a small, sad smile. "Not every creature is a periwinkle flower. Some are quite vicious, only existing to destroy."

"And would you hunt and destroy the creatures you didn't believe to be a threat? Would you be the conqueror?"

"I have questioned assignments before, if that's what you mean."

"Hmm," the man muses. "You are the first witch I've ever heard say that, Brielle Tresillian."

Brielle's eyes cut to his. "You know my name."

He smiles. "I'm Rue. An . . . ambassador for the ruling

council. And now you know mine."

"Brielle?" a voice snaps at her back, and she turns, finding the mal waiting for her. "Time to leave."

And when Brielle turns to say goodbye to Rue, she finds she is alone. She frowns, gaze sliding to the flowers in the bed, the riot of tiny periwinkles and the creamy, manicured roses.

"Brielle, now."

She strides across the courtyard, falling into step next to the malefant as they make their way back through the cold marble corridors. Just before they leave, she looks back at the palace, at the once-opulent sprawl, now clipped and regimented and cold, and finds Rue standing in the entrance, watching her.

CHAPTER
TWENTY

THE SIREN GRAVEYARD IS JUST AS I REMEMBER, A stretch of watchful sea pressed under a sullen gray sky. I tread water, finding a thin veil of mist floating just on the surface, the peaks of jagged rocks brushing the air like seeking fingers.

The journey took two days aboard *Phantom*, and Elijah's reluctance was only worn down by Tanith's cool insistence. Traversing wasn't an option; it drains Elijah too much over long distances, and as Amma pointed out in the kitchen over lunch before we departed, he's still learning his limits with no guide through the dark. We need him strong and ready if he needs to use his magic over the coming weeks.

Joby came with me, with Merryam at the helm. I noted all the times her eyes rested on Pearl's bunk belowdecks, or she held Pearl's mug before placing it carefully back on the shelf. This is another reason why this has to work, why we have to drive out the watch and break Renshaw. Pearl is with Bryn in hiding, and Merryam is needed on Ennor. Until we succeed, they are divided, and the longing Mer feels when she is away from her love is clearly costing her.

I take a breath, knowing I could be underwater for some time, and dive. I cannot hear my mother's song anymore, yet her presence is everywhere. In the way the sea undulates, the current as it flows between the rocks, the pale sand on the seabed. I brush my hand over a rock as I pass it, the rasp of granite softened by the sea urchins clinging to its back. The sea is dark shades of navy and teal with the overcast sky, but there are still glimmers of light. Tiny starfish, clinging to the rocks, silver fish darting in brisk shoals. This place makes sense to me; it feels like a piece of home. All at once, my heart calms, and my whole body relaxes as I float through the hidden waterways to where I know the sirens will be waiting.

When I reach the outcrop of rock where I found my mother's chest, I catch a flash of movement from the corner of my eye. It's them.

I smile, speaking without moving my lips, hoping they can hear what I say in my head, as before.

I need to ask some questions. I come alone.

At first, the sea quiets, as though all the life surrounding me, those brisk silver shoals, the exploring starfish, has darted away. Then I feel it, a shift in the water, a presence. I turn and find the siren I spoke to the last time I visited this place, ethereal in the water, a soothing painting of pale blues.

We had to make sure.

Of course.

She indicates that I should follow her, diving down to the small opening of an underwater cave. It's not the same place where I joined her before, and I hesitate. She turns, beckoning, showing her teeth in what I can only hope is a smile. They claimed me as their own last time, but was that just a show of grief for my mother? Was it just to dispatch a promise made to her? They said I have a very human heart. Just how loyal are they to my mother's memory? Loyal enough to answer my questions, and not feast on my heart afterward? After all, that's how they survive. They drag sailors down to the depths of the sea . . . and feed.

They promised help if I ever needed it, but how long does that promise extend for a siren—years, weeks, moments?

I've come too far to leave now. I swallow my fears and dive down to the cave. Pulling myself through a dark passage of smoothed rock, I catch glimmers of light above. Song, haunting and strange, drifts through the water, and when I surface in the underwater cave, I gasp softly. I'm floating in a pool entrance to the cave, which is designed the same way as the siren's treasure cave I visited before.

But this one is huge. The roof of the cave must be a crop of jutting rocks just above the waves, as the middle of the ceiling is open to the stars. Those swollen storm clouds must have passed on, because the stars blaze overhead in a tapestry of light, and as I lower my gaze to the walls themselves, I see that the pattern of night and constellations is repeated. The cave walls are dark, speckled with mica that glitters and reflects the light from above. There are orbs of light floating, bowls that seem to hold glowing phosphorescence, lingering overhead. And everywhere I look . . .

Sirens.

Draped over rocks cut like thrones, curled up on the floor of this cave, standing with their otherworldly features all turned on me. My heart stutters in my chest and I blow out a breath, squashing the nerves. There are so many more than I believed there would be. Hundreds. All gathered here, in this secret place. It must be some kind of ceremony hall, a sacred meeting space. And mine is the only human heart among them.

"Gallena, introduce your companion," a siren says, her pale hair shimmering down to her waist, her eyes wide and ice blue. "I take it she is the one?"

"She is," the siren says beside me, rising gracefully out of the water. I pull myself from the pool, aware of the water streaming ungracefully from my shirt and breeches, so human and awkward compared to their wild elegance and grace. I wonder how far I'd make it if this many thirsty sirens turned on me.

Gallena continues. "Her human name is Mira Boscawen, and she is the living land daughter of our sister Lowenva. She has been given the map in witch-spelled parchment, the knowledge passed down from mother to daughter, and we promised to help her, if ever she has need of us."

I relax a little as Gallena finishes speaking, murmurs running like ripples through the cave. This is just like a meet on Rosevear. The only difference is that on my island, we do not eat human hearts.

"Are you here to call in the promise my sisters made to you?" the siren asks. She's imperious and cold, and I notice the other sirens leave space around her as she moves toward me, heads lowered in deference. She must be their leader.

"Not exactly," I say. Then I raise my chin, even as my heart thuds too loud, too fast, and I'm sure they are all marking every charged beat. "My mother left me a letter, with the map. It said things that I don't understand yet. About what I can do, who I may become. And I believe, that is . . . *I think* I called a storm. Not once, but twice."

A hush falls over the gathering.

"You called a storm to yourself? On land?" the siren leader asks, her tone suddenly jagged and sharp.

"Yes. On my island, on Rosevear, the watch torched our homes, and we needed rain. I willed it, and a storm appeared from nowhere. I didn't realize I had called it, but then a few days later I awoke in Ennor Castle to a shattered window, a storm raging outside. . . ."

Whispers begin, getting louder and louder, and I turn my head to find many sets of eyes fixed on me. Not with hostility, but with something more akin to . . . awe.

Gallena steps toward me and holds out her slender hand to take my own for a moment, before dropping it. "Lowenva could summon a tempest," she says quietly. "It took much out of her, and she only did it twice. But it's in your siren blood. Storm bringers are revered, as sirens with this ability can lure in food for us. Ships, hearts. If you are a storm bringer . . . there are no others living that we are aware of."

Heat washes over me as I take this in.

"My mother said in her letter, '*Be the storm the world needs to right itself.*'"

Gallena smiles. "Lowenva loved the human way with words. Poetry and riddles delighted her. She likely considered that you might have the ability she had."

I nod, looking down at my hands, salt streaked and chapped, ruddy from the cold of the sea. And I wonder just what these hands can do. What havoc I could wreak without knowing how to tame it? Or how to stop myself?

"Could any of you train me? Show me how to control it?"

The siren leader shakes her head. "Lowenva was the last storm bringer. No others have been born since with the ability. If you have the same power as she . . . you will have to learn control for yourself. Lowenva described it as a fever at times, and we tried to help her, but there are very few records of sirens with this power. The first tempest she brought was a bounty to us, a fleet, and we feasted on many hearts. But the second . . ."

"The second?" I prompt.

Gallena flinches. "The second killed some of our own after she lost all control. After that, she left us for a time, turned to the witches, stole aboard human ships, discovered your island. She didn't just want to be human out of love for your father. She wanted to change her nature because she hated herself for what she had done. Her words to you in that letter may well be a warning, or a hope that you will be able to control what she could not."

Silence descends. I take a breath as the horror of what Gallena has said settles over me. If my mother couldn't learn control here, if none of the sirens know, how will I learn?

Who could I end up hurting?

"Why now? Why can I suddenly do this now?" I ask, frustration tearing at me.

"For sirens, abilities usually manifest after an emotional event, like a death," Gallena says carefully. "It may be that when your father died, it sparked more than fury within you. It drew out your siren side. With your mother's death, you were young, and possibly you did not have those same feelings of fury and rage."

I swallow. Since my father's death, I haven't felt like myself.

It makes sense now that this was more than grief, more than pain. It's all-encompassing, truly as though a tempest has lodged itself inside me. And I am different now. What if that outpouring of rage and horror really did unleash something within me? It was different when my mother's body washed up on the shoreline. I still had my father. I had the comfort of him as a constant. And when he was ripped from me, in front of my very eyes . . . suddenly I had nothing.

I push down the fear and panic, knowing I need more answers. "I also came to ask—the map. Is there no way for it to be just in my head? A part of me? If it falls into the wrong hands, if someone else deciphers it, or if I lose it—"

"The watch and Captain Renshaw are tightening their grip," the siren leader says. "We saw what befell the Far Isles. You want to use it to help your people, the humans. To bring the watch down, to learn their secrets. But it wasn't us who created that map, Mira, as you know."

"It was the witches," Gallena agrees. More murmurs ripple through the cave, a few hisses in grating tones. "Lowenva may have sought their help, but we try to avoid them. Not least because of their hunters. But your mother was desperate. She made a bargain with a coven against our advice. Witches are greedy, untrustworthy creatures. Powerful, yes, but selfish. They are not our allies."

"And if I go to this coven, these witches, will they help me?"

Gallena and the leader share a look. I realize some of the sirens are slipping out, retreating into the shadows. This meeting is drawing to an end.

"Please, you offered help, and I am asking for it. I need to save my island, save the people I care about. More will hang;

more will starve come winter."

"You may not like the answer," Gallena says.

By now it is just the three of us, and the dark has gathered us together in its grip. The stars are blotted out above, the mica no longer glittering and glinting. I shiver, wrapping my arms around myself. Finally the leader speaks. "Ask Lord Tresillian. It was his aunt, the malefant of her coven, who made the bargain with your mother. It was she who took Lowenva's blood as payment. He deals with the coven still, and there is something hidden there, something he dearly desires. Elijah Tresillian deals in bargains and secrets, Mira. Did you ever wonder why he chose to bargain with you?"

"I don't . . ." I hesitate, thinking back over my first encounter with Elijah. How he promised to help me off Renshaw's ship, and earlier, how he tailed me on Ennor, how he'd wanted his crew to get to know me. He knew I was different, suspected, possibly, that I was part creature. "What does Elijah want from the witches?"

"The coven has a locked jewelry box that belongs to him. His mother left it for him, and it was supposed to be passed to him on her demise. But her sister locked it away in a chest spelled with siren blood. Your mother's blood. Elijah begged her for the key to unlock the box, begged her for what was inside. But his aunt tricked him, used it to tie him to her. She made him promise to always be loyal to her and only her, and when he agreed, she sealed that promise with a binding spell.

"She gave him the spindle key but wrapped it, and said that anyone who bears it—anyone who touches it who does not possess the blood of a siren—will be driven to madness and die." The siren smiled sadly. "In return for that key, as promised, Elijah Tresillian must work for her, delivering the creature blood to apothecaries. He must be the courier, forever loyal, forever at her beck and call, even though he must surely despise her for her trickery and her hold over him. But he's never stopped looking for a siren, for a creature with our blood who might walk into that coven, turn the key in the lock of that chest, reveal the jewelry box, and release its secrets to him. We know what he seeks, and none of us has any reason to put our lives in danger for him."

It all clicks into place. Elijah wanting me to work for him, to stay near him. It was all for this. My fingers touch the bargain mark on the inside of my wrist, pressing into it as I try to contain the thrumming of my heart. "What's inside the jewelry box?"

"The answer he's been searching for his whole life," the siren says quietly. "Who he is, and *what* he is. Where his magic really comes from."

CHAPTER
TWENTY-ONE

"JUST WHEN DID YOU PLAN ON TELLING ME THE truth?" I say, throwing back the doors in the entrance hall as I stalk inside Ennor Castle. Elijah is waiting there, arms crossed, gaze narrowed. As I expected. I cross my arms, mirroring his own, and stop a few feet away. Merryam and Joby slip through the door behind me. "I want it all, not just you shrugging and sending me off to practice with Caden."

Merryam and Joby skirt around me, whistling softly as they quickly dash to the door leading to the kitchen. "Well?"

He sighs. "Come with me."

We walk into the town in silence, the breeze ruffling our hair and clothes, spiked with sea salt and warm pollen. I keep my temper in check, clamping my jaw around the torrent of questions, the accusations like poison on the tip of my tongue. But Elijah says nothing, barely nodding to the islanders we pass, until we arrive in a familiar square, a shop before us that I visited a couple of months ago.

"Here?" I say, eyeing the forlorn objects, the desk at the back, shrouded in shadow.

"Here."

This time when I step inside, I feel the insistent, strange pull of it, like fingers twined around mine.

"Like calls to like, just as blood calls to blood," Elijah says softly, his gaze sweeping over me. "I thought when you first stepped inside here, when you crossed to the shelves . . . I was watching you through the window, and I had an inkling . . . call it intuition . . . that you were the one I'd searched for: one of a kind, impossible and brilliant. But then you hesitated, you reached for it, but you didn't pick it up. And I wondered if I'd been mistaken."

He swallows. "So I followed you. And when I spoke to you, I realized you couldn't be as you appeared. All human. You were like a storm wrapped in a girl, and I had to make sure. Had to know. So I asked Mer to carry you aboard *Phantom*, to get a sense of you, to see how you were tied to Seth. And when she told me the coordinates, where they were . . . I knew what they meant. And where you were heading."

I step toward the shelf, slowly, cautiously. I had no idea who Elijah was, what he wanted. But now . . . I look at the object, navy as the sea, dazzling with promise.

The spindle key.

"It's in this shop and not locked away in the castle because I wanted someone to find it. I wanted it to be so obvious that if it called to a passerby, they would be lured toward it. I needed to find a person who could hold it and not be cursed."

Now the events of the past couple of months spill over my mind differently. This key did call to me. Even then, in this shop, on this lonely, dusty shelf. But I ignored it. I listened to the shopkeeper, figured he was right, that it was an odd lure, a trap. And that if it was indeed magic, I should keep away. But now I reach for it. I curl my fist around it, and a sigh, just like my mother's, shudders through the room. I close my eyes and hear her song. For a moment, she is with me, her blood woven into this key calling to my own.

Opening my eyes, I turn to Elijah, the spindle key cold in my palm. "You want me to go to your aunt's coven and open the chest she has hidden there from you."

"Yes."

"You think it contains something precious, something that will tell you who you are, what you are made from."

He eyes me warily and nods. "Yes."

I release a breath, then place the key in my pocket. After Seth's betrayals, the secret Elijah kept is grating. It explains a little of why he was unsure about me going to the sirens, knowing they would likely tell me. But he didn't stop me from going. He ensured I had a crew to take me to the siren graveyard. And I chose a bargain with him, knowing that our ultimate goals aligned—but he's never opened up to me completely.

I can choose to hold this against him, to see it as a betrayal of my trust. But I value this alliance too much, and I understand the desperate urge to understand who you are, and where you belong. I understand why he kept this from me. Perhaps I would have done the same.

"You and I are more alike, Elijah Tresillian, than I ever could have imagined."

He shrugs, a small smile lifting up the corners of his mouth. "Call me Eli, Mira. There are no secrets between us now."

"Eli," I say, rolling it along my tongue. My temper, consuming me for the whole journey back from the siren graveyard, dissolves into the air around us. There is relief somehow in knowing what Eli seeks. He's no longer some elusive young lord, but someone solid and real . . . someone like me. I do not trust those who claim complete altruism, those who only want to save the world. But something like this? Something personal? That makes sense. It means he is human. "All right. Now tell me everything you know about the witches."

We leave the shop, taking the meandering path through town, out to the beach with the pale sand and pearly shells. We sit in the sunshine and he tells me about Coven Septern, about how his mother died shortly after childbirth, and how his aunt, the malefant, insists that she's protecting him by keeping him tied to her. That it's what her sister would have wanted.

"But you and Caden grew up here without her or your mother," I say, shaking my head. "How is that protecting you?"

"She doesn't like my father, never trusted him. So now she won't tell me a thing about him, where my magic may have come from. But . . ." He shifts, picking up a shell. "I'm sure it's all in that locked jewelery box. And meanwhile, we can ask her if there's a way to bind the map to you, so it's useful. We'll both get what we want."

"You mean so that *I'm* useful."

"So that you're the weapon we need. And so we'll know if we're about to be ambushed, instead of Amma having to keep the map under lock and key."

I frown, tipping my face up to the sun. "I can't ask her about my abilities though, even if my mother might have confided in her, or if she has research of her own. It's too risky. The sirens don't trust her." Then I tell him about what my mother could do, and what she couldn't control. I tell him what happened down there in the siren graveyard.

"Then we'll ask someone in the coven who we *can* trust," Eli says, flicking his wrist to throw the shell into the waves. "Caden's sister, my cousin. Lowri."

The note arrives two days later, granting our request and inviting me and Eli to visit Coven Septern in Highborn. Eli calls us all together.

Joby shuffles into the kitchen after Merryam, shaking his hair from his eyes. He squeezes my shoulder before sprawling on an armchair closest to the hearth, where Amma usually sits and does the mending. He's salt stained and wiry, his usual glow deepened to a tan by the sun from his work with the crews and a swift visit to a drop point with Merryam.

"No food aboard *Phantom*?" I ask, loading up a plate with Amma's saffron loaf and sandwiches to pass to him.

He nods in thanks, wolfing down several bites before responding. "Had to be careful after going to the drop point and visiting Pearl. The seas were not kind between here and the safe house, couldn't rest for a moment. No talk of where they've gone though, and no sign of them anywhere."

"Who?" I ask, grabbing a scone and buttering it.

"The people of Finnikin's Way," Merryam says. "They've got some of our goods. Eli needs it all back, but they've left.

No trace of them, no whispers in any of the ports."

"Goods for the . . . apothecaries?" I ask delicately.

Joby nods once before shoving a whole sandwich into his mouth and taking a swig of tea.

"And how is Bryn?"

Eli strides in, flanked by Caden and Tanith. I don't know if I'm imagining it, but I'm sure I see Tanith's eyes widen and her cheeks flush when she sees Joby by the hearth. She edges around the room, choosing a seat at the table as far from him as she can possibly get.

Eli drops onto a chair across from me, next to Merryam. "He's well. The limp is improving with the spring weather, at least."

I expel a relieved breath. "Code for, he's complaining like a sailor at sea after the drink has all been drained."

Joby smiles. "Pretty much."

"This isn't why you summoned us though," Tanith says, eyes flitting to Joby, who seems to be incredibly interested, suddenly, in the mug he holds in his hands. "Is it?"

"No, it's not," Eli says, sitting back, the picture of apparent ease. "Mira and I are visiting my aunt. Tomorrow."

"We're spread too thin, Eli," Caden mutters, crossing his arms across his chest. My eyes dart from him to Eli, but Merryam seems completely unconcerned, scooping up bramble jam from a dish to smother over a scone. "Highborn isn't the isles—you need cover."

"That's why I want you to come with us," Eli says smoothly, raising an eyebrow. "Any thoughts? Objections? Mer, Tanith, Joby?"

"None," Merryam says around a mouthful of scone. "I'll do a much better job than Caden anyway. We all know those muscles are just for show."

"Oh yeah?" he says, flexing them. "You want to take this to the yard?"

"Er . . . no?" she says. "I'm eating?"

Joby snorts, quickly covering it with a cough, and mutters, "No objections here."

We all turn to Tanith, who hasn't touched the cakes or sandwiches. She places her empty teacup on the table and rises gracefully. "You children have fun. Don't annoy your aunt again, Elijah. Amma and I will guard Ennor until your return."

With that, Tanith drifts out on a cloud of jasmine and the faintest hint of smoke. We all watch her leave, then busy ourselves with the last of the saffron loaf and scones.

"Can I ask a question?" I say, looking around at them all. "How old is Tanith?"

"It depends what you mean," Merryam says, glancing at Joby. "Do you mean in her current human form, or in her true form, which she has not assumed in some time . . . ?"

"Never mind," I say, taking a quick bite of my scone. I'd heard that firedrakes could live centuries, the same ones cropping up in stories passed down through generation after generation. But now I know for sure.

"It's settled then," Eli says. "Caden, Mira, and I will leave for Highborn tomorrow, and Merryam will stay here. Joby will stay too."

"Excellent," Amma says, appearing by the hearth and leaning over to pat Joby's cheek. "This one needs feeding. Gaunt as a ghost." Then she rounds on Eli, fear flitting briefly across her ethereal features, and I only just catch it from the corner of my eye. "Be careful. No bargains you can't break this time. Don't underestimate her lack of humanity, or her loyalty to the coven above all else."

"Amma . . ." Caden says.

"I mean it," she says softly—so softly I almost don't catch the rest. "She does not deserve to be your kin."

CHAPTER
TWENTY-TWO

WE MEET IN THE FORMAL DINING HALL, WHERE shadows gather at the corners. The spindle key and map are folded away inside my clothing, as hidden as they can be. I take a breath, holding my hand out for Eli's, but he hesitates.

"If things . . . don't go well, Caden will bring you back here."

I frown, realizing now why he wanted Caden to come with us. I swallow, wondering just how dangerous this side of his family is, how ruthless these witches are. "And why do you assume I would need an escort?"

Caden grins, but the humor doesn't quite touch his features. There is no sunlight today. "Let me rephrase that for Eli. If my mother decides to get shitty with him for one of his *many* misdemeanors, and if Eli chooses to challenge her on being completely insufferable, you and I will be traveling back the slow way."

"Right," I mutter. "Got it. Do you think your mother will help us?"

"Who knows?" says Caden, also holding out his hand for Eli to take. "Witches are a mysterious breed. Depends what's in it for her and the coven."

"When we land in Highborn, the ruling council and all five of the main covens in Arnhem will know we've arrived. There are wards on the city. Like spiderwebs with invisible bells," Eli says, rolling his shoulders. "There'll be spies everywhere, so stay together."

"Do we have to traverse? Could we not travel the slow way there?" I ask, thinking of the cost, having seen how it depletes him after traversing a great distance, or using his magic many times, like the night on Rosevear. "You'll be drained before we step foot inside the coven."

"It's a show of strength. The malefant despises weakness."

Bracing myself to traverse, I wait for Eli to take my hand. I glance up at him, and for a heartbeat, I see a glimpse into what lies beneath the surface of him. We both have much to lose, and much to gain, by visiting the coven. His gaze slides away, fixed on a point across the room.

I close my eyes and take a step backward into the ether.

The sharp scents of old stone and smoke billow up around me. When I look around, I'm on a street, but none like I've ever seen before. It's like the merchant streets of Penscalo and Hail Harbor, but grander. I gasp softly, releasing Eli's hand to turn in a circle, taking in the huge, solemn buildings lining the street, the wide pavements, the street clattering with glossy black horse-drawn carriages.

"Welcome to Highborn, Mira."

"You never said it would be so . . ."

"Loud, smelly, crowded?" Caden says, wrinkling his nose. "Grand."

There are people everywhere, pushing past us on the pavement, dodging between carriages to cross the street, hawking newspapers and buns and flowers, a copper a stem. The men everywhere wear suits, some patched and faded, some smart and sleek as a raven's wing. One man passes by us, wearing a hat as tall as his head, mustache bristling as he steps around Caden with a frown. And the women, always in twos and threes, wearing hats and small smiles, whispering and giggling behind their finely gloved hands. I catch the eye of a woman in a carriage, jewels strung around her throat, a whole necklace of coveted glitter. . . .

I swallow and look at Eli and Caden, then down at myself. At Agnes's old shirt, my black jacket, the holder at my waist with Agnes's blade thrust into it. My hair is half-unbound, a wild sheet of gold, and I realize with a jolt that every woman and girl I can see has her hair carefully styled, either immaculately straight and glossy, or crimped and curled in ringlets. I brush a hand over my own hair, feeling the salt still clinging to the strands. "I don't fit in here."

"You look just as you should," Eli says quietly, so quietly I almost think I imagine it. I self-consciously run my fingers through my hair, wondering if he means that I look as outlandish as I feel, but that it's a good thing. I hope that's what he means. I've never been very good at fitting in. Then he strides off, Caden trailing behind him, and all I can do is follow after them, weaving through the crowds on the pavement.

We turn right onto an equally grand street, and the crowds fall away behind us. This street has trees growing along the pavement, every few feet, already green with the signs of spring. It's strange, how they've sprouted, how this city keeps the nature here tamed like this. And I realize that's what it is. In Highborn, there is no *wild*. Everything I can see and smell has nothing of home about it at all. I wonder how far it is to the sea, or the fields, or the hills. I wonder just how landlocked and contained the people who dwell here are.

Eli and Caden stop outside a tall townhouse that seems more imposing than the rest. With wrought-iron railings circling it, dark windows that seem to go on and on, rising up several stories, and carefully clipped gardens of grass and low hedges on either side of a brick path leading to the front door, this house does not look as if it particularly likes visitors. On either side there are townhouses similar in stature, like wise elders judging those passing on the street below. But this house . . . it whispers of magic. Of captured wilds, dark and thorny, straining to snatch unsuspecting passersby.

"Coven Septern," Eli says grimly, eyeing the closed black front door. "Caden, you'd better go first. The mal will want to greet you."

"The mal?" I ask as I walk through the wrought-iron gate, letting it swing closed with a sharp screech.

"The mal—short for the malefant. It's the title given to the leader of any coven," Caden says. "If I called her Mother in greeting, I'd be out on the street quicker than a curse."

"She sounds . . . motherly."

Eli chuckles. "Nothing like a family get-together."

"She thinks that by favoring Eli with the creature blood for his apothecaries, that she is doing her duty by both of us. I say favoring, but as you now know, he's bound to her. We both are," Caden replies. "Not a motherly bone in her body."

Caden raps on the door, stepping back to wait. I notice the shape of the door knocker, a hooded eye, and shudder.

The door opens, framing a young woman with severe dark bangs and hair spilling in a sleek curtain on either side of her cheekbones to nearly her elbows. Her pale face cracks into a wide, blissful grin and she squeals, dashing down the steps to throw herself on Caden.

"You promised you'd be back two whole months ago. I've been waiting and waiting!"

"Sorry, Lor," Caden says, hugging her tightly back.

"Mother's getting worse, I swear, and there's more—"

"Not here," Eli interrupts softly. "Later. We're being watched."

The witch releases Caden, turns to Eli, and throws her arms around him next. I catch one muttered word, breathed in his ear.

"Beware."

Then this young woman, who I'm beginning to realize must be Caden's sister and Eli's cousin, turns to me and holds out her hand for me to shake. "Lowri Tresillian. Witch in training. Daughter of the malefant, but please don't hold that against me."

"Mira Boscawen," I say, her smile infectious as we shake hands. They are cold, bone white with the strangest black nails. "Just an islander. Tagging along."

"Of course," she says, barely blinking. "Come in. She's expecting you."

A cat darts from the open door and winds around our ankles before flanking Lowri as we walk up the steps. Somehow, it's colder inside than out, and as we follow Lowri through the entrance hall and up the wide staircase to the first floor, I catch glimpses of watching eyes, half-hidden in shadowy doorways. Sconces line the walls, casting pools of light over paintings of stern women dressed all in black, portraits and groupings with the occasional cat seated on a lap, or at the subject's feet.

"Their familiars," Caden murmurs.

"What's a familiar?" I mouth back.

A creature of nightmare.

I startle, looking around for where the voice came from. "Did you hear that?"

Lowri's footsteps stutter and she turns to me. "Did you just . . . hear Nova speak?"

Nova meows unconvincingly, rubbing up against my leg.

This one isn't like the others.

I jolt, staring down at the familiar. It blinks slowly up at me, a small white star of fur twitching in all that sleek black, and I catch a shifting, the merest glimpse of something with fangs and hunger, something patient and loyal that is many, *many* years old. . . .

Lowri frowns, then quickly reassembles her features. "She only lets Brielle hear her occasionally, aside from me. . . . Anyway, come along. We're late."

Before I can question Lowri, we're swept into a room stuffed with books and armchairs and huge windows overlooking the street below. There's a hushed quiet to the space, the only sound the insistent tick from a clock on the far wall. And there, seated on a sofa, prim and petite and wholly unassuming, is another witch. She has dark blond hair, a shade deeper than her son's, keen eyes, and the same black nails as Lowri. And although she seems perfectly ordinary, the room echoes with her presence. I am instantly wary.

"Malefant," Caden says stiffly, nodding to her. Eli and I stand back next to Lowri as he walks forward, kissing her on each cheek.

The malefant's eyes, cold as the winter sea, fix on mine. Her lips twitch in something that could be a smile or a grimace, and she says, "Come, sit. Despite what my nephew and son may have told you, I won't bite."

Lowri and Caden exchange a look, and we all sink into seats around her. Two witches walk into the room, discreetly setting a full tea service on the table. As tea is poured, the witches hurrying from the room, the malefant—Caden and Lowri's mother, Eli's aunt—fixes her piercing stare once more on me.

"Now tell me, my dear. Why are you here with my son and nephew?"

I hesitate, and Eli growls a response. "She's here to discuss a witch-made map, one we are fairly sure was created by this coven."

"Interesting," the malefant says, taking a small sip from her teacup. She places her cup back in its saucer, eyes narrowing on me in a way I am all too used to. "Why should I help a murderous creature like you?"

Caden splutters tea back into his cup and frowns at her. "Mother . . ."

"It's a valid question," the malefant says with a sniff, stirring a sugar lump into her tea. "She's murderous and she's a creature. Would you prefer I called her a monster?"

"Mira will suffice," I grit out, reminding myself that I need this witch's help. But I'm starting to see why this was a last resort, why coming to Coven Septern was not the first option—certainly not before going to the sirens first, an actual pack of ravenous monsters. "I need your help with the map."

"Interesting. Go on."

"The map is from the sirens," Eli says, spreading his hands. "The knowledge that would usually be passed down from mother to daughter, innate, has been given to her on parchment. Mira needs that knowledge to be a part of her, just like any other siren."

"A binding is a tricky thing with a steep cost," the male-fant murmurs.

"Can you help me?" I ask, not breaking eye contact for a second.

"Perhaps. I should like to study you. And the map. How you read it, how your interpret—"

"No," Eli says quickly.

The malefant sighs. "It'll take something from you if we do a binding. Something of weight and value to you." She raises her eyebrows. "I suppose the question you have to ask yourself is . . . what could a spell take from you that you do not wish to lose?"

I take a sip of tea, saying nothing. Giving nothing away as she studies me.

"Until we perform the binding, we will not know just what it will take from you. But I will confer with my coven about the price and bring you an answer. In the meantime, no straying to the lower level of the house or interfering with our work."

"So it is possible?"

"It is." She sniffs, already rising from the sofa. Clearly our meeting is concluded. "Caden, I expect you at dinner."

The malefant sweeps from the room, leaving the three of

us looking at each other. Then Caden shrugs with a rueful grin. "At least she didn't say no. I'd say she was practically obliging."

"She didn't give us a price either," Eli says carefully. "And I've never known Hillary Tresillian to do anything that isn't to her advantage."

CHAPTER
TWENTY-THREE

IN ANOTHER LIFE, THIS VAST ROOM MAY HAVE
been a ballroom, filled with symphonies and trysts and scandal. Now, once a week, the young hunters and casters of
Coven Septern gather for a formal lecture, and Brielle tries
to remind herself it's not a total waste of her time.

"Who can tell me the uses of charms in the different
countries across the continent?" the witch apparent, Theine,
says in a nasal voice that always leaves Brielle on edge and
irritated, like one damp sock squelching in a boot on a long
walk, or a hangnail she's yet to cut away.

Peony's hand shoots up and she answers—with that ever-
present sneer that she apparently can't help because it's, as
Lowri says, "Just her face."

"Arnhem uses charms mainly for power, Leicena for
beauty, Skylan for persuasion, and the Spines for protection."

"Excellent," Theine says, scanning the crowd of seated
witches. She turns to the board and begins discussing the

process of creating a charm, from the hunted creature blood to its application by casters.

Brielle takes the opportunity to lean across to Lowri, who is sitting next to her, and whisper, "What's she like, then?"

Lowri's mouth twists as she flicks her eyes to Brielle, then back to the board, Theine still droning on in nasal tones. Ever since Brielle had confided in Lowri who or what she had been assigned to hunt, the human name on that scrap of paper and the reason why she had been summoned before the ruling council, Lowri had been ominously quiet. "She's completely ordinary. Dresses and looks like Eli and Caden. Nothing monstrous about her."

"I wouldn't be so sure," Brielle says with a snort. "Did you notice a weapon?"

"A small blade slung at her waist. Mother didn't seem concerned—"

"Lowri and Brielle Tresillian, are we disturbing your afternoon?" Theine says with no small amount of smug triumph. She clasps her fingers in front of herself, ash-blond hair framing her watery blue eyes and colorless skin. "Lowri, what was I just discussing?"

Lowri sighs as Brielle winces, knowing what's coming. No one picks on Lowri. She may *seem* diminutive, but she is the malefant's daughter. Even the senior hunters don't cross her. "You were discussing charms, specifically the evolution of charms across the continent, their applications, and the revenue they bring in to the coven. You just used the example of the royal court in Morgana, and how we send three witches there at the beginning of the season to work with the most discerning families, who wish to see their offspring well matched. These charms usually include thimble-sized bottles of potions or powders locked in a ring or locket, dusted at a pulse point to make the wearer seem, temporarily, more alluring. Funny. Kind. *Charming.* These charms are developed by witches, not apothecaries, because the subtlety can only be wrought by a being with magical aptitude. They are an important source of income for the coven." Lowri allows herself a small, knowing smile. "Would you like me to go on?"

Brielle shrinks in her chair as Theine's eyes bore into Lowri's. Theine snaps back to the board, ignoring the unspoken challenge. Whispers and murmurs echo around the room, but Lowri stares ahead, unruffled. Brielle has a creeping sense of foreboding, about what her sister is, and what she may still become.

"The only real question to ask yourself . . ." Lowri says as she turns to Brielle, "is why does the ruling council want her alive?"

There are four place settings for dinner, where usually there are just three. It's always held in the private dining room beside the malefant's study, and despite her working only in the next room, Lowri and Brielle are always the first to arrive and be seated. Lowri snaps her napkin open over her lap and takes a sip of cherry-red wine before fussing with the overly ornate cutlery. Brielle rubs a hand over her face, hoping this won't become like every other Tresillian family dinner when Caden visits.

Caden wanders in, stooping to kiss Lowri's cheek before ducking into the chair on Brielle's right. "Mother does love a cozy family dinner. I'd forgotten."

"If you visited more, you would know how fond she *also*

is of standing us up and sending a note with a messenger to apologize," Lowri retorts.

Caden sighs, lounging back in his chair. "But apart from her lack of motherly qualities, is all well here? You're both happy?"

"I have Nova, and Brielle. We have each other." Lowri shrugs. "I've just come out on top at Presentation, and now I have the best rooms. I have access to every spell book, every ingredient, all the knowledge of our coven. . . . What more could I ask for?"

Caden toys with the stem of his wineglass, glancing to Brielle, who shrugs, then back to Lowri. "Any friends?"

"Have you met another witch? Ever?" Lowri chuckles, taking another sip of wine. "Besides Brielle, they're all about as insufferable as you can imagine. Peony and Ellowyn are tolerable, but they're all mini malefants in training."

"Whereas you actually *are* a mini mal in training."

Lowri rolls her eyes. "Don't remind me. My life is the coven and nothing else."

"And you?" Caden turns to Brielle. "Mother keeping you busy?"

"Why do you ask?" Brielle says.

Caden looks between them. "There's something you two aren't telling me."

Before Brielle can deflect, the malefant bustles in, sniffing as she takes the final seat. She snaps her napkin over her lap, and Lowri winces. Are their mother's ways rubbing off on her? "Caden, Lowri, Brielle. What a pleasure to eat with a full complement."

"You could have invited Elijah," Caden rumbles as the first course is brought in. Wide white dinner plates are set before each of them, a construction of slivers of duck, plum sauce, and layered greens. Caden picks up his fork and demolishes the food in two mouthfuls before sitting back once more. "He is family too."

The mal clears her throat, her pincerlike stare settling on her son. Brielle busies herself with her food, used to the biting and hissing between the Tresillians. She knows it isn't about her place in the family, and entirely about Hillary and her lack of motherly qualities. "Elijah is not *close* family."

"He's your nephew."

"But not a son or daughter like the three of you." She places her fork on her plate and smiles. "Tell me news of Ennor."

Brielle tops up the wine, listening for any details she can glean about Mira Boscawen, her prey. They discuss Ennor, the repairs recently carried out on the castle, and the mal reminisces about her childhood home and her love of the library as her children pick at the main course. Caden is growing quiet as he downs yet another glass of wine, but their mother doesn't seem to notice. Brielle notes the frown pinching his forehead, the troubled swirl in his features. He's hiding something, just as she is. She'd bet coin on it.

Immediately after dessert is cleared, Caden pushes back his chair and stands up. "Mother, Lowri, Brielle, it's been a pleasure. I have a headache, so I'll retire and leave you to finish the wine." And before Lowri or Brielle can protest, he leaves the room.

"That went as well as can be expected," the mal says, ringing the bell for tea to be served. "Your brother did manage to remain pleasant, at least."

Brielle barely hides a snort as Lowri sighs with impatience.

"Why don't you scrap the rule about boys at the coven? Surely from your own experience of being divided from him at birth, and your own sister's child—"

"Boys have no place in a coven," she says, raising her eyebrows in surprise. "They are not witches. Every single coven in our world follows that rule."

"But you must have missed him, having to send him away to Ennor, not getting to know him, or love him. . . ."

The mal chuckles indulgently, reaching for her wineglass, black nails glinting. "Oh, Lowri. Witches do not have space in their lives for such a human emotion as *love*. Really—"

"What about loyalty?" Lowri asks, the words spilling from her mouth.

Her mother freezes. "What do you mean?"

Brielle kicks Lowri's foot under the table, but she plows on, even under their mother's cool, assessing gaze. "Mira is with them, here at our coven. She's here seeking our help. And yet you've accepted an assignment from the ruling council to hunt her, haven't you? She's Brielle's assignment. The human name."

The malefant's nostrils flare briefly, her skin growing deathly pale. "I don't know how you know of this, Lowri. Has Brielle been confiding in you?"

Brielle inches back, wondering if she might slink out unnoticed.

"She tells me nothing," Lowri lies smoothly. "Not that it would matter. Surely it's all *coven* business."

The mal exhales, leaning back in her seat. Brielle, despite herself, exhales as well. "Mira will not be hunted while visiting the coven. This house is a neutral space, and we stay out of the politics of the continent. To carry out the assignment here would be . . . damaging. To our reputation, and to relations with our courier. Brielle knows this. It is merely a chance to observe—"

"You mean Eli, don't you? He's not a *courier*, mother. He's not just some business associate of the coven's. He's family."

"Even more reason to remain neutral during their visit. The work of our hunters must be carried out quietly, with discretion. It is of the upmost importance. If word got out that we hunted our visitors and guests, no one would trust us again—"

"And what of family loyalty?" Lowri demands quietly, cutting her off. "Is that not important too?"

Lowri and Brielle leave the dinner with their mother's words ringing in their ears. But Brielle fears that far from placating her, they have enraged Lowri.

"Lowri . . ."

"No. Not this time. Not again, Bri." She twists to look at her, shaking her head. "When I am malefant, the first thing I'll do is overturn that damn rule."

Brielle groans, trying to keep up with her. "You know she's fond of tradition. Just stop for a moment, let's talk about this."

"Go and ready your traps, Brielle, or whatever it is you're planning to catch Mira with. I want to be alone." She stalks away down the shadowy corridors, and this time Brielle doesn't bother trying to stop her. She heaves a sigh, slumping against the wall, the sconce by her head bathing the far wall in soft light. There's a painting hung there, a painting of a hunter and a witch. Her birth mother and Hillary Tresillian. Brielle gnaws on her lip, thinking.

Whatever way she cuts this, there's no way of joining all the pieces up afterward. It'll be her on one side, on the coven's side, and Lowri on the other. Next to Caden, next to Eli. Standing with this monstrous girl, Mira.

She understands the careful path the malefant must tread, placing the needs of the coven above family, above all else. It's the only way the Tresillian witches have survived so long, how Coven Septern still thrives. Brielle has always followed orders, grateful to have been adopted, grateful not to have been cast out when her birth mother perished. But faced with this girl, this assignment, in the very halls she calls home . . . it's the first time she's ever wanted to disagree.

It's the first time she's ever wanted to behave as Lowri does, to speak her mind and damn the consequences.

CHAPTER
TWENTY-FOUR

A HAND COVERS MY MOUTH. I GASP, DRAGGED from a dream of night and stars, and stare up into eyes dressed in shadow. My fingers curl around the blade under my pillow instinctively, ready to thrust it into my attacker's side, but then—

"Murdering someone for disturbing your sleep is a *little* drastic, even for you."

I relax, loosening my grip on the blade as Eli grins in the dark and removes his hand from my mouth. "There are better ways to wake someone," I grumble, pushing my hair from my face and sitting up. "I was having a good dream."

"Was it about me?"

I snort.

"All right, don't tell me. Just get dressed and follow me."

That clears the last of the sleep from my mind. "Why? What's happened?"

Eli moves toward the door. "I'll be outside. Just hurry, and be quiet."

I mutter darkly but do as he says, throwing on my jacket, a clean shirt, and breeches before slipping on my boots. Everything about this visit to the coven has been unsettling, from the familiars winding around the ankles of their witches, to the stern, bold stares of the portraits lining the walls, to the witches themselves, almost hostile in their silence. And all I can think about is what their malefant said, the payment I must offer in return for binding myself to the map.

I find Eli in the corridor, silver slants of moonlight from the window several feet away trickling along the walls. I shiver, feeling his eyes on me, and wrap my arms around myself, heart fluttering in my chest. "This had better be worth losing sleep for."

"Surely a nighttime jaunt with me is always worth losing sleep for?" he says with a wink.

Before I can squeak a retort, he beckons me with a finger at his lips, and we slip away from the guest wing. The coven is silent. We step past closed doors, down a narrow, cramped back staircase, Eli ducking his head in front of me as the ceiling lowers. He leads me through the empty kitchens at the back of the house, the silvery light dancing over polished marble surfaces, pots and pans, and a huge, modern-looking oven unlike any I've seen in an island home, not even in Ennor Castle.

Then we're outside, in a kitchen garden filled with raised beds of herbs. Eli's hand finds mine, sending a jolt through my veins. I take a quiet breath, willing my heart to calm. He's just taking my hand to lead me through an unknown place. What of it? The teasing, his eyes, the way my blood heats like I'm in the sea when I'm around him recently . . . it means nothing. It's only his nature, and I'm just reacting to it.

"All right, Mira?" he whispers over his shoulder. Can he feel the pulse at my wrist quickening? I swallow and nod. He pulls me toward a back gate, then out into an alleyway beyond.

"Why are we not traversing if we want to stay hidden?" I ask as quietly as I can when we turn left, moving farther into a dank alleyway littered with crumpled newspapers, empty glass bottles, and the shining, ocher eyes of cats in the dark. Or at least . . . what I hope are cats.

"If I use magic anywhere in this city, a witch will know. Just like when I traversed in through the city wards. It's too unusual, too . . . different."

"And we don't want your aunt to know we've left the coven?"

"Exactly."

We walk on in silence, avoiding the main streets that still echo with the occasional beat of horses' hooves pulling late-night carriages, the sound of snickering laughter and grating voices, the scent of smoke and manure and drifts of floral perfume worn by the women who work late at night. Instead we navigate a complex web of alleyways until I know I wouldn't be able to find my way back to the coven without Eli guiding me.

Finally we stop before an unassuming door, much like every other we've passed. Eli knocks once and waits, never releasing my hand as if . . . as if he would traverse, if he had to. Even if it did alert the whole damn city, he would traverse through shadow and risk the wrath of his aunt and her coven, to keep me safe.

The door opens, allowing a slice of light to spill out. Eyes peer at us before the door opens wider, and the person moves back. Eli tugs on my hand, never letting go. Not even for a heartbeat as he closes the door in our wake, turning to the person in the room. No, two people.

Caden and Lowri.

It's a narrow, neat sort of townhouse, lit by candles and flickering oil lamps. We have stepped into the front room, three neat armchairs flanking a cold, empty fireplace. It smells clean, of polish and beeswax and soap, but there's a stale tinge to the air, as though this house is not aired and loved as it should be. As I regard Lowri, she straightens a lamp on a low table, fussing with it, a slight tremor at her wrists. Perhaps this is a safe house for Coven Septern, seldom used.

Lowri speaks first, breaking the silence, her syllables clipped and cold. Much like her mother's. "Were you followed?"

"No."

"Are you sure? Because if—"

"If he says he wasn't, then he wasn't, Lor." Caden says, crossing his arms over his chest. "Now tell us why you disturbed our beauty sleep. Eli needs his."

Lowri peers through the small window beside the door, and it's only then that I notice the cat-shaped creature, her familiar, threading around her ankles, tail twitching. The witch murmurs a word, and it's as though a blanket falls over us, like the stale air has thickened. And still Eli does not let go of my hand.

"That should do it," Lowri says with a nod, rounding on us. I realize then that she's scared. But there's more than just fear there—there's determination too. A will of iron. She reminds me of Agnes. "I need to tell you something, and no one else will. Especially not Mother. But if I don't warn you . . . well, Mother says there are always consequences. I believe our coven will pay dearly for this one."

"Spit it out, Lor," Caden says. "What's Mother done now?"

Lowri hesitates, wrestling with herself. "You must understand, if anyone knows I told you, if anyone so much as suspects . . ."

"You can trust us," Eli says. "We're your kin."

"Right, well. The coven received an assignment a few weeks ago, from the ruling council directly, to hunt a monster."

I feel Eli's fingers tighten around mine.

"Brielle, our sister . . . Mira, she's a hunter. And she's been assigned to hunt you."

I inhale sharply, the room spinning around me as Caden and Eli both reach for their blades.

"Lowri, if this is a trap, so help me," Caden begins, eyes darting everywhere.

"No! No, absolutely not," Lowri replies quickly, holding out her hands. "This is a warning. I . . . I couldn't lie. Not anymore, not with you at the coven, not with you being . . . kin."

Eli loosens his grip on my hand slightly. "Lowri, thank you."

"That's not all. What I'm going to tell you next, you cannot breathe to another living soul. And I will deny all knowledge of this conversation. I'd be sentenced to a witch trial, I'd have to prove my innocence, which is almost impossible to fake, and at best, I'd be cast out. At worst . . ." She bites her lip.

We all stare at her, and Eli moves an inch closer to me.

"Mother won't tell you anything, Mira. She'll deny all knowledge of sirens and the research we have gathered over the centuries. But Coven Septern *does* have research. Specific, plentiful research, kept in a book under lock and key and trap, only accessible by the highest witches of the coven. Tomorrow she'll help you with what you have asked of her, she'll perform the binding, and it will be at great personal cost to yourself, and to Eli's pocket." Lowri takes a breath and continues. "But she will swear we know nothing else about a siren's abilities or about your bloodline, when really she gleaned a lot from your mother on her visits. Previous generations of witches have had only rare opportunities to speak to sirens, so it was all recorded in this book."

"I . . . Why are you telling me this?" I ask. "I understand helping Eli and Caden, they're family, but why me? Why risk your life, your place in your coven?"

Lowri smiles sadly. "Call it defiance."

"We'll call it what it is. Bravery," Caden says.

"Lowri, you know that if you ever need it, Ennor Castle is always your home too," Eli says quietly. "Never think the coven is your only place in this world because you're a witch."

"Thank you," she says, and there is a glint in her eyes, like unshed tears. "Now, to plan. Mira, you must go through with the binding spell tomorrow as though nothing is amiss, and you must accept whatever lies Mother spins. She must not suspect a thing. Then, in the night, before you leave . . ."

"We steal the book." I look to Eli and Caden, and they both nod in agreement. Of course I don't mention the other thing, what we might find locked away with the spindle key, but as Eli does not say a word, I keep quiet. This may well be our way in, to find where it is kept within the coven. And all I must do is give up some elusive, precious thing. Something of weight, something I will dearly miss. I grit my teeth. I'm sure it will all be worth it. I remind myself why I'm doing this—for my home, for my islands.

"All right then," Lowri says, motioning for us all to sit. I take one armchair, Caden slouches against the wall, and Eli sinks into another chair. Lowri stays standing, her black nails glistening as she talks, hands moving along with her mouth. "Here's what I know."

CHAPTER
TWENTY-FIVE

"TELL ME WHAT YOU'RE THINKING," ELI SAYS AS we make our way back to the coven. Lowri and Caden have chosen to go a different route, and if they're caught, they can spin a lie about meeting for a drink. Just two siblings catching up.

"I'm thinking I need to stop for a minute. Take a breath. Now that I know I'm being hunted, that the *ruling council* has given this assignment . . . the risk I am putting us all in *every minute* we stay here . . ."

Eli tugs on my hand. "I know a place. Come with me."

He leads me to a walled garden shrouded in darkness. As we step through the gate, the air becomes muffled and quiet. The scent of loam, of new life and wild things, lures me in, and I fill my lungs with something that feels more like home. There are winding paths between looming trees, and when we follow one through the night, it opens onto a lawn edged with benches. Spring flowers are nodding in borders and I imagine that during the day, courting couples stroll along these paths, their lives spread out before them, sparkling like jewels. So unlike Eli and I in this moment, but maybe in another life, at another time . . . I flush in the dark at the turn in my thoughts.

"Thank you," I say after a moment of soaking it in, reveling in the quiet, in this captured piece of wild pressed between the houses and streets of this maze of a city. "It's beautiful. I've never seen a garden like this, made just to enjoy. Our gardens always serve a purpose: to grow medicinal plants, for herbs, for cut flowers to sell on market days. . . ."

Eli bends to examine a white teardrop-shaped flower, and I catch his smile illuminated in the moonlight. "I used to bring Lowri here when she was younger. When I first started dealing with my aunt's coven, many years ago, she could barely be contained. Always trying to escape, half-wild, that familiar forever at her heels. Here at least she could be surrounded by nature and I didn't have to worry about losing her in the city."

"You're fond of her," I realize, eyeing him carefully. This young woman, this unknown witch who now has as much at stake as us. She's as dear to him as Caden.

"If I could, I would take her back to Ennor tonight. But a witch has to learn to control what's within her. Witches don't drink the blood of creatures to gain magic; it's already there, waiting. It's a catalyst. It means they can channel the raw power in their own blood. If Lowri were never to learn spellwork, even if I ensured she had a supply of wild blood to imbibe, her own raw power would consume her. It's an outlet. And Lowri . . ." He sighs. "Lowri is like her mother. Formidable."

"Has a witch ever been . . . consumed by her own power?"

Eli hesitates, as though unsure how much to share. "Yes. The hunters of a coven don't just drain monsters. If a witch is left undiscovered for too long, their magic manifests in other ways. Dangerous, destructive ways. You have heard of wraiths?"

"No," I say, searching my memories of the stories I've been told. But there has never been any mention of wraiths.

"They are creatures of yearning and sorrow. Half spirit, half monster. The souls of witches who were consumed by their own magic. They feed on emotions, leaving the person or family they attach themselves to in great anguish. Sometimes, a hunter will be sent on an assignment to find the wraith and untether it. They can't be killed, but they can be dispelled. It's the hardest assignment a hunter ever has to face, because it's like looking into a mirror of what might have been, if she didn't belong to a coven. Or if she had been cast out before her training was complete."

I shudder. "So Lowri must remain at the coven and finish her training."

"Yes." Eli sits on a bench, and I sink down next to him. "Of course, the opposite is that a witch can use too much of her power. You've noticed they have black nails? Well, when a witch uses too much power, the darkness spreads along her veins, and in some cases, to her eyes. And she will burn that way, not from too little use, but far too much."

"It's a balance then," I say. "Lowri is learning control and balance."

"There was a time when I worried she would become like those other witches. She can be impulsive, strong-willed, rash . . . but then her familiar, Nova, appeared, and it seemed to calm her."

I consider Nova's voice in my head, the way she seemed so much more than the cat she appeared to be. "What is a familiar, exactly? And why don't they all have one?"

"Some witches, usually the strongest, are chosen by familiars, and Lowri is one of them. But the true nature of familiars, well . . ." He shrugs a shoulder. "Don't ask me what kind of creatures they are, what prowls beneath their fur. . . . They're as old as firedrakes. They have their own magic, their own hungers."

We sit in silence for a moment, and I begin to understand what Lowri is risking by telling us about the book of siren secrets and that I am being hunted. If she had to leave her coven, if she didn't get her full training . . .

"I have to go through with it. All of it. Not just the binding spell, but we have to take that book. And we can't allow any suspicion to fall on Lowri."

"Are you sure, Mira?"

"Lowri's done her part. Now it's up to me, isn't it?" I look over at him, to find his gaze fixed on me. A rush of heat suffuses my veins, and my breath hitches. He's mere inches from me, our bodies almost touching. I want to twine my fingers through his again, I realize. But I push the thought away, and focus on what I'm trying to say. The decision I'm making.

"If I don't, we're all at risk. If you say a witch must live with this, this fight for balance and control, is that not the same for me? The magic may not consume me, as it does a witch, but it's worse than that, isn't it? I could hurt someone else. I could lose control and kill."

Eli is quiet for a moment. I'm learning to read him, and

when he is like this, he's thinking through strategies. "And if we're caught taking the book?"

"Then you get out, you get Caden out, and you leave me to deal with—"

"You know I could never do that, Mira."

I laugh softly. Looking down, I see the bargain mark etched in my skin, glowing in the moonlight. A compass with a blade shot through it. Our promise to work together. "Then we cannot fail, and we cannot be caught."

"I've known worse odds," he says, and I can hear the smile in his words. I glance up and find his eyes glittering, those twin dark stars. "And the map, are you absolutely sure? The cost to you could be great. When my aunt gives a warning about a working, it's best to heed it. It's usually more terrible than she lets on."

I nod, pressing my lips together. "I'm ready. I can't risk losing it, and without using it on the water, when it's actually useful, we can't defeat Renshaw and the watch. I can't keep my home safe. It has to become a part of me; we have to know exactly what they're doing. It's the only way."

"If you're sure."

"You know, I haven't forgotten the other thing. The key, the jewelry box. When I look for the book, I *will* find it too. Like calls to like, just as blood calls to blood. I will hear my mother's song and find it for you."

He exhales. "Thank you."

"I understand what it means to you. We are both out with lanterns, searching for ourselves."

I angle my face, sweeping my gaze along the planes of his, and find only sureness. Only trust. I glance at his mouth, inches from mine, and feel my heart swoop in my chest. To

find someone with secrets bound in their blood, a whole history tightly wrapped around their very soul, just like me . . .
It's no wonder I felt he was an anchor in the dark aboard
Renshaw's ship. We are two jagged halves of the same
strange, unique whole.

What would it be like to kiss him? To close this distance
between us, and feel his mouth on mine? My pulse thrums
quicker and quicker as my knuckles brush against his. That
connection sends sparks—tiny, blissful sparks—racing through
me, and all I want is to feel him. To press my body into his as
his arms wrap around me. I imagine his hands on my sides as
his lips graze mine, heat washing over us. I can almost taste
him, midnight and stars, dark and sweet and velvet—

"We should get back," he says softly, and I blink, my
imaginings dissolving around us.

"We should." I leap from the bench and turn away from
him, willing the night air to cool my restless, galloping heart.
I could so easily have leaned in, claimed a kiss, a touch. But
what if Eli doesn't want that? He is only here with me to
protect the bargain we made, to ensure that we both find
what we are seeking within the coven's walls. Surely his
concern is the same as what it would be for any of his inner
circle. And these feelings, this sudden wretched torment . . .
I blow out a breath and turn back to him. I must extinguish
this before *I* risk everything between us.

He holds out his hand, a small smile playing across his
beautiful mouth. "Just as a precaution."

I swallow as his hand closes over mine. In case we have to
traverse, to leave quickly. Not to be close, not for those tiny
sparks to continue dancing between us.

★ ★ ★

The next morning I wake with his name on my tongue and curse myself afresh. "You're a fool," I mutter to myself as I dress, thrusting my feet into my boots and braiding my hair. It's just the situation. The overwhelming nature of all that is to come, the binding spell, the risk, the cost I do not yet know. I can't fall for Eli. Can't grow attached. Despite these past few weeks, getting to know him, to see how his island feels about him, the way he encourages, coaxing the best from his people . . . the thought of losing anyone else I care about, anyone else I love, leaves me breathless with fear. I've already lost too much. All I have left are the memories.

I fix my gaze on the mirror and point a finger at my reflection. "You do not have feelings for Elijah Tresillian. Focus on the binding spell and on the heist."

A knock sounds at the door. They are ready for me. I give myself one final moment to stare at my reflection, gathering my strength. Then I turn, and get ready to face what the binding spell will take, and what it will offer in return.

CHAPTER TWENTY-SIX

WE WALK TO THE FIRST FLOOR IN SILENCE, FOL-
lowing Lowri down the main staircase, through the entrance
hall, and onward to a door to the left, which leads to a chamber at the back, far from the street and any curious eyes. The
only light is from flickering black candles, shifting over the
walls to illuminate pieces of the paintings adorning them.
All of them are abstract, filled with harsh lines and darkness.
I can make out a figure in one of them, a small, bone-white
being in the middle of what appears to be a forest. They are
so very different from the formal portraits scattered through-
out the rest of the coven.

"The depictions of wraiths," Eli murmurs.

I glance over at him, but his eyes don't leave his aunt, who
is standing at the other end of the chamber. There are seven
witches present. Lowri, the malefant, three witches dressed
like her in black, and two witches wearing sets of blades in
sashes across their chests, their hands clasped behind their

backs, feet shoulder-width apart.

The hunters.

And I know, deep in the marrow of my bones, which one of them is hunting *me*.

She eyes me curiously, the hunter who must be Brielle Tresillian, barely moving as the mal steps forward. Her braid matches my own, plaited tight to her scalp, winding down over a shoulder. She wears fighting leathers, her muscles evident beneath them, her waist thick. Where I am slight with a curve to my hips and chest, she is honed like a weapon. If it came down to it, if she cornered me alone, I know who would win.

And yet she does not appear menacing. If anything, the hunter at her side seems far more poised to strike a killing blow. If this is the hunter assigned to me, then why? Is she more devious? Ruthless? I catch the flicker of her eyes as they rest on me, then flit to Lowri. Doubt, so fleeting I almost miss it, plays across her features, but is quickly blinked away. I wonder if she knows Lowri has told us. If she knows that *I* know who she hunts, that I will be her quarry as soon as we return to the islands.

"Mira Boscawen, step forward into the circle." The male-fant's voice rings out, swiftly drowning my thoughts. I bunch my hands into fists and take three steps into the center of the chamber. "There is an unbroken chalk circle surrounding you. Do not smudge it. It's the only thing containing the power we will pour into you with this binding."

"Understood."

"We have collected payment from House Tresillian. But you understand that the spell to bind the siren map's knowledge into you will require something of you as well?

Something unimaginable, something you would give your very soul to protect?"

"I . . . I do," I say, keeping my fists clenched. Tremors shiver through my entire body, fear at what will be asked of me. What unimaginable, precious thing I will have to give up for this spell. I have pondered it endlessly since she told me, but the imaginable has already been taken. I'm not sure what more could be ripped from me.

The mal falls silent, watching me. She joins hands with the other three high witches, like a row of foul crows ready to tear me apart. They close their eyes as one, and all the candles save for one extinguish. Smoke, thick and cloying, curls around me, and I fight to keep my eyes open as they sting and water.

The witches' eyes fly open. Their gazes bore into mine, and I feel a tug in my chest. Almost as though someone were testing a rope's strength. Then the feeling dissipates, and I blow out a breath.

"Mira Boscawen, the cost of this binding spell will be every memory you have of your father."

All the air leaves me at once.

"Wh-what?"

"Every memory. Every moment. You will know you had a father, you will feel the shape of that love. But you will have no memory of the details, his voice, his features, his scent. The way he held you as a child, the way you mended nets together in the sun on your step. The stories he told you, the gloves he made you wear before swimming out in a storm. This spell will take it all."

I choke, the smoke seeming to thicken around me. I fall to my knees, the sheer weight of what they will take—

"It is your decision, and yours alone. Will you go through with the spell? Is the cost worth paying?"

I picture my father, his soft, sea-blue eyes. Our home, our nights by the hearth in our cottage. I picture his grave, the coffin Kai made, carved with so much love—

Tears fall on the ground, and I realize they are mine. My heart is breaking.

Then I picture Rosevear. I picture my people, every time we met with the people of Penrith and celebrated, every feast day, every wedding. I picture the children, remember their hunger. I feel it gnawing at me. I think of that night when our island burned. The terror, the bodies, the screaming—

I take a jagged breath.

And I know he would want me to do this. He would do it himself, even if it killed him. He would do it to save everyone; he would give and give and give.

I rise to my feet, forcing breath, in and out, and face the witches through the wall of smoke and silence. "The cost is worth paying," I say, even as my entire being shatters with the words. I raise my chin, steeling myself, and take out the map, placing it at my feet within the chalk circle. The islands, the rocks, the eddying waves are scrawled across it in black, flowing ink. Knowledge that I need to keep safe and carry with me, always. "Take it all."

I find Eli's eyes in the dark, two stars illuminated by that single flickering candle. I hold his gaze, as his holds mine, and in it, I find strength. Purpose.

Hope.

I cling to a memory of my father from childhood, when we walked down to the beach together, his hand in mine, and I looked up at him, the sun glancing off his smile, and he seemed as a tree, tall and ancient and forever. . . . I smile through the tears, holding this moment in my mind for as long as I can. As long as it will last.

There is a single uttered word, and lightning explodes inside me.

I scream, falling back to the ground as heat, white-hot and searing, floods me. I cradle my head in my hands. The pain is unbearable. I can't see, can't think. Make it stop—

Make. It. Stop.

I hear something. A voice. Calling my name. Crying it over and over.

Mira, Mira, Mira . . .

He's laughing, and we're in the meeting house, heat washing over me, music and dancing and the people of Penrith weaving around. I grasp his hand and he twirls me, my mother smiling, watchful at the edge. . . .

It's deep winter and I'm helping him with the pots, drawing them in on his boat, checking for lobster before tipping them back over the side. The sea churns around us, frothing and gray as gulls wheel overhead, a drip of rain shivering down my nose. . . .

It's just the two of us, on our sun-warmed step, the nets in my hands and a yarn on his tongue. I can smell fresh bread, it's a good day, a spring day, and we have fish for the market at Penscalo. . . .

Then we're on the old quay, mist clinging to us. He's wearing his green wool jacket. I search for his soft blue eyes, reaching for him, knowing what's coming, waiting for the blood, but he's just out of reach. . . .

Then suddenly, nothing.

I curl into a ball, the heat seeping away, leaving nothing

but cold. I can't open my eyes. Can't bear the brightness, the light . . .

"It is done," the malefant says in all that light.

Warm arms come around me, lifting me, carrying me away. I whimper as the light dims, as I see the shape of what I once knew, now empty. Gone. And in its place, there is something new. Places and people and sea and rocks and tide, so much that my mind cannot hold it all, so much knowledge, so many secrets.

My body convulses and the arms tighten around me. "We're nearly there, Mira, hold it together—"

A door creaks, and finally I open my eyes to an unknown room, a pair of witch's eyes full of fear before me. Lowri's eyes.

"It's the shock," she's saying to the person holding me. "We have to keep her cool, keep her anchored. It could kill her. . . ."

I don't hear the rest as my whole body spasms, turning rigid and hot, waves of nausea ripping through me. I scramble to the ground and retch. I collapse on my side as cool hands brush the hair from my face. I see Lowri's lips moving, talking to the person who carried me, telling them to hurry, to bring something—

A ringing starts in my ears, quiet at first, then louder. I try to block it out, this terrible raging noise, this sound of hate and love and hunger and dying and life and power and calm, and I realize . . .

It's the sea.

I can hear it all. I *know* it all.

Before, the sea surrounded me, her moods fickle and hungry. But now I can feel her moods, the sweep and curve and roar. It's insistent and epic and everything I was teetering on the edge of, but now I've tumbled down into a wicked abyss and the side of me that is creature and monster and other—the side that is siren—is awakened.

I look around me, finding Lowri and Eli, their eyes wide with horror and awe. "I know everything," I whisper, my voice strange even to myself. "I see, I hear, I feel . . . everything."

Then the dark reaches for me—

and I go under.

CHAPTER
TWENTY-SEVEN

I AM FALLING.

Falling through a world of sea and storm. I tumble, forced under by a current so powerful I cannot breathe through it. I reach for anything to break my fall, but the sea is vast and I am so small. No one hears my screams.

No one can rescue me from myself, except me.

So I give in. I stop fighting, stop trying, and allow myself to fall. Down and down, farther than I've ever been, deep into the recesses of who and what I am. And at the end—at the very end of this world of sea and tide—I find a glimmer. A glint. It is a key. I grasp it, holding it close, and when I hit the rock at the very bottom, I gather everything I am, everything I have ever been.

Everything I will become.

And I *push*. Soaring upward, I climb and climb, slicing through the current, through the waves, through this endless world. I surface.

When I open my eyes, there is no key in my hands. But somehow, I know I've unlocked what's within me. I know what I am, what it is possible to be. I know how the sea flows around the world, how storms form and bruise the sky with their darkness. I know all this, and more. And yet . . .

There is a space where something should be. Someone I can't quite remember, can't quite shape in my mind . . . someone integral. Important. But it's slippery, this sense of loss. I can't quite grasp it.

I blink my eyes open and gaze around at this room that isn't mine, knowing that beyond these walls is a landlocked city and beyond that, green and woods and fields and beyond that, the sea. . . .

"Where is Eli?" I ask Lowri. She startles, moving toward me, checking my pulse, my eyes, my skin. "Where is Elijah Tresillian?"

The witch blanches, stepping away from me, and looks over my head, nodding to someone behind me by the window before her gaze fixes on mine. "The binding spell worked. You're more siren than human now. The map is a part of you, and those memories of—of the person you lost . . . are gone."

As day wanes into night, we assemble. We are meant to be leaving before breakfast tomorrow morning, but if everything goes according to plan tonight, we'll be gone long before dawn touches Highborn. Eli and Caden, even Lowri, keep sneaking glances at me, as though I'm about to keel over. Or blast this coven apart. Although I can feel my siren side singing clearly in my veins now, I still don't know how to control the storm-bringer ability that's woven through it.

I can feel the shape of my power more clearly, can understand how storms form and re-form, but if I willed one to unfurl, I'm sure I would not be able to control its violent delights, or violent ends.

"Will you stop?" I hiss at Caden as he holds out his arm to guide me down a set of steps. "I went through a binding spell, I didn't turn into a brittle-boned hundred-year-old."

"I *know* he's infuriating, but you really all have to shut up beyond this point," Lowri whisper-shouts up from a few stairs below. Nova purrs in agreement.

I look over my shoulder and see Eli shrug. He hasn't mentioned the binding. None of them have. I'm still unsure how much it took from me. I know there's something missing—there's a huge jagged hole in my heart—but every time I try to find the edges of it, it shifts. I just know now it's my father. I can no longer feel the same love and grief for him.

But I can sense the map as a living thing within me, where every rock, every stretch of sand, every hidden cove awaits. This knowledge is tremendous, and I find myself fighting with every breath to stop it from consuming me. We have to succeed tonight, because if I don't know how to harness this knowledge, how to be greater than this new part of myself, I fear it will overwhelm me. And I made a promise to Eli. We both have much to gain from this night.

Tomorrow is for answers.

Tonight is for stealing.

The weight of the spindle key in my pocket is the reassurance I need of our plan, and our goals.

Lowri wants you to know that only you can go with her. The others will have to wait. Even I cannot always go where a witch goes.

I look down sharply and find Nova's glowing eyes fixed on mine.

Noted. And stop getting inside my head, creature.

Nova hisses, tail twitching back and forth, and slinks ahead at Lowri's heels. When we reach the entrance hall, Lowri takes my hand, pointing Eli and Caden to a room just off it. Caden places his hand briefly on my shoulder, and Eli gazes at me, nodding once, before they both silently close the door behind them. No one must suspect. We know what's at stake, and if I don't make it out with Lowri, they have to leave. We've given ourselves an hour. Then it's likely we've been caught, and I'll face the judgment of the coven. As will Lowri.

"Are you sure about this?" I murmur to her as she says a word softly, unlocking a door to reveal another winding set of steps. I peer down, and find nothing but darkness.

"Am I sure about helping you? Yes," she says, flicking a smile at me. "But am I sure of what I'm doing? Honestly, no."

I hesitate as we look down into the gloom, wondering if this is a mistake. If Lowri is forced to leave the coven, if she is excluded . . . would another coven take her in to complete her training? Or would she become a wraith, forever cursed to linger at the edges, full of sorrow and regret, haunting Ennor Castle with only Amma to try and tether her?

You'd better hurry, monstrous girl, Nova's voice purrs. *When my witch is determined, there's no dissuading her.*

Right. I glance behind me, checking that the entrance hall is still deserted, and step down. The winding staircase has narrow and uneven steps that remind me of the trick steps that lead to our secret cove on Rosevear. I feel along the wall, heart in my throat, and after a while, it feels like I've been walking for hours. Or maybe it's less than five minutes. I cannot tell.

"Lowri?"

"I'm here," she replies. "Nearly there."

When my feet hit solid ground, I take a deep, shuddering breath. Lowri speaks a word I don't understand, and her features illuminate. She holds a storm lantern, much like they use aboard ships. "Couldn't risk using one on the stairs. This level is warded—if a light is used to guide your steps, then a witch apparent is summoned to check who passes below." She shrugs. "It's a deterrent."

"But not a trap?"

She flashes a grin, beckoning me onward. "If a witch wanted to trap you, you'd not escape it. The only reason you can walk down those steps and every alarm doesn't clatter through the coven is because you have magic in your veins, just like we do. And the wards can't distinguish between different kinds of magic."

"But Eli . . . surely he—"

Lowri shakes her head. "Eli is . . . different. His magic is unlike any that exists in our world. I'm not even sure his power to traverse would be classed as magic, but rather a rare ability. I couldn't risk it." She casts the lantern upward, the pool of light revealing a flagstone floor and a wide hall lined with wooden doors. "The doors switch around, and we must be careful because they keep monsters penned in here for research. But I am *fairly* certain where it would have been hidden."

"And if you're wrong and we enter the wrong door?"

"Then we may be locked inside, until someone lets us out, or worse . . . at the mercy of one of the captured monsters."

I suppress a shiver. Lowri moves to a door on the left, no different from the others. But after a moment she tuts, moving along to the one beside it. "I locked the workroom I use behind me the other day, and I know that door. It is in a different place, but I was sure the door we seek would be next to it."

She turns, and in the pool of light I catch indecision flickering over her features. "Lowri, if you're uncertain—"

"No, we can't turn back now," she says firmly. "I just need a moment. . . ."

I watch as she moves from door to door, standing in front of them before moving on to the next. A prickle of fear begins in my chest, spreading to my throat. The air is thick down here, and musty. I push the hair from my forehead and loosen the top button on my shirt. It feels warmer, and I am beginning to struggle to draw a full breath. As though the air is seeping out . . . as though the hall itself does not want us here.

I open my mouth to tell her we should leave, to ask her if this feels all wrong to her too. And that's when I hear a keening song, the faintest notes of sorrow and love. And I freeze. That song, the notes . . .

I gasp.

It's my mother's song.

I whip toward the sound as it calls to me, luring me closer. I take a few steps across the hall, listening for the cadence of her voice, and stop in front of a door. It is just like all the others, just as plain, and yet—

"Mira?" Lowri whispers. "What is it?"

I raise my hand and place it on the wood. The song, her voice, grows louder. And the spindle key . . . it warms. "This is the door. Trust me. I—I can hear her singing. My mother."

Lowri's footsteps tap across the flagstones, and she draws to a stop beside me. She eyes the door, lifting the lantern aloft. "It could be a trick of one of the monsters. If you're wrong . . ."

I swallow and look at her. "This is the door. I know it."

Lowri hesitates, but then her features settle and harden. "All right. Stand back."

She places a hand on the door and says a single word in a voice that does not sound like her own. For a moment, I see a black vein throb in her wrist, twisting like spilled ink before disappearing. She sucks in a breath, sagging against the door, panting, and we both hear the click of a lock. "Quickly now."

She straightens and moves her hand to the handle, opening it, and we step inside. The room beyond is small, and empty shelves line the walls. I cast around in the glow of the lantern light, Lowri searching down one side and me searching the other. There doesn't appear to be anything inside, but I can still hear it, her song, even louder than before.

"It has to be here," I say, running my hands along the shelves.

"Wait," Lowri says softly. I turn and find her standing completely still, staring at a space in front of her. "This room is completely empty, isn't it? Unusual for a room that should contain many things, many items and books . . ."

Understanding dawns on me, and I walk around the room again. "You think there's a spell on this room? Everything's been hidden somehow?"

"In plain sight." Lowri nods grimly, chewing on her lip. "But I don't know what spell has been used to bind it. It could be an illusion, or the contents of this room could have been bound."

Lowri begins saying words in that strange witch language, tapping points along the walls and shelves. I fight my agitation, walking to the opposite wall, raking my fingers through the shadows, searching for the lure of the siren song. And there in a dark corner, so small I almost missed it, is a box. Not hidden inside a chest, as Eli believed it would be, but out in the open, a turquoise-and-pearl jewelry box, the kind that a siren might covet, the kind that could have been found on a ship she had wrecked. I bite my lip and draw the spindle key from my pocket, turning it in the keyhole to release the catch. Inside there is a single silver charm on a thin, glinting chain.

In the shape of an eight-pointed star.

"Is that—" Lowri says, breaking off her own search.

"It's what Eli is seeking. This star . . . it's symbolic. My mother used it before to guide me, and if this jewelry box was created with her magic, imbued with drops of her blood, this must be it." I reach down to lift it from the jewelry box. The chain falls like water through my fingers, like no metal I've ever seen. Something else. Something . . . otherworldly.

As we stare down at it, barely breathing, I'm suddenly aware of a stillness. The air is thickening in here too.

The door slams shut.

I flinch, whipping toward it as the lock clicks. Then the lantern almost gutters out. But in its dwindling glow, I see we are now surrounded. Books, rolls of parchment, an oddity of objects, feathers, talons . . . The binding spell on this room has been broken. "Lowri?" I whisper.

Her hand grips my arm, fear slicking my skin. "They know we're here," she says. "They're coming."

CHAPTER
TWENTY-EIGHT

"WE'RE TRAPPED," SHE SAYS. "THEY'VE SEALED us in. They must have felt the binding break."

"Lowri, think." I pocket the necklace and cast around desperately for the book. It has to be here. I run my hands over countless spines, reading them quickly, my thoughts tripping over one another in my haste. "*Think.* There must be another way. A tunnel or a hidden door, or—"

"Not in my mother's coven," she says, making a desperate kind of choking sound. "You don't know her, what she'll do, what she's capable of. . . ."

"Shit," I say, drawing a blade. We haven't found the book. All we've found is the necklace, and now . . . "When that door opens, get behind me. And when you can, you *run.*"

A sound like thunder shakes the room, and my heart leaps to my throat. I grip my blade, dropping back from the door, but for some reason, my other hand strays to the necklace in my pocket. The necklace that was hidden in a jewelry box coated with magic suffused with my mother's blood.

Then I realize. The malefant may have sealed us in here, but if my mother has been in this room . . .

"Did my mother have a hand in crafting that jewelry box and key? Lowri, this is important," I say quickly as another boom shakes the room, making my feet skitter across the flagstones. "Did she enter this room? Was she allowed in the lower levels?"

"I . . . yes. I think so," Lowri says, and I can hear the fear in her voice. It's choking her. "When she visited, she would have had to seal the necklace in here herself to ensure the potency of the binding."

"Good." I thrust the blade at Lowri. "Take this, and if anyone comes through that door, cut them."

I move to the farthest corner, imagining my mother here, listening for the soothing notes of her voice, the haunting timbre of her song. Lowri screams, but I ignore it, falling deeper into myself, listening for my mother's voice, for what I know she will have left here, in case the witches ever tried to trap her. An escape route, another path. A way only a siren could find. I step back, place my hands on the cold wall, and drink in the stuffy air, thick now, warming and stifling.

"Mira!" Lowri gasps, and I open my eyes to see a split in the door, as though it's being hacked at with an ax. Lowri's hand is out in front of her, but her eyes are turned to me, wide and desperate with terror. "Mira, I can't hold them much longer!"

Then, suddenly, I hear it.

Her voice.

A murmur, like the sand shifting in the tide. I turn toward

it, this hush of sound in the far corner, to a wall that appears to hold only a vast collection of old books.

"Mira!" Lowri says again, but I walk toward it, placing my hands against the wall. I knock, moving my fists over it, pressing my ear closer, listening, trying to make out—

There.

A hollow ringing, as though there is empty space behind. I feel with my fingertips, brushing the brick, and find one in the corner with the faintest of markings. An eight-pointed star. I grit my teeth, and push. The wall falls away, and I nearly fall with it, as a dark yawning appears beyond. The wall swings inward, and I turn to Lowri. "Let's go."

She makes a choking sound . . . then her eyes suddenly widen. She says a single word, and I swear it sounds like "*Sirena.*" A book lands at her feet, silver and gleaming, etched with waves. She glances at me in wonder, scoops it up, then shoves me toward the opening in the wall. The door splinters at our backs, and I whip the wall closed in our wake, just as the sound of cracking fills the room beyond.

We stand in the dark, barely breathing, listening to the sound of voices—of hunters.

I touch Lowri's arm and she flinches, but in this depthless dark, she murmurs a word. "Lumiere." A spark of pale light appears at her fingertips, and she holds it between us, her gaze meeting mine. As the hunters shout instructions, thumping around the outer room and calling to other witches, we grin at each other. I look around, taking in the space, illuminated by the soft glow Lowri created. We're in a stairwell, narrow steps peeling up into more darkness. I point upward, eyebrows raised. Lowri shrugs, as if to say, "What choice do we have?"

Lowri goes first, hugging the book with one arm, her

pale light leading the way as we begin our ascent. The air is cool here, unfettered and sweet, and I realize the very air was spelled down in those rooms. Another witch ward that somehow hasn't permeated this secret staircase. We step as quietly as we can, moving up and up, and I wonder where this leads, if we are stepping into a trap. . . .

Lightning cracks below us.

I gasp, falling to my knees, gripping the step before me to stop from tumbling down. Lowri gets to her feet first, terror filling her voice as she says, "They've found it."

I sprint up after her, even as the staircase seems to shift and buckle. I stagger, holding on to anything I can, pulling myself upward, keeping that light Lowri twists between her fingertips in sight—

"Hurry!" Terror laces her voice as the sound of the hunters grows louder.

Sweat prickles along my hairline as we run, taking two steps at a time, stumbling, then finally bursting through a door.

I turn to kick the door shut behind us. Lowri leans against it with me, and we both gasp for breath as I look to see where the secret passageway has led us. The front parlor, draped in shadows and night, and behind us, the great hearth, disturbed by our sudden entrance. A dark chuckle sounds from the deepest shadows, and I tense, moving to hide Lowri in case it's a hunter, in case they see that it's her who helped me . . . but when Eli steps out, Nova at his heels, I sag in relief. He smiles at us both as Nova's eyes roam over her witch.

Took your time, monstrous girl, Nova says, licking a paw nonchalantly before us.

"Time we left," Eli says. "I think we've outstayed our welcome."

"How?" Lowri asks between breaths. "How did you know we'd appear here?"

"Your familiar is quite insistent. Only stopped yowling when I followed." Eli shrugs, holding out his hands to Lowri and me. "Caden's keeping your mother occupied, Lowri. I'll drop you on the way, then come back for him. Nova, make yourself scarce. You don't need to traverse."

The familiar twitches its tail, hisses once, and vanishes.

I grasp Eli's hand and feel the ground fall away. We spin through the night, so fast I can't breathe, landing in Lowri's bedroom for a handful of heartbeats, just long enough to ensure she's safe and for her to thrust the book into my empty hand before spinning onward, through nothing but shadow and midnight and still I can't breathe—

Eli releases my hand and I fall. I jolt with the impact, the book skittering away. I get slowly to my feet, drawing air, fumbling for my blade, scanning the near-dark for witches, for hunters—

"You're safe," a voice says, and I whip around, finding Joby. I choke, placing my hands on my knees, bending forward as my mind tilts and wanes. Joby's at my side immediately, holding me up as my legs turn to water. "Fast getaway?"

"Never again . . ." I gasp, finally able to stand on my own. Then Eli and Caden appear across the room.

Caden dusts off his jacket and turns to Eli. "I don't think she'll forgive us this time. She knows we took something—"

"Have you got it?" Eli asks me, eyes intent, edged with the strain of traversing quickly over a vast distance.

I nod. The necklace falls between my fingers in a river of

silver as I pass it to Eli, letting it pool in his palm.

He releases a charged breath, closing his eyes, something akin to grief passing across his features before he opens them again. "Thank you, Mira. I can't tell you . . ."

I smile up at him, reveling in the victory that I can't quite believe is ours. "You're welcome." I cast around, walking to where the book has slid into a corner, the silver-etched waves glinting as I pick it up. All the answers I need, all the secrets that may help me . . . they're now mine.

Caden strides over, scooping me up and spinning me around. "Well done, fierce one."

Joby grins, leaning against the wall—and that slouching movement, it reminds me of someone dear to me who slouched against the wall in the meeting house on Rosevear many times, someone I know is important. But I can't quite . . . it's almost as though I've forgotten a whole part of myself. There's a gaping hole of nothing where my father used to be. . . .

"Mira?" Eli asks, his grin fading. "What's wrong?"

"Nothing." I shake my head, looking down at the book. "We got away, didn't we?"

A scream rends the dawn.

We all freeze, turning to the sound, but it seems to have come from everywhere and nowhere, from the very walls of the castle itself.

A cry, full of pain, echoes from far away.

"Amma," Eli breathes, eyes wide with fear before he steps back into shadow and vanishes.

I look to Joby and Caden, whose fear and confusion mirror mine. Then the walls begin to moan and shake, rattling with anguish.

"Oh shit," Joby whispers, darting for the door.

"She's hurting Amma," Caden says. "She's breaking her, the malefant, trying to pull down the wards on Ennor."

He too hurries from the room, and I race after him as the corridor seems to ripple and shudder.

"The malefant knows we stole the necklace and that book," he says. "She's taking her revenge."

CHAPTER
TWENTY-NINE

WE THUNDER THROUGH THE HALLS, SEARCHING
for Amma as, all around us, the castle buckles and sways.

"She'll bring down the walls!" Caden says, sprinting
through the hallways.

I keep up with him, slamming down the main staircase,
the sound of Amma's pain echoing louder. We reach the
back of the castle and the anguish intensifies, slicing through
my mind, and I double over, feeling every inch of it with
her. It feels as forceful as the binding spell did in my mind,
and I realize it's the malefant, Hillary Tresillian, the weight
of her power bearing down on this place. On Amma. And
now I know how that feels, the vicious power of a Tresillian
witch. I sense it immediately as it fills these walls. "She's . . .
cleaving her in two," I gasp. "She's trying to pull her apart!"

Caden blasts through the kitchen door and I follow,
stumbling inside. We find them all there, surrounding her.
Tanith holds Amma in her arms as she convulses, again and

again. The gossamer threads of her dim and fade, pulsing briefly, before stuttering to almost nothing.

I fall to my knees just as Joby says quietly, "Is it time, Tanith?"

Her beautiful face turns to his, full of sorrow and raw longing. "Not yet."

Joby sags, his whole being crumpling, his head in his hands. I look at Eli, then at Tanith, wondering what he means. But Tanith's eyes are fixed once more on the being in her arms, the last wisp of magic made into this form by Eli's mother, this being who holds the castle together, who has held her son together without her here.

Tanith soothes her as the malefant tries to break her. The spell slams into her, and all we can do is watch on, powerless against the mal's wrath and vengeance. As Amma chokes, eyes bulging horribly, clutching at her throat as she stutters in and out of focus.

"Can't you do something?" Caden asks Eli desperately.

"I don't . . ." Eli swallows, gazing down at Amma's thread-bare form. He's blinking back tears, trying to hold himself together. "I don't know how to save her."

"There is a way," Tanith says. "You *know* there is, Elijah."

"I can't ask that of you," he says, anguished eyes straying to hers. "Please, Tanith. Don't make me ask that. I can't sacrifice one of you to save another."

Tanith smiles sadly. "You don't have to. I give it freely. For Amma, for this castle . . . for my home." She looks at Joby. "Some things just cannot be. However much we want them."

Joby's gaze locks with hers. I look between them as an unspoken agreement seems to pass. Something I don't quite understand. Then Joby nods, almost imperceptibly, before turning away again.

Tanith lowers her eyelids briefly, a wave of unbearable sorrow passing over her features. But when she opens her eyes, they turn down to the being in her arms, and they're filled with nothing but love. "Amma, I tie my mortal body to you. Let my strength be your strength. Until the walls shatter, until the wards on this isle fall and I must return to my true form and forget my life here, forever."

I stifle a gasp as Joby flinches as though struck. If the castle falls, if Amma dies, Tanith will lose her mortal body. She will have no memory of being Tanith; she'll be a firedrake once more, bound to the skies, bound to the wild north. I realize now there is something between her and Joby. I did not imagine it the other day. And if Amma should die, if Ennor should fall, that something between them is doomed. Tanith will have to shore up the walls of this castle, shore up Amma by binding herself to her. Bolstering the last of Eli's mother's power to keep Eli and Ennor safe.

Tanith gazes down at Amma, speaking words in a language older than I've ever heard, words that don't sound human, or witch, words as old as the earth itself. Words that sound almost siren, but different, less sea and salt and storm, more fire and earth and wind. Gradually the walls stop buckling, the castle quieting around us. Amma glows softly, still insubstantial, still threadbare and wrong, but she relaxes in Tanith's arms. Tanith looks up at Eli and smiles sadly.

"I'll never forget this," he says softly. "Not ever. I owe you an unpayable debt. Thank you."

Tanith nods. "I'll take her to the library. She needs rest.

But she'll live on for now, as will the wards your mother placed over Ennor. She's weakened—only a Tresillian witch could have done that, and skies know your mother would *never* have thought that your aunt . . . but, anyway, her legacy lives on, Elijah. Amma won't die today. Ennor will not fall."

Amma murmurs something, her voice weak as she searches around herself. When she finds Eli, she crooks a finger at him and he leans closer, kneeling before her. "Find the door," she whispers, so quiet I almost don't catch it. "Find the door. I can feel the necklace. I know you have it. Find the door and *step through it*."

The next day, I find Eli alone on the ramparts. Shadows curl around him as he leans on the wall, staring out to sea. I step from the tower at the far end, the wind whipping my hair, and walk toward him.

The rampart is built for defense, straddling the sides of the castle between the towers at each point of the star. And this side faces the mainland, Arnhem, and beyond to Highborn, where Coven Septern lies.

I lean on the wall beside him, watching the waves as they dance toward the shore. For a moment, we don't speak. The shadows waver like smoke in the breeze, finally dissipating, and Eli sighs deeply. "I should have anticipated it."

"That your aunt would seek revenge, or that it would be on Amma?"

"Both," he says, frowning. "Amma isn't . . . She's not real, exactly. She's a protection spell. The physical embodiment of a ward over the castle and the isle of Ennor. My mother created her in her dying moments, poured all of her magic into her. She left this world after giving birth to me, and Amma raised me here. A fragment of her. Amma . . . she looks like my mother did. Speaks like her. To me, she is my mother—all I have left of her."

My breath catches. "So your aunt was taking away the final piece of your mother to *punish you*?"

He closes his eyes, pain flitting across his features, and nods. "Hillary and Elena, my mother, were very close. They went through everything together. And then they both fell in love and gave birth on the same night. My aunt had Caden, and my mother gave birth to me. That was the last time Hillary saw my mother, and she cursed my birth when it killed her sister not long after, cursed my father for abandoning her, and sent both Caden and me here."

The thought of the woman we met sending away two baby boys, of cursing Eli's birth . . . My stomach knots and I blink back tears. "That's so *cold*."

"She's a witch. A creature of sorts, not human, and one that needs to bond with the monsters of this world to access what is inside her. Witches can far surpass humans in age span; they can live centuries. And if you can live that long, and are raised by other witches, I suppose you lose the semblance of humanity over time. You perhaps do not value what you deem to be lesser lives." He stares at the sea with unseeing eyes. "My father left before my birth, hoping to find a way to protect both of us. He was not of this world, and he knew the pregnancy might not go smoothly. There was too much magic, too much power surrounding my mother and her unborn child, and he feared for our lives. He stepped through a doorway, promising to return in time for the birth. Only he never returned."

"Is that what Amma meant? About a door?" I ask, watching him.

"Yes," he says, finally looking at me. The sorrow in his eyes twists deep inside me, and all I want to do is reach for him. But I maintain the small distance between us, waiting as he works through his thoughts. "My father left a letter for me, and Amma shared it when she deemed me ready. He could step through shadows like me; he called it traversing in his letter. He stepped through a door to his own world, and I've never been able to work out how. How to move between worlds, as he could." He sighs, shaking his head. "But I knew that whatever was left for me in that jewelry box was an important component. And now I understand why: the necklace is *from* his world. It's what I need to focus on to traverse there. If I can figure out how to use it, I'll go. As soon as the isles are safe, as soon as Ennor is safe, I'll go to his world and find him." His voice cracks slightly. "I'll demand to know why he never came back for us."

This is the truest, most vulnerable Eli has ever been with me. He's opened a window into his very soul, and I ache with the heaviness of all he carries. A tear forms at the corner of my eye, falling slowly down my face as my heart breaks for Eli. For the little boy, abandoned. "What did Tanith mean? When she said she will tie her mortal body to Amma?"

"Ah, that," he says darkly. "Tanith is a firedrake. She has a human form now, but she only fixed on that form because she fell in love, at great personal cost. Remaining human meant that she would remember her love for him. It's a fleeting moment in her vast lifetime, and the person she loves . . . is human. When she tied her mortal life to Amma, she also tied it to Ennor. If the wards of Ennor fall, if the walls of the castle are breached, then Amma will cease to exist, and Tanith will return to her true form. She will no longer remember us, or the one she loves. She'll no longer be Tanith."

I take a breath, the pieces falling into place. The magnitude of that decision. "It's Joby, isn't it? She knows it can never be, so—"

"She's protecting him, in her own way. Joby, of course, does not see it like that. That's why he rarely stays on Ennor anymore, choosing to be at sea instead of being here, reminded at every moment of the love and life he will never have."

"How did they meet?" I ask.

Eli smiles wistfully. "Joby freed Tanith from a curse. She was shackled to a lonely place in the Spines, and when I sent him there to deliver to one of my apothecaries, he heard tales of the monster in the mountains that fed on the brave people who went to slaughter it. They didn't have money for a hunter from a coven, and so Joby offered to go and slay the monster.

"He found Tanith, barely alive in her true form, shackled there by a spiteful witch's curse. Tanith didn't try and hurt him; she just lay there, quietly dying, starving and alone. Joby sat with her in the ice and the cold and talked to her. He told her stories about Ennor, and without knowing it, he broke the witch's curse."

"How?"

"He showed a monster kindness. Her shackles broke, and she transformed herself into her current form after arriving here, knowing it would only be fleeting, a mere blink in the span of her existence, but she wanted to spend more time with Joby. The rest of the story is theirs to tell."

Another tear falls, and I brush it away quickly. So much loss, so much longing for all that can never be in this place. "Is there no way Tanith can stay as she is? In her human form? And not forget him?"

"There is not. However much she researches, however many books she reads. If she resumes her true form, she will forget him."

"The library," I say softly, realizing. "That's why she is Ennor's librarian."

"The Tresillian witches hold a vast collection of books here," he agrees. "She hangs on to a thread of hope, searching for an answer every day."

Eli's hand tightens around mine, and I look at him. Without being aware of it, I've edged closer, standing right beside him. The wind catches at my hair again, blowing it around the two of us, as though a cloak is drawn against the world. His eyes, so much darker, so full of sadness and pain, lock with mine, and all I want to do is lean into him. He brings his hand to my face, tracing the path of my tears with his thumb, his mouth forming the shape of my name.

"Mira."

It would be so very easy to give in and find some comfort in this connection with him. We're two sides of the same coin. So much more alike than I ever imagined. He's not all arrogance and swagger or teasing words. He's kind and loyal and filled with an aching sadness I would do anything to take away.

But . . .

I can't.

I can't risk my heart anymore. I can't lose someone else;

it would be unbearable. To lose Eli, the person I am seeing now, *truly* seeing every piece of—it would break me.

I pull away from him, feeling the wrench in my very soul. Then, with one final look at him . . . the troubled lord, the boy with a heart as big as an island, smoke and shadow curling afresh around him . . . I turn away.

My heart pounds like a drum as I walk through the castle, all the way to the sea. I pull off my boots and dive in, the feverish heat exploding in my veins. Then I swim, directionless, weightless, spearing like an arrow through the deep. I needed to get back to the ocean, to feel the wild freedom of it, to lose myself in the vast blue. I feel everything now. Know everything. The winding shape of the currents, the way the tide swells and retreats, the vessels afloat in the vast waters. Now the map is a part of me, twining around my soul, I feel more at home in the ocean than ever before. Its song is my song. Its blood is my own.

When I surface, though, I only see him. His eyes, his smile, his huge heart, and I burn with it, even though I know it cannot be. I am too afraid to lose again. It hurts too much. It would consume me.

But I burn with wanting him anyway.

So I stay in the sea, until the day falls to dusk, until the dark deepens to night and I begin to cool the flames inside me. I dive down to the seabed and brush my fingers along the sand. I listen to the sea, to a storm rumbling miles away, and slowly begin unraveling it all. The world surrounding me and everything within me.

Everything I might become.

CHAPTER THIRTY

THE DAMP FOG OF HIGHBORN LINGERS LIKE A curse. Brielle turns up the collar on her coat as it creeps around the back of her neck, shivering over her skin. She waits on the corner of Bread Street under a lonely lit lamp-post, the only one on the street. The five-story buildings on either side of the street tower over her, dark windows like wide, staring eyes.

At a quarter to midnight, the sleek black carriage appears, no insignia stamped on its side. The horses paw at the ground, spectral forms of white, the only indication that this is not just any Highborn carriage. Only the members of the ruling council keep white horses of such breeding in their stables, glossy coats luminous under a full moon. Brielle sighs, approaching the carriage door.

So much for secrecy.

The driver doesn't get down to help her inside, so she unfastens the door herself and climbs in, shutting it behind her with a quiet click. The carriage is colder than outside, and she's glad for her coat and leather gloves. She settles back on one side, facing the man occupying the other. In the court, he was the man standing by the window—Nero, with the ash-colored eyes, gazing out over Highborn.

There is a metallic tang about him, hidden by a sweeter scent of roses or violets. His blond hair is swept back, revealing an unlined, delicate, pale face, as though he doesn't often venture out into the sunlight. His chin is weak, lips soft and pink, but it's his eyes that don't seem to fit his features. They're hard as firedrake scale, a sharp gray color that doesn't appear human.

He looks at her for a moment in the soft witch light of the carriage, the light he must pay a coven to charm. Then he grips his silver-tipped black cane, taps it on the ceiling, and barks, "Drive on."

The carriage jolts and sways as they pull away from Bread Street. Brielle licks her lips, wondering why a member of the ruling council himself has met her to hear a report. Usually, they would only deign to meet with the malefant of a coven; her summons to court was a rare occurrence. A discordant ringing begins in her ears, one she hears sometimes before an ambush or a slaughter. She flexes her fingers and grazes the handle of her hidden blade. "I was expecting one of your minions. Rue, perhaps."

"Why would I want to hear your report secondhand?" The man smiles coldly, and it sets Brielle's teeth on edge, warnings clattering in her ears. "But interesting that you should mention Rue. I had not realized you were acquainted with our ambassador."

"We met. That is, we spoke when I visited court."

He narrows his eyes. "And what did you speak of?"

"Flowers," Brielle says softly, picturing him now. For some reason, she has thought about him often since they met, hoping to meet again.

"So, come now, hunter. Report."

Brielle blinks, jolted from her reverie, and outlines her foray to the south of Arnhem, describing the ambush on the secret cove near Port Graine. She keeps her report far briefer than the one she gave to the malefant on her return. She doesn't know why, but for some reason, she can't bring herself to give details to this man.

"And did you witness any siren traits, anything monstrous?" Nero asks, waving his hand to indicate he was done listening to her talk.

Brielle sets her jaw. "She appeared as a girl with a blade."

The man snorts, twisting his cane in his hands. "I assure you, hunter, she is far from human—"

"There is more."

His features take on a ravenous twist. "Some signs of magic, perhaps? Power?"

She steels herself, knowing his spies will inform him soon and it is best for the coven if she delivers the information first. "No, not exactly. She visited Coven Septern with the cousins of House Tresillian."

"Did she now?" He grows deathly still. "Why?"

"A visit between relations. Nothing more. As you know, the malefant and her daughter are Tresillian witches."

"And you didn't think to inform us at the time? Or better yet, *complete* your assignment and bring the girl to us?"

The carriage takes a sharp turn and Brielle fights to stay upright, slamming her feet against the carriage floor to steady herself. Nero just smirks, preternaturally still, as Brielle growls, "You know very well that coven houses are neutral territory. No hunter works inside their own coven house, or that of another. The five main covens have lived by these rules for centuries, dispelling any need for infighting, or war, preserving reputations and good will—"

"You witches and your *rules*," Nero cuts in, tearing his gaze from her. He yanks back the curtain on the window, staring out into the streets of Highborn as they pass. "You had her there. She was right under your nose, and you refused to act. Need I remind you that your coven was *chosen* for this assignment? And it can still fall out of favor. Perhaps I will seek out another malefant, another hunter. As you say, there are four other covens in Highborn. Strong and loyal, perhaps more loyal than Coven Septern."

"That is your decision to make. If you prefer another hunter—"

"Now, now," he says, darting her a sly look. "This is, after all, your chance to prove your strength, cunning, and loyalty to the ruling council. Can I rely on you, Brielle Tresillian?"

Her name on his tongue is like a hundred paper cuts. She suppresses a shudder. "Of course. I go where my malefant commands."

"Excellent," Nero says, wiping his hands against each other as though ridding himself of something unpleasant. "I shall look forward to celebrating a victory at our next little get-together. Driver!"

Brielle winces as the last word is projected at her head. The carriage screeches to a halt, jolting Brielle forward, almost into the man's lap. He chuckles as she flings open the door and scrambles from the carriage.

"Until next time," he calls, slamming the door. The horses set off at a steady clip.

Brielle drinks in the night air, watching the fleeing carriage as it disappears into the fog, which seems to have thickened. It takes Brielle a few minutes to orient herself. When she realizes where she is, she swears in a muffled hiss.

"Bastard," she mutters, setting off at a trudge. Of course he's dropped her at the farthest point from the coven house within the confines of the city. "Unnaturally pale, smug little bastard . . ."

An hour and a half later, she arrives back at the coven. Soaked through from the moist air, a tickle at the back of her throat, and nothing on her mind but a warm fire, hot tea, and bed.

But when she reaches the front door, it's yanked open, revealing a flushed Peony.

"What . . . ?" Brielle says, frowning as light pours from the entrance hall. It's half past one in the morning. She was expecting to be able to slink upstairs and close her bedroom door until long past dawn, perhaps even sleep late.

But here Peony stands, shoulders shaking as she stutters and whimpers, tugging on her black sleeves. "It's Lowri. She . . ."

Brielle moves inside, cold dread sharpening her as she closes the front door and rounds on Peony. "Is she hurt? What is it?"

Peony gulps, eyes straying to the door leading down to the lower levels, ominously wide open. A prickle of unease passes over Brielle, a knowing that settles over her. "Something's been stolen. The Tresillians and that girl have disappeared overnight, and Lowri—"

Brielle doesn't wait for the rest. Hitting the stairs, she leaps up two at a time, careening down the corridor and straight for the mal's office. Lights blaze everywhere, pockets of witches and hunters gossiping, eyeing her coolly as she passes. She reaches the door, throws it open, and stares around in a panic as she finds the malefant deep in conversation with two high witches.

"Lowri? Where is she? What happened—"

The malefant raises a finger. "Taken care of. You needn't worry, Brielle, it's all in hand."

"What is? Where's Lowri?"

"Awaiting trial, as is right in the circumstances," one of the witches says, eyeing her imperiously. "Lowri Tresillian has been accused of conspiracy against the coven, and theft. She will stand trial at first light."

CHAPTER
THIRTY-ONE

A WITCH TRIAL.

Rare in a coven, especially one as established as Septern. And for it to be Lowri, her sister, her friend . . . Brielle spent the last hours of the night awake, staring at her bedroom ceiling, ransacking her mind for any way out of this. Witches seldom survived a trial, and if they did, they never escaped the taint from the charges. And now Brielle knows what Lowri stands accused of. Theft. Stealing a book and a precious item . . . and aiding in the escape of her fellow thieves. All treasonous, all grounds for instant expulsion from the coven—or death if proven to be true.

At dawn, Brielle rubs her gritty eyes, feeling the room sway around her, before striding down to the lower levels. She'd tried to get in to see Lowri, begged the mal for a few moments to check that she was all right, and of course had been denied. But with Nova winding frantic figure eights around her ankles and her voice scratching in Brielle's mind, telling her to find her witch, Brielle decides to try one last time to see her.

"Stay," she hisses to Lowri's familiar in the entrance hall, and Nova's tail twitches as her claws rake the parquet flooring. Brielle disappears through the door before Nova can react, stepping quickly into the belly of darkness and magic below. There is one hunter on guard duty, and she could weep with relief when she sees her face.

"Thought you'd be down here sooner, Bri," Niamh says, unlocking the door. "Five minutes. The malefant's crones will be here to collect her soon."

"I owe you," Brielle says, touching her friend's shoulder before shrugging through the door.

A shaft of light from the corridor outside outlines Lowri's silhouette in the corner of the small, square room, knees up under her chin, without a lick of light in the stifling dark. Brielle sighs, whispers a word, and light pools in the wall lamps, throwing the small room into stark lines of shadow and pale light.

"Are you all right? Do you need food or water?" Brielle asks softly, passing her a water bottle and a bundle of biscuits she had hidden in her jacket.

Lowri waves Brielle away. "I'm fine. I knew this might be a possibility."

"A possibility? Lor, what were you thinking—"

"That Mother wouldn't lock me up like a criminal. That I could get away with helping the people I love." She laughs harshly, a rush of bile and bitterness that makes Brielle recoil, finding someone she doesn't know. Doesn't recognize. "I know what creature they'll use. What I'll have to fight to prove my innocence."

"There are only two outcomes here, Lowri. You survive and are cast out, forced to plead with another coven to complete your training. Or you die."

"Or a third," Lowri says, hair falling like ink around her. "I win, I survive, and if I beat this creature, my training will be complete. I'll have proved that I am a full witch. That I am *just* as powerful as them. That I'm absolved of all charges."

"Lowri . . ." Brielle swallows uneasily, fear dancing at her fingertips. "You cannot win. No witch ever has in our coven. Apologize to her, *beg* her if you have to. Make Mother see reason."

Lowri smiles and stands up, finally raising her eyes to meet Brielle's. And Brielle, despite herself, takes a step back. For Lowri's eyes are no longer those of her sister, her friend. They are pure obsidian, burning with darkness. And as she extends a hand, pointing at Brielle, her sleeve falls back, revealing twisting, thorny veins. Brielle shudders, knowing what this means. Lowri isn't just dabbling with her power, exploring it as any witch in training does. She's plunged into the depths of it, drawing it up and up, letting it fill her, consume her. "Then perhaps I will be the first."

The door cracks open, Niamh peering around at them both. "Brielle, you need to leave. They're coming."

Brielle backs away, spluttering warnings about burning out, about what she might do to herself . . . but Lowri has been swept all the way under. There is only the witch in her now.

The Tresillian witch.

For the first time, Brielle is not afraid *for* Lowri. She is afraid of what Lowri might do.

★ ★ ★

Brielle hurries to the training courtyard, already packed with witches and hunters. She fights her way through, ignoring the string of mutters as she reaches the malefant and the other high witches.

"I beg of you, don't do this. It won't end well," Brielle pleads, heart in her throat as Lowri is brought in, dark hair obscuring her changed features. "Malefant . . . Mother. Please reconsider—"

"Your loyalty is commendable, Brielle," the malefant says, sweeping an imperious gaze over the coven. "But what Lowri did cannot go unpunished."

Brielle can only watch as the roar of the coven intensifies, witches and hunters hissing or cackling in turn, as a filthy, cuffed creature is dragged into the center of the courtyard. A snarl rumbles up Brielle's throat as she beholds it, this monster that's been chained in the lower levels for too long.

A fury.

Brielle battles through the crowd and lunges for Lowri, even as a high witch follows, trying to restrain her. "Just remember who you are. Remember—" Brielle whispers hurriedly, brushing her fingertips over her sister's hand, over the darkened veins, already writhing and twisting under her skin. "Remember I'm your friend, your sister. Remember you're not alone. I am with you. Remember when we manifested on Clarus. Remember how we fought side by side and you came back to yourself."

Then Brielle is yanked from her, cruel fingers digging into her arms as the expectant faces of the crowd all melt into one and there is only Lowri. Only her sister, and the monster she must fight.

The malefant, garbed in a flowing crimson robe that

Brielle is sure is meant to remind the accused of blood, begins speaking in an emotionless voice. "Lowri Tresillian, you are on trial today for the theft of two significant objects belonging to Coven Septern, and for aiding the escape of your accomplices. Your trial will begin when the sun is fully risen. Confess, and it will be over and you will await judgment."

Brielle holds her breath, silently begging Lowri to concede, to face being cast out, but still alive, still whole.

Lowri barely seems to register the disdain, the hunger of the other witches for her downfall as she meets her mother's cold stare and nods. "I'm ready for my trial."

The malefant's eyes flare wide. "That is your choice. Shayle, Hira? Unleash the creature."

Brielle watches in horror as the courtyard becomes a few degrees colder. Lowri is mouthing something over and over, even as tremors catch on her fingertips. "I am not afraid. I am not afraid." She twirls her fingers, black nails glistening as the light dims.

The creature massages its unbound wrists and raises its head. Brielle's heart thuds in her chest. The fury, a creature captured by Hira and Shayle on an assignment six months ago, is a monster of manipulation. Sometimes it can be heard crying like a child, forcing a shudder from Brielle as she passes its cell.

But a fury is no victim or helpless creature. It's made of pure loathing, with dark hanks of hair twisting over its features and slender hands that are unnaturally long, ending in claws. Brielle's breath hitches as the creature crawls across the courtyard, staring at Lowri with its angular bleached-white face.

"Bind the fury to your will and prove your worth to the coven," the mal calls out. "By besting a fury, you prove that your heart is pure and true, empty of guile and malcontent toward the coven that raised you. Lowri Tresillian, your trial begins."

Lowri raises her gaze to meet her mother's, as though searching her face for something. Anything. But Brielle knows what she'll find staring back at her. The imperious gaze of the malefant. Not a mother. Not her kin. Brielle's heart bleeds for Lowri as she clenches her fists and nods once, a wince the only sign of the pain deep in her chest. Then Lowri finds Brielle's eyes, her features softening as she mouths, "I love you." And Brielle knows she will do this for herself, for her brother, for her cousin, for the people who would never damn her to a trial such as this, to a fate of fighting a fury. A single sharp tear falls down Brielle's cheek as she mouths back, "I love you too, sister."

Lowri looks back to the fury before her. "I accept my trial and my fate."

The malefant brings her hands together, and a crack like thunder echoes around the courtyard, sealing Lowri in with the fury and the rest of the coven outside. "Begin."

Lowri laces her fingers, then pulls them apart, saying a single word as gold tendrils of light float around her.

"Protegere."

But the fury is swift, slicing a finger through the air, severing the spell. Lowri stumbles back, her mouth already forming the word of another spell when a voice scrapes down her mind and somehow . . . somehow Brielle can sense it too.

You are nothing and no one.

Brielle stumbles back, the fury's wrath somehow slipping

through the wards placed around this trial and finding her. It echoes around and around in her head as Lowri screams. Pain laces her in place as the fury creeps closer, limbs all angles as it crawls across the courtyard. Brielle knows what's happening. She knows what a fury can do, how they shred your mind and then, when you're helpless, feast on your soul.

But she learned this in a textbook. She researched and listened in on the hushed conversations between the hunters. She has never faced one, nor seen this one they keep in the lower levels, until now. Until the moment her sister's life hinges on finding a way to defeat it. And somehow the fury has also gripped *her* mind. Her fate now rests in Lowri's hands too.

"*Protegere.*"

Lowri tries again, desperately spinning the spell around herself.

"Protect me. *Protegere. Protegere.*"

But the creature just giggles, the sound hideous and high-pitched, shredding the spell to ribbons once more.

You are less than nothing. Kneel and succumb. Give in, why fight? You are nothing. No one loves you. No one cares for you. Kneel.

Brielle falls to her knees with that vicious, foul weight in her mind, watching helplessly as Lowri buckles, a great weight pressing on her shoulders, the fury's power clutching her.

Kneel or I will take your sister too. I have her mind; she is in my thrall. Your souls are as fragile as eggshells.

Kneel.

Lowri gasps, dropping to one knee. Brielle knows that somehow the fury has linked their fates, has joined their souls into one crushable whole. She sees as Lowri sees, feels as she feels, and yet she is powerless to protect her. Her heart thumps harder, fear pumping like poison.

You are mine. The fury grips Lowri, fingers like talons clutched around her throat. Brielle is aware of each puncture, each claw piercing her sister's delicate throat. But Lowri doesn't move, doesn't even struggle. Instead she raises her head—

And *smiles.*

Brielle holds her breath, unable to move, unable to wrench herself free as Lowri does the impossible. She draws upon that deep well inside herself, viscous and cool as oil, pulling it up and up, until her veins glow obsidian. Suddenly images flash in Brielle's mind, and she realizes they are from Lowri. As the fury holds them both in its thrall, their minds are linked; they are one. Brielle sees the two of them manifest together on Clarus, hugging and crying as they survived the night. She sees Caden winking at his little sister; she sees Eli through Lowri's eyes in a park in Highborn. He's making a daisy chain with her, sitting in the dirt and grass. Then she sees herself again, travel worn and depleted, but somehow braver, stronger, after her trip to the Spines when she vanquished the monsters that killed her birth mother.

All these memories. All these moments. Lowri draws on them.

She draws on love.

"I am Lowri Tresillian." Her voice booms all around the courtyard. "And I am not nothing and no one. I *am* loved. I *am* someone. And I am *not* afraid of you."

Then her hands whip out, wrapping around the fury's throat, and squeeze.

Brielle trembles as the sound of a thousand mirrors

shattering forces the witches and hunters to their knees around her. The wards are broken, the spellwork blasted to pieces, her sister erupting with the true power of a Tresillian witch. Lowri only laughs as the fury's grip loosens on her throat, as she wrings the fury's neck, veins bulging black at her wrists. She gathers all her power, her darkness, her strength and whispers a single lethal word. A word of fire and ash and glory.

"*Incendere.*"

The fury's eyes widen in terror—

and it explodes with burning light.

Brielle collapses to the ground as the tie between her and Lowri is severed. Smoke fills the courtyard, obscuring everything within it. The malefant chokes out a word, and the worst of the smoke is swept skyward as the witches blink and cough, tears streaming down their cheeks. At first, there is only silence and ruin.

Then the last of the smoke clears, and there stands Lowri at the center. Alone in a pool of white ash, eyes blazing with pure defiance.

She takes a few steps toward her mother. The high witches nearby shrink away, watching her warily. She flicks a piece of ash from her nightgown and asks in a low voice, "Am I excused?"

Without waiting for an answer, she turns on her heel, moving to the doorway that leads back into the house.

Brielle forces herself to stand, and lurches after Lowri, shoving witches and hunters out of the way. The malefant and high witches try to instill calm over the coven, chaos breaking out as Brielle slams through the corridors. Their voices cut off as she mounts the stairs.

She finds Lowri on her bedroom floor, crumpled and unconscious, darkness leaking from her like mist. She locks the door and crashes to her knees beside her, shaking her sister.

"Lowri, wake up. You have to make it. You can't have burned out—"

Lowri's eyes flutter open, still gleaming onyx. "No one is allowed to hurt you. No one is allowed to hurt those I love."

Brielle sobs as Lowri's eyes close again. She scoops her up from the ground and places her on her bed. She smooths back her hair, understanding now what gave Lowri the strength, what drove her to delve too far into her power.

Brielle rests her forehead against Lowri's. The fury had made a mistake when it reached past the wards, capturing Brielle's mind. It gave Lowri a reason to fight. "I would have done it to save you too."

Lowri Tresillian—witch, thief, survivor—is utterly, helplessly depleted. And as she succumbs to an oblivion Brielle can only hope she'll wake from, she considers the Tresillian family. The mother who would cast her own daughter out of her coven; the cousin who used her to steal and lie; the brother who left her here to her fate. The people she has been devoted to, who would use her and throw her away as if she means nothing to them, when all Lowri ever does is love.

And Brielle is filled with a cool, steady rage. A certainty. They are undeserving of her.

She whispers fiercely to her sister, "Don't worry. I will avenge you."

CHAPTER
THIRTY-TWO

I SPEND MORE AND MORE TIME IN THE SEA, learning the hidden ways of the water now the map is a part of me. Tanith pores over the book, raking through every sentence, which we find is written in a language none of us can decipher. It's siren, a language as old as the world itself, and I do not know it. It was not a piece of knowledge I absorbed with the map. But Tanith relishes the challenge, and I'm unsure about going back to the sirens to decode it. It's far safer hidden in the library on Ennor, with a firedrake translating it and unlocking its secrets.

Since stealing the necklace and book, we have not heard from Lowri. The only contact from Coven Septern was the spell intended to break Amma, and the wards of Ennor with her. She's weak as frayed thread, but under Tanith's care, she is slowly flickering back to life. Joby has proved himself adept in the kitchen, baking bread, buying meats and cheese at the markets on Ennor, and serving every meal before taking a plate up to the library. None of us mentions it, but I know it's more than concern for Amma. It's an excuse to see Tanith.

Caden trains all the time. Dawn training has turned into all-day training, his sunny nature becoming brooding. At first I thought it would pass. But for him, knowing that the witch who birthed him would strip him of every protection out of spite has darkened his spirit. A restless rage burns like an ember within him, and even a ravenous siren would seem approachable in comparison.

"He'd burn the coven down if it weren't for Lowri needing the place," Merryam says, watching him one morning as he squares off against Eli.

I cross my arms over my chest, leaning against the wall at my back. "I'll light the match when he's ready."

"We all will. Especially since now we're not tied to the coven, Eli can deal with whoever he chooses to get supplies to his apothecaries."

Eli turns to us then, and a small thrill rushes through me as he strides over. He's breathing heavily, cheeks ruddy from training, hair tousled and eyes glittering. My breath catches and I have to hide it, plucking a practice blade from the air as he throws it my way.

"You're up. Caden's meeting with our scouts."

My gaze slides to Caden, then back to Eli. "Are you expecting anything?"

"Renshaw's fleet is maneuvering around the islands as you told us, and we're keeping tabs on it. But the watch has only a small number of men stationed on Penscalo. It's unnerving. I want him to meet with Kai, for a start."

I ignore the knot in my stomach at the mention of Kai's

name. Not getting to go home, to see Agnes and Kai, is beginning to grate on me. But I have to maintain my distance; I can't bring the watch down on their heads again. If the watch even suspects I've visited, it won't be worth the precious hours of being with them. It's not long until the full moon now, and we cannot be sure the watch's threats won't still be carried out. We need to break them before they can.

"That's a good plan. From what I can feel, there are more ships in the water. But they're not moving into formation. It's more like they're . . ."

"Waiting?"

I nod. Eli rubs his hand over the back of his neck, saying nothing. But we're all wondering the same thing. What are they waiting for?

Caden's hand claps down on my shoulder. "I'll tell them you've found a handsome lad to train with."

Merryam grins. "He's traveling on *Phantom*. Joby's taking him. I hate to think how two massive egos will fit on board."

Caden tosses us a wink and begins walking out. "You love to talk, but you're still watching my fine behind as I walk away."

I chuckle and glance up at Eli, who's looking between me and Caden. The red in his cheeks has paled slightly, the glitter dimming as though he's turning something over. Then his gaze snaps to mine and all the hard edges soften, a glimpse of the boy I met out on the ramparts shining through. He cocks his head. "Come on. No slacking."

I face him from ten paces away. We go through drills, working through the steps, and I'm pleased they're second nature now, my limbs moving and shifting before I've actively thought about it. We go through the steps as the sun climbs, and I wipe the sweat from my forehead before going for a drink of water. Eli puts away our practice weapons, joining me.

"You're swimming again."

"Since our visit to the coven, I've wanted to more and more. It's as though a weight has shifted, and now the sea feels like home again."

For a moment, I swear he looks troubled before he smiles. "What do you say you and I go somewhere where you can really work out what you can do as a storm bringer?"

"With the knowledge of the book Tanith's decoded so far?"

"If it's away from people, maybe you'll be able to relax. Figure out how to control it, rather than worrying it's just going to unleash like before and bring a tempest down on us."

"I've tried," I admit. "I've swum as far offshore as I can. But I can't seem to unlock anything. I don't know how—it's like I get closer, and my power shifts out of reach. I still have no idea how I did it before, or what triggered it."

He squints at me. "Maybe you're just too close to the islands, even swimming out. Maybe you need to be somewhere where you're not worried about hurting anyone. Somewhere far from the Fortunate Isles."

"You have somewhere in mind?"

"I do," he says, gaze trained on my features as he crosses his arms. "Meet me at dusk in the main entrance."

I walk down the main staircase, wearing fighting leathers and boots and my blade strapped at my waist. My hair is plaited tight to my scalp, ending in a braid that I leave hanging between my shoulder blades. Eli is dressed similarly, watching me as I approach. His eyes travel slowly over me, a small smile lifting the corners of his mouth. He looks rakish, like the lethal stranger I first met here on Ennor. The kind of boy to steal a kiss, then press the tip of a blade to your chest.

For a moment, as his gaze hits mine, I feel a delicious purr in my blood. My face heats, pulse thrumming, but I don't look away as I reach him. I don't try and hide it. Since he admitted so many of his truths on the ramparts, this dance between us has slowed. And even if there is nothing between us, I can revel in his nearness, in being alone with him.

"We'll be traversing farther than you're used to," he says in a low voice. "Are you ready for that?"

"Sure," I reply, and swallow. Then I hold out my hand to him. Traversing is chaos to me. I can't breathe, can't work out where I am, *what* I am in the dark. But that constant, the thing I cling to, is him. I know I'm not alone and he will guide me until my feet meet solid earth once more. "I trust you."

His smile widens as he takes my hand. Sparks dance through my veins all the way to my middle, which tightens and fizzes, not unpleasantly. "Good."

"Are *you* ready?" I ask, raising an eyebrow.

He shrugs. "There's always a cost. But for you, it's worth the way it drains me."

I smile, and his answering grin lights me up in a way I never want to end. Then we take a step into a waiting shadow and fall into a world of night.

Smoke swirls all around me, the ground dropping away, leaving me weightless. His hand is my only connection as we fall, no . . .

Fly.

I blink as stars ignite around us and I chance a breath. Cool darkness fills my lungs. I gaze in wonder, the night sky all around us, a vast world of starlight. I laugh, looking at our joined hands, and I feel . . . a jolt. Like I've been here before with him, a thousand times. I find Eli's eyes burning into mine. Like a home, a place I've been searching for. I whisper his name into the dark and he smiles, his eyes depthless and velvet, those twin dark stars.

Then his smile turns wolfish as he grips my hand tighter and pulls. I'm ripped from this world, this perfect midnight. A scream rakes up my throat as we fall.

Wind rushes past us, tearing at my hair, my skin as we travel from this in-between place of shadows into the world I know.

We plunge down, and Eli twists, stepping left into a seam of deeper shadow. . . .

Then out.

He releases my hand and I fall to the ground, feeling sand beneath my fingers as I gasp and cough. I push myself up and look around, finding an islet: a strip of exposed sand and a gathering of jutting rocks. Beyond that, there is nothing but ocean. I feel for my connection to the sea, and find just ocean surrounding us.

"We're alone?" I ask Eli, turning to him, wanting to make sure. "Truly, totally alone?"

He nods. "No one for miles and miles. The wild north of Arnhem is that way . . ." He points in one direction. "And the Spines are in that direction. You can't hurt anyone here. Even if you whipped up a storm so great it blotted out the sky. It's just us."

I exhale, turning to stare at the waves. Then I close my

eyes, and sink into myself, deep into that place that for so
long was hollow and empty. But now it's filling with light,
and desire. Now it's no longer empty and cold. I open my
eyes and smile.

Then, as though something has unlocked within me, I
hold out my hand and beckon the wind. A few tendrils of
air thread over the water, like ribbons weaving through and
reaching up to the shore. I concentrate, trying to hone the
feelings of desperation on Rosevear when the storm arrived,
and then when I dreamed on Ennor. I imagine the wisps of
wind spinning around me, circling me, and I focus on that
feeling of heat and light in the center of my chest. The wind
swirls around me, and I laugh. Then almost as quickly, it
collapses around me, spraying the sand in an arc around my
boots.

It's the first time I've felt any measure of control. The first
time I haven't felt powerless. Tanith said that the book spoke
of how a storm bringer might coax the threads of a storm—
the wind and clouds—and learn to channel their power.
Knowing I can whip up a breeze is one thing, but I need
to be able to call a storm and then control it. Once I can do
that, I could break a fleet. I could deter the watch, the ruling
council. I could ensure we are safe on our islands forever.

I turn to Eli and shrug. "I guess it's time to get to work."

I practice all through the night, learning how the power
feels, how it crackles like fire in my veins. By the time the
sky begins to lighten around us, the sun blazing in a line of
gold on the horizon, I can call a flurry of clouds overhead
with a flick of my fingers. I can pull a fog bank to surround
us and cloak us. But I still don't want to chance calling any
more than that, and I find that it drains me. I know I can do

so much more . . . but what if I cannot control it?

Sinking to the sand beside Eli, he passes me a hip flask and I take a small sip, the amber smokiness burning my throat. I pass it back to him, wiping my mouth. "We should head back," he says. "I need a shadow big enough for us both to travel through."

I lean back on my arms, watching the sea as it turns molten and hazy, the sun rising slowly, lighting it up. "Just another moment. Life is never like this anymore. It reminds me of Rosevear."

"Do you miss it?"

"Always," I breathe, thinking of Agnes and Kai, the gorse and heather, the sand, powder soft beneath my feet. And somewhere else, a place by the cliffs, somewhere I left a piece of myself, marked with carved wood. But when I try to find the exact shape of that memory, it eludes me. I know it must be where my father rests, but I cannot feel it anymore. "But I know it'll be waiting for me when we defeat Renshaw and chase the watch from our shores. All this, and no hunger. No scraping by. A future."

I glance at Eli and find him watching me. He lowers his eyes and begins to speak. "Mira, I need to tell you—"

Then a blade flies out of nowhere, thudding into his chest.

CHAPTER THIRTY-THREE

SHADOW BLOOMS AROUND THE BLADE IN ELI'S chest. I whirl, leaping to my feet. A girl, dressed for war, stands across the sand.

The hunter I saw at the coven.

Brielle.

"You!" I gasp, drawing my own blade. "You're my hunter."

She tips her chin, features grim. "That was for Lowri. You used her, and you left her alone to face the consequences. And this? This is for me."

I barely have time to move as another blade flies for my face. It grazes my cheekbone and I twist, already moving for her, blood beating hot in my chest. I reach her in three strides, slashing with my blade as she spins. I catch her side and she grunts before I dance away. She's taller, bigger, and built for combat. And I've only been training for a handful of weeks.

And yet she isn't holding a sharp blade. The one she's

extracted from the sash across her chest is dull and small. If she wanted to, she could have killed me already. She has another blade strapped at her waist, and I wager a few more secreted in her leathers. Her plan isn't to kill me today.

It's to capture me.

"Why are you working for them?" I call, taking another step back toward the sea. I need to lure her down to the water, away from Eli. My gaze strays to him. He hasn't moved, and the shadow is leaking like smoke from his chest, mingled with blood. It's as though the magic infuses his veins as it does mine, and if he loses too much . . . what if he can't traverse? I swallow, panic ripping through me. I have to get him somewhere safe. I cannot be captured and leave him to his fate.

My heel brushes the edge of a wave. The hunter's eyes dart to my feet, then up to me. And in that split second, I aim and throw. Her cry of pain tells me I have hit my mark. She looks up at me and gasps, "Because you're a monster," before saying words I don't recognize, a spell. And then she vanishes.

Shaking, I run to Eli, taking in the blood and the thundercloud around him. I take his hand in mine and pull his face toward me. Pale, so pale, and cold.

"Eli, we have to get you somewhere safe. We need an apothecary. We need—"

"I can take us," he rasps, voice strained from the effort it took just to say those few words. "Help me find a shadow. I'll pull us through."

"Are you sure we can traverse?" I ask, pulling his arm over my shoulder. I snake my other arm around his waist and help him stand. His shout of pain echoes across the beach, but he stays on his feet. Shuffling, so slowly, we make it to a shadow by the rocks a few feet away. And this time, all I can do is hold on and hope.

We crash through the dark, my arms wrapped around him, falling through howling night. I catch glimpses of other places in our world, forests and mountains and cities, but it's suffocating, fractured. I can barely breathe from the chaos; the jumble of shadows is too much, too intense—

Then we're falling.

We land in a tangle of limbs. I roll over, groaning. Everything hurts. My head, my lungs, my limbs from the impact. Blearily, I turn to Eli, his name on my lips, and find him on his side, eyes closed, barely moving.

No, no, not like this, not like this . . .

I look up, seeing where he's taken us, and my heart skips. The apothecary in Port Trenn. The one I visited with the crew of *Phantom* just months ago. I stagger toward the door. Just as I reach up a fist to knock, it opens. The apothecary, Howden, inhales sharply and calls back into the shop. He hurries out; then his assistant, the girl from before, hurries after him. They pull Eli to his feet. I help them walk him inside, boots dragging across the ground. The apothecary looks left and right up the street before bolting the door behind us.

"Get him to the workroom, Stas. We need warm water, cloths, and my full set of equipment." We carry him to a table in the workroom and he collapses onto it. He's almost white now, shadow no longer seeping from him.

Only blood.

"Was it a poisoned blade?" the apothecary asks, nimble fingers dancing over Eli's shirt, cutting it away.

"I don't know. It was a hunter, from Coven Septern."

The apothecary swears and gathers supplies from the workroom shelves. "A tonic to put him under, and a draft to refresh the blood he's lost. My lord," he says, looking down into Eli's blanched features, "this will not be pleasant."

Eli's eyes flutter open and he almost smiles, then grimaces. "We've been through worse, Howden."

The apothecary nods once, clasps Eli's hand, and tips the draft to Eli's mouth. I hold up Eli's head, trying not to look at the blade in his chest, the blood. . . .

He manages three swallows and Howden removes it before tipping a few drops of tonic from another bottle into his mouth. "Sweet dreams, my lord."

Eli's eyes meet mine for a heartbeat, and all I can think is, Don't die, please don't die, as my heart blooms in my chest like a feral wound, and it's as though I can't breathe, like I'm seeing him for the first time, not just as Eli, or a lord, or an elusive, handsome boy I made a bargain with, but as . . . him. My safe harbor. And I cannot, I *cannot* face losing him. His mouth forms my name and I reach for his fingers before his features slacken and he's under.

It's nighttime before the apothecary finishes his work. He leaves me alone with Eli in a room just off the workroom, in a big bed with clean sheets pulled around him. I hesitate, then get onto the bed beside him, curling up on top of the covers next to his still form. He's sleeping now. He's alive, blood replenished and the wound in his chest healed. Silent tears track down my face as I realize what could have happened. How close he was to . . . to . . .

And all because he was trying to help me.

I take a deep breath and place my hand on top of his,

where it rests on his stomach. His chest rises and falls, his features peaceful in sleep. I wonder what he dreams of. Where he travels in his own mind. With his tousled dark hair, he seems almost vulnerable. Not like the lord of a castle and island, a lord who protects us all. Who protects me. Who . . . maybe even cares for me.

I turn my wrist, catching the gleam of the bargain mark in the low light. What would have happened if I hadn't agreed? If I hadn't gone with him? Suddenly that seems unimaginable. My hand tightens over his, and I curl in closer to his warmth. He smells so familiar now, it's like he's home, the compass point I can't help navigating toward every time we're apart. Somehow, he's become so much. So much more than a boy I made a bargain with. I trust him, and I care about him, and every time I picture that blade in his chest, it's like it's sliced open my own, like I'm dying next to him.

I swear he knows I'm here. I swear I hear him murmur my name, like a promise weaving on the tendrils of air between us.

Mira . . .

I want more than the bargain to link and bind us. I want more of him. I want to feel his mouth pressed to mine, the feel of his hands on my waist, the touch of his skin, his scent wrapping round me.

But.

I placed him in danger today. I am the one who is hunted. I am the one who stole that necklace and the book from the coven. And what did the hunter mean when she said, "That was for Lowri"? That Lowri is facing the consequences? We should have sent someone to check on her. It was too strange that we heard nothing after the malefant took her revenge on us.

I wipe the insistent tears prickling my face. Then slowly, so I don't wake him, I get up from the bed, move to a chair in the corner, and wrap myself in a blanket. I consider what would have happened if he hadn't been able to traverse at all. I imagine him bleeding out on the sand, the light in his eyes dimming to nothing, another person that feels like home wrenched from me, forever. And I can't stand it. I can't stand how close I came to losing him. We've become so tangled up in each other; we've shared our beating, vulnerable hearts, so slowly I almost hadn't noticed it happening. If I allow my roots, my heart to tangle even more with his, if I allow us to fuse together in the way I now long for . . . I shudder. The possibility of that loss is unbearable.

Eli and I can never be. I know it now, more than ever. I cannot put someone else I care for in danger like this again. What happened today, the blood, the blade, his failing breath—

I shake my head. I'm a coward for not releasing him from our bargain. A coward for ensuring an alliance with him for Rosevear, for sealing it with a bargain mark neither of us can break. I cannot fall for him, just as he cannot fall for me. At least this way, I am the only target of the hunter, the watch, and behind them all, the ruling council. At least this way, when we return to Ennor Castle, I will not place him in danger ever again.

It isn't until later that I realize the hunter hesitated. She could have captured me, could have taken me to the ruling council and left Eli alone to die in that lonely place. But she seemed to only want to harm Eli, to vent her fury. I am still puzzling over this as I finally fall asleep.

CHAPTER
THIRTY-FOUR

"MIRA, IT'S TIME TO LEAVE." A HAND SHAKES ME awake, and I blink up into Eli's face. He smiles, but it's strained, eyes hollow, features still drawn and pale. "We need to head back."

"Are you well? Can you manage? Eli, about what happened—"

"It wasn't your fault," he says. "If anything, I put *you* at risk. I should have known that she would be tracking you. Maybe that binding spell had an additional component, maybe that's why she was there when my aunt performed it at the coven."

I gaze up at him, my eyes straying to his chest. Only a few hours ago, shadow and blood leaked from there. From where a blade sliced into his heart. "How are you still alive?" I ask quietly. "How did that not kill you?"

He shrugs. "Call it a parting gift from my father. His blood—his magic—makes it *very* hard to kill me. It's almost as though I forced the weapon to become something else, something less substantial, as it flew toward me. Something that would pierce me, but wouldn't be fatal."

"But it's not impossible to kill you. If your magic hadn't shielded you . . ."

"Everyone has to die someday, even someone as monstrous as me."

"You're the furthest thing from monstrous," I say quietly, startled that he'd believe that about himself.

"And yet I put you in danger, and Lowri, unwittingly." His gaze locks with mine, and my breath hitches. Even wounded, on the very brink of death, he's still devastating. With his dark, ruffled hair drifting over his forehead, muscular forearms outlined under his white shirt, tanned skin just visible at the base of his throat . . . and those eyes. Piercing, deadly. Even now, everything about him screams lethal, screams predator . . . and yet all I want to do is touch him. Run my hands over that place the hunter's blade sliced into and know that he's truly all right.

But then I remember. I force myself to untangle my feelings, to see him merely as an ally, nothing more.

I rise from the chair, hiding my tangle of thoughts and desire as I put some distance between us. I feel every inch of the bruises bestowed on us during our landing the day before as I straighten out, tired and sore.

"Ready?" he asks quietly, as though he knows how I truly feel, and how I will fight these feelings with every bone in my body. For his sake, and for mine. I nod, not trusting myself to speak as I take his hand and we step into shadow.

★ ★ ★

Tanith finds us first. I stumble to stay upright as we land in the entrance hall of Ennor Castle. Eli sags, throwing out a hand to steady himself, gripping the end of the banister. Tanith appears from outside, hair and clothes streaming wet.

"Rain shower?" I ask her.

Her eyes assess us. Then she hurries to Eli, worry sweeping over her features. "Where did you go?" she asks, helping him to the great hall through the doorway just off the entrance hall. It's a cavernous space, scattered with worn sofas and rugs. There's a huge fireplace, unlit, and Maggie lumbers up, picking her way toward us. She nuzzles at Eli, clearly realizing he's hurt. Tanith takes a breath, continuing, "We've been trying to locate you. Mer is at her wits' end, we nearly went to the coven to see if they had taken you, if you were there—"

"I'm fine," Eli says wearily. "Nothing but a scratch. Good practice for Mira. Just exhausted and a bit battered."

"Good practice?" a voice booms through the double doors leading to the entrance hall. Caden rushes over the threshold, features pinched. "Brielle?"

Eli nods grimly.

Caden swears, worried eyes sweeping over every inch of me.

"I'm fine too," I say, swatting him away. "Starving though. Is it eleven?"

"Long past eleven."

I whip around, and there, standing in the doorway of the great hall, is Amma.

Eli makes straight for her, Tanith at his side, and she beams at him. "Causing trouble, young lord?"

"Of course," he says gruffly, bowing his forehead close to hers. "Only the good kind."

She leans in, placing her ethereal hand on his cheek. "Your mother would have been so proud." Then she looks at all of us, beckoning. "Come, come. It'll take more than a Tresillian witch curse to send me into the afterlife. The scones are going cold. Bread's baked, and there's fresh butter and sliced apples and cheese."

I follow the others, collapsing in an armchair by the fire in the kitchens. I'm still in my fighting leathers, tired and aching. But as Merryam runs in, seeing Eli and me and hiding quick, relieved tears before thumping him on the shoulder, I know I have to do this now.

Caden fills a plate for me, thrusting it into my stiff hands. "Eat, then we talk," he says. "Did you remember the steps we practiced at least, when you faced her?"

I stuff a scone into my mouth, groaning as the buttery thickness slides down my throat. "Put it this way—you should see the hunter."

He grins. "That's what I like to hear."

I scarf down two more scones, slathering them in butter and jam, then gulp down hot tea, and finally feel human again. I watch Eli out of the corner of my eye as Tanith hands him mouthfuls of food, then forces him to drink, even as he winces. With each passing moment he seems more himself. My gaze meets his, and he raises his eyebrows in question. But I look away, busying myself with more tea. After what happened, I'm shoving the door closed on my feelings, on the way my blood heats just to be near him. I can't see him hurt again because of me.

★ ★ ★

When we've all finished, I take a breath, fixing each of them in my mind. Eli's inner circle, his trusted people. And somehow, now my people too. I never thought I'd have more than those I grew up with, the people I've known since birth. But here I am. And the thought of a single one of them getting hurt or worse . . . I suppress a shudder. I have to put our plans in motion now, before it's too late.

"I want to attack Renshaw's main fleet," I say, pushing my plate away. "We've trained. We're ready. And I don't think we should wait any longer. I've been sensing her ships, following them through the tide. I know where they'll be berthing soon; there's a pattern to her movements. I had to wait and be sure. I know we can't make any mistakes. We have to be swift and strike true. It's only two weeks till the watch will carry out its threat against Rosevear if I'm not handed over. I need Renshaw to bleed. I need the watch to have *no* allies in our waters."

Caden nods and rests his forearms on his thighs. "How long do we have?"

"If the pattern of her movements stays consistent, three days," I say. "Renshaw will berth her main ships to the east of here, toward the siren graveyard. It's far enough from the isles that the watch wouldn't be able to assemble and move to aid her. We should set an ambush. It's time to take her out, show the watch what we're capable of. It's time to break their alliance and their grip on the isles. It's time . . ." I pause, setting my gaze on Eli's. Thinking about the necklace, his plans to find his father, to find a door and step through it, to understand who he is. What he can be when Ennor and the rest of the isles are safe. I want him to know he is not a monster. "It's time for *all* of us to be free."

Eli closes his eyes, a small frown carving his forehead. He knows what I really mean. It's time for me, for us, to be free of our bargain, to go back to how things were before. It's time for me to lock that door forever on my feelings about a young lord with lethal grace and a ready grin. I hope he knows that I'm doing this to save him. To save all of them. That I would tear the world apart to keep them all safe, even if that means stepping away.

After a long moment, Eli opens his eyes and sighs. "All right. In three days, we strike, and we end Renshaw for good."

CHAPTER
THIRTY-FIVE

THE ONE THING BRIELLE DESPISES IS FAILING.
Ever since she became a hunter, she has never lost a creature
or returned empty-handed. And yet today . . . she hisses as
the witch healing her thigh finalizes the spell. The witch
whips out the blade, letting it clatter to the floor, and Brielle's blood swiftly clots, the muscles stitching back together.
It doesn't hurt, exactly; it's more a deep itch. The kind you
can't scratch. She flinches beneath the witch's hands, bunch-
ing her own hands into fists.

What annoys her the most isn't that she's been injured. It's
that she failed. She returned to the coven without that monstrous girl, without avenging Lowri, and all she had to show
for her effort was Mira's blade, stuck in her thigh, immobi-
lizing her. She growls as the spell does its work, closing her
eyes as the itchiness, deep under her skin, spreads. It heats,
turning to flame, intensifying and forcing her to grit her
teeth.

"All done," the witch says with a sniff. "You can report to the mal now. She's waiting."

"Of course she is," Brielle mutters, swinging off the starched white bed and planting her feet on the floor. She scoops up Mira's blade, eyeing the blood still spattered along its length. Her blood. "Damn siren," she spits, and leaves the room.

The malefant is indeed waiting for Brielle, drumming her obsidian nails on her desk. Brielle slinks in, drops into a chair across from her, and raises her chin to match the mal's cold stare.

"Report, hunter."

"I tracked her to an isolated islet using the spell we planted in her binding, some way off the coast of Arnhem, to the north."

"And?"

Brielle digs her nails into the arms of her chair, reminding herself to keep her tone measured. "She got away. Her parting gift was this." She places the blade on the mal's desk and notes, with a small thrill, the look of disgust on her face. The malefant does not deal in details. She likes to delegate, hear reports, and keep her hands spotlessly clean.

"You may remove the evidence," she says. "And give me one good reason why I shouldn't send you to Valstra to hunt down fire sprites for the next ten years."

Brielle's blood turns cold. Would she? She isn't sure how empty the threat is. The malefant may have adopted her after her mother passed, but she could be cruel, cold . . . and at times, malevolent. Like the way she had cursed Amma, the spirit protecting the isle of Ennor and all its inhabitants, including her own son, in retaliation for stealing a book and a necklace. Or accusing and subjecting her own daughter to a witch trial to prove her innocence . . . In Brielle's eyes, that was irredeemable.

Brielle's mouth turns dry and gritty. Yes, the witch before her could and *would* send her to Valstra if she failed again to capture Mira. Of that there is no doubt. To lose the coveted position of favored coven in this city would be a disaster in the mal's eyes. Her reputation is more important than the lives of her daughters. She would separate Brielle and Lowri without a second thought.

"The assignment is not over. I have never failed you before—give me one last attempt, and I will drag the creature back here. I will ensure we are still favored above all covens in Arnhem. I will ensure you are favored most by the ruling council." Brielle says all this in an urgent, hurried string of words, but in between them, silent, are the real words: "I will do anything. Anything. Just don't separate me from my sister."

It's the right thing to say. The malefant's features relax, and she sits back in her chair, eyes beady, dark, and calculating as she measures Brielle beneath her gaze. "Do not fail me again, hunter."

Dismissed, Brielle rises to her feet, limping for the door. Pins and needles shake the leg that Mira buried a blade in, and it takes all her composure not to sink to the ground.

"One last thing," the malefant says at her back. "Not a word of this to Lowri. She may have triumphed in the trial and therefore is no longer accused, but the last thing I need is a wayward witch in my coven. Ensure she does not meddle further."

★ ★ ★

Brielle grunts her way up two flights of stairs, swearing occasionally when the witches in training titter as she passes. They are all so prim and pretty on the outside, but Brielle knows what a witch is capable of. Hillary Tresillian was once a witch in training like them, and she chose to place her coven above her family. But Lowri . . . she's different. And that's why, even with her leg still mending, Brielle will go and visit her, as she has at every moment possible since the trial. She is fairly certain her mother hasn't so much as asked after Lowri's welfare, let alone gone to check on her personally in the days since the trial.

Brielle reaches the final staircase, grips the banister, and prepares to drag herself up. She contemplates how she will draw the siren creature out . . . if she will wait until she is alone, or capture her when she is surrounded but distracted. The hunter pauses a few steps from the top, catching her breath, and kneads the muscles in her leg. It has gone past the itching stage, and now it is just weak. Lacking blood flow, a quivering mess. It will take a day or so for her to be able to train again. Precious hours of rest she does not have.

She resumes her climb. One thing is certain: she can't capture the siren on Ennor. It's too protected, too heavily warded by Amma, and she'd never get out alive. No. To be successful means biding her time. And being ready to strike at a heartbeat's notice. Only . . . she had the opportunity, didn't she? And she hesitated. Brielle pushes this treacherous flit of a thought aside. Hesitation is weakness. Compassion is weakness when it comes to her work. She cannot allow it to taint her thoughts, and she certainly will not examine her actions on the islet. The only way is forward now. The only outcome can be success.

"At last," Brielle gasps, conquering the staircase. She wipes the sweat from where it prickles at her hairline and makes for the most sought-after rooms on the witches' landing. Lowri had won them fairly at Presentation, but that doesn't mean the other witches are happy about it. Brielle has already had to intervene when another witch complained loudly about how Lowri has held on to them, even after her disgrace, the accusation, and her subsequent trial. Witches are indeed self-serving creatures.

Brielle knocks softly before entering, knowing the wards that Lowri has set will admit her. Lowri is sitting up in bed. Nova is on her lap, and her hand brushes her familiar's back absently as she stares out the window. Brielle's worry deepens. The trial seems to have left Lowri a shell of her former self, as though the fury succeeded in consuming her soul before Lowri bested it.

"They brought me soup, before you ask," Lowri says dully. "Vegetable. Too much pepper."

"But you ate it?"

She sighs. "Cleaned the bowl, just like I promised."

"Good." Brielle sits down in the armchair by the window. She grimaces as the weight shifts off her leg, the ache in it deep, near the bone now.

Lowri watches her for a moment before speaking. "You've been on assignment, haven't you?"

"I still have to hunt."

"You only have one assignment right now. The one my mother gave you."

Brielle eyes her warily. "That's right."

"So who hurt you?" Lowri says, scrunching up her nose. "Was it Mira?"

"It was," Brielle says, trying to make light of it. "It'll soon heal."

"You should refuse the assignment. It's wrong. Surely you see that by now? I helped her, I helped all of them willingly, and—"

"And look at you now," Brielle snaps. "Bedridden, a shadow. Whereas they're unmarked, unscathed, and haven't even deigned to check on you."

Lowri's eyes widen. "You didn't tell them—"

"Didn't get the chance."

Lowri grows quiet. Then she sniffs. "I smell blood on you. And magic. But not the creature kind, or the witch kind . . ." She gasps. "You hurt Elijah, didn't you?"

"So what if I did?" Brielle explodes. "You have to see how it could have gone for you in that trial! Surely you see? What if you hadn't survived? What if you'd been bested by the fury, and cast out—"

"What my mother chooses to do is not my family's fault. She shouldn't have hidden that necklace from Eli all these years, denying him knowledge of himself, or the book from Mira that her own mother helped compile. Just as she shouldn't have . . ." Lowri swallows, looking away. "I've nearly completed my training, I can sense it. When I beat the fury, everything changed. It's like I was reborn, like the ties and knots that held me here snapped. When my strength returns, I shall do a working, and we shall see if my training is complete, if my powers are whole and separate from the web of the coven. And when I have all I need from Coven Septern, my place will be there with them. With my family on Ennor, with the people that love me. Not here with her."

"What about me?" Brielle says quietly. "Do I not figure into your plans?"

Lowri's gaze flickers, catching on Brielle, the harsh angles smoothing, softening. "Give up the assignment, and join me on Ennor. Your training is complete; you don't need Septern. Leave the coven behind, leave all this—"

"And what happens to you in the meantime? What if your training isn't complete and I abandon you here?" she says, leaning forward. "Don't think I don't question this assignment, or wish it had been given to another. If I have to leave the coven, I'll be a target. For every creature's kin I've drained. I'll be a hunter for hire, living assignment to assignment, going where the coin is good. I won't be able to stay on Ennor, it's not my way. It's not in my nature." She sits back, crossing her arms. "That's what happens to hunters that are cast out, Lowri. It's not just witches in training, but hunters that are doomed to wander the world until we are bested. I've met other hunters, know the stories, heard the warnings. Your mother may be a piece of work, but you have family still, as you say. I have no one. I have this coven, and that's all I'll ever have."

"Then you've made up your mind."

Brielle scrubs her hand down her face, moving to stand. "I made up my mind the moment your mother, *my* malefant, asked me to take on the assignment. I know what's waiting for me if I refuse, or fail. The fact is, we're not the same, Lowri. I guess we have to accept that." She reaches for the door handle. "Get out of bed, Lowri. Get back on your feet and do a working. See for yourself if you are ready, if your training is complete. You worry about yourself, and I'll worry about my own future. We have to remember—you're a witch. I'm a hunter. And maybe there's a reason why we don't mix."

Then, before she can hear Lowri's response, or regret the bitterness pouring from her lips, Brielle yanks open the door and leaves.

CHAPTER THIRTY-SIX

I GRIP THE WOODEN RAILING, MY NAILS BITING into the wood. *Phantom* cuts through the waves like a ghost, leaving barely a whisper as we sail to where we will find Renshaw.

I can feel where her ships cluster. Feel the tug and pull of the waves around them, how the tide is high, how the rocks are few. They're anchored beside an island unmarked on any map, near Port Graine. There are eight ships, including her shadow ship. We have six, but we are hungrier.

Deadlier.

Over the past three days, we have drawn all our resources together for this strike: the people of Ennor, Rosevear, and Penrith, our fighters. Those who do not accept the watch and Renshaw burning homes and taking what is ours. I know Renshaw wants me—she may have heard by now that the map is bound into me. I am bait, but I also know so much more now. I can feel each one of their ships in the water, the weight of them held by the ocean. We will come for her, and then we will break the watch's hold. I am powerful, and I am not alone. These are our waters, our lives, and we will fight for them. We will end Renshaw's hold over the isles.

I catch a flash of teeth in the dark and feel for Agnes's hand. To have her at my side gives me strength and certainty. As I squeeze her fingers briefly, the embers stir in my chest. This is war. This is vengeance. The rest of the seven are with us too; Kai is on a ship with Feock, ready for the ambush. Ready for blood. Tonight, we are not here to search for survivors. We are working as one.

We are the storm.

"Watch out for Renshaw's thugs—they're brutal," I murmur to Agnes.

"I'll gut them like fish," she hisses. "They burned our homes. Killed our people and the people of Penrith. The healer, she hasn't been the same since her brothers . . . since we laid them in the earth. I have a score to settle for Rosevear."

I press my forehead to hers. "Make our people proud."

Eli steps over to us, the night seemingly darker around him. Deeper. He stares out over the water to where we know the fleet rests. "My shadow ships will take out the right flank. We'll move in on the starboard side, secure the grappling hooks, then jump across. Mira, you'll be in the water, circling Renshaw's main ship and ready to attack when my shadow ships have purchase. Agnes, you're with Kai on the port side. Caden will lead, all as we planned."

"And you?" I ask, feeling for the handle of the blade strapped at my side. I chose a black one from the armory at the castle. Sharp and slightly curved, perfectly weighted in my hand. It gleams as it catches the light, like a wink of pure night. But I still want to find my hunter, and win Agnes's blade back. Tomorrow, I tell myself. Tonight is for breaking; tomorrow is for reclaiming.

"I'll be searching for Renshaw." He smiles. "That is, if Mer doesn't find her first. She's waited a long time for this."

I look at Mer, a few feet away, booted feet planted, shoulders back. She's staring out at the water, features unreadable. Pearl is miles away now, hidden with Bryn in Leicena. I'm sure she's missing Mer, missing their life together on the waves aboard *Phantom*. There's Seth as well. Ever since he tricked us, Mer has refused to speak his name, almost as though he's already dead to her. She's realized he'll never defect or leave Renshaw. He'll never have the strength and courage she did, and it's fractured her heart.

"Are you ready for this?" Eli asks me.

My heart thuds in my chest, once, twice, spreading warmth through every inch of me. I study his face, the worry etched there. "More than ready," I say. "We're close now. I'll get in the water, circle round when we're near. Are you sure I shouldn't try to bring a storm—"

"It's too dangerous," he says softly. "I cannot risk you. I cannot . . ."

"It's all right," I say, hesitating before placing my hand on his arm. His eyes search mine and he moves his hand, capturing mine in his. "It's too volatile. I understand."

He nods once. Then his fingers release their grip on my hand, moving down to touch my waist, sending sparks along my veins. "I cannot risk *you*," he says again, dropping his hand from my waist and swallowing. "See you on the other side."

I smile, taming the insistent clamor of my heart, and tear

my gaze from his. I look to Agnes, fixing her in my mind one final time, then to the others gathered around us, then farther, to the night and fleeting stars. I climb over the railing and slip as quietly as I can into the beckoning sea.

The ocean ignites within me. I glide through the water, cutting away from *Phantom*, and as I move farther out, I feel the shapes of Renshaw's ships above, and dip down to graze the seabed with my fingertips. There's hardly a current here, and oddly, no life. No fish or scuttling things, as though every creature has hidden itself. Frowning, I twist in the water, casting my mind over the seabed, feeling for the tide, the ships, the swirl of soft wind as it dances over the water. But there's something strange. Something I haven't seen or sensed in the sea around the isles before. Something vast and watchful, a looming presence. Something is waiting.

But all I see are our ships, and Renshaw's. The shadow ships moving into position. This map bound into me, this siren knowledge, is new. Perhaps I do not fully understand it yet; perhaps it is nothing and I am just on edge. I kick up, slipping to just beneath the surface as the grappling hooks fly across the water, sinking into Renshaw's ships. The sound of voices rises, muffled by the sea, and I smile. It's all going according to plan. Soon I'll be needed on the starboard side of the ships. I dart over to get in position—

Then I sense it again.

Something lurking, something that can't possibly exist . . . the same size as the largest of the ships overhead, maybe the breadth of two. I turn in the water, facing toward whatever it is. The whole ocean seems to shudder, then grow still. Bodies begin hitting the water, plunging down, blood streaming from them. Fire lights the surface above, painting the sea in golds and reds. Above the sea, the strike is going as planned; soon they will need me. I need to shake this feeling. It's just nerves, just my restlessness reflected in the sea. I squint, circling slowly, and freeze. There's a shape in the water now. The sea is darkening, like spreading night, moving toward me at an unnatural pace. . . .

Then it emerges.

I fumble for my blade as the thing from the darkness reaches me, wraps, twists around me like rope. I gasp, the air squeezing from my lungs.

Writhing, finding I am bound completely, as though a rope as thick as a man's waist has snaked over me, I look up, screaming into the water, but only a stream of bubbles breaks this silent dark. There's no one to save me. No one to stop this thing, this vast shape, this monster, as it glides ever closer.

More bodies hit the water, cries and the clatter of blades echoing like hollow bells from above. I realize more ships are arriving, somehow hidden from me, lurking close by. . . . I shudder, twisting and bellowing in desperation now, trying to get free. But I'm powerless, caught in what feels like a tentacle, slick and oily as it constricts my chest. And the ships I can sense now, flying toward Renshaw's fleet—

The watch.

It's a trap. They must have been cloaked by a spell and there are so many, a dozen, *too* many. . . .

And what lies beneath them, tangling me in its grip . . . they have no idea, Agnes and Caden, Eli and Merryam and Kai, no knowledge of what's looming, poised to consume them all. The tentacle wrapping me squeezes, and I choke, vision turning black at the edges.

At last I see its foul form. How huge, how terrifying, this deep sea beast, closer to the Fortunate Isles than ever before, and now lured toward us by the scent of blood, lured by so many hearts in the water. And it has me in its grip, its first heart, the beginning of the end—

The watch has arrived to crush us.

And the kraken, tentacles darting toward the falling bodies, is here to feast.

I scream again, powerless to pull away, to warn them, panicked breath bursting from my lungs as the kraken lurches toward the ship to my left.

Toward *Phantom*.

CHAPTER
THIRTY-SEVEN

SHOCK WAVES RIPPLE THROUGH THE COVEN. BRI-
elle lurches toward Lowri's door, sensing the spell build and
build, coaxed and molded into a wide cloak. The coven
house grows as still as the moment before a thunderclap,
before the walls shudder, as if shrugging off that cloak, casting it free to whip over the gusts toward the Fortunate Isles.
Toward the watch's ships.

Brielle reaches for the door handle and finds Lowri standing there, framed in the doorway. She's in her nightdress,
feet planted on the bare floorboards, veins like threads of
ink on her exposed wrists. She's still recovering, still lost in
sleep for most of the day and night, and as she stands there,
shivering, she babbles about teeth and rattling and a roaring
like the sky unleashed.

"Back to bed, it's all right, have you eaten?" Brielle fusses,
she knows she's fussing, but Lowri is still so pale. She should
have waited outside, should have done as she was bidden and

stopped Lowri from leaving her room. But seeing her like this, as Lowri senses the spell cast out by the coven, toward the Fortunate Isles, her heart constricts. She's still her sister. They can fight, they can argue, but it means nothing when one of them is in pain.

Lowri ignores her, stepping back only far enough to allow Brielle inside, then crosses her arms, lank hair falling around her features. "It's a spell, a cloaking, don't lie to me. What's Mother up to? What is she doing?"

Brielle sighs, locking the door quietly, standing in front of it. "A working for the ruling council, for a fleet of ships . . . near the Fortunate Isles." She figures Lowri will find out soon enough anyway. With most of the coven involved in creating the working, Brielle can hardly be expected to conceal it from Lowri. All the mal asked of her was to stop her from meddling.

"An ambush?"

"We do not concern ourselves with politics—"

"Don't give me the party line!" Lowri snaps, fists tightening at her sides. "She's sent you here, hasn't she? To stop me from leaving. Or interfering." Lowri's eyes widen. "It's Eli, isn't it? Is Caden there too? Are they fighting the watch?"

Brielle opens her mouth and then frowns. "I'm sorry."

"And Mother is working for the ruling council. She may as well be on their side." Lowri barks a humorless laugh. "She may as well be sinking my family's ships herself."

"Lowri, please—"

"You're going there, aren't you?" Lowri says, growing still. "It's the perfect opportunity to capture her. Perfect for the hunt, all that death, all that chaos—who would miss a single monstrous girl?"

Brielle bites back a harsh retort. It's everything she's thinking but not allowing herself to give voice to. Everything whirling inside her mind, about what the coven stands for, what *she* stands for, her place in her adoptive family, the lines she's unwilling to cross, even for her malefant. "I will look for Caden. I will keep him safe, I promise you. And Eli, whatever my anger over their abandonment of you. But this is our work, Lowri. The assignments our malefant takes on, *we* take on, without question."

Lowri closes her eyes. And her hair begins to shiver around her cheekbones. Lifting up around her. "I fought a fury in her trial. I trained. I've stayed obedient. I've followed every rule. . . . *Enough.* Maybe we *should* question."

"Lowri, don't—" Brielle gasps, eyes widening in fear. "If you disobey now, if you leave the coven house, she won't let you back, your training—"

"Is complete." Lowri's eyes whip open, chips of obsidian, and the room contracts inward. Brielle grabs for the wall to steady herself, shuddering at the pressure. "She's gone too far this time, Brielle. She won't hurt my family."

Lowri utters a single word.

"*Traversa.*"

And vanishes.

Brielle's breath whooshes from her lungs as the room steadies around her. Lowri is gone. She's disobeyed, she's . . .

"Calm down, take stock, then act," Brielle mutters quickly to herself, controlling her racing heart. She checks that her weapons are all in place, the blades fastened on her sash, at her waist, and at her ankle. Lowri cast a spell to go to where Caden is, she's sure of it. And now Brielle has a choice: protect Lowri, or hunt. She knows what she'll do—in fact, it isn't really a choice. It never has been. She'll side with her sister, fight for her, lose for her. The coven may have raised her, but Lowri is her home. And Lowri is right. Maybe she should have questioned more. She closes her eyes, says the same witch word as Lowri, and focuses on her as she tumbles through time and space.

When she lands on the deck of a ship, all around her is fire and death. Screams of the dying, roars of battle, and as she steps forward, gaining her bearings, there is Lowri a few feet away. Her white nightdress dances around her ankles, black hair shimmering down her back. Lowri turns around, finding a man of the watch swiftly loading a rifle, eyes trained on her. She smiles pityingly and twists her fingers, speaking under her breath. The man's rifle flies from his hands, overboard into the sea. Then he's lifted, arms outspread, a gasp in his throat. Up he rises, and Lowri raises her hand, watching as he shouts, panic filling his eyes—

She clenches her hand into a fist, and he plummets down onto the deck. His body hits the boards with a crack and Brielle winces, blood pounding in her ears, as he twitches. He does not get back up. Lowri steps over him, the black veins snaking over the backs of her hands, reaching up her wrists, disappearing under the sleeves of her nightdress.

"Lowri!" Brielle shouts. Lowri angles her face toward Brielle, tipping her chin, and Brielle's blood turns cold. So much like the malefant, and yet so much like . . . like the fury she destroyed. Like every malevolent creature Brielle has hunted, and killed. "Lowri, we'll find them, just remember who you are, don't let her win, don't burn out."

"They're here to kill my family! I can't just stand by and

watch, waiting in the shadows, being an obedient little witch, biding my time!"

Brielle swallows, reaching her side, stepping over limbs and rifles and flames. The sea around them is awash with ships, the scent of burning and blood and the metallic tang of magic crackling as the cloaking spell falters. Three fleets are engaged. The ship they're on is more or less drifting, abandoned, the water boiling up around them as though hungry to drag it down. She grips her sister's hand. This isn't safe. They need to leave; it isn't *safe*. "Do not become something *because* of her, Lowri."

Lowri hesitates, a flicker of something appearing in her eyes, something soft, almost breaking through the flint and rage. But before it does, her gaze snaps to the sea. Brielle's instincts scream at her, the instincts of a hunter. The ocean parts before them.

A tentacle, as wide as her waist, mottled and purple, launches from the deep—

Striking a main mast.

The sailors on board fire into the water, shouting, calling to one another, but a second tentacle joins the first, then a third, a fourth. . . .

"Skies . . ." Brielle gasps as she realizes what this is, what it means.

The ship is clutched in those tentacles like a toy, shaken and tipped, and the sailors begin sliding, unable to hold on, unable to stop—

They all, one by one, fall into the water.

None of them resurface.

"Lowri, we have to leave, go back to the coven, that's a . . ."

But Lowri is moving, hurrying to the other side of the

ship, and Brielle can hear it, a voice, faint over the sounds of the fire and the dying, a voice calling Lowri's name.

"Caden!" Lowri shouts, dodging debris and the fallen to barrel toward him. She climbs up on the railing, eyeing the ship where her brother stands, the grappling hook and the rope slung between them. Then she raises her hands, says a short, sharp word, and a witch wind lifts her up, then drops her on the deck of the other ship. Brielle follows, heart in her throat as she uses the same word, the same witch wind, sensing the darkness in her veins already spreading like flame. She's using too much, too fast. Traveling here, manipulating the elements . . . She reaches Lowri and Caden, this deck not like the other, clean and free of bodies and blood, and she knows it's Eli's shadow ship.

Lowri speaks hurriedly to Caden, who is grasping her shoulders, staring into her eyes. "It's an ambush, the watch and Mother—"

"She cast the spell," Brielle says, approaching them. Caden's eyes whip to hers.

"We realized," Caden says, crushing his sister to his chest. "What are you both doing here? Lowri, your eyes, your veins—you're using too much of your power."

"It's worth it," she says fiercely, staring up at him, and Brielle's heart aches with worry. "I'm not going back."

"But your training—"

"I'm ready. It's complete," she says. "After the trial, and beating the fury—"

"What trial?"

"Never mind." She shakes her head. "Just know I no longer need the coven, or Mother. Tell me what to do. Tell me what you need."

Caden frowns, a war playing out across his features. Brielle knows what he's thinking. He's only ever wanted to protect Lowri, but here, now, they *need* her. They've been ambushed, they're outmatched, and they need a witch. She puts aside her frustration with him, with all the Tresillians, for so recklessly using Lowri. For not seeing what she sees, a witch dancing too close to the edges of her power. "Stay hidden. But we need you to find Mira. We think the kraken has her, and she can't get loose." He looks at Brielle. "And Brielle, you must promise not to harm her, or capture her. Not here, not now. Please."

"I'll find her," Lowri says, already moving away from him. "Now go. Fight for Ennor."

Caden gives them both one final, reluctant look and sprints away, leaping for the next ship. Eli's shadow ship is deserted now; it's only them in this sea of war.

"You won't, will you? You won't hunt?" Lowri asks Brielle.

"I won't hunt Mira, no," Brielle says quietly, eyeing the tentacles as they pull the last of the ship beneath the waves. "You are more important than an assignment. But to hunt a kraken . . ."

Lowri's face splits into a grin, and Brielle realizes she can't remember the last time she saw her sister smile. Did Lowri really doubt her loyalty? Her love? There's never been anything to test it, she supposes. But she knows in her bones what matters more. Her sister. Her home. The one person who has always stood by her side. "I'll cast; you hunt. Let's at least remove one enemy for our family."

Lowri climbs from the deck to the helm, leaning out over the water. "It's time—long *past* time—that Mother learned what I am capable of."

The spell Lowri casts is like a web, falling over the water in a wide net and vanishing. A searching spell. She is gripping the rail with her black nails, eyes closed, her onyx hair whipping around her. Brielle watches as she feels along every loop and kink, every piece of the net she's cast across the sea. She watches as, at first, there are only human hearts. Beating with panic, sometimes rage, and more often still and silent. Lowri continues her search, feeling, seeking out the siren, the monstrous girl in the grip of the sea monster.

"There, Brielle—" She points. "The kraken lurks just over there."

Brielle grips Lowri's shoulder. "Do as your brother bids— stay hidden. Stay safe. No heroics." She climbs up onto the railing, her heart thudding with the wild beat of the hunt, and leaps into the ocean's waiting jaws.

CHAPTER THIRTY-EIGHT

I WRITHE IN THE WATER, FIGHTING THE KRAKEN's ever-tightening grip. It loosens a little, and I try to wriggle free, but the tentacle pulses, circling me, squeezing. I feel as if my bones will crack. I'm unable to even gasp, to *scream*—

Then a bright light flashes, and I sense the kraken curling back into itself, wounded or stunned. In that fleeting moment, I reach down, pull my blade free . . . and slice. The kraken roars, somewhere to my right, and I finally spring away.

I dart like an arrow, circling a dying ship, splintered wood floating above, a mast sinking into the water. . . . There are bodies everywhere. Bodies and flame and desperation. I claw my way up to the surface, fill my lungs, and search around me.

Chaos.

I can't tell which ships are ours, which are Renshaw's, and

which belong to the watch. Tentacles whip out of the water, grabbing at ships, ripping them apart. Rifle fire breaks across the shouts and screams, and I turn in a circle, looking for Eli, Caden, Agnes. . . .

That's when I see Lowri.

Hair in a black shroud all around her, ebony eyes, veins obsidian, crackling like dark lightning over her skin . . .

She stands like a figurehead at the bow of the ship, staring at me, and my breath hitches.

Then she grins, turning toward the rest of the fleet.

Lowri dressed in magic, in darkness, in *power* . . .

I take a deep, shuddering breath, realizing what this means. She's left the coven. She's defied her mother, her malefant.

She's chosen *us*.

She'll protect the others now as they fight. I grip the curved blade tighter in my fist. Their battle is above.

Mine is below.

There is a sudden gasp and I turn, scanning the waves to find my hunter, Brielle Tresillian, watching me. She's treading water, a small blade in her fist, keeping her distance from me. "I'm not here to hunt you. Not today. I'm here to protect Lowri."

"And the kraken?" I ask, the blade in my own fist gripped tight.

"A prize, if I were to hunt it . . ." She sucks in another breath, gaze wandering over the ships, to Lowri and then back to me. "It's very tempting. But I'm here for Lowri, not for glory. Can you defeat it?"

I grin, the answering flame in my heart burning brighter than ever. "Protect Lowri, help her keep our people safe, and leave the kraken to me. It's injured now, and I have a sense of its style of killing. I can defeat this monster. The sea is my battlefield. The ships are yours."

"So be it. Happy hunting," Brielle says with a small smile. "When we meet again, I will be your hunter once more. In another life, perhaps we would have been allies. Maybe even friends."

"Perhaps," I say, already preparing to dive. "Perhaps in this life still."

Then I leave the hunter on the surface. Just beneath the lip of the waves, I cast out, feeling for where the monster lurks, where the darkness is deepest. Happy hunting, indeed. I slip into the water and fly. Down, down, piercing the deep like the swift cut of a blade. Aiming for the heart of darkness, the maw of the kraken as it feeds. It senses me, a tentacle slithering out, slightly more sluggish than before from its wounds. I grit my teeth, then slash. The creature roils, a second tentacle darting out, and I kick up, willing it to give chase.

It does.

I wait on the surface for it to find me. Then, in a mass of ancient flesh, it emerges. I look up as it towers above me, this beast of myth, this huge monster that lurks in every sailor's nightmare.

It lunges—

But I'm faster.

I leap, sticking my blade into its side, pulling myself up. Then I twist, leaping back as I rip the blade free. I land on a tentacle, getting my feet under me, then run and jump, swift as I can, leaping from tentacle to tentacle. I have its full attention now. I can see its eyes, two orbs of hate and hunger. This beast is waiting for me to slip. Waiting for me to fall.

I feint to the right, a great tentacle coming down, and then dive straight for it, blade outstretched.

The blade cuts deep, skewering the kraken's right eye. There's a roar, tumultuous and terrible, and I hold on, feet braced, blade tearing down. Thick blood, hot and stinking, gushes from it.

Pain, a great howl of agony, echoes from the kraken, and a tentacle snakes out, smacking me in the back. Gasping, I tumble, crying out as I hit the sea, plunging down farther, tentacles wrapping round me, squeezing, pulling. . . .

I reach out, desperation driving me. I reach up to the clouds, to the rumbling thunder—

Lightning splits the sky, magic and searing light hitting the kraken. It jolts, convulsing, and its tentacles slacken. I slither down, stunned, looking up from the water at the kraken, a blot of darkness with the rippling surface all around it, inky blood leaking as it convulses again. It's stunned, slow as a slug, and I eye it carefully, treading water just out of reach. There are rocks below, sharp rocks that it can't see, but I can sense them. I know they're there. And if I can guide it, if I can somehow lead it down to that jagged rock . . .

I grip the blade in my fist, dancing toward it, taunting it, pulling its attention my way. It turns its head, blood spurting from one eye, but the other sees me.

That eye narrows to a slit.

It lunges again, but I'm ready.

Darting down, I swim for the seabed, for the vicious rocks waiting like fangs. The sea shifts and quakes behind me, a slow rumble, a roar reverberating from the monster, its war cry, its final push for the kill.

I slip and curve, stretching my body around the rocks,

and turn back to see the kraken plunging. It sees the rocks, the sharp tilt of them, but it can't change course, it's too late. The beast screeches, an unnatural sound of pure fear.

It slams into those vicious rocks, skewering itself through the middle, and falls still.

The kraken, the monster of myth and tide, monolith of a sea beast, terror of the deep, takes its last rattling gasp, and dies.

I close my eyes, and sink slowly down to the seabed. A ribbon of current carries me away from the jagged rocks, across the bone-pale sand, and I go with it. I'm depleted, nothing left to give. Not even enough to kick to the surface, to find the others. I spread my arms, the water warming me, curling over me. And in that place between sleep and wake, I allow myself a moment of rest in a place of shadow.

Then a hand I know, warm and strong, covers mine. I open my eyes, looking into his, eyes I would know anywhere, full of soft velvet and deepest midnight hues in this hushed darkness. For a heartbeat we watch each other and he pulls my body toward his, his arm circling the small of my back, pressing his chest to mine. He pulls me sideways, into the smoky dark.

We thump onto the deck of *Phantom*, and I lie on my side, panting. My whole body shakes, as though freezing, and a warm hand massages my back. "You're safe; you're alive."

I look up, finding Eli staring down at me, features pinched with exhaustion, streaming as I am with sea and salt, smoke shrouded, but whole.

"Eli," I croak. "Where's Agnes? Kai?"

He sits beside me, scrubbing his hands down his face, the signs of depletion all over his body. "They're fine. I've taken them back to Ennor. Agnes took a hit, but her healer is working on her."

I bolt upright, searching his face. "A bad hit? Where?"

"Her side," he says, looking over at me. "I promise you, it'll just be a nasty bruise tomorrow. Kai's with her."

"And the others? Eli, I saw Lowri, and Brielle—"

"I'm here. We're both here," Lowri says, her voice deeper than before, but strained.

I lean around Eli, finding the witch huddled against her sister, leaning against the main mast, her hair in her eyes. She lifts up a pale hand, showing me two black veins now tracking almost to her elbow. "I delved too deep. But you did it. You defeated the kraken."

I press my hand to my heart. "Thank you, Lowri, for what you did."

Her bloodless lips widen. "That lightning you called from the clouds was all you."

Eli stiffens at my side. "No—"

Grappling hooks thunk into the railing. Three of them, thick ropes streaming upward, thrown from another deck. Renshaw's shadow ship. I scramble to my feet as *Phantom* sways, tipping toward that mighty vessel.

Then she appears. Dark red hair, wild eyes, twin blades gripped in her fists. Renshaw chuckles, staring down at us, her prey.

Her captives.

CHAPTER
THIRTY-NINE

"LOOKS LIKE I'VE CAUGHT MY HAUL," RENSHAW says, beckoning more of her thugs over. "Get down there. I want the siren." Then her eyes stray to Lowri, flaring wide. "In fact, bring the witch too."

It's only then I realize that Eli is no longer at my side. He's . . . gone. Vanished into a pocket of night. I grit my teeth and stand, hiding the sway in my body, my sheer exhaustion as I plant my feet. My blade is lost somewhere deep in the ocean, skewered through the kraken's eye.

"You want me, Renshaw? Come down here and claim me yourself," I call up. "Or are you the coward everyone says you are?"

Her mouth tightens. "Say what you like, little monster. But you're not the first siren I've captured."

My heart stutters in my chest.

"That's right, work it out. What *other* siren have I known, Mira?"

No.

No, no, no . . .

"Yes," she hisses. "I dragged her from the ocean that day with my own two hands, and when she wouldn't agree to give me her blood, I took it. I gutted your mother, and I threw her back for you to find. And now I'll gut you too."

The deck tilts beneath me. "You . . . you . . ."

She leans forward, looking down at me. "Yes, Mira. I killed her. I killed your mother."

I gasp, doubling over. Blood pounds in my ears, the sea roars in my veins, and all I can see is her body, her broken body on the sand . . . and the red in the water that day. Red, so like blood, so like a siren's eyes . . . but not quite. It was the exact shade of Renshaw's hair.

"I saw you in the water that day. . . ." I whisper. The horror of it, of my mother's final moments, her act of defiance, slams into me. *"Murderer."*

I scramble across the deck for a blade, a weapon, anything to cut her with. I'm going to carve her up, piece by piece. I'm going to break every bone in her body until she *screams*—

Lightning cleaves the sky at her back, thunder rolling in a few heartbeats later. But I don't care. I don't care if it's me, if I damn them all, if a tempest comes and washes us clean away. She killed my mother.

"And now you've traded away every memory of your dear father. How does that feel, Mira? How does it feel to be utterly alone? You should have come with me that day on the quay. Maybe now you realize just who holds the power in these isles," she says with a laugh.

"My . . . my father?" I rasp. A shadow flits through my memories, a feeling of emptiness, the binding spell, the trade for the knowledge of the sirens in my head . . . my father. I've lost every piece of my father. How could I . . . how could I have forgotten?

"You don't remember him, do you? You don't remember how much you gave away for that binding spell." She huffs a laugh. "I hope it was worth it, embracing your siren side. Losing your entire family, forever."

Clouds bruise the sky overhead, flaring over us in shades of sullen gray. They rip apart, rain pelting the deck like sharp little knives, and all I feel is rage. Despair. A certainty that I have no control, that I don't even want it. This tempest, this storm, is everywhere, in my heart, my head, my soul. Let it rain.

Let the ocean burn.

I find a blade on the deck at last. Shaking with fury and grief, I turn, finding Renshaw still standing by the grappling ropes on her own deck as it looms over us. And I aim for her chest. "This is for my mother. For all of us." I lean back and—

A blade flies past my ear, skewering Renshaw in the gut. She gurgles, clutching at her middle as blood blooms like a scarlet cloud across her shirt.

Merryam steps up beside me, cool and calm. "That, dearest aunt, is for *me*."

Renshaw's eyes widen in surprise. She pulls a pistol from the holder at her waist, aims it at Merryam's head. "A rotten apple *never* turns sweet . . . and must be crushed."

But before she can pull the trigger, it's knocked from her hand. There's a boy holding her back, turning desperate eyes on Merryam.

Seth Renshaw.

"No, Mother. Not her. Not Mer." He hauls her back, and she stumbles and sways, pain and hate twisting her features as Caden and Joby surge forward, releasing the grappling hooks from *Phantom*. Eli appears beside me, doubling over, and I catch the gray wash of his skin. "Had to . . . get Lowri to safety. To Ennor. I'm sorry. The hunter helped, then went back to her coven. To placate the mal."

I drop the blade to the deck, placing a hand on his shoulder as he blows out breath after breath, the traversing taking its toll. Then I turn to find Merryam there, hands at her sides, eyes still fixed on where Seth stood only moments ago. A small sob escapes me, and she whips her gaze to mine.

"She—she killed my mother. All this time, I thought it was the ocean . . . but it was her."

Mer's features fracture and she lunges, wrapping me in a tight hug. "It's over, Mira. It's over." I cling to her, as Eli, grim featured, stumbles to the grappling hooks, helping Caden release the last of them.

Then we set sail for Ennor, under a constant cover of rain, the world crying with me.

When we return, shivering, exhausted, I move in a daze toward my room. Through the entrance hall, hand on the banister, pulling myself up, one step, two, three, four—

"Mira, wait." A hand comes down on mine.

"Eli, I can't, not now . . ."

He removes his hand, and I turn to face him. Dark circles ring his eyes; his clothes are torn and bloodied. He reaches up tentatively, brushing at my cheek.

Tears. I didn't realize I was still crying. He brushes away another tear, and I close my eyes. "She told me what she did to my mother. And the memories, my father . . . I can't remember him. I can't . . ." I gasp softly, and Eli's arms come around me. I drop my head to his shoulder, tremors running up and down my body. "It's too much, Eli. It's all too much."

He takes my hand, pulling me up a step, then another, and another, as we make our way through the castle, which seems to bend around us, shortening the distance. Suddenly we're outside a door, then we're in my bedroom, cocooned in the dark. His hands move up and down my spine in rhythmic sweeps, soothing me. I sob into his chest, the feel of his hands slowly calming my heart. He leads me to the bed, and I curl up on my side. His arm falls over me, his body curved around mine, and we both lie there, spent. I close my eyes and give in to the night within me. A small, distant part of me notes how it is to be with him. That he has become a constant, a place I need. Safe in his arms at last, I let oblivion take me.

When I wake, it's the next day, but twilight is already taking hold. The sky blazes through the window, the sea dipped in molten gold reflecting it. Eli has gone. I rise from my bed, still in the clothes I fought the kraken in, salt stained and worse. I hobble toward the window, watching the sun sink toward the sea. I'm ravenous. But before I can eat, it's time to bathe. I make my way to the bathroom, stiff and sore, and find a warm, bubbling bath awaiting me.

After sinking in and scrubbing the death from my body and hair, I choose Agnes's shirt from my wardrobe, tight-fitting breeches, and a fresh pair of socks and boots. I hesitate at the door. I don't wish to see anyone, not yet. My stomach grumbles, and I press my palm into my middle. As though the castle hears me, as though it understands—or perhaps it's Amma, back up to strength, protecting me as she protects Eli and his home—there's a rattle behind me. I turn and find platters on the low table before the fire, which roars to life in the grate. There's a glass of red wine, thick soup, and crusty rolls, steaming and fresh. I sniff, whispering a grateful thank-you into the silence, and collapse into the armchair before the fire and eat.

When I've had my fill, cake, sweet and soft and rich, appears, along with hot tea. I sit back, sipping and eating, watching the flames dance in the grate. When the knock comes at the door, I feel renewed, refreshed. I move to open it, turning the handle to find Eli, a tentative smile playing over his mouth. He looks over my shoulder at the fireplace and the finished meal and chuckles. "Amma likes you more than me, it seems. I had to go and hunt for food in the kitchens and give her a full report of the battle, then reassure her I'm definitely not dead."

"Jealous?"

"She always has her reasons." He rubs his hand over the back of his neck, looking down. "I just wanted to check on you, to see how you were, after . . ."

"Everything?" I supply.

"Yes."

"I'm all right," I say, unsure how to answer. "Safe, warm, clean, fed—"

"You're describing a horse."

I chuckle and catch his answering grin. Gentle, warm, tender—the side of himself he only shows to those he trusts and cares for.

"Is everyone safe and well? Agnes, Kai, Lowri . . ."

"They're alive. We lost two ships, but the watch and Renshaw lost more. Some lives were lost," he says quietly. "Brielle will be busy for now with her coven, taking stock. For now, we can take a breath."

I allow this reality to settle in. A partial victory at most, but not a defeat.

"Take me somewhere," I say on impulse. "Somewhere safe, where we can just . . . be. If Brielle isn't tracking me, we can take stock too. If you've recovered enough to traverse."

I wonder if he'll refuse. Make up some excuse, back away and leave whatever it is between us to cool. I wonder if I've misjudged this. If he's naturally like this with any girl. But his gaze locks with mine, steady and sure, and he nods. Then he extends his open hand toward me. "I've recovered enough for a short trip. I'll take you anywhere, Mira. Anywhere."

"Take me to see the last of the sunset." I place my hand in his, warmth flooding me at his touch, his closeness. Being with him suddenly seems so much more important now after the battle, the brush with death. And after knowing the true fate of my mother. "Before we do anything else, I just need a moment."

He pulls me toward him. His grin is gentle and soft, so different from the wild, rakish boy I first met. My blood stirs, and we fall into a fold of darkness.

We step out into a twilit world. There's a hazy landmass to our left that almost looks like a cloud bank. To the right, nothing but open sea and sky. The beach is powder soft and bleach white. My breath hitches as I sink into it, reaching down to sprinkle the tiny grains through my fingers. It reminds me of Rosevear. The sky and sea before us are on fire, golds and reds consuming the horizon. It's so beautiful, so still and peaceful, that I just sit for a moment, taking it all in. Eli hunkers down beside me, watching the world with me.

Our world.

I sigh as the sun dips farther, painting the sky in deeper shades of crimson. And when I look over at Eli, my stomach clenches pleasantly. He's lost in the horizon, his features calm and watchful, his skin tan and gleaming from our hours outside training and at sea. He's washed away the signs of battle, opting to wear a white shirt like mine and cut-off breeches. His feet are bare, digging into the soft sand, and as the breeze ruffles his hair, I catch his scent. Midnight and citrus. I inhale it, turning fully to him, and he glances at me, his eyes dark and depthless. The kind of eyes to fall into, to get lost in.

"The other day, when we were training," I begin, "when we traversed, it was through starlight. And I looked down at your hand in mine and I remembered, I thought . . ."

"The dream?"

I gasp. "How did you know?"

He chuckles and moves closer. His face, his mouth, is inches from mine. "Because I've had that dream too, Mira. For years. I didn't know it was you at first, your hand linked with mine. But when I recognized you, when I realized . . ." He takes my hand gently, turning it over so the bargain mark on my wrist is exposed. Our link, our unbreakable tie. "I couldn't let you go. I needed to know if it meant something to you too. If it made you feel less alone."

"I . . . Eli . . ." My heart leaps in my chest, and I move my hand to touch his cheek, his eyes burning into mine. That dream carried me through for so long. It gave me hope. That feeling of flying, of weightlessness, of freedom . . . it promised something more. A better world. "I've been searching for you for so long."

His mouth touches mine, and it's like the very world explodes around us. His touch, his scent, the feel of his lips. His fingers brush strands of my hair from my face, his kisses gentle, exploring my mouth, my jaw, then down to the base of my throat. I groan, tipping my chin up, twisting my fingers in his hair, needing him closer. Needing all of him.

"Shall we go back to Ennor?" Eli murmurs into my neck, kissing up to my ear. He breathes gently into the shell, that sensitive place that makes me unfurl with want. With desire.

"My bedroom," I say. He laughs softly, taking my hand in his, and pulls me up to standing. I brace my other hand on his chest, allowing myself another kiss, his mouth on mine.

He pulls back slightly, eyeing me in the growing night. "What happens when sea meets sky?"

"I don't know."

"Care to find out?" I grip his hand tightly as we fall into the deepest shadow, into nothing but stars and night.

CHAPTER FORTY

IT'S JUST LIKE MY DREAM. WE FLOAT THROUGH A sky full of stars, molten and glittering in the deepest, velvet dark. I am flying, soaring through a world that's suffused my dreams, that's followed me from night to day, always at the edges of my thoughts. And now . . . now I look down and his hand, Eli's hand, is holding mine. My heart thumps, spreading heat, blazing delicious heat, all through me.

When I look up, I see him.

I see Eli.

He smiles and my breath hitches—that mouth, those eyes, everything—and then we're falling. Slowly, drifting down, down through a seam of shadow. When I blink, we are in my room at Ennor Castle, his hand still wrapped around mine.

"The dream," I murmur.

"The dream," he agrees.

I step toward him, his hands drift to my waist, and we collide. His mouth is on mine, tasting of salt and stars, my hands against his chest, reaching up for his hair—

"Mira . . ." he whispers. "May I?"

I know what he's asking. I know what this means. And like I'm still falling, through stars and endless night, I snake my arms around the back of his neck, deepening our kiss. I've realized I was wrong, so wrong, to be afraid. I lost my mother, my father and all the memories of him. But I know now—it is better to love, to trust and open your heart, to risk losing it all, than to stay closed and cold and never love at all. And it's all because of our shared dream. A dream of flying. A dream of hope.

"Yes," I say with my whole, aching soul. "A thousand times, yes."

His hands move from my waist, down to my thighs, and he lifts me. His hands stay there, holding me up as I straddle him, my legs wrapped around him as he kisses me. I moan softly, body pressed against his, heat radiating between us. He steps forward, lowering me to the bed, and I pull him down toward me.

He pauses, watching me, brushing my hair gently away from my face. "You're beautiful."

My stomach flips, sparks dancing through my middle, and I run my fingers through his hair. Then I kiss him harder, deeper, drawing him down to me. I arch into him, his hand moving up my ribs, stroking gently. There is no turning back from this moment. Not after the dream, our shared dream, and finally realizing it was him, his hand in mine all along. The alchemy of that, how he infused my dreams, how he guided me away from nightmares . . . He's been here all along, just across the sea. And now—now it's us, here in this moment together.

"Give me more," I whisper.

We are a tangle of limbs and hearts; we are the dream I return to, night after night. We are two souls, cleaved and cut from the same whole. Two beings that have searched a lifetime to feel complete. We found each other in the stars, in the dusk of distant night. He is home. He is my anchor, my harbor, my equal. And now I am with him, I know what it is to love with my whole body.

"Mira, I have to tell you something," he begins hesitantly, slowly, when we have given ourselves to each other. "After I was born, I was cursed. Cursed never to be loved, except by someone as monstrous as me. Someone not all human. I was fated to be forever alone. But then, in that dream . . . I saw you. I saw your hand in mine, and I knew you existed. That maybe, maybe I wasn't destined to forever be cursed."

"Eli . . ." I murmur, looking up at him. I place my hands on his cheeks, drawing his mouth to mine. I kiss him, wanting him to feel it. To feel how I feel, this deep sense of home. Of knowing that he is the one, that our souls have cleaved together. Then I pull back, locking my gaze with his. "You've found me. You're not alone."

We spend the night together. When morning light filters into the room, I draw his arms around me. In that warm cocoon, that tangle of bedsheets and limbs, we sleep. And we dream together, of a sky filled with stars.

"We should get up. Get some food, find the others," Eli says the next day. Judging by the sunlight streaming through the gaps in the curtains, it's around midday. I stretch against him and he groans, burying his head in my neck. "Or we could stay here. . . ."

I laugh, wriggling away from him, and shuffle toward the bathroom. "Hopefully the castle agrees that we should get up and has run me a bath."

I smile as I shut the door, finding a steaming, sweetly scented bath waiting for me. I sink into it, inch by inch, feeling the ache in my limbs, and sigh. My skin is still tender from his touch, his kisses. And all I want to do is climb back under the covers with him.

But . . . the others. All that happened, Lowri delving deep into her magic, Agnes getting wounded . . . He's right. There was nothing we could do for the wounded last night; we all needed rest and peace to regroup. I reach for a cloth and soap, foaming it up. "I'll see you in the great hall in half an hour," I call through the door, and a moment later, I hear him retreat from my bedroom, off to his own bath, his own clean clothes.

I emerge wearing a clean shirt and cut-off breeches, my hair freshly braided. Walking to the great hall, I find Maggie outside, as though waiting for me. Her tail thumps on the ground as I scratch behind her ears, telling her she's a good girl. She yawns, exposing a full mouth of huge teeth, and follows me into the hall. Merryam and Caden are waiting. I assess them quickly, searching for injuries, but find them in good shape. A few cuts, a bandage around Caden's right arm, but otherwise only a bit bruised and battered. Caden grins at me, sitting back in his chair.

"Restful night?" he asks, and Merryam snorts, hiding it quickly by taking a sip of her drink.

I saunter over, take a chair opposite him, and reach for a bread roll. I wink at him, refusing to be ruffled by his teasing. "The sweetest of dreams."

Caden's eyes widen in surprise, then he bursts out laughing. Just then, Tanith wanders in, sits elegantly beside me, and leans over to murmur, "You look like you didn't get enough sleep."

I shake my head and roll my eyes as she titters, swirling her drink in a large goblet. Eli prowls in a few moments later and sits down at the head of the table. He reserves a smile just for me, features relaxing into the boy I know, the mask of the young lord slipping away. Then as his eyes travel around everyone gathered, noting the absences, all ease vanishes. "Lowri? Has anyone seen her?"

"Here," comes a voice from the doorway. As she walks in, I suppress a gasp. She looks like herself and yet . . . altered. Her skin is still the same delicate porcelain, hair a sleek black waterfall. But the veins at her wrists are all black. Usually they would fade back to a pale blue after spellwork, but the inky lines on her skin seem far too permanent. She pulls down her sleeves, hunching her shoulders, and scurries to the table. Then she catches us all watching her and manages a tentative smile. "I used a lot of power. It takes its toll." Then she squeals as a cat leaps seemingly from thin air, landing on the table beside her. "Nova!"

No, not a cat at all. The familiar purrs, huddling into her, allowing Lowri to scoop her up as she drapes herself contentedly over her shoulders like a shawl. Nova nuzzles into her, and she beams around the table. I swear, the darkness in her veins recedes with Nova's presence.

"You know you can't return to the coven, right?" Caden says. "Mother will be twitching."

"Let her," Lowri says, smiling at him. "I've been training in secret. I can't be sure, but I think I can control my power enough not to become a wraith. I realized after I beat the fury, like I told you about last night, I don't need her or the coven anymore."

Eli leans forward in his chair, clasping his hands on the table before him. My heart flutters, and I reach for some more bread, crumbling it in my fingers. "Stay then. Stay with us and join my circle, Lor. If you want to. You know Ennor is as much yours and Caden's as mine."

Lowri bites her lip and nods, a flush creeping over her skin. "Thank you. I'd love that. I haven't been with my true family in so long, other than Brielle. This place feels more like home than the coven ever did."

"Well, now that's settled . . . Amma? Would you mind?" Eli looks at Amma hovering in the doorway.

"It would be my pleasure," she says, smiling warmly at Lowri as more food begins filling the platters before us.

After lunch, we discuss the battle. Merryam is quiet at first as I describe the kraken, how I killed it. But then she sighs, saying what we've all been avoiding acknowledging. "Obviously we won, but Renshaw is still alive. Perhaps so injured that she is incapacitated for a time . . . but still. However, her fleet is scattered, her routes are for the taking, and Seth isn't commanding enough to draw her people together while she tends to her wounds."

"And how do you feel about that?" Caden asks delicately. We all know what he means. Seth stopped Renshaw from shooting at Merryam. He saved her life without a thought for his own. We believed him irredeemable, but after seeing that, I am not so sure, and I know Merryam feels the same.

"Conflicted," she says with a shrug. "I feel nothing for Renshaw. But the battle itself, and the outcome? Not victorious, not happy or sad, but . . . conflicted. Seth saved my life, and now he will surely face her wrath. I should hate him after his betrayal, but . . . I don't know. I suppose more than anything, it's opened up that old hurt, and I want to shake him afresh for all he put us through."

"Give it time," I say quietly, and hold out my hand to her. She takes it, squeezes my fingers, and nods, frowning. I look to Eli. "Have you heard how Agnes is?"

"Not yet, but Joby is on the way there. He took *Phantom* this morning with a skeleton crew and supplies for Rosevear. I caught up with him just before he left."

I shoot him a grateful smile. "Thank you."

"But circling back to the most *important* matter for discussion . . . is anyone going to say it, or should I?" Caden says, pointing between the two of us. "This is new."

I blush, staring down at the table, then over to the window. Now that we've claimed each other, I want it to just be between us. Just for us, and no one else. Growing up on Rosevear in each other's pockets, it was hard to keep any sort of secret, or keep anything for just myself. And finding Eli, giving my heart, feels too integral to my being to discuss glibly over lunch.

"Caden," Eli says in warning.

Tanith folds her arms with a smirk. "No, carry on. I'm enjoying this."

Eli runs a hand down his face, glancing at me as I bite my lip, then back at Caden. "You'll get used to it."

I blush even harder. "*Anyway* . . . we need to regroup. Plan for the watch's retaliation. Caden?"

"Yes, yes," he says, bracing his hands behind his head and grinning. "We should absolutely move on and discuss strategy."

"Ignore my brother," Lowri says, rolling her eyes.

"Mira's right though," Merryam says, biting the tines of her fork before setting it down. "Renshaw and the watch's grip on the isles is buckling. Renshaw will likely not risk her own fleet so soon. But the watch is still present, still a threat. We need a plan, and we need to send spies."

"Already done," Eli says. "But, Mer, I need you with Joby as soon as he returns from Rosevear. Caden, you'll train the crews for close combat on land. Also, Mer, a report on our ships, any damage sustained, any repairs we need to undertake. And, Lowri . . ."

"Yes?"

"I need you to tell me anything you can about the coven and its involvement in this matter."

"Well, that's just it," she says, stroking Nova's head. "Brielle may be Mira's hunter, but as we know, the assignment came from an unexpected place." She glances at me and continues. "The ruling council wants you very badly, Mira. They want you alive. That's why Brielle is being so careful. They want you captured unharmed and brought to them, and I don't know why."

I turn cold hearing this again. "All right. So the watch still wants to tighten its hold on the isles—we can be sure of that after the battle. The threat remains over Rosevear if they don't hand me over. I'm still the main target, and the ruling council is doing everything to guarantee my capture."

I pinch the bridge of my nose, then push back my chair. It always comes back to this. Back to me. "I need to train.

Alone," I say to no one before turning on my heel and heading for the door. There is much to consider, but right now I need the sea. And I know, if I turn, if I stop and look back, whose eyes will be on me.

CHAPTER
FORTY-ONE

BRIELLE SITS THROUGH THE MEETING OF THE hunters, a hand on the blade strapped at her waist. It's not that she dislikes her fellow hunters or distrusts them—she's just distracted. Distracted by the ultimatum issued by the malefant and now, now . . . She swallows, dread filling her stomach. She's distracted by Lowri's absence.

She couldn't keep it together this morning, not when the whispers whipped through the coven about what Lowri had done, when Brielle knew the truth. Brielle knew how Lowri had dug so deep and given so much in the battle. And now she had been cast out, forever banished from the coven, and Brielle hopes desperately that Lowri has indeed mastered herself enough to contain the witchery in her blood. Brielle sniffs, just falling short of actually gripping the blade handle her fingers hover over. Anything to anchor her, to bring her comfort in this sea of a coven, which she must now navigate alone.

Looking around at the hunters at the table, she meets steely gazes, cold stares. They are hardened, the hunters of Coven Septern. Trained to be ruthless, to survive. There is little room for warmth or kindness. She doesn't blame them, not really. But if it weren't for Lowri, she would only have had her mother's brutal love to mark in her memories, in her soul, and the malefant's cool interest in the skills she possessed, that perhaps wasn't really love at all.

". . . and of course, Brielle will be reassigned soon." Brielle jerks her head in the direction of the head hunter, Lessifur. Her dark brown skin gleams as she thrusts her chin up, pointing at Brielle across the table. "The capture is days away. Isn't that right?"

"Yes," Brielle murmurs, reaching for the tumbler of water before her, her throat suddenly dry as dust. "Mere days. She trusts me enough to let her guard down. To allow me to get close, as planned."

Lessifur fixes her with an assessing stare, and Brielle raises her eyes, meeting the challenge there. Lessifur nods, satisfied, and moves on to the next hunter. Brielle sags internally, taking a small sip of her water. She hides the tremor in her fingers as she places the tumbler firmly on the table, sitting back in her chair with a predator's grace. Her mind is a swirling tempest, fractured by thoughts of Lowri, of where she's gone, of the statement she is making. Defection. That's what the witches call it. She will never be allowed into this coven—nor any other—ever again.

After the meeting, more training. But her heart isn't in it, distracted as she is, and she earns several bruises and a sharp reprimand that hurts more than the inflicted wounds.

Dragging herself to the bathing rooms, she hears a male voice. A distinct, nasal voice that makes bile rise in her throat. As she turns the corner into the entrance hall, there he stands. Captain Spencer Leggan. His face a mask, as always, of unerring politeness, his uniform pressed and spotless, his shoulders back, hands clasped at his back. The only indication of the person beneath, the cold, hard monster Brielle knows him to be now, is the slight sneer at the corner of his mouth.

"Brielle," he says, turning from the witch who greeted him, who is already hurrying to the mal's office to announce his presence. "What an unexpected pleasure."

"Oh, cut the polished crap, Spence," Brielle says with a sigh. "I'm not in the mood. We both know I'm the last person you wanted to run into here."

He chuckles. "You haven't changed a bit. How refreshing. Tell me, how goes your assignment? The little monster hard to catch, is she?"

"None of your business."

"Actually, it is very *much* my business," he says, eyes flashing that shale gray, that hard, unrelenting hue, a window to who he is inside. "After the Far Isles went so spectacularly well, I was stationed in the Fortunate Isles. And Mira Boscawen is causing me more than a little difficulty."

"You want her out of the way so you can bring the isles to heel, suffocate another set of people into miserable subservience, and—"

"You don't get it, do you?" he cuts in softly, shaking his head. "Still, after all this time, you don't see the truth."

Brielle grits her teeth. "All I see is a bully."

He leans toward her, speaking in short, sharp syllables.

"The Fortunate Isles are mine. Not Mira's or House Tresillian's. Mine. As the head of the watch on those isles,
appointed by the ruling council itself, I will bring order.
Control. And *prosperity* for Arnhem. Do you think it's right,
what Mira's little community of thieves and wreckers gets up
to each winter? Luring ships in to pillage and plunder them?
Do you?" He straightens, sniffing. "I will raze Rosevear to
the ground. There will be nothing left, and we will rub the
name from our history books, from our maps. Trade will be
plentiful and unhindered between the Arnhem ports and the
Leicenan capital, and I will be lauded. I'll have my pick of
future posts."

"That island *is* part of Arnhem though. Have you ever
considered that? How they starve each winter, how they're
desperate? Have you ever considered that they may need
help, not erasing?"

"You can't help people like that." He snorts, suppressing
a laugh. "Brielle, you are funny sometimes. I had forgotten.
How fond you were of those people on the Far Isles . . ."

"Where's your humanity?" Brielle shudders, really looking at him. She can't remember how she ever loved the
serious set to his features, the blond hair that she had once
imagined glowed like threads of sunlight, the passion. Now
all she sees is cruelty. A lack of humanity, an excess of self-
interest. And all she feels are stirrings of bitter hate.

"I uphold the law," he says coldly. "The law set by the
ruling council, the law we *all* must obey. You know, the
ruling council has allowed these covens to exist as they are
for so long. . . ." He looks around. "But magic in any form is
an abomination, Brielle. It breeds greed. It breeds monsters."

"*You* are the monster—" she begins, but then she sees

the witch hurrying back, beckoning the captain. She smiles, inclining her head. "A pleasure, *as always*."

Captain Spencer eyes her. "Shame. We'll be needing hunters in the watch with your capabilities. Keeping Arnhem safe, allowing it to thrive and flourish, to become mighty. But with your opinions and sensibilities . . ." He tuts, turning from her, and follows the witch toward the malefant's office. "So much promise, wasted."

Brielle is left with a world of feeling, of anger and nowhere to throw it. She paces the entrance hall before a snarl rips from her throat and she leaves the coven, choosing to beat the pavements of Highborn with her boots. If what Captain Spencer says is true, then Rosevear will soon be no more. And now Lowri is there on the Fortunate Isles as well.

Another group of isles. Another people, suffering. And yet again, she will have to stand back. Coven Septern will never interfere in the watch's plans, never risk losing the favor of the ruling council. It leaves a bitter taste on her tongue. It leaves her questioning everything once more. Is her coven truly staying neutral if it stands back and watches this destruction? She isn't sure anymore.

She isn't sure of anything.

CHAPTER
FORTY-TWO

MIRA.

Your island is surrounded.

Mira.

Mira.

I inhale sharply, bolting upright. Moonlight floods the bedroom, sheets tangled between me and Eli. I slip from the bed and the whole room tilts—

I slam to the ground, screams filling my ears.

"What is it? What is it?" Eli crouches beside me, lifting my face to his. I blink, hearing only screaming, crying, endless pain. My eyes snap to his.

"The sirens—they're warning me. I think it's Rosevear, you have to check, you have to go—" I can see nothing beyond the shores of Ennor, as though the map, the knowledge bound into me, has been shrouded. As though the witches have found a way to cloud my senses. I try searching for the thread of that siren voice, try to call back, but it's silent. As though that was the only message they could give before their senses were severed too. "The witches. They've done something, something terrible. . . ."

Eli moves faster than I thought possible, shrugging on a shirt, breeches, grabbing his blade. "Hang on," he says, before stepping into shadow.

I get to my feet, move to the window, then pace back, quickly dressing, getting ready, thoughts crowding in panicked, bleating circles in my mind—

Eli reappears, grim and wild-eyed. "The watch is attacking Rosevear. I've just seen Joby aboard *Phantom*; they're still offshore. Get ready to fight."

Then he braces himself, as though digging into the deeper well of his magic to traverse once again, and he's gone, ripped back into shadow. A moan tears from my chest as I tug on my boots, tying back my hair as I rush to the armory. Is it a trap? Or is this a punishment for ambushing Renshaw and her crew, for breaking her hold, for damaging the watch's ships? Then I realize. It's the full moon. It's been a month since the watch's warning, and Rosevear didn't turn me in. And now they're not just rounding people up. They're back to destroy my island for good.

Caden's already in the armory, suiting up. He frowns at me, his sweeping gaze running up and down my form. "Fighting leathers. At least four blades. Find Agnes on Rosevear and partner with her. Go through the steps, just like we practiced. And, Mira?"

"Yes?"

He grips my shoulders. "I like you. Don't die."

I press my forehead briefly to his. Then he turns to two of Eli's crew as they rush in, bleary-eyed, barking out orders to suit up. I change quickly, fixing two blades at my waist, two smaller ones on my arms, and try to calm my racing heart. I close my eyes, falling into that part of me that is one of the seven. That fearless, fierce heart of myself that looks on storms and doesn't flinch, never waivers. I grip my hands into fists, knowing this is the moment. We are balanced on a knife edge, Rosevear poised to fall.

When I open my eyes, I am ready.

Eli appears as Merryam runs in, already in her leathers, six blades strapped at her waist, thighs, and arms. She nods to me. "Ready to dance, Mira?"

"Oh, I'm so ready."

Eli holds out his hands to us, bracing himself once more to traverse, and we are swept away on a wave of dark.

He drops us on the cliff top, on the other side of the healer's cottage. Every home is aflame, the scent of smoke and ash swirling in noxious clouds around us. I turn to him, fixing him with a look, taking in every inch of him. He squeezes my fingers and I feel the tremor in them, the toll the traversing is already taking after so much recent use of his power. We say nothing—there are no words for moments like this—but he leans in and kisses me fiercely. Then, in a blink, he's gone.

Merryam draws twin blades, circling them in her fingers. "Eli will start pulling the children to Ennor first. Good hunting, Mira. Make the watch pay for this."

I draw a single blade, just like the one I lost to the kraken, the curved obsidian winking in the night. I feel the rage already burning. A storm crackles overhead, and I feel it inside me, every spark of lightning, every heavy cloud. I don't know what I can do with it yet. I don't know if it will answer to me, as it did to my mother. But I called it here, this storm, called it to me with all the fury in my heart.

And now I ask it to unleash.

"Good hunting," I reply, a strange coolness sweeping over me from that burning rage in my center. "No prisoners, no mercy."

Bursting from the cliff top, we hurtle toward three members of the watch holding torches. I slash, feeling muscle, scraping bone, and leave two at my feet. Merryam takes the third. A gurgled cry in his throat, and the blood of all three drenches the torches as they drop. The torches hiss as they're extinguished, leaving a copper tang in the air, and I'm already leaping over the bodies, my dark blade ravenous for its next prey.

I find two men of the watch wrestling a woman to the ground. I whip a blade across one neck, pulling back his arm with a feral twist until it snaps. Baring my teeth at the other, I kick him to the ground. Bracing him there, shoving him into the matted heather and gorse, I see the white in his eyes as I hand my blade to the woman. It's the mother with the children in the cottage beside mine, Rowena, a woman I've known my whole life.

Her whimpering ceases as she rises to her full height, and unleashing a wild battle cry, she grips the blade and plunges it into his stomach. When she wrenches it out, I release my hold on the man and turn to grip her tightly in my arms. Her whole body shakes as she slumps against me.

"Where are the children, Rowena?"

"Safe," she gasps, finding her feet as she pushes her hair from her face, meeting my gaze. There is iron there, and relief floods me. They have not beaten her spirit from her yet. "The young lord from the shadows, he took them."

I expel a relieved breath and press her fingers tight around the handle of the blade. "Find the other women. Tell them to get the fish-gutting knives and arm themselves. Eli will get you out when he can. Show no mercy. No prisoners, no survivors tonight."

She nods, hugging me fiercely again, and says, "Thank you." Then she disappears into the dark. I hope I see her back on Ennor. I hope she keeps that fire burning inside herself and survives the night.

Merryam grabs my arm, pointing to a girl with flame-colored hair looping a rope around a man's neck and pulling, with a roar twisting her lips.

"Agnes!" I scream, finding her features in the dark as I race for her, the man of the watch kicking, turning purple, the flickering flames illuminating his desperation, his terror. I punch a blade into his chest, ripping it out in a spray of red, and he slumps down.

Agnes looks at me, feral and blood streaked, and grimaces. "Kai reckons it's a company of at least fifty. I haven't seen him since . . . since—"

"We'll find him," I say, pulling her into me. "We'll find him."

She trembles in my arms, then takes a blade out of the holder on my left arm. "I didn't think to grab a blade when we ran. The bakery is burning. . . ."

Fire explodes from a cottage nearby, the heat so intense I shield my eyes, coughing. Agnes claws at my hand, tugging me away as my eyes water, the world awash in flame and smoke. She grips the blade in her fist, already darting for another man of the watch. He's trying to load a rifle, and as we reach him, she releases my hand to slash. But he's faster. Raising the rifle, he jabs her with the butt of it, hitting her in the chest, and she crumples. He pulls out a knife, gripping her hair, and in that moment, everything seems to slow. I watch in slow motion as he yanks her head back, as her eyes flare wide, as the knife arcs down. . . .

Suddenly he jerks, a long blade piercing his chest.

He stares at nothing, the knife dropping from his fingers, then collapses to the ground. Dead.

And behind him, behind him is our healer, all five feet of her, grim faced and furious, brown hair tumbling around her, down to her waist. I barrel into her, hugging her tight, then reach for Agnes, checking them both, checking they're all right—

The healer's hand catches my own, and she smiles. "I do not intend to leave my island, Mira. Give me another blade, girl."

I nod, handing her one with shaking fingers. She grips it fiercely, then presses a kiss into my forehead, then Agnes's.

"I brought you both into this world. I will not bury you as well. When you get the chance, you run. You hear me? This is not your last battle. This is not the end for you. We refused to hand you over. Don't let them take you." And with that, she nods to us both before hurtling down into the heart of the village, with a cry like the howl of a wolf.

A sob catches in Agnes's throat and she turns to me, sorrow and pain warring over her features. I see her painted in the flicker of burning light and darkness, in the razor-sharp lightning that forks the sky. She is darkness and light, fire and ice. Like all of us. "They mean to kill us all. They mean to leave no one and nothing behind. Our home . . ."

"The healer's right," I say, swallowing down my own pain, my own grief. "You have to survive this. *We* have to survive. Rosevear isn't just an island, it's our people. They can't kill our island if we've escaped their flames. Start rounding up anyone you can find. We need to retreat."

Agnes nods, blinking. "I'll start with the meeting house and work my way down."

"Good, good," I say. "I'll sweep behind you, help any survivors you find. We need to get to the cove, get into the gigs if we have to, pile in as many as we can, and leave these shores."

We set off at a run, ducking into shadows, chaos erupting all around as the watch flows through our island. We can't take them all. There are too many of them, too many. . . .

Agnes darts around the smoldering meeting house, searching for someone, *anyone* we can save. . . .

I open my mouth to call out that I've found a body on the ground—a man, someone with breath still fluttering in their lungs—when a stirring of wind to my left makes me pause—

And a fist pummels my face.

CHAPTER
FORTY-THREE

STARS EXPLODE BEHIND MY EYES. I LAND ON MY side, the whole world tilting and hazy. Then sharp, searing pain.

"Get up," the hunter grunts. "We can do this the easy way, or the hard way. But you're coming with me, creature. Don't make this difficult. They're all here for you. This ends with your capture. We have no choice in this."

Creature?

I turn to face Brielle towering over me. More lightning cracks, forking across the sky, a rumble of thunder swiftly after. Then the rain. It tumbles down, dousing the fire leaping between cottages, drenching us. Plumes of smoke, of misty ash, envelop us both, and the island fades into the background. It's just me and her. Me and my hunter, the witch who has plagued me, who plunged a blade into Eli's chest, who wants to hand me over to the ruling council—

I see nothing of Lowri's sister in this moment. She is a

hunter carrying out an assignment, a hunter working for her coven. I won't go with her. I won't make it easy for her.

Leaping to my feet, I extract my final blade, holding it close. It's short, wicked, designed to be thrown rather than for combat. But it's all I have. I spit on the ground, tasting copper blood, and grin at her.

"You really think the watch will stop when you capture me, hunter? You really think there is any honor in this night? They will burn everyone and everything." I catch a flicker of hesitation, a heartbeat's pause, and I laugh, wiping the blood from my chin, staining my fingertips. Then I look at her. "That the best you can do?"

She growls, taking up a fighting stance. Then charges. I duck, rolling to the side, the ground already slick from the storm. Thunder shakes the island again, and my breath catches as she stumbles, and misses. I land a swift kick to her lower back, scrambling away. If she gets hold of me, that's it. One word from her, one witch spell, and she'll use her magic to transport us. I'll be a captive of Coven Septern. Ready to be delivered to the ruling council, and my fate. And Rosevear will still burn.

Brielle whips round, eyes narrowed, and hisses. Faster than I can move, a tiny blade hits my arm. I scream, looking down. A trail of blood and steel. I hold the handle and rip it out with a nauseous gasp. Then I take aim, and fire it back, releasing a feral, wrathful cry along with it. It pierces her thigh, and she grunts.

My arm throbs, blood leaking through my leathers, but I raise my chin, wipe the rain from my eyes. The storm is crowded over us now, and I realize I have no control. Whatever course it takes, it's up to chance. "You want more, hunter? You want to bleed?"

"*Monster . . .*" she gasps, pulling the blade from her thigh. It clatters to the ground and she heaves once, twice, and looks at me. With satisfaction I realize it's the same thigh where I hit her before, on that islet when she ambushed me and Eli. She winces, but stands, drawing herself to her full height as she squares up to me. "I am bound to my coven, and I *must* bring you back. So it's the hard way, then."

I brace myself. I know I cannot win. But her assignment isn't to kill. And I can make this hard for her. I can land a few kicks, dance around her until I'm spent. She'll capture me—she's strong and swift and lethal—but I won't go down without a fight. I can land a few blows to that pretty, hardened face. And if I aim for her thigh . . . maybe she'll never hunt again.

She moves to leap, but her footsteps stutter. Eyes widening, mouth dropping open. She whispers a single word. A name. "Lowri."

I turn and freeze.

The witch is surrounded by the watch, among the burning cottages, the night illuminated in flashes of flame as the islanders fight or flee around us. Power twirls around her in ribbons, just like on the ship. It's as though she's weaving ribbons of light. Her eyes are jet-black, veins darkening up to her throat. I cover my mouth. It's ghastly and tremendous, magnificent and horrific to witness all at once.

She's using too much, and she's only one witch, one person. . . .

"She'll burn out," Brielle says.

Lowri holds up her right arm and clenches it into a fist. My heart stops as her mouth forms a single word—that I cannot hear over the sounds of the storm.

Ribbons of light and power whip out, striking their targets. Five men of the watch fall to the ground. She cackles, as black veins snake up her cheekbones. . . .

"She can't handle that much power," Brielle yells to me. "She'll die. Lowri, *no*—"

Lowri turns, as though catching the hunter's words. She looks past us, to the cottages scattered nearby. I follow her gaze, and I see what she sees. A loaded rifle, a scarlet jacket. A man taking aim. At Brielle.

Brielle stills, horror freezing her features, knowing what will happen, knowing what Lowri will do, that she would do anything to save her sister—

A crack.

Lowri moves to shield Brielle. She is faster than sound. Faster than light. The bullet thuds into her chest.

In slow motion, Lowri falls.

Brielle catches her sister before she hits the ground. I heave, breathing wildly, racing for them. I'm in reach of the man who did this to her. I fling my last blade, the killing blade, and it thuds into his throat.

Then I kneel in the rain and mud, pressing my hands to Lowri's chest, to the power and blood leaking from there, so like that moment with Eli, who was so close to death—

"Eli!" I scream into the night. *"Eli!"*

Suddenly, Eli is there beside us. He pulls Lowri into his arms, out of the hunter's, cradling her carefully, his face limned with pain and exhaustion and fear as his eyes meet mine for a heartbeat, and then he staggers away into shadow, traversing with her. Then it's just Brielle and me, alone in the center of chaos surrounding us.

The hunter kneels on the ground, rain falling all around. Staring at nothing. At everything. At the devastation wrought this night.

She turns to me, hair plastered to her cheeks, eyes desolate, empty, and offers me her blade. "I—I picked the wrong side. I've always been told, always thought . . . but I *am* on a side. And it's the wrong one. And now Lowri, my sister, the only . . . the only person I . . ."

I run a hand down my face, clearing the rain from my eyes. I want to sob. I want to howl. Rosevear, my home, my heart, has fallen. And all that's left, all that's here in this hollow place, is me.

And my hunter.

I offer her my hand. "It's not too late," I say. "Join us. Leave your coven. Help me save who we can."

She's fighting down a sob. Fighting back unimaginable, bone-deep sorrow as the world she knows crumbles to ash, exposing the harsh singular truth. The people in charge of our lives, the watch and the ruling council, are the real monsters. The people her coven works for.

Then she takes my hand and rises. "Together," she says.

I nod. "Together."

CHAPTER
FORTY-FOUR

WE SAVE WHO WE CAN, BUT IT'S STILL TOO FEW.
Eli reappears over and over, swaying and stumbling as he
nears burnout, the hunter cutting down any men of the
watch who come close as we rescue those who are left. But
more of the watch arrive on ships from Penscalo, overrun-
ning our island. As the sky lightens, rain still crashing all
around us, we know we have lost.

I drag my limbs through my village one final time, checking pulses, covering bodies as bile slicks my throat, a tight
knot of grief and fury writhing in my stomach. Eli appears
beside me in a slice of darkness, his face drawn and pale as
he throws out a hand, steadying himself against me. The
remaining buildings are burning; even the meeting house
smolders. A month ago, after the attack, there were still cottages standing. But now my island, my home, is ash and ruin.

"It's time."

I nod, ducking low to avoid rifle shot. Brielle looks

uncertain, unsure of whether she can accept a way out like this, but then she seems to steel herself, choosing to trust him, and thrusts out her hand. Eli closes his eyes for a moment, scraping the last of his strength together, the final fleeting glints of magic in his blood.

Then we step into shadow and spin through the dark. Landing with a thump, we're in the entrance hall of Ennor Castle. I sit on the floor, just sit there, and put my head in my hands. I'm too tired to cry. Too tired to do anything. This weariness is soul deep, something even sleep couldn't mend. The exhaustion of deep grief. For my island, my home, my people. Generations dead. Families huddled in this castle, stripped of everything. And still, it won't be enough for the watch, for the ruling council.

They will take and take until they have every isle under their control, or destroyed.

Eli collapses beside me, breathing heavily. The weight of near-burnout and failure pressing down on him. I put my hand in his again, our tether to each other. We have no words.

"Lowri?" the hunter asks, her voice a reedy rasp of wind. I look at her, this solid warrior of a witch, and see her cut and bloodied, bruised and shredded. She sways on her feet, blinking slowly. She's as exhausted as we are, just as defeated. "Take me to her, please. *Please.*"

"Tanith is working on her with my best apothecary. Second floor, third door of the east wing. Do not—" he begins, and sighs. "Help them save her if you can."

The hunter nods, rubbing a hand down her face, and sets off, using the banister to pull herself up the central staircase. Eli gestures to me and swallows. "I can't traverse anymore. I'm sorry. . . ."

I brace myself, then get to my feet, blood flowing once more from the wound the hunter dealt me. I sway, dizziness fracturing my vision, a tinny ringing in my ears. But I hold him as he staggers, helping him to stand, should he fall. "Don't say sorry, not ever. You're weakened because you fought for my island, my people. Don't ever apologize for that."

There's no way we'll make it up the stairs. So I half carry, half drag us both through the double doors to our left, into the great hall, and we collapse onto the sofas by the hearth.

Platters of bread and cheese and scones appear before us, along with tea and tumblers of something smoky and strong. I sigh deeply. Amma has prepared for this moment, wherever she is in Ennor Castle right now. Most likely with Tanith, nurturing Lowri, or seeing to the displaced families of Rosevear. Gratitude wells in my throat like a sob, eyes smarting as I take a steadying breath. Across from me, Eli cracks a smile, and I tremble. I lean forward, pour two fingers of the smoky drink into two tumblers, one for me, one for him. He reaches for his glass with shaking fingers, holding my eyes with his, and clinks his glass against mine.

"To Rosevear," he rasps.

"To Rosevear," I echo.

We down the drink, all honey and smoke and burning, and I cough, banging the tumbler on the table. Then I slump back, the warmth of the drink and the bone-deep tiredness sweeping me somewhere far away in my mind.

After we've eaten just enough bread and cheese to give us the energy to keep going, I check on Agnes and Kai an hour later and find them in the thick of sorting arrangements and care for our people. I leave Eli with Lowri, still unconscious and under the watch of the apothecary, Howden. The hunter is at her side.

Then I go down to the sea. I wade into the water, feeling it igniting within me, washing over my thighs, tugging me by the hand. I drift away from the shores of Ennor, carried on a soothing, steady current into the deep blue. It's healing, this world of peace and depth and quiet. It mends my battered soul. The salt tends to my wounds; the pull of the tide tends to my heart.

I fill my lungs, sipping on the briny breeze, and dive deep. The light on the seabed is mesmerizing. I lose myself in it, twirling my fingers through the pinks and greens of seaweed fronds. We have come so far, and yet they are herding us. Penning us in on Ennor, this one remaining island, until they can tear us apart. Stamp us out. Whenever I believe we have conquered our enemies, they multiply and shift, showing another side to themselves, united against us. And behind it all, lurking just out of sight, pulling all the strings of the watch, Renshaw, the witches and hunters, is the ruling council.

The watch's puppeteers, the people who made an alliance with Renshaw. The people who want me alive. Alive and in their control. I shudder, still not understanding this. Why they hunt me, why they sent a hunter to capture me.

I sigh deeply, bubbles streaming from my nose, and gaze up at the shimmering bowl of sun far above. I can feel them. The ships clustered around Penscalo. More still, anchored near Ennor. Not bothering to hide now, or cloak themselves from my sight with some witch spell. The watch is waiting for the perfect moment to strike, waiting to take us down.

And Rosevear—I blink, my tears melting into the sea—
Rosevear is a shell. An empty, scarred husk. My island, my
home, is no more.

The ships surround our shores, poised to overwhelm us.
We have two choices. We can submit to the watch. I can
offer myself up, a sacrifice to keep us all safe. Or . . .

We fight for our islands. We don't wait until they're ready
to attack. We attack first, and we take out their stronghold.

We take out Penscalo and let them burn.

CHAPTER FORTY-FIVE

"DO YOU REALLY TRUST HER?" AGNES ASKS, STARing stubbornly at Brielle across the meeting table. We're all in the formal dining hall. Maggie is at my feet, tail thumping at dust motes in a slant of sunlight. Brielle keeps her eyes trained on the table as Agnes sits back, arms crossed. "She could be spying, gleaning information, then run straight back to that coven and bleat to the ruling council—"

"Lowri trusts her, so we do too," Eli says with a small smile. "She has left her coven. She fought for us alongside Mira on Rosevear."

Agnes pouts, glancing at Kai, who raises his eyebrows. I run my hand down my braid, eyeing the odd gathering around the table. The inner circle has widened. Caden, Merryam, Joby, and Pearl sit on one side. Then on my right there's Bryn, quietly chewing on the end of a pipe, Brielle, Eli, Tanith, and Feock. Agnes and Kai sit across from me, making us twelve. With Lowri, we number thirteen.

Thirteen standing against the ruling council and its watch. Monsters, witches, islanders, smugglers, wreckers . . . and yet we all stand as one. Committed to beating back the watch and reclaiming the Fortunate Isles.

"In the Far Isles, the watch used the same tactics," Brielle offers.

"Also led by Captain Spencer Leggan?" Merryam asks.

Brielle flinches at the name and nods slowly. "I was there. I was there before it fell, and I've visited since. It's a place of ghosts now. I would not wish their fate on anyone."

Agnes hisses. "This is history repeating. And when the ruling council has us in their grip, what then? Is there even a future for us?"

We all grow silent, contemplating this. The Fortunate Isles, a place of ghosts. A place where we no longer exist, where Rosevear exists only as a tumble of rock and rubble.

I swallow. "We have to fight, and be smart about this." I look around at them all, these people from my past, my present, and—I hope—my future. "If we take out Penscalo, we cut the watch off at the knees. We ruin its supply line into the isles, take out its prison, its stronghold . . . and that sends a message to the ruling council."

Caden's eyes gleam. "I like your thinking."

"I'll stay on Ennor, with Lowri, and with Amma, in case Coven Septern decides to weaken the wards again while you're all distracted," Tanith says. "But I agree with the siren."

I nod to her gratefully.

"Where Mira goes, I go," Agnes says quietly. I hold my hand out to her, brushing her fingers with mine. "But if you do anything self-sacrificing, if you pull any of *that* kind of—"

I hold up my hands and grin. "Wouldn't dare."

"All right then," Kai says. "Rosevear is with you."

"As is Penrith," says Feock.

"And Ennor," adds Eli. My gaze locks with his, and he winks. "Let's make some good trouble."

"The best kind," agrees Caden.

"Indeed," Merryam says.

"If you're even *considering* leaving me behind on this one . . ." Pearl begins.

We all laugh, and Caden says, "Wouldn't dream of it, little ghost. If everyone agrees, we should discuss Pearl's aptitude with poisons. . . ."

Lowri's veins are flourishes of ink, twisting back and forth under her alabaster skin. Brielle is at her side once more, monitoring every breath, every twitch. The witch sleeps, a forced slumber from an apothecary-made brew.

"She should be healing by now," Tanith murmurs.

"But she's not," Eli finishes. It's not often I see him lose his composure, or seem uncertain. But now I have a glimpse of that abandoned young lord, the boy who was suddenly left on an island. Left to grow up as the head of a family, utterly vulnerable, alone save for Amma and Caden . . . and not having a clue what to do.

"Is there anything witch made? A spell, or a charm, or . . . ?" I ask, watching Brielle's shoulders heave, then sag. I made my peace with her quickly, seeing how devoted she is to her sister, knowing the risk she took by turning her back on her coven. It was barely a decision for her; it was instinct, choosing her sister over them. If they find her, she's dead. They wouldn't let her live with all the knowledge she holds about the inner workings of Coven Septern.

Tanith shakes her head. "Not that I can find. The Tresillian witches left a lot behind, but none of their cures are working. She needs something more. Something else. Her magic is leaking out, and not even . . ." She darts a glance at me and winces. "Not even creature blood is strengthening her. There's nothing in the siren book you took from the coven either, Mira. I don't believe anything in our world can help her now, but luck and patience."

I look at Eli. "You should tell Caden to stop training the crews. He needs to be here with her, in case. . . ."

Eli's eyes fall on mine, sorrow pinching the corners. I can't finish the sentence. I can't imagine a life for Caden—so full of sunshine, quips, boundless energy—in which he loses his sister. But this is our reality. This is war and we won't all survive, unless we find a solution soon. Eli squeezes my fingers, thanking Tanith with a nod. "You're right. His place is here."

That night, we lie, limbs entwined, my mouth swollen from his soft kisses, bodies tired and spent. He moves closer to me, running his fingers over my brow. "Mira, what if I told you . . . I've found a way? Something that could change everything."

"Tell me."

"You know that my father left a letter for me that Amma shared, about our magic, and the necklace?" I nod, silently bidding him to continue. "This traversing, this stepping between worlds . . . he said that worlds are layered on top of one another, and that you need something from a world in order to step into it. Well . . . I tried to, just before what happened on Rosevear."

My heart thumps in my chest. "And?"

"I think it's better if I show you."

I sit up as he reaches for the necklace, holding it in his fist. He looks at me, his face cast in silver light and shadow from the moon outside, nearly full now, as though she is spilling liquid in a path across the sea through the window.

Eli rises, pulling on his breeches, and I sit up as he steps across the room. "I imagined a world like this necklace. I pictured my father and thought of him wearing this necklace. And then I imagined carving a doorway between those two points. This necklace, and his world."

He turns from me, staring at the space between the bed and the door. And in that slip of shadow, an opening appears. At first there is only smoke and stars and midnight, the world we spin through when Eli traverses in our world. Then it . . . ripples. Realigning. At first there is a manor house surrounded by wild, frost-tipped moorland, then it ripples again and beyond is a dense, dark woodland. The scent of loam and pine gusts from the opening, a doorway, and I gasp softly, stepping from the bed. Eli shakes, and I notice the pinpricks of sweat at his hairline, the flush to his skin. "Don't . . . Eli, be careful . . ."

The doorway ripples again, changing back to smoke and stars, before disappearing completely. Eli gasps and doubles over, breathing deeply. "That . . . I believe that is my father's world."

I bring my hand to my mouth, staring at that slip of shadow that was something else, something other, only heartbeats ago. . . .

Another world.

A whole other world.

"You did it."

"I did it."

We say nothing for a moment as he collects himself, then sits on the edge of the bed. The necklace chain trickles through his fingers like water, glinting in the silver light as he places it on the bed next to him. I sit down beside him, this boy who has just done the unimaginable, who may be able to step between worlds. "This is beyond anything, Eli. This is new magic. I don't think the witches can even do this, and no creature—"

"I wonder if I can find something in that world to help Lowri. What if my father found something when he left to get help for my mother? What if he found something that could heal any witch, or maybe even just the Tresillian witches? If I could locate him, if I could take Lowri to him, maybe I could save her. That's why he went back—to save my mother. I have to believe he found something, a way to help her, but couldn't return."

I close my fingers around his hand. "You have to find help for her."

"Not until Ennor is safe. Mira, he put something in the letter I didn't understand until very recently, and I think it's connected to you." He hesitates. "He says the ruling council are conquerors. That they mean to use magic to conquer."

I frown. "The ruling council? I don't understand."

"Nor did I, for a long time. Then with Brielle sent to *capture* you and not to drain you, I began to wonder."

Chills run down my spine. "You think they want to use me in some other way, to use my magic. . . ."

"Yes." Eli says. "And I never wondered before why the

covens had to give some of the blood they collect to the ruling council, like a tax. I thought it was about control, profiteering off our work, but now I think I'm beginning to understand. With the factories in the north, the buying up of silver, the rifles . . ." He holds me closer. "I have to know. I believe the only way to protect you is to know the kind of enemy we face and what it is they're planning."

"You think they'll send another hunter?"

"Yes." He eyes me carefully. "That's why I must ensure Ennor is safe first, for all of you. Amma and Tanith can protect the island to a certain extent, buy us some time. But I do not want them laying siege to our home. I cannot risk the innocent people who live here."

I blow out a breath, the plan that's been forming in our minds now firmly planted. "We take Penscalo, we secure the Fortunate Isles, then you leave. You leave with Lowri, you find your father's world, and you save her. Find out who you are, *what* you are. Find answers your father may have about the ruling council and their plans."

"And I'll come back for you," he says, turning my face to his, our gazes locking. "I'll always return. I'll find you on Rosevear, rebuilding with your people."

We sink back down on the bed and I nuzzle into his side. "Traverser. World walker. Bring me back a piece of another world," I whisper into his neck, dusting kisses there, moving up to his jawline, thinking about that doorway, the woodland, the impossible thing I've just witnessed. "But mostly . . . bring me back yourself."

CHAPTER
FORTY-SIX

UNDER A CLOAK OF PURE NIGHT, WE READY FOR a reckoning. I sail aboard *Phantom*, Agnes at my side, a blade strapped at my waist. Just as it should be for the final take-down. The watch took my home and killed my father, and I still cannot find my memories of him. They twist away from me still, since I made the bargain with the witches. In a way, the watch took the memories from me as well, forcing me to make that impossible trade and to lose those precious, irreplaceable jewels.

We land at the old quay on Penscalo in a drift of mist and silence. I glance around at this crew—the seven I swam out to wrecks with, and the crew of *Phantom*. Each of them has a place in my heart. And each of them is ready to reclaim what is ours. The islands. Home.

"We'll move straight for the prison. Kill any men of the watch on sight," I say. "Kai's our anchor. Everyone else, fall into your roles. We need to warn the people of Penscalo to stay away from the streets near the prison, and if they want to take up arms and join the uprising, they are welcome."

Kai nods to me, strong and serious, and I nod back. I shutter off that part of me that worries if I'll see him again. If we'll make it back. I can't think like that, not in a storm, and not now. I grip Agnes's hand, squeeze her fingers, then release it before leaping for the quay.

The town is slumbering in the hours before dawn, and we wend like ghosts through the streets. No one is about. No one dares break the watch's curfew. And as we get closer, I see the posters. Hangings. Five men, two women. I swallow, heart in my throat. All islanders, and they're to hang today.

I point out the posters to Kai, whose face sets in grim, harsh lines. He understands. My role in any wreck is to search for survivors. And these people, our people, islanders of Penscalo, *will* survive. The reign of the watch is ending, and it cannot claim any more lives.

We wait in the shadow of an alleyway close to the prison, listening for the signal. Merryam grips her blade beside me, the silver glinting in a dash of stray moonlight. We hear three cries. I take a breath, steeling myself, and follow Kai as he makes for the main door. It opens, revealing Eli framed there, and I grin at him, filing past. He silently indicates where the watch is, and we split into pairs, scattering. I'm with Agnes, and as we enter the main prison, I point to the staircase winding downward. Where the prisoners await sentencing. She nods, and we disappear together into darkness.

When I was last here, I was so afraid. Unsure, unnerved, unsteady. But now . . . now I am fury and rage and certainty. They've already taken everything. Now they will feel my wrath. I press my fingers to the bargain mark on the inside of my wrist, pulse like the thump of a war drum. I feel the power in my veins as my blood rushes through me, the answering spark that is all siren, and I grasp it. I mold it, twisting it into something I can hold. Something I can *throw*. Control isn't something I've mastered, but fury is. Fury is something I can hone, something I can craft into a weapon. I stand before the rows of locked doors, the thick wood, the old iron hinges, and picture the desperation, the hunger, the fear waiting beyond. It fuels the power within me. I nurture it, pouring in everything I have, then I hold out my hands, just as I practiced on the beach.

I unleash it.

The power blasts out of me, like lightning, like a whirl of raw storm, and the doors crack back, hinges shattering. I breathe hard, placing my hands on my thighs, taking in the destruction I've wrought. There's no more. That's all I can grasp, all I've been able to mold and unleash with the scant control I've taught myself. But it's enough, just, to free the people in this place. And when they begin creeping out, the prisoners, the islanders, a shamble of ragged limbs and wide eyes, a slow smile spreads across my face.

"You're free," Agnes says to them, stepping forward. "Get to the main door, go home, and *hide*. Tell your families to lay low, and if the watch comes calling, don't open up. Tell them the tide is turning."

I straighten, still trying to catch my breath, as though I've swum all night. It's one thing to summon a storm that's already in existence, quite another to create lightning with a spark from my own veins. They slink past me, these people, half-starved. Men, women, even some that are only just past being children. I nod to them and swallow down the pain at their angular faces, sharp cheekbones, hollow, staring eyes. We search through the cells, making sure everyone has escaped.

"Remember Bryn," Agnes says. "And your father . . ."

She doesn't say any more. We're both thinking it. How Bryn is not the same after his time here. How the seeping damp of the granite floor and walls, the meager food, the fear and uncertainty, haven't left him. He's a shadow of the leader he was. I grip my hands into fists. No more.

We hurry back up the stairs. The crew moves in packs, hunting down the men of the watch as they spring from their beds, cries in their throats soon stifled. I point up, up to the captain's office, and Agnes nods. We both want to find him. Captain Spencer Leggan. I move up the staircase on silent feet, Agnes just behind me. There's no one on the landing. I pull out my blade, knowing I have no power left to draw on. My heart thrums in my chest, ready for the fight as I open the door to his office, throwing it back.

Empty.

I sigh, taking a few steps inside. There's the chair I sat on as I begged him to spare my father and Bryn. There's his desk . . . his chair . . . the windows with a view over Penscalo. I turn in a circle, eyeing all the small tells of wealth, of power. The portraits on the walls, the clock ticking on the mantelpiece, the framed medals, and the glinting crystal decanters filled with smoky amber liquid. I want to burn it *all*.

"He's not on Penscalo, is he?" Agnes says quietly, picking up a framed miniature, then dropping it back down. "It's just the watch here. His minions."

"We'll get him, Agnes," I say. "Maybe not today, but we'll . . ."

I pause, listening. Then I motion to the door, and we both hide behind it. There are footsteps. Slow and muffled, but coming this way. A figure walks in, a boy, casting about in the dark before making his way to the desk. He moves toward a drawer, shuffling through papers, picking up then discarding one before rifling through the next.

Rage erupts inside me. I know those shoulders. I know that curling hair. Pressing my fingertips around the door handle, I twist and push the door closed. When he looks up, I'm there, bathed in shadow, blade glinting in a slant of moonlight at my side.

"Hello, Seth."

His eyes widen in horror, but before he can cry out, I've crossed the space between us and forced him to his knees, my blade kissing his throat. Agnes stalks toward us, a feral smile on her lips as I press the tip of my blade a little harder against the skin of his throat. He swallows, staring up at me and Agnes, and I can sense the wheels and cogs of his mind turning, readying to twist his way out. But there is no way out this time. Not for him.

The boy who tricked me, betrayed me, who broke my heart. I've waited for this moment. Waited for him to know fear, true fear, for him to beg for his life at the point of my blade.

"Give me one good reason why I shouldn't slit your throat," I hiss.

He blinks up at me, panic straining his features. "Because if you kill me now, they'll know you're in here. And they want you, Mira. They're coming for you."

CHAPTER
FORTY-SEVEN

"THEY'RE COMING FOR *ALL* OF YOU."

Silence permeates the office as I exchange a glance with Agnes. The song of battle erupts outside suddenly, and I resist the temptation to turn and thrust the curtains back to look out the window. The fight for Penscalo has begun.

"We already know they want to wipe us out," Agnes growls. "Old news, betrayer."

"I don't mean islanders," Seth says, his gaze flickering between us. "The ruling council is after creatures like her. Monsters with magic in their veins. *People* with magic. They aren't after what you think, they aren't—"

But he's cut off by more footsteps in the corridor outside. I drag Seth back behind the heavy curtains, keeping the point of my blade pressed to his throat in warning as Agnes moves around the desk to crouch at my side, flicking the curtain to conceal us. The footsteps stop, and the door creaks slowly open. My breath hitches as two sets of footsteps thud inside the room and we hear cleared throats, the scrape of chair legs.

They're settling in, as though unbothered by the chaos just downstairs and outside. As the sound of clashing metal and the pops and crackling of hungry fire echo through the office in waves, receding, then returning like the tide on the turn, I realize whoever is on the other side of this curtain cares little for the watch being slaughtered in this ambush.

"I trust this office is warded?" a man's voice rumbles.

"You have my word. None of them can break through that door while you're in here, and we'll have you on your way as soon as my men have cleared the route."

"Excellent, Leggan. As always."

"A drink, your grace?" There's a jostle of crystal and the slow glug of a drink being poured. A clink rings out in the quiet, and I stiffen. They're toasting. They're bloody toasting as though this is some kind of *victory*. Agnes's hand snakes out, clamping over my wrist. I bite my lip, focusing on that point of pain as her nails crease my skin, that sharp sting, until the sparks in my veins, clustering and fusing, begin to calm, to quiet. I blow out a silent breath and nod to her. But she keeps her hand right there, wrapped around my wrist.

"Any sign of the girl? Would have thought she'd be leading the charge."

"We believe she released the prisoners. My men will find her; she can't have gone far."

"Good, good." The man sighs, the chair creaking as though he has leaned back to lounge in it. "We need her, you know. When I pass the law, there will be resistance. All that magic, all that power. It should be ours. Not in the hands of those witches and apothecaries and those *creatures*.

They should be coming begging to us. I hope you're ready for the next stage. We'll need to show them some might."

"Always, your grace." The captain clears his throat. "And the . . . islanders, your grace?"

"Burn every island. Burn them all, for all I care. They've blocked the trade routes, damaged relations with Skylan and Leicena for too long. Just like the Far Isles—can't get a damn bolt of fabric from our ports to Leicena without an escort nowadays. Merchants don't like it. Not one bit."

"Right you are."

"Good man. What is this vintage? It's excellent."

"You gave it to me, after we established your rule on the Far Isles."

"Did I? Hmm. I clearly have good taste." The man chuckles, and my stomach twists.

"So you'll take the siren creature back to Highborn, your grace?"

"We have plans for her. The hunter at Coven Septern failed, so we'll have to take matters into our own hands. Can't trust a single one of those witches. Too tied up with House Tresillian. Bad blood. Bad, bad blood."

There's a discreet tap at the door and the men shift in their seats. I hear the sound of one set of footsteps crossing the room and a muffled conversation.

"Your grace, the route is secured. You can be safely on your way."

"Good stuff."

"Can I ask, your grace? What about Renshaw's crews? Her son?"

"She's useful for now. Couldn't care less about the boy—always sneaking around, that one. If you catch him red-handed, flog him and imprison him. Hang him along-side the wreckers if you must. Renshaw won't care, I'll wager. More concerned with keeping favor."

Seth stiffens beside me.

Their footsteps recede, the door clicks closed behind them, and I release a charged breath. Agnes thrusts back the curtain, narrowing her eyes at the two empty tumblers, sticky with residue, the crystal decanter swirling with amber liquid.

"Bastards," she mutters, stalking around the room like a caged cat. "Talking about us like we're nothing. Like we're something to be squashed under their boots."

I lower the point of my blade from Seth's throat. He blinks at me, then moves, shuffling over to the desk as well. "Now do you believe me?" he says bitterly, turning to us. "Mother thinks she's so clever, aligning herself with them, but she's just a pawn as well. We all are."

"Is that why you were in here? Going through the desk for information?" Agnes asks.

Seth shrugs. "If I'm to get away from them all, I need something I can hold over them. Blackmail them with. Just a threat, so they won't come looking for me when I go."

"So you're defecting? Truly?" I ask, narrowing my eyes. "Took you long enough."

"When she pointed the pistol at Mer on the ship, every-thing changed. She would have killed her, my cousin, her sister's daughter . . . and thought nothing of it. Thought nothing of her." He swallows. "You know how there's always a line, even if you're not wholly aware of it until it's crossed? Well, that was mine."

I think back to that moment, when she admitted to

murdering my mother. . . . She is a killer. Cold, calculating, inhuman. I don't trust Seth, and frankly, I never will. But I owe Merryam this much, to have the chance to speak with him and make her own choices. I've hated him as a storm ravages the land, but looking at him now, I realize it's not worth losing my own humanity by ending him. We're all pawns in a wider game.

"They want all the magic," I say bleakly, turning it over. I look down at my hands. This isn't about the Fortunate Isles. We're merely an inconvenience, a blot on the landscape. This is about power shifts, about money and control and the continent. I steel myself, looking at both of them. "I have to tell Eli. We have to tell . . . everyone."

"But why you, Mira?" Agnes says. "Why do they want you?"

"I don't know. Magic, I suppose, if that's what they prize above all else." I shake my head. "We should go. Get back to *Phantom*, get everyone out. Find the other crews, let this place burn. Let the people of Penscalo take back what's theirs."

"And me?" Seth says uncertainly. "Am I coming with you?"

I look at him, then at Agnes. "You heard them. They'll flog him if they catch him. Likely hang him after."

Agnes shrugs, feigning nonchalance. "Probably deserves it."

I raise my eyebrows at him and shrug as well. I know I'll take him to Mer. I've already decided. No one deserves to be left at the mercy of Captain Leggan. But the part of me that's still smarting over his actions in all this wishes to twist the knife a little deeper, just to see him suffer. "*Do* you deserve it?"

Seth's gaze shifts between us, and he crumples before my eyes. I realize I don't hold the same anger toward him anymore. He betrayed me. He used me. But I don't feel hatred. I no longer want to see him suffer.

What I feel for Seth is pity.

"We'll take you to Merryam," I say quietly. "You're her kin. It's for her to decide."

Seth's shoulders slump. "Thank you."

Agnes rolls her eyes, and I know what she's thinking. I'm too soft. We should leave him to the watch. But . . . there's been so much death already. So much hate. I can't have another soul on my conscience, even a Renshaw. And we have far bigger problems now.

We check both ways, slip out of the office, and disappear back down the staircase. Smoke billows up like a cloud, shouts and screams and chaos ripping through the prison. I cover my mouth, dashing after Agnes's red hair, and hope Seth keeps up. We take the same route out of the prison, back to the old quay, and find others on the way, bearing grins and ash streaks and the watch's blood on their clothes.

Merryam joins us as we walk the alleyways back through the town. "Good trouble?"

I point to Seth. "What do you think?"

Merryam chokes and swings her fist, punching him on the arm. "Ow," he says, scowling at her. "Was that necessary?"

"Are you going to run off to the watch?"

"No," he mutters, rubbing his arm. "I just ran *away* from them."

She swings her fist again, connecting with his jaw. "Mer! What the . . . ?"

"That's for ambushing us. For turning on us."

He rubs his jaw and spits blood on the ground. "I deserve that."

"You do."

"He's your problem now, Mer," I say as we round a corner past a tavern, still quiet before curfew has lifted. "I'm leaving it up to you to decide what to do with him."

She eyes him quietly, sorrow and anger and frustration mingling with something else. With love. With relief. "No promises I won't tip you overboard. But you can escape with us on *Phantom*. I'll decide what to do with you after that."

Seth shrugs, managing a small smile. "I would deserve to be tipped overboard. I'm . . . I'm sorry."

"I know," she says quietly, taking his arm. "Believe me, I know. But you're not off the hook just yet. I don't trust you to not break my heart again, cousin."

We reach the old quay, crews already climbing aboard their own boats and ships, setting sail, away from Penscalo. *Phantom* waits, Joby leaning on the railing, and when he catches sight of Seth, he rolls his eyes. But still, we all climb aboard. Eli and Caden are already there. Eli's eyes narrow as they slide over Seth, landing on Merryam, who raises her eyebrows, shrugging one shoulder. He purses his lips, looking away. A discussion for later. Eli trusts Mer enough to give her that grace.

I almost expect the watch to spring out. For Renshaw to appear, with her crew and her blades. My heart catches in my throat, looking beyond the old quay, to the town, to the plume of smoke from the prison at its heart. And I imagine the people coming out, seeing it burn, and taking back control of their island. With no stronghold, the watch is no more on Penscalo. The islanders here are liberated. Free. We cast off, the sail filling with the sea breeze, and as I lean on the railings, I see the first lick of red flames crowning the prison.

With a twin flame of victory burning in my heart, the watch's stronghold burns.

CHAPTER
FORTY-EIGHT

"THE WATCH IS ALREADY HEADING FOR ITS SHIPS. Leaving the isles," Eli says, coming to stand beside me. I lean into him, smelling ash and smoke. "Bryn, Feock, and Pearl, along with a few others, are staying behind to restore order with Penscalo's leaders. The next few days will be chaotic at best."

"But we did it."

"For now, yes. The islands are safe."

I release the breath I've been holding for so long, for months. Since the watch first swarmed the beach on Rose-vear, since they took my father and Bryn away. It still stings, piercing like a knife, that I can't capture my father's likeness in my mind. That I can't remember his face, his voice . . . anything real.

But I know I loved him. I know he would have been proud. No more curfews for the people of Penscalo. No more fear and retribution, no more hangings and floggings, no death on their shores. And no stronghold for the watch to rally and break our islands when we begin to rebuild. There is so much to do, so much to mend and grieve . . . but the tide has turned at last.

I turn to Eli, moving his jacket aside to snake my arms around his waist. I tilt my head up and kiss him, really kiss him. My blood heats, head dizzy and light as I sway into him, allowing this moment with him to consume me. His scent, his skin, everything about him is intoxicating. I soak up every heartbeat, knowing it could be the last for a while.

Knowing he has to leave.

I pull away, gazing up at him. His soot-dark eyelashes, his tan skin, his eyes, navy as the ocean. If I could, I would pull him into shadow and steal another night with him. "You have to go. To get back to Ennor, collect Lowri, and traverse. Find help, find your father." I swallow. "Save her. Then come back to me."

He groans, pressing his mouth against mine, moving along my jaw, to my eyes, my forehead, before finally wrapping me close in his arms. His warmth spreads all through me as he holds me against his body. I don't want to let him go. I don't.

But it's the only way.

"Remember, a piece of another world," I say, moving away to brush a tear from my face and smile at him. "Bring me something back. And if you have nothing . . . just return. Just come back alive and safe and whole."

His eyes darken, his knuckles brushing away my tears. "Mira, for you I would walk through flame," he says. "I'll bring you back a whole world in the palm of my hand."

I laugh, smiling through my tears, and nod. I can't say it

yet, the word that I feel. That fills me, consumes me with warmth and energy and light. But I feel it. I feel it in the very marrow of my bones. I feel it in my soul. This young lord, traverser, world walker . . . he is mine, and I am his. We are two beings in a world that would call us monstrous. And I will wait until the end of my days if I have to, for him to return to me.

I gather myself and turn to our crew. Eli spies Seth lurking at Merryam's shoulder and points to him. "You're Merryam's problem while I'm gone. Don't mess it up."

Merryam flushes, running at Eli and hug tackling him. He wraps her in a bear hug, whispering in her ear, telling her to take care, that he trusts her. Then he turns to Joby, clasping his fist, then Pearl to kiss her cheek, Kai to clap him on the shoulder. Agnes throws her arms around his neck, crying more than I am. I sniff, brushing away more tears, and turn to watch Penscalo drift away. I lean on the railings, watching the horizon as it blazes purple, pink, and scarlet. As the sun rises higher, and our islands are once again our own.

Eli's arms wrap around me, and we watch the waves for a few moments together. I tattoo this moment on my heart, print it in ink so I can carry it with me. It's time to rebuild, to rally our community. It's time for me to return to Rosevear.

"I have to go," he murmurs, pressing his lips to my throat. "Imagine this is just one long kiss, and when you turn around again, I'll be standing there. Waiting for you."

"Eli . . ." I breathe, the word cloying as it rises from my heart. I have to tell him I love him, before he crosses to another world, before we are parted. Suddenly I'm desperate to say the words, every doubt and hesitation swept away.

His arms drop from around me. And when I turn, that word like a pearl on my tongue, my heart all his—

He's gone.

I suppress a sob, remembering why he is doing this: for me, for us, and for Lowri. For our future. But there's still a part of me that wishes he had stayed. That he wasn't able to traverse, that he couldn't follow his father across worlds. Because what if the same thing happens to him, and he never returns?

Agnes pulls me into her arms and I fight back the tears. She strokes my hair, and I close my eyes, mentally pulling myself together. When I look up, Merryam is talking quietly with Seth, Kai is chatting with Joby, and Pearl is at the helm. I steady my gaze on Seth and shrug. "Third time's the charm, I guess."

"I promise I've learned. No more chasing something that doesn't exist. No more lies."

"We'll see," I say, folding my arms. Knowing what he's been chasing, what he'll never have . . . his mother's love. It softens me, despite myself. At least I knew that. "No pulling anything—"

A gunshot cracks.

Seth stutters forward, then stares down at his stomach. Blood blooms, fast and red, spilling out around him. He raises his head, eyes wide and confused, before tumbling to the deck.

"Seth!" Merryam screams, racing for him and pulling him into her arms, trying to hold her hands over the wound, blood everywhere, spilling scarlet, his features paling, drawn—

Witches appear. More and more of them, hunters as well,

and I fumble for Agnes's hand. I turn, searching for her, and find a witch with a blade at her throat. Her eyes are wide with fear, and I mouth her name as the witch whispers a word in her ear. . . .

And she screams.

I gasp, reaching for my blade, a hand clamping down on my wrist—

As I gaze up, a witch with bright blue eyes, with steely features, a witch I don't recognize, plants her hand on my forehead.

"*Inferna.*"

My mind roars with flame.

And I burn.

The last face I see, the last cruel, twisted features, is a man with pale hair and piercing eyes. He's staring at me with something sharper than triumph. I realize with horror that it's hunger as he says two words, "You're mine."

Then flame engulfs my mind.

The burning is endless.

Inferna.

That single whispered word.

A touch to the forehead, a witch's ice-blue eyes . . .

I burn.

And burn.

In a maze of fire, drowning in flame, I scream and scream, crying into the heat. But everywhere I turn, there is nothing, there is no one. Only me, trapped in a world that begins and ends with that one whispered word, with that witch, with those eyes . . .

Inferna.

This is what it means for the world to end. For the sky, the earth, the very air to be on fire.

This is what it means to burn.

Then, when I am sure that I am nothing, that they've erased who I am, what I am entirely, it ceases. I open my eyes, curling into a ball, cringing away from the faint light from a lamp.

"You're awake," says a voice, a boy's voice. Cool fingers touch my forehead; a glass is held at my lips. "Drink. It's water. It'll help."

I do, allowing a mouthful down my parched throat. My mouth feels blistered, as though I've been burned from the inside, but when I blink up at this boy, then down at my body, I find I am unchanged. Still in the clothes I wore when I stormed Penscalo, the clothes I wore when . . . when . . .

I push the glass away, water sloshing over the sides. "Where am I?"

The boy hesitates, then moves away, putting several feet between us. He crouches down, and I note my surroundings— whitewashed walls, a single bed that I'm curled up on, a pitcher of water on a table, and not a lot else. "Where am I?" I ask again, coughing.

"Highborn. They brought us to Highborn. I'm Kell. They took me when they saw what I could do. I'm from the Far Isles. I didn't answer the call. I stayed quiet, like the hunter . . . like Brielle told me. But they found me anyway, brought me here."

I frown, trying to make sense of this. Then I realize what it means. Where I must be. The witches . . . Highborn . . . *no.*

As I scramble from the bed, my vision dips and sways, but I make it to the small window. My heart shudders in my chest. A courtyard far below. High walls. And the watch. Patrolling in pressed scarlet jackets, rifles slung across their shoulders.

"The ruling council brought us to court. We are their champions, against the other contenders from the continent." He swallows. "The trials begin in three days."

EPILOGUE

SHE SLIPS IN AND OUT, POISON RATTLING through her veins. At times there is a roaring, like a water-fall, or the sea. But mostly there is silence. Aching, endless silence. She cannot move, can barely breathe, but somehow she holds on to life. As her magic spills from her, she weakens. And then she hears a voice. A bridge, linking her from this cold, tired world to somewhere familiar, somewhere good and warm . . .

Brielle.

She hears Brielle, and she follows that thread until she wakes.

"Lowri? You're going with Eli. He's going to get you help. Lowri?"

"Lowri?"

It's Caden's voice.

"It's all right, I can hear you, you don't have to shout. . . ." she mumbles, gripping her brother's big, scarred hand. He squeezes her hand, twice for fine. Just like when they were little, and he would visit the coven for one of their family dinners after going to a walled garden in the city, full of wild and green and loam, where she would be free for one precious afternoon. She smiles, trying to open her eyes, wanting to ask him if Brielle is really there, or if she imagined it—

"Can she stand?" she hears Eli ask. "Has she moved at all?"

"She wakes a little, then she dreams," Caden says, worry injecting his voice. "Are you sure about this? What if you can't find him, or you get lost in the wrong world . . ."

"We're out of options," Eli says gently. "Say goodbye for now, Caden. I'll carry her."

"Go quickly, and use the necklace as a bridge, like we practiced." Another voice . . . maybe the librarian, Tanith? Although the feeling she gets from her . . . she's sure she sees scales when Tanith moves. . . .

Nova crawls into her lap, and she blinks down at her familiar. Nova tilts her head, tail twitching. *I'm going with the hunter. Be safe, witch. I do not want to choose another.*

"I love you too, Nova," she rasps, weakness already filling her, dragging at her thoughts. She looks up, finding Brielle, fierce love brimming from her features. "Look after my sister. Don't let her do anything too heroic."

"We're going to find the wraiths, Lor. It was Nova's idea. Any that have been cast out, and try to help them. We'll bring them back here to form a new coven. A true Tresillian coven. Tanith thinks we can save them."

Lowri sighs, eyes already closing. "Save a space for me in this new coven."

"She's fading." Strong arms circle her, lifting her up. She

opens her eyes just enough to know it's Eli, to see his calm, capable eyes staring down at her. "Sleep, little one," he says. "Don't worry, I've got you."

Then they slip into a shadow that is not a shadow but a doorway, and on the other side is forest. Woodland and the scent of wild things. It warps, twisting into shadow, then snow, then a mountain range.

"Eli . . ." she whispers, but her voice is a thread. She clings to him, fighting to keep her eyes open as he steps and steps again. And again. This is not like traversing between shadows. This is not a spell, or witchery, this is . . .

This is something else.

"Hold on, Lowri. I have to find the right doorway. . . ."

They step first into a library, a place of moorland and snow outside the windows, a single book sitting before a young girl with brown hair, a book about fairies, her eyes flaring wide as they pass—

Then they're under trees and frost and stars, blazing overhead, and when Lowri twists in Eli's arms, she sees an old woman, a cut on her finger, the blood dripping on the ground in a shaft of silver moonlight. Behind the woman is a vast landscape, a tapestry of lights, a town, and Lowri realizes they are very high up, on the side of a mountain. The woman shakes her head, pointing away, as though to say, *Not this world, not this place. . . .*

And Eli steps again, passing elsewhere, onward.

Then the sky blanches to gray, a steady drizzle misting a garden, surrounded by trees, that forest she first saw. No, not a forest, not with carved marble stones, flowers in neatly arranged bunches, already picked—

A graveyard.

Lowri can feel Eli's heart pounding inside his chest. He's holding the necklace, the eight-pointed star tight in his fist, the chain draped over his fingers, glowing softly. She glances around, to where he's staring, where a single black-clad figure stands before a grave. The drizzle thickens, rain slipping down her cheeks, but she forces her eyes to stay open. Fights to stay awake. Eli carries her to this figure standing beside a black gravestone. Gleaming black, flecked with white and carved with a name.

Isaiah Kellinick

"Excuse me," Eli says, and the figure turns toward them. Lowri's breath catches. She's staring into Eli's mirror. Black-brown hair, the same deep, soulful eyes, green rather than blue, set under thick brows, the same set to her shoulders. But this girl is slightly younger, Lowri's age. She blinks away her shock, seeing what Lowri sees, similarities that outweigh the differences between them.

"I'm afraid you just missed him. He's been waiting. He always hoped . . ." The girl's gaze trails to the necklace in Eli's fist, then over to Lowri's obsidian eyes, before she jerks up her chin, lower lip trembling. "You're too late by five days. Your father is dead."

ACKNOWLEDGMENTS

FIRSTLY, TO MY WONDERFUL READERS FOR FALL-ing in love with this world and these characters as I have. The love this series has gained is truly breathtaking. Thank you.

To my brilliant agent, Mads, for being the most fabulous wingwoman and for always fighting for my stories. You're the best. To the wider team at DHA for all the unseen work. I appreciate everything you do so much.

Megan Reid, how are we already on the second book in this series? Working with you is an absolute joy—you make my stories so much stronger, and in fact, working with you never really feels like work at all. To everyone at Harper Fire, particularly Charlotte Winstone, Sarah Lough, Isabel Coonjah, Matthew Kelly, Cally Poplak, Nick Lake, Jane Baldock, and Sarah Hall, thank you for making publishing fun and for genuinely caring about the books you publish. Still counting my lucky stars to be working with you all.

To my US publishing team, Karen Chaplin, Kamille

Carreras Pereira, Ro Romanello, Audrey Diestelkamp, Allison Weintraub, Hannah Neff, and the many people who thoughtfully and carefully publish this series across the Atlantic, thank you for all you do.

To Jim Tierney, the illustrations you create for the US covers are gorgeous. To Nico Delort, I gasped when I saw the first sketch for *Shadow and Tide*. And now it's a complete cover, and it's a work of art I will treasure forever. Your talent knows no bounds. To Daisy Davis, mapmaker extraordinaire, I'm forever thankful you created the map of Mira's world.

Finally, to Joe, Rosie, and Izzy. My whole world. Joe, thanks for being the best dad and the most wonderful partner so I could write this book. Rosie and Izzy, this whole series is for you. May you always be as feisty as Mira, as loving as Agnes, as strong as Mer, as clever as Pearl, and as loyal as Brielle. My island girls. And Iz, Maggie was created especially for you.